DATE DUE

JUN 0 5

GAYLORD			PRINTED IN U.S.A.

Rhythms

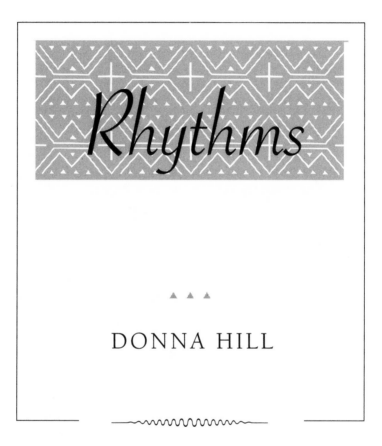

Rhythms

▲ ▲ ▲

DONNA HILL

ST. MARTIN'S PRESS
NEW YORK

www.stmartins.com

Design by Susan Walsh

ISBN 0-312-27299-5

10 9 8 7 6 5 4 3 2

To my Mom, who loves me unconditionally, rejoices in my achievements, and shares my pains. All that you are, I can only hope to one day become.

Acknowledgments

My deepest thanks are extended to the St. Martin's team who believed in this project from the beginning and worked to make it a reality.

To Robert, who remains both my anchor and my compass, keeping me grounded while opening up a world of possibilities.

To my family, a constant source of inspiration!

To all those who came before me and paved the way, I only hope that I will continue to honor your legacy by doing the same.

Most of all to God, who continues to watch over me and all that I do, for this wonderful gift of words and its ability to touch lives. I am blessed.

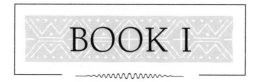

BOOK I

Cora

One

~~~~vvvvvvvvvv~~~~

Down in the Delta, somewhere just beyond Alligator, Mississippi, rests the colored section of Rudell, a community of less than five hundred, divided unequally by race, wealth, and religion by the Left Hand River. It was named such because from the top of the highest tree in Rudell the rippling river looks like a man's left hand. Yes, it sure does.

Well, today all the folks, black and white alike, moved heat-snake slow along the dusty, unpaved roads, pressed down by the heavy hand of the July sun.

Towering yellow pines raised their angry fists toward the blinding white sky demanding a long, cool drink. Mosquitoes buzzed and bit, zealous in their hunt for sweet, moist flesh, especially the plump legs of little brown baby boys and girls. Good chewing grass, razor thin, glistened like emerald fire, fanning out as far as the eye could see.

Funny how nature plays its tricks. Earlier that same year, the spring of 1927, the mighty Mississippi River rose higher than ever before in its history. Before its floods were over, the river had turned the Delta valley into lakes of despair. Dikes and levees crumbled, while the river swallowed whole towns and farms with an insatiable appetite that could not be stopped by man.

The war between man and nature rode the ever-increasing tide. Still, months after the devastation, lost land and lost lives, recovery was a slow and painful process. The Father of Waters had spared no one, colored or white. But times being what they were, the colored who already had so little now had even less. Yet even the oppressive, relentless heat and untold

1

tragedy couldn't stop the parishioners of First Baptist Church from stomping and shouting on this Sunday morning just as on any other.

The white clapboard building, put together plank by plank by the men of Rudell, offered them little refuge as the steam ascended from the momentum of the congregation bunched together along the crowded, wooden pews.

The sun streamed in through the handblown windows casting rays of shimmering color across the wooly heads of the congregation to explode in a ball of brilliant light that gleamed off the ten-foot cross of Christ. The strongest members of First Baptist, male and female, had carried that cross in through the narrow door five years ago, piece by piece, nailing it together in silent reverence. It stood in proud testament of all they had endured. And they were grateful.

Today, more than ever, they had much to be thankful for. They'd been spared.

"We done seen the wrath of the Lord," Reverend Joshua Harvey ebbed and flowed, his voice an instrument of persuasion. "His mighty hand swept the Mississippi from Arkansas to the Gulf of Mexico. Wiped out sinners and nonbelievers with a puff of his breath."

"Amen! Yes, Lord," shouted the pulsing throng.

" 'The great flood of '27' we hear tell it called. I say it be the great cleanser. The Lord's way of riddin' this earth of those who continya ta do us harm." He stretched out his arm and passed it over the packed room. "And y'all know who I'm talkin' 'bout."

"Praise the Lord!"

"But many of our innocent sistahs and brothas have suffered, too. They been left with even less than the nothin' they had."

"That's why we's here t'day, Reverend," shouted Deacon Earl, looking 'round to see the nods of assent.

"Amen," again came the response.

"I knows y'all don't have much," the Reverend continued. "You works hard to feed yo' families from sunrise till set. But it's up to us who have little to share with those who have less."

Government relief had come to those stricken by the devastation of the flood. But it was slow coming, if at all, to some of the colored sections along the Delta.

Joshua gazed out at his congregation, the beaten, the downtrodden. His dark, all-seeing eyes peered into their souls; his heart heard their prayers. He witnessed the unflinching pride in the bent backs, the clawed hands, and leatherlike faces. Sorrow shadowed their eyes, but hope hung on their lids. In each one he saw strength from a people who had seen much for any one lifetime. Still, he knew he could ask for more.

"I knows what I'm askin' is gon' be hard for the lot of ya. But I needs ya to dig deeper than yo' pockets. I needs ya to dig inta yo' hearts to help those who cain't help themselves. We here in Rudell gotta come to-gether once again as a community and as a people." He paused to let his words rest a spell. "The doors ta the church gon' be open all day. Brang what chu kin. Deacon Earl gon' be in charge of collectin' whatever y'all kin brang."

Cora sat in the front line of the choir. The flick of her slender wrist moved the circular cardboard fan in a steady flow in front of her face. She gazed out at the rows of black bodies, a melody of color, size, and shape. They were hypnotized by the power of her daddy. Pride puffed her chest. Papa Daddy could do anything. He could make you believe the impossible, give you strength when you had none. He made it so easy for her to lift her voice in praise, as much for him as she did for the Lord. She wanted to do them both proud.

Like so many colored communities, the heart and soul of Rudell could be found in the church. Reverend Joshua Harvey was the bedrock upon which Rudell was built. Their lightning rod. The calm during the storm. It was to him the white folks came when they had trouble with their coloreds, Cora thought. Daddy always found ways to make the peace. But, of course, he made them think it was their own doing. He knew white folks in a way few coloreds did in those parts. He spoke their language, knew the power of their words as well as those of his flock. Daddy carried the weight for all of Rudell on his back.

While he was not seen as the equal of the whites, something in Daddy's bearing made them tolerate his uppity ways. He was like the esteemed Booker T. Washington with the powerful white folks up north. Daddy was just like that. White folks feared as much as respected him and the quiet power he held over the town. His church was the visual symbol of that power.

"I want y'all to stand now and join our choir in song." Joshua turned briefly toward his daughter, a smile of pride on his thick lips. "Lift yo' voices to the Almighty in thanks."

The choir stood in unison and Cora stepped forward.

▲ ▲ ▲

David Mackey stood out on the dusty road, his starched white, high-button shirt clinging to his moist back. Even his sweat tried to find a place to hide from the beating sun, securing sanctuary beneath his stiff shirt collar.

He whipped out a spotless white handkerchief from the pocket of his blue serge pants and mopped his brow, then set his straw hat squarely atop his close-cropped head.

He'd fretted for hours about what to wear, wanting to make the best impression. His customary work pants and clean but frayed shirts were fine for visiting his sick and laid-low patients, but not today. Today was special.

David drew up a deep breath and checked his scarred, gold pocket watch, a gift from his father.

Service would be over directly, he calculated, and then he'd see her again. As a matter-o'-fact, if he shut his eyes he could see her face plain as the day is long, as he was sure it would appear while she led the choir through the strains of "Swing Low Sweet Chariot." Her powerful contralto voice poured out of her tiny body, entered the soul, grabbed and shook it.

The age-old cry of the weary souls seeped through the walls of the one-room building. But it was Cora Harvey's rapturous voice that soared above them all.

Cora Harvey. She was something else. A right pretty thing. He'd spotted her months ago, and upon discrete inquiries he'd found out who she was. That discovery compelled him to keep his distance as much as he wanted to do otherwise. Since then, they'd passed each other on several occasions when she made her monthly shopping trips into town. However, up until the other afternoon, she'd never paid him no never mind other than a passing wave or flashing that smile of hers. Then they'd run into each other at Sam's market earlier that week, and she'd given him his first look of encouragement. Of course her daddy wasn't looking. But he dared not approach her, not with the good reverend close at hand.

David sighed. They came from different sides of town. Cora Harvey was a sharecropper's daughter turned preacherman who worshiped in the Baptist Church. He, on the other hand, was the one and only colored doctor in Rudell, the surviving son of the now prosperous Mackey family, who paid his homage—at least some of the time—at the Episcopal Church on the other side of the dividing line.

It shouldn't matter none, he mused, but it did. The Baptists were considered common, while the Episcopals were made up of the few educated coloreds, those with a bit of money. As much as colored folk had endured since they were brought in chains from Africa and stuffed like garbage into the bowels of death ships, one would think that now they would band together. That was not to be. It wasn't enough that the white folks made no secret of their disdain for the coloreds; the coloreds did it to themselves.

David snapped out of his woolgathering at the sound of voices surging through the now opened church doors. He took a quick look at his shoes—which still held their shine—wiped his face one last time and walked forward.

▲ ▲ ▲

Cora stood on the plank wood steps of the church, flanked on either side by her parents, Pearl and Joshua. She looked so soft and beautiful in her pale peach cotton dress, David thought, just like one of those dolls he'd once seen in the Sears Roebuck catalog. Her smooth, pecan-colored skin, with undertones of red, glowed as if lit by an inner sunbeam. Her thick, neatly plated hair was pulled back in one braid that fell to the center of her back, protected by a sun bonnet that matched her dress. She sure did look pretty.

She shook hands with each of the churchgoers, accepting their praises of her singing with grace and the right amount of humility.

"Sister Cora, that voice of yours gon' take you straight to heaven, chile. Lordhammercy! Mark my words," professed Lucinda Carver, as the sweat rolled in waves down her plump face.

"Thank you, Sister Carver. I sure hope so."

"You just make sho' you hold them pearly gates open for this old sister," Lucinda chuckled, patting Cora heartily on the arm.

"See you tomorrow, Cora," Maybelle said, giving her friend a kiss on the cheek. "I's goin' to meet Little Jake at the river," she whispered in Cora's ear, before running down the steps.

Sassy, Cora's friend since they were both in diapers, stepped up beside her. "That girl gon' get herself in a heap of trouble if her mama ever finds out." Then Sassy giggled. "Harold Jr. say he gon' come by and sit on the porch later when it cool down some. I'll see you later." Sassy, it wasn't her real name, but that's what she was always called, skipped down the stairs.

Cora watched her two friends leave and wished she had someone waiting on her, eager to see her under the stars.

When the last of the parishioners filed out, Joshua slipped into his role as father, husband, and protector. "Come along, ladies. We best be gettin' on outta this here heat," he instructed them.

Pearl eased up alongside her towering husband and slipped her arm through his.

"Comin', Daddy." Cora took a step down when movement across the road captured her attention. She felt the muscles in her heart expand and contract, creating a moment of light-headedness. It was him, that handsome, quiet doctor who made her stomach feel funny inside.

Pearl's eyes followed the trail of her daughter's. "Oh, Joshua, here come that nice young doctor." She gave his arm a "come on" squeeze and a quick wink to Cora.

"How nice kin he be ifn he thinks he's too good to worship in a Baptist Church? Humph."

"Joshua," Pearl hissed in warning as David crossed the first step.

"Afternoon, Mrs. Harvey, Reverend." David tipped his hat and looked at Cora. "Miss Cora."

"Dr. Mackey." Cora gave him her sweetest smile and wished her mother and father would leave her be.

Silence hung over the quartet as heavy as the heat. The poor boy looked so nervous from the glare Joshua was hurling his way that Pearl's maternal instincts leaped to his rescue. "What brings you to First Baptist this hot day, Doctor?" Pearl asked, finally breaking the silence.

"Well, ma'am," he paused and looked from one parent to the other, wishing that his heart would stop hammering long enough for him to take a breath, "I was hoping you'd allow me to take Miss Cora here over to Joe's for a soft drink, maybe some ice cream." He swallowed down the last of his fear and plunged on. "That's if Miss Cora is willing." He snatched a quick look at Cora. "I have my auto-mo-bile right 'cross the road. I'd have her back in plenty of time for supper. I—"

"What 'chu know 'bout what time we has supper?" Joshua pulled his black, wide-brimmed hat a little farther down on his brow, with the intention of giving his dark features an even more ominous look.

Cora's face was afire, and it had nothing to do with the heat. She was mortified. Here she was seventeen years old—eighteen in six months—and her daddy was treating her like a knee-high. When would she ever be able to court like the other girls she knew? Daddy was always preaching about how she needed to settle down. How was she ever supposed to do that if he wouldn't let no respectable man near her? Not that marriage was her goal no how. It was just the whole notion of having someone interested in her, especially a doctor. All the girls would be green with envy.

She wanted to know what it felt like; wanted to know what she'd heard some of the girls of the church whisper about. She had yet to be kissed. How could her daddy embarrass her this way? Maybe the earth would just open up, like she'd read about in the picture books, and swallow her whole.

"Joshua, for heaven's sake, let the young man speak his piece," Pearl cajoled, seeing the possibilities in the union. "That sounds right nice that he wants to take Cora for a soft drink. Matter-o'-fact, I could use a long, cool glass of lemonade myself." She looked at Cora, who flashed her a smile of thankful relief. "You ought to take the good doctor up on his offer, Cora. Don't you think so?"

"Sounds invitin', Dr. Mackey. Is it all right, Daddy?"

Joshua heard the soft plea in his daughter's voice and saw the eagerness shining in her eyes. In that instant he remembered all too clearly what it felt like to be young. What it felt like when he'd met his Pearl. He weren't nothin' more than a paid slave workin' the cotton fields. When he'd drag his weary body home after a day under the Mississippi sun, Pearl would run down the road from her beaverboard shack and bring him a tin of water and a piece of dried beef or a biscuit.

"I figured you'd be thirsty," she'd always say.

"Right kind of you," he'd answer.

She'd walk with him part way down the road till he finished his water.

"Thank you much, Miss Pearl."

She'd duck her head all shy. "Tomorrow," she'd whisper and run off.

That musta gone on for months. That and things they didn't talk about no more, till Joshua said the two of them would do much better as one.

"Whatchu sayin'?" Pearl had asked, taking a seat on the top of a flat rock.

Joshua squeezed his hat in his hands, trying to find the right words. He shifted from one foot to the next. "You what I look for at the end of the day, Pearl," he finally said. "Thinkin' 'bout you out in dem fields makes me remember I's still a man, not some pack mule like Mistah Jackson make me out to be. I kin be somethin', Pearl. Somebody. You believe that?"

"I knowed it from the first time I saw you hitchin' down that road yonder."

"I got dreams, Pearl. I want to have my own church one day, preach the word. I—I want you to be a part of that."

"That yo' fancy way of askin' me to jump the broom wit you?"

Joshua grinned like a young boy, seeing the challenge in her eyes. "I 'spose."

"Then I 'spose I will."

And she'd been by his side ever since, sunup to down. Never complaining, no matter how bad times had gotten. Pearl was his strength, his reason for everything. Her faith in him, her unwavering love, was his joy. And Cora was just like her.

Truth be known, he'd like nothing better than to see his strong-willed Cora married off and secure. It would sho' nuff make Pearl happy. A good, solid husband may just be the thing Cora needed to tame her willful ways. But that didn't mean he had to make it easy for any man who thought he was good enough to come a courtin' his baby girl. Especially an Episcopal doctor—and one from the other side of Rudell at that.

"I 'spose," he finally grumbled. "We have Sunday supper at four o'clock sharp."

Pearl briefly lowered her bonneted head to hide her smile. "You might think 'bout joining us, Doctor. I fix a fine table."

Joshua threw her a cutting glance, but kept his own counsel.

"I just might, ma'am. Thank you." He looked at Joshua, who gave an imperceptible nod of approval. *The day is beginning to look better every minute,* David thought.

Cora gave her mother and father each a peck on the cheek and stepped down.

"I'll be sure to have her back in plenty of time for supper, Reverend."

"Be sho' you do," Joshua added for good measure.

Cora couldn't believe her luck as she walked side-by-side with David down the church steps out onto the road. The saints must surely be with her today, she mused, tossing up a silent prayer of thanks. Her father had never so much as entertained the notion of her courting, even though all the other girls her age had a steady beau. "You're not other girls," Joshua Harvey would boom in his preacher voice. "You the daughter of the reverend of this town, and you ain't gon' be seen with just anybody."

Well, Dr. David Mackey must sure be somebody, she thought, delighted.

"I'm right happy your folks let me take you out for a spell, Miss Cora," David said in a hushed voice as they crossed the road to his Model T.

She looked up into his dark face, eyes like polished black opals, and her young heart panged in her chest. "So am I, Dr. Mackey." She batted her eyes demurely as she'd seen some of her churchgoing sisters do, and she would have sworn David blushed beneath his roasted chestnut complexion.

Strong, large hands caught her waist as David helped her step up into the seat, and Cora was no longer sure if it was the force of the blazing sun or a fire that had been lit inside of her that caused the surge of heat to run amok through her body. Settling herself against the soft, cushioned seat, she adjusted her hat while David rounded the hood and hopped up beside her.

"All set?"

Cora nodded, suddenly unsure of herself.

The Model T bucked, chugged, coughed up some smoke, and finally pulled off down the rutty road, bouncing and bumping all the way. As they drove by the rows of makeshift shacks, half nude children playing in the river and old wrinkled women smoking corn pipes all stopped and stared at the handsome couple in the automobile. To see colored folks driving was rarer than having meat for dinner once a month.

But instead of feeling like a specimen under glass, Cora felt like royalty. She smiled and waved to everyone who came out on the road, wide-eyed, to greet them. Little children ran alongside the car until they grew weary, and the old Model T chugged out of sight.

"Did you go to Sunday service today, Dr. Mackey?" Cora asked, needing to break the silence that hung between them like clothes drying on a line.

David cleared his throat. "No. Not today." He shrugged, then chuckled lightly. "Truth be told, it's awhile since I been to church."

Cora angled her head in his direction, surprise widening her sparkling, brown eyes. "Why? Don't you have anything to be thankful for?"

"Sure I do. Except I don't think you need to set up in a building to give thanks. I believe that God can hear my prayers and my thanks from wherever I am."

Cora frowned, tossing around this new idea. What David was saying may well have been Greek for all the sense it made to her. It never occurred to her not to attend Sunday service. She'd been brought up and reared in the church. All of her friends attended. They had social functions, did things for the community, helped each other out in crises. Why just the other week, the sisters got together and took turns sitting with old Miss Riley, who'd been feeling poorly for months. She didn't know what she'd do if she didn't have her church and her church family. Besides, on Sunday mornings, she could do what she loved more than anything, raise her voice in song.

"But—it's more than that," she protested, convinced that she was right. "It's about belonging to something that has meaning, being a part of something."

"That may be, Miss Cora, and I don't fault no one for going. I don't want you to get me wrong. I do set foot in from time to time, just not right regular." He turned briefly to her, hoping that his revelation hadn't put her off, especially with her being the preacher's daughter and all. But the reality was, he wanted to be honest with her.

"If Christians are supposed to love all men, then what's the difference between your church and mine? What makes one better than the other—the amount of money you put in the collection basket, how large the congregation, what side of town you worship on?" he asked with honest sincerity.

Cora crossed her arms beneath her small breasts. She listened to what he said. Secretly she'd wondered the same things, but she'd never dared to voice her concerns, ask her questions.

"You're a very interesting man, Dr. Mackey," she said, still unwilling to give in. "You done put something on my head to ponder."

"That's a start," he said, turning to her with a grin.

It was then she noticed the deep dimple in his right cheek and knew, that barring everything else, whatever differences might separate them, she wanted to see more of him, hear his strange thoughts, and maybe become exposed to a side of life she'd never known existed.

Shortly, they arrived in the center of town and pulled to a stop in front of Joe's. David quickly hurried around and helped Cora from her seat. She immediately felt the curious gazes from the townspeople as they went about their Sunday business, the surprised look from friends of her father and mother as she took David's arm and walked toward the shop.

Voice by voice, conversation ceased as heads turned toward the open door. The heat stood like a man between them, separating them from the brown, tan, and black bodies, then was buffeted about by the slow, swirling ceiling fan—the only one in town.

The interior was dim and it took Cora a moment to adjust her eyes from the glare of the outside.

David glanced down the narrow aisle and cleared his throat. "There's a table in the back," he said, indicating the vacancy with a stretch of his arm.

They proceeded through the gauntlet of probing eyes.

Cora's gaze faltered for a moment, then darted briefly about, a taut smile drawing her mouth into a thin line.

"Afternoon, Miss Wheeler," Cora, said, remembering her manners as she recognized her nosey neighbor from down the road.

"Cora Harvey," Sarah Wheeler droned, long as the quitting whistle at the cotton mill. "I didn't know the good Reverend let you keep comp'ny." Her tiny eyes skipped across David's face. "Dr. Mackey, ain't you lookin' fine this bright day."

"Comp'ny in general, or me in particular, Mrs. Wheeler?" David asked, with a tip of his hat and an extra drawl, his smile as fixed and direct as his stare.

An ungloved hand fluttered to her chest. "I . . . I just meant . . . she, Miss Cora seems so young still. Well I recall when she was just a bitty thing." Sarah's forced laugh flapped like the wings of a feeble bird.

"She seems all grown up to me," David replied smoothly, tipping his hat in dismissal. "You take care of that foot now," he added. "Let me know if it gives you anymore trouble. Have a nice day now."

"Why . . . I . . ."

David ushered Cora down the aisle, not interested in what the old bird had to say or what she thought. What he wanted to do was ask them all to tend to their own business. But proper manners dictated that he act accordingly, especially in the company of the Reverend Harvey's only daughter. Even he'd been taught that much on his side of town.

Cora felt her chest swell with pride. He'd come to her defense, just like the gentleman she knew he'd be, even if he did have some strange notions. She raised her head a bit higher as she moved now with a slight sway to her hips, the strut of a confident woman. After all, she wore her best Sunday dress. That alone made her feel womanly, made her feel pretty and special.

David pulled out the shaky, wooden chair and helped Cora get settled. He took off his hat and placed it on the corner of the table. "What can I get for you, Miss Cora?" he asked, still standing.

Cora looked up and her stomach did a little dance. "A banana split with nuts would suit me just right."

"Extra syrup?"

"Absolutely," she said, her eyes sparkling with mischief.

"Be right back."

Cora folded her white-gloved hands atop the table, threading her fingers neatly between each other, being certain to sit with her back straight and away from the chair and her feet planted on the floor. "That's the sign of a true lady," her mama would always say. "A lady is proud. Holds her head up and covers it with a hat, and she wears gloves in public. Don't matter that you colored. You's a lady first. Don't you forget that, Cora, chile," Pearl had warned on too many occasions.

Cora tucked in a smile. That was one of the things she always admired about her mama, her sense of womanly pride and her strength. Her daddy, too. Especially, Daddy. Daddy didn't back down from no man, colored or white. He didn't duck his head or lower his eyes when he passed white folks on the street. She'd heard "uppity nigger" so often when she was coming up, if she didn't know better she'd swear that was her daddy's name.

Joshua Harvey may have been a man of the cloth, but he didn't turn the other cheek, and he preached that to his parishioners as often as they would hear it. His outspoken ways had made for many a tense moment with the white folks. He and Mama had even come to shouting about it.

"You cain't just go 'round sayin' and doin' what you want, Joshua," Pearl said one night, sounding on the verge of tears. "They lynch us for just 'bout nothin' as it is. If you not gon' think 'bout yo'self, at least think 'bout me and Cora."

"It's a man's right to speak up for hisself and his family. I may be a preacher, but I'm a man first. I gots to stand up, not just for myself and my family, but for all of us. We gots to have a voice. I'm that voice."

"Here's your split . . . Miss Cora," David said, liking the sound of her name on his lips, while scattering her wandering thoughts like chickens on the run. He placed the glass tub on the rickety table.

Cora's eyes widened in delight as she ran her tongue hungrily across her lips. Chocolate syrup slithered down the side of the split, forming a rich, dark pool. "Thank you."

"I don't see how a tiny thing like you gon' eat all that."

"One mouthful at a time," she said, dipping the spoon into the concoction and bringing it daintily to her mouth.

David shook his head in amusement and took a seat, wrapping his long piano-like fingers around the glass of root beer.

For several moments they were silent, the only sounds between them were Cora's spoon tapping against the glass and the cubes of ice cracking as they melted in the soda.

The fan swirled in a lazy, buzzing circle.

David watched her lift the spoon to her mouth and slip the creamy sweetness inside. He swallowed and took a sip of his drink.

Her dress clung to her young, damp body, the moisture binding it to the soft curves.

A trickle of sweat ran along the line of David's hair. He turned his gaze away from temptation and buried it in the bubbles that bumped and bounced inside his glass.

"You sure know how to lick that ice cream," he said into the glass.

Cora's face heated. She waved her hand back and forth in front of her then flapped the top of her dress in and out to circulate the hot air. "There's an art to it," she said. She slipped the spoon into her mouth.

David pulled out his handkerchief and mopped his face. "Fan don't do much good on a day like today."

"Don't seem so, Dr. Mackey." She smiled and licked her lips, feeling her womanly powers. "Doctors have to get real personal . . . intimate with folks, figure out what ails 'em," she said thoughtfully. "You like being close, Doctor?"

David's eyes rose from the depths of the brown brew and landed on a dot of ice cream, no bigger than a pinhead, hugging the corner of her mouth. The tip of her tongue slowly peeked out and dabbed it away.

His heart pumped faster.

"I mean . . . did you always want to be a doctor?"

David cleared his throat. "I suppose," he finally answered, twirling the thick glass in his hands. "When I was about six or so, my older brother, Cleve, got real sick. He'd got caught in a terrible lightning storm out in the fields. Fever about made him crazy. His chest rattled like rusty chains every time he took a breath. My mama tried everything to break the fever; cold baths, roots, prayer, nothing helped."

He sat back in his seat and looked off to a place Cora couldn't see. "I remember it being so hot, the grass had curled and turned brown. . . ."

The house smelled of sickness, sweat, homegrown medicines, and fear. He didn't know until his brother came down low sick that fear had a smell. Smelled like something gone bad, but you couldn't find the source. Unnatural moans came from beneath the thin, white sheet.

"Why cain't a doctor fix Cleve, Mama?" he'd asked, watching her dip a rag into a pan of cool, well water. She rung it out and placed it on Cleve's fevered head.

Betty Jean turned to her son, and the dead, empty look chilled David even in the heat. "Ain't no colored doctors, son. And ain't no white doctors gon' treat him."

David felt a sinking sensation in his belly like falling from a high place. "So what's gon' happen to Cleve, Mama? You gon' make him better?"

Betty Jean didn't answer her son; she couldn't. There was things he couldn't understand, things he wouldn't understand until he was growed, things about white folks and colored. About the stone-cold colored line and how a life could hang in the balance and wasn't nothin' nobody could do about it. There was nothin' she could tell him but the truth, and the truth terrified her. "We got ta pray," was all she said, before lifting the pan and shuffling to the makeshift kitchen.

Cleve grew worse during the night. Low sick. Fever so high you could almost see the steam rise from his burning flesh. Frantic, Betty Jean did all she could to break it: bathed him in alcohol, put cool rags on his head, fanned him until her wrist got sore. All night. All night she never left his side.

When sunup came, Betty Jean, eyes red from no sleep, body bruised from the pain of watching her son suffer, wrapped her child in a hand-washed sheet and toted him the long, five miles into town.

David went along, helping to hold up her thin arms as best he could when she grew weak. Finally they reached the white part of town. Folks walked by them like they were invisible.

"Don't y'all nigras knows you 'spose t' step aside and let white folks pass?" one white man with a heavy, black beard demanded.

David's body trembled, but he didn't budge. To tell the truth, he paid the white man no mind, for his thoughts stayed on Cleve.

The man pointed at Betty Jean. "Don't make me have t' teach you a lesson, make an example outta ya and yo' boy."

Betty Jean's arms shook from exhaustion, but she wouldn't lay her burden down.

"I needs a doctor for my boy, suh," she said, eyes fastened to the ground. "He powerful sick, suh."

"You done come t' the wrong place. I's the doctor and I don't take care of no coloreds. Now get on." He waved his hand the way you shoo a fly. "Use some of dem roots y'all nigras have." He guffawed as if it was the biggest joke, turned and walked away.

Tears of heart-pain hopelessness streamed down Betty Jean's face. She was wore out, drained. Still she clutched her near lifeless child to her thin chest, spinning 'round and 'round in a circle, raising her face to the sky. Her mouth opened. The muscles of her throat pulsed as a howled cry tore from her throat.

Where was her Lawd? Where was He when she needed Him most?

Meanwhile, David ran down the street, his legs windmilling underneath him in desperation. He moved from one white person to another to stop whoever would listen. The words tumbled from his lips in a stream, beseeching their kindness, their compassion, to do something, anything. "Please help my mama," he begged of everyone who passed. One white woman tossed him a coin and told him he was cute as a little puppy before patting him on the head and moving away.

David turned toward his mama, her face partially buried in the sheeted bundle. Agony ran in a ragged crisscross on her face. It was then that he fully understood that he could never risk loving anything as much as he loved his mama and his brother ever again. To do that would leave him with this feeling that was too dark and ugly to express.

David absently lifted the glass to his lips and held it there, still trapped in the memory.

"What . . . happened then?" Cora asked, almost afraid of the answer.

David blinked, brought Cora's face into focus. He saw the tears there, glimmering like diamonds on her lashes.

He took a sip of his root beer. He didn't answer.

"David?" She wiped at her eyes, forgetting formalities.

"He died."

Cora reached across the table and placed her hand on his, not caring what anyone thought.

Trouble had never touched her life. Not really. She'd felt trouble when the mister was paid in chits for a crop rather than cash money, heard about trouble in the whispered tales of the hooded night riders who did the devil's handiwork. Yes, Lawd, she'd seen way too many folks put under the earth much too early. But trouble, not that kind of trouble, had ever touched her life. Her parents protected her from the ugliness of it all as much as they could.

She remembered standing outside of their bedroom door right after they'd heard about another lynching on the outskirts of town.

"Don't never wanna see my baby girl suffer like how other coloreds done suffered," Joshua said. "It's up to us to make a better place."

"But she needs to understand what's real, Joshua," Pearl protested. "What life is like for colored folk in the South. You got that chile thinkin' she can do what she please down here, and she cain't."

"Cora gon' be just fine. She's strong, like I taught her. Cora got dreams bigger than a husband and a houseful of younguns, Pearl."

Cora covered her mouth to keep from shouting out loud with pleasure at her papa taking her side. She pressed her ear a bit closer to the door.

"That's 'cause you got her thinkin' that singin' of hers gon' get her somewhere. Church singin' is jes fine; it's the Lord's way. But that's it. Cora needs to get behind a man, help him make his way in the world. Be his support, raise the family. Womens is what keeps mens strong, able to deal with the trickery, backbreakin' work, and no pay. Cora gon' make a good wife one day. You'll see. She'll settle down."

"But children need to have dreams of their own, Pearl. Make their own way. We can only guide 'em, give 'em strength to stand on they own two feet."

"That's what I intend to do," her mama stated. "Guide her. The right way. The Lawd's way."

"His way ain't always so plain," Joshua said, his heavy voice weighed down by the simple truth. "We just wait and see what He has planned."

Cora tiptoed away, confused. She couldn't spend the rest of her life in Rudell, with no hopes, no dreams of being any more than an old, broke-down woman with children and a husband to look after. She had hopes. Hopes of going someplace like New York or Chicago, where coloreds were making names for themselves, like Bessie Smith, Ma Rainey, Duke Ellington, and Zora Neale Hurston. All the folks she'd read about in the magazines she hid away in her room. If her mama ever found out . . .

But what of her mama? Was she right and papa wrong? A sadness settled over her. She didn't want to be the root of what grew between her mama and daddy. Yet even as much as she quietly fretted about her fate, she couldn't imagine life without either of them.

She clasped David's hand a bit tighter, sniffed back the last of her tears. "So . . . that's how you reckoned with . . . it, huh? By becoming a doctor and all?"

"I think I have. Looking after folks keeps my mind busy. Don't make me feel so . . . helpless. Make me feel like I'm not . . . invisible." He forced a half-hearted smile. "Stay so busy I don't have time to think about much else. Too tired at the end of the day."

"Prayer helps when you have a heavy heart and a tired body," Cora offered, in the only language she knew.

David flinched at Cora's last statement, looked off, then his voice grew distant. "I was the first one in my family to finish schooling. The only one who can read and write."

"My mama is a teacher in the colored school. Papa taught me to read straight out the Bible."

"I worked my way through doing odd jobs, field work, dishwashing, cook, whatever would feed me and pay for my books. Saved up my money after I finished school and bought a piece of land for my folks."

"I help out at the church every Wednesday and Saturday," Cora said. "We collect clothes and such for some of the poorer families. Then there's always choir rehearsal."

"My pa works the land and does real good with crops and his chickens. Ma is a dressmaker. Makes fancy dresses for Ms. Harriette's shop in town."

Cora's face brightened. Now that was something she could understand, a reality in her life. "That's where I buy my church clothes," she said. "I probably have some of yo' Mama's dresses in my closet."

"All the fine ladies in town wear something from Mama's hand," David proudly stated. "Don't seem to matter much what side of town you live on or who your folks are when it comes to clothes."

Cora felt the bee-sting of his bitterness as if he was trying to say somethin', but couldn't fix his mouth to say it, so it just hung there on the tip and dripped over them both like molasses. What had she done? she wondered and realized she still held his hand. Slowly she pulled away, wrapping her fingers around the spoon instead.

"Seems you have ideas 'bout everything, Dr. Mackey," she said, with an edge to her voice.

"Only about the things that matter, Miss Cora," his tone easing back to the one she could understand.

"What things?" she questioned.

David looked at her a moment, seeing the youth, the naive view of the world, the eagerness and daring that sparked her eyes, the sensuality that begged to be released. Cora Harvey would be a handful.

"Doing what's right. What's inside my heart," he said simply.

Cora peered into David's eyes, studied the angles of his face, saw the truth of his convictions on his lips. "How do you know when it's the right thing?" she asked, needing this answer more than any other.

David pressed forward. "It's not the knowing if it's right, Miss Cora," he said, his voice propelled by a deep urgency. "It's knowing *when* to do the right thing. You've got to believe in something, have something that matters, want it more than anything; and when the opportunity comes, you got to know when it's right to take it," he said, snatching his hand into a fist.

Cora was transfixed, held there for that moment when sleep eases toward awakening. She knew what she wanted, what she wanted more than anything. When would her time come?

"That's how I feel 'bout my singin'. When I sing I feel . . . like I can do anythin'." Her eyes glowed. "It's a gift and I want to share it with the world." She lowered her eyes. "But I'll never get out of Rudell if my mama has anything to say 'bout it."

"Ain't nothing wrong with sharing what you got right here. These folks enjoy your gift much as anyone. Maybe even more." His eyes trailed across her face. "I know I do." He swallowed, suddenly shamed for having exposed himself. "I could have gone away after I finished with school," he went on, regaining his footing. "Could have gone North. But then I figured, who needs me more, folks who can walk right into a clinic, doctor's office, or a hospital, or the folks no one will touch 'cause they's colored?" David slowly shook his head, a gentle smile on his mouth. "The choice wasn't hard."

"We's 'bout ready to close up, Dr. Mackey, Miss Cora," Joe the owner interrupted, lifting the anchor that held them in place. He picked up the remnants of their fare and wiped down the table with a steamy, white rag, making the old table shine for as long as it could stay wet.

Cora glanced up, hiding her disappointment behind a forced smile. She wasn't ready to give up the time between them. She wanted to hear more, learn more.

David pulled out his pocket watch. "Didn't realize it turned late so quick." He returned the watch to its nesting place. "Don't want you to be late for supper." He stood and Cora reluctantly got up as well.

"Have a nice evenin', now," Joe said. "And tell the good reverend I'll be sure I'm at the next meetin'."

"I will," Cora mumbled, and followed David outside.

The air had cooled considerably in the time since they'd left church. Long, fingerlike shadows crept across the road. One by one the few open shops on the short, ramshackle street began to pull down their shades, like tired lids drifting over weary eyes, their owners heading home for Sunday supper. Soon the small community would be no more than a whisper, a rush of dust and hot air, until life bloomed again tomorrow.

Everything would be closed long before dark. No colored folk in their right mind would be out after dark in Rudell. It wasn't safe.

"Didn't mean to keep you so long, Miss Cora," David apologized, helping her into her seat. "Time got away from me." He came around to the other side and hopped up next to her.

"I didn't mind," she said softly, looking up at him from beneath her lashes. "I never met no one like you before, with big ideas and new thoughts."

He turned toward her for a moment. "I didn't mind either. Your company sure is pleasant. I, uh, hope it won't be the last time." David started up the car, and they chugged down the road.

Cora knew he could hear the pounding of her heart. It sounded like angry thunder in her ears. "Neither do I."

They were silent for a part of the ride, the sounds of evening turning 'round every corner—creek water running over rocks, hoot owls preparing to settle down, unseen critters pressing the grass beneath their four feet— kept them in familiar company.

From the corner of her eye, Cora snatched glimpses of David's side view. He was handsome for sure. Tall and lanky, a right pretty brown, like tree bark. Even, white teeth and serious, dark eyes, rimmed with thick, long lashes. Hardworking. Had ideas about things, made her think. But he was reserved, cool almost. Even when she cried at his horrid story and held his hand, it was like she weren't there. Mama and Daddy was always huggin' and kissin', showing affection. She was accustomed to being wrapped up in their love, embraced by the church folk. But she wanted to know what *it* felt like for herself, just once. Thought David would be the one, but he didn't seem to have much more interest in her than in a housefly.

She folded her arms and pouted. Weren't she pretty enough? Maybe he figured he was too good for her, he being a doctor and all and educated at college and such, and her just being a preacher's daughter. Or maybe he was just taking her out to be nice, felt sorry for her or something. She didn't need nobody feelin' sorry for her.

The car came to a stop. Cora looked around. They were in front of her house.

"Safe and sound and on time." He turned to her, surprised by the hard set to her mouth that had only a short time ago seemed petal soft. "You all right, Miss Cora?"

She turned, her dark brows crocheted in knots. "Fine. Thanks." She quickly opened the door and got out before he had a chance to help her and slammed the car door, the noise ricocheting through the woods.

David hurried 'round to the front of the car, seconds before Cora was ready to stomp off to the house.

"Miss Cora." He touched her arm, careful not to grab her. He looked toward the house and saw the curtain lift in the window. Cora saw it, too.

"Have I done somethin' to offend you, Miss Cora?"

His voice sounded strained, confused, as if he really didn't know what he'd done.

"You ain't done nothin'," she answered, suddenly ashamed of her unlady-like behavior.

"So what's wrong? Did you have a nice time?"

Cora looked up at him, to the sadness that hung in his eyes. "Yes. I had a fine time."

David bobbed his head, relief easing the skin on his face. He glanced toward the window again and knew if he didn't speak soon it might well be too late. "I, uh, was wondering if you might like to go inta Jackson with me next Saturday to the picture show. If it's all right with your folks," he added quickly.

Her stomach started feeling funny again. "Yes," she blurted out, a smile like sunrise moving across her mouth.

David ducked his head a moment. "I'll come for you 'round noon."

"I'll be ready." She smiled coyly like a young schoolgirl.

They stood there, uncertain of what to do next. David stepped closer, almost reached for her. Cora felt her heart beat out of time. She tilted her face upward, anticipating.

The sound of her house door opening halted any further discussion, any further hope. Cora knew her mother was watching, but still she didn't want to leave, not just yet. But she had to.

"I better go," she said, breathless and disappointed.

David waved to Cora's mother, who returned the acknowledgement but didn't move off the porch.

"Maybe I should ask your folks now if it's all right."

Cora pressed her hand to his chest. "No, I'll talk to 'em. It'll be fine. I'll see you Saturday. At noon."

She turned, quick as a butterfly, and ran toward her house.

$\mathcal{T}wo$

No sooner had Cora stepped up on the front porch, than the cry of her father's name halted her steps and seized her heart. She spun toward the dust cloud on the road.

"Reverend Harvey!" Deacon Earl hollered, charging down the path on his russet-colored mare. "Reverend Harvey, you got ta come."

David froze with his hand on the car door. The deaconesses who routinely gathered inside the Harvey home on Sundays, hearing the ruckus, poured out of the narrow door, forming a wall of color on the porch steps. Their rising voices cackled in an off-key symphony heard too often.

Pearl's hand flew to her mouth to beat back the cry that rushed to her throat. She knew Earl's news was bad. She could feel it. She could feel it sure as she could sense a storm comin' from days off.

Joshua came around from behind the house, his booted steps slow and measured.

Silence passed over the gathering, loud as thunder when Joshua took his place among them. He still wore his preaching shirt and good black pants. Had wanted to set a spell before supper, think about his sermon for next Sunday. No time for that now, he reasoned. He let his eyes rest on Earl and waited—for trouble.

"They done found the Willis boy," Earl panted. Sweat dribbled down his mud brown face. "Down by da river."

A chorus of "Dear Lawd's," "God help Mamie," and "ham mercy," lapped like waves among the womenfolk.

Cora pressed her head against her mother's bosom as if she could somehow hide from the horror—hide from trouble. There was no hiding. This was their life, such as it was. The way it had always been.

Pearl looked toward her husband, just like the others. Needing him to find the words to salve their wounds, give them strength, give her strength.

How many times would he be called upon to make things right, bear the weight of other's sorrow? Joshua thought, his spirit as heavy as his steps. How many Mamas and Papas and children would he have to tell to be strong, it was the Lord's will, that their kinfolk was in a better place? How much longer would he believe it to be true?

Joshua looked toward the dusky sky, watching the heavens shift from day to night. Why? he silently cried. Why have we been forsaken?

Squeezing his hat between his thick fingers, Joshua stepped down from the porch and the procession of solace formed behind him.

By the time everyone had gathered in front of Mamie Willis's house, the sky was full of stars peeking out from between the treetops. There was near a hundred colored folks gathered outside Mamie Willis's door. Most of them came because they were secretly relieved that it wasn't their own house the folks of Rudell were standing in front of. Then there was the rest who were there because they'd want to see friendly faces if it was their boy or girl turned up in the river.

These were the members of First Baptist Church, Joshua Harvey's church.

David looked around in amazement, taking in the somber faces that stood ten deep. They all just stood there in solidarity—for Mamie and her boy Frank. Is this what Cora meant by being part of something—a family—a community?

Joshua moved forward, toward the front door of Mamie Willis's house, and entered, slowing closing the door behind him—barely muffling the sounds of sorrow from within. All along the walk toward this place, Joshua had prayed for strength. Prayed that his words wouldn't sound like a voice bouncing in a bottomless well—empty.

▲　▲　▲

Finally, the door to Mamie Willis's house creaked open, shattering the stillness, scattering the thoughts. No one moved. Even the birds stopped their twittering, not a critter scurried, and the wind settled down to a hush.

Joshua's somber eyes gazed out across the congregation. There was nothing he could say that they didn't already know, already feel. But they expected words of comfort and wisdom. They wanted him to tell them that it was all a mistake, that Frank was playing possum. They wanted him to reassure them that this kind of trouble would never happen to them. And he couldn't. He folded his hands in front of him. "Mamie Willis's son Frank is gone. Gone on from this place to a better place."

A weak "Amen," could be heard in the distance.

Joshua drew in a ragged breath. "But his place here with us is only empty in the body sense. Frank Willis's spirit will always be with us."

"Amen."

"Who we needs to be strong fo' is his mama and his sistahs and his brothas. Our annual church picnic will do honor ta Frank, and our collection for the next three Sundays will go ta the Willis family."

Joshua could see in each of their eyes the unanswered question: How much more can we give, when we ain't got nothin'?

He stepped down off the porch, intending to send his people home, when the sound of a car chugging down the road broke through the night.

The sheriff's car pulled to a stop in front of the Willis house, pushing a cloud of dust and dirt over those nearby. Everybody instinctively moved back when he stepped out of his car.

Joshua approached. "Evenin'."

Jessie Moss's small green orbs cast a look of disdain upon the brown and black faces that dared not look him in the eye.

"You's a long way from yo' church, ain't cha, Reverend?"

Joshua raised his chin a notch. "Church don't have to be a buildin,' Sheriff."

"You sassin' me?"

Joshua didn't respond, merely stared back at him with the same look of controlled contempt.

Jessie cleared his throat loudly and put his hand squarely on his holstered gun. "I think you should tell yo' people to get on home." He hitched his pants up over his protruding belly, then wiped the trickle of sweat that leaked down his face.

"We's here to comfort Mamie Willis," Joshua responded, in that river-deep tone that bespoke authority, the tone he used to soothe his flock—clear and unflinching.

Jessie pursed his lips and looked out on the unmoving crowd, wishing he'd brought his deputy along. "Shame 'bout the Willis boy," he said, loud enough for all to hear. "Heard he turned up in the river. Must have been doing somethin' unseemly." A leer stretched his thin lips. "The rest of you nigras best be careful, too. Ain't safe. There's some right bad folks out here."

In a lower voice he said to Joshua, "Get these people on home, Reverend"—he paused for effect—"I'd hate to see anything else happen."

"So would I," Joshua returned, in the same pseudowhisper, straightening his field-built shoulders.

Jessie clenched his jaw, his face turning crimson before he tipped his hat to the crowd and returned to his car.

Joshua watched it slowly disappear down the road until there was nothing left but the cloud of dust the sheriff rode in on. Joshua walked to the head of his congregation and led them home.

▲ ▲ ▲

Cora hung up her good, peach Sunday dress in the cupboard-like closet in her bedroom. From the top drawer of her bureau, the one her father made when she'd turned sixteen, she took out her short-sleeved, sky blue nightgown and let it drift over her weary body.

A day like today makes you feel older than your years, she thought, running a boar's hair brush through her thick, black hair. It clouded everything pretty, shook up your dreams like a hurricane, and tossed them out of reach.

Cora walked to the window and pushed the thin, white curtains aside. The deep blue sky was lit like a Christmas tree full of stars. Peaceful like. Yet less than a mile away, sorrow kept company with Mamie Willis and her kids. It made what she wanted to do with her own life seem so unimportant and small.

She turned away, decided to set a spell on the back porch before turning in for the night. Cora tiptoed down the stairs and opened the door to the porch, expecting to be alone.

Joshua sat still as a tree shadow on two cinder blocks, staring it seemed, sightlessly beyond the horizon.

Cora approached quietly, peering into the black-as-pitch night. "Daddy?"

Joshua turned his head and gazed upon his daughter. A whisper of a smile stretched his lips. "Thought you'd be 'sleep by now." He picked up a twig from near his feet and twirled it between his fingers.

Cora stood above him, wrapping her arm around the post that held up the overhanging roof. "Couldn't sleep."

"Hmm. I knows how that can be," he said, in a voice so sad she could hardly recognize it as her daddy's. Her heart thumped.

"Gonna be another hot one tomorrow," he said. "Kin tell by the way the heat band rings the moon." He pointed toward the heavens with the twig.

Cora gathered up her gown in her hands and sat down on the step. For a while neither of them said anything, just sat in the company of each other.

"Didn't get a chance ta ask ya 'bout yo' afternoon with the doctor."

Cora felt her face heat and was grateful for the darkness. "It was nice. Real nice. Dr. Mackey is a gentleman." She paused a beat. "Thank ya for lettin' me go, Daddy."

He nodded. "You like this fella?"

Cora lowered her head. "I reckon I do."

"Hmm. How's he feel 'bout you?"

She wasn't quite sure how to answer that. David Mackey was a hard man to read. One minute she thought he didn't give a hoot, the next he was asking to see her again. She wasn't sure what that meant.

"I don't rightly know. I think he does. I, mean . . . I don't have nothin' to compare him to."

"I 'spose it is hard to tell with some mens." He continued to spin the twig between his fingers. "They's raised up to hide their feelin's, but that don't mean they don't have none." He turned to look at her. "Understand what I'm sayin'?"

"Yes, suh." But she wasn't sure she did.

"He ain't tried nothin', did he?"

"No, suh!" she answered, shocked that her father would ask her such a thing.

"Good."

"He, uh, asked to take me to the picture show next Saturday coming." She waited, listening to nature and the beat of her heart.

"Hmm. He gon' come pick you up in that fancy car of his?"

"Yes, suh."

"Hmm. We'll see what yo' mama has ta say."

"What do *you* say?"

He looked at her and smiled. "I'll talk to yo' mama 'bout it, and we'll come to a decision." He lowered his head to hide his grin. "But I'll be sho' ta put in a good word for ya with yo' mama."

Cora felt like she'd burst with joy. "Thank ya, Daddy," she said, and immediately began to think of spending time with David Mackey in a dark theater. What would she wear?

They fell into silence again.

"What you think happened to Frank, Daddy?" she asked suddenly.

Even in the darkness, she could see her father's features tense, the jaw squeeze.

"What happens to a lot of coloreds; they disappear then turn up dead."

"Was it the night riders?" Her flesh prickled when she thought about the white-sheeted men who periodically rode through town terrorizing the coloreds, setting property on fire, or making people disappear.

"I can't say." He dropped the twig. "What I do know is that Frank Willis is in a better place. No more sufferin', no more struggle."

"But he was only sixteen," she protested, thinking how easily *she* could just disappear. "He didn't get a chance to see nothin', do nothin', get way from Rudell." She was breathing hard now, just imaging the possibility that maybe she would never get out, would never realize her dreams. The thought terrified her.

"Age ain't what makes the difference, Daughter. It's what you do with the time you have. Nothin's promised."

She followed the direction of his gaze, out and beyond Rudell. She pointed. "What's it like out there, Daddy?"

Joshua pushed out a breath. "Mississippi is all I ever knowed. Around these parts it's all the same for colored folks. We try to make a life, do the best we can."

"They say it's better for coloreds up North, in New York and Chicago. We get treated good, get jobs, and have nice places to live."

"So they say," he agreed, nodding his head slowly.

"Deacon Earl's niece lives up North. He say she's doing right fine," she added, needing to press her point.

Joshua rubbed his hands along the length of his thighs, then pointed up toward a brilliant star that shone brighter than all others in the heavens. "If you had one wish, what would you do?"

Cora pulled in a breath, letting her eyes follow the stretch of his arm. "I would go to a big city up North and sing," she said, without hesitation.

Slowly Joshua rose, towering above his daughter. Gently he looked down into her eyes. "Sometimes wishes come true, Daughter." He lovingly kissed her forehead. "Just be mindful of what you wish for."

He stepped up on the porch and headed for the door. "Better get rid of them magazines fo' yo' mama finds 'em," he said lightly, and went inside, shutting the door quietly behind him.

▲ ▲ ▲

Cora lay atop her quilt and opened the secret box she kept hidden beneath her bed. She had to keep it away from Mama. Mama didn't take to her reading nothing but the Bible. Thought all those fashion books and singing in clubs was sinful and wouldn't lead to nothing but devilment.

She was still shocked that her daddy knew about her treasures and didn't lecture her none. Now it was their secret. Hers and Daddy's. She smiled, feeling warm and loved. Not that she didn't feel her mama's love, 'cause she did. It was just that her daddy understood her, understood that she had dreams bigger than Rudell, and he wanted to see her get them.

Mama's love was a protective love, borne out of knowing how hard life can be. Mama didn't want to see her get hurt, didn't want her to lose her way or lose sight of the Lord. But she believed she could live her life and still love God. She didn't have to give up one for the other. Mama. Daddy. How different they were, yet they were both the same. They loved her something fierce and only wanted what was best for her. She was lucky.

Sighing, she flipped through the Montgomery Ward and Wanamaker catalogs, her fingers grazing across the pages, imagining herself in the fancy dresses she saw on those pages. Tossing those aside, she opened her copy of *Colored Citizens* one of the few colored papers in Mississippi, and haltingly read an article about Duke Ellington, who was the rage in Chicago with a kind of music called jazz that was gaining in popularity. There was also a story about the blues singer Bessie Smith, who was performing with Coleman Hawkins. She wished she could hear that kind of music. But her folks would never allow it.

Cora lay the paper on her chest. What was it like to sing something other than church songs with a big band behind you and bright stage lights shining down? She could almost hear the sound of applause vibrate in her ears.

If she could get away from Rudell, she would buy fancy dresses and go to the nightclubs she'd read about. She would sing for the crowds and make lots of money to send for her folks so they could join her. She would meet all the famous people she'd read about, and she'd be famous, too. She'd be somebody. And maybe, just maybe, she thought, with a little beat of her heart—maybe David would come, too.

Cora gazed toward the window. Hope was just beyond the horizon. She could almost touch it. Almost.

Hypnotically, a slight breeze pushed the lightweight curtains in and out of the opened window. Just beyond its frame she could hear the sound of crickets in the trees and hoots owls settling down for the night. And if she listened real carefully, she could hear the faint rumbling of the railroad heading North—to freedom—to her dream.

Three

~~~~~~~~~~~~

In the solemn days following the reclaiming of young Frank Willis from the receding river, a dark shroud of sorrow draped itself over the town of Rudell, robbing it of its vibrance, creating a sort of hush much like a tragic secret shared by everyone.

From both sides of the Left Hand River they came. One by one and in pairs, bringing food and clothes they couldn't spare but did nonetheless; Baptists and Episcopals alike.

The deaconesses of First Baptist held prayer vigils at the foot of Mamie's bed. The women of Big Bethel bathed her like a newborn. Both sides took turns spoon-feeding her when need be. And the men, young and old, did their own fishing—for a change. All compelled by a single force—loss.

It was no longer Mamie Willis who'd lost Frank. The town of Rudell had lost him, too—their ray of hope. Their beacon. As such, they moved through an unfamiliar darkness, guided only by what came naturally.

Cora, her mama Pearl, and Sister Lucinda Carver, having paid their respects, continued the business of gathering supplies for the flood victims of the Delta. They worked from sunup to set, packing, weeding, and talking woman talk in the one room of First Baptist.

Everywhere the eye could stretch was row after row of sacrifice, sacrifice overflowing in the tiny, white church. Clothes, worn shoes, sheets, canned fruit, dried beef, and even children's toys with missing arms or legs were piled high. It was up to Cora, Pearl, and Sister Lucinda to see to it that only the best of the worst was packed in the cardboard boxes and burlap bags.

If Sister Lucinda had her dithers, she'd do it all herself. Being in charge, taking care of others, was her way, and all the women of the church knew it and knew it well. If there was a job to be done, a church member laid low, an errand to run, Lucinda Carver was at the head of the flock, directing the women like a farmer scattering his chickens. And the folks of Rudell just accepted it.

Lucinda never married, never had no young ones. Whisper was she was too bossy and would run the men away. Truth was, when Lucinda lost her folks to that coughing sickness, and she'd wandered along the roads alone and hungry, from Alligator to Rudell, it was the women of First Baptist who took her in, made her welcome. Most of those women were long under the ground, and folks forgot the real story. Truth was, Lucinda was so grateful she decided to devote her life to good work, helping others. As such, there wasn't time or room in her life for much else. And she was happy just the way things were. At least that's how one of the stories went.

Cora watched Lucinda's quick, thick fingers, thinking of the times Lucinda had squeezed her between her meaty thighs and plaited her hair, fussing with each thick braid. "Got enough hair on top of yo' head fo' two!" Lucinda would mumble, twirling and tugging and twisting those braids into shape, sweat running down her face and into her eyes. When that would happen, Lucinda would let out a yelp like a pup whose tail had been stepped on. And it took all of Cora's good home training to keep from laughing.

Cora smiled at the memory, while she neatly folded a threadbare cotton shirt and put it in a box marked MENS.

Just two more days, Cora thought quietly in her head, taking a jar of dried beans and wrapping it in newspaper. Two more days until her outing with David Mackey. Sometimes when she thought about it, thought about him, her heart would start beating so fast she could hardly breathe. She'd get a warm feeling inside, like the onset of fever. Was that love?

She wanted to talk to her mama about what an outing was like, what it was like to be with a man, what her and daddy did when they were courting. But when she opened the subject at the breakfast table—after Daddy left, of course—Mama only told her, "Make sure he stay a gentleman and you be the lady I raised you up to be." With that, Pearl got up from the thick, hand-carved wood table and started collecting the breakfast plates, as if that was all that needed to be said.

It wasn't. Cora had so many questions, so many emotions spilling around inside her that she didn't understand. She couldn't ask her two best friends,

Maybelle and Sassy. Those two fools would laugh, sure enough, until they cried, and tell her she was a baby. She wouldn't be laughed at. No sirree. She'd thought about talking with Sister Carver, but since she'd never had a man, Cora reckoned it would be a waste of time.

"Cora, chile, you gon' daydream or work?" her mother asked, giving her a tender poke in the arm.

Cora blinked and gave her mother an apologetic smile, absently putting the jar of dried beans in the box with the other food stuff. "Sorry. Just thinkin' is all."

"You got plenty of time for that. We got ta get this place squared away fo' Sunday service," Pearl said, waving her thin arms to emphasize her point.

"She thinkin' 'bout that young, handsome doctor," Lucinda said, chuckling deep in her throat. She glanced at Cora from the corner of her eyes, then winked.

Cora's face burned. She lowered her gaze, moved to the far end of the pew, and began sorting through the clothing.

"Ain't that right?" Lucinda pressed, holding up a pair of work pants for inspection.

Pearl stood still as a photograph, waiting for her daughter to answer. What was going on in that head of hers? Ever since she'd gone to Joe's with that boy, she'd been walking around like a ghost. She'd been too feared to ask her daughter if anything happened. All she could pray for every night was that Cora stayed a good girl till the time was right.

Lawd knows she remembered too well the fire between her legs when she was Cora's age, and Joshua starting coming 'round regular. Sometimes it got so bad she'd beg him to touch it, just once, to put the fire out. And he did. More and more every day, until her skirts were up around her thighs and her ripe breasts ready for picking pushed through her thin shifts.

They couldn't help what they did. And no amount of praying could stop them. They'd laid together before their marriage day, right there on the grass beneath the canopy of trees along the Left Hand River.

It was hot that night. So hot. Hotter than she'd ever remembered. Hardly nothing moved, not a leaf, not a blade of grass. Even the water was still.

She was sitting in her favorite spot, atop the flat rock waiting, as always, for Joshua to come down the road from the fields. The instant she spotted him cresting the ridge, she'd felt a tumbling in her tummy and the warmth spread like an overflowing river. She'd folded and unfolded the napkin covering the biscuit she'd saved him from her supper. Her eyes widened into twin pools of reflective light as he drew closer.

Joshua walked with a heavy foot, slow and plodding, moving like a man beaten down by a hard day's work.

Pearl's heart panged in her chest to see him so weary. She wanted to lay his head against her breasts and lull him into a restful sleep. What she wouldn't give to take some of his weariness away.

At first he didn't see her there, shadowed as she was beneath the umbrella of tree leaves. Then all at once, there she was, like a sweet vision from his dreams. He felt a slow flow of energy sludge through his veins, giving him the last push he needed.

Pearl stood. Joshua's eyes met her gentle, eager ones, and he knew what it felt like to be loved, to be lifted with just a smile. But what could he offer this woman but his dreams, this woman who deserved to have fine clothes, a bed she didn't have to share with cousins and neighbors, a good meal and a better life? He had no more than what was on his back and the satchel he carried on his shoulders. Still he knew he would be less than what he was if Pearl wasn't in his life.

Joshua snatched his beat-up, brown hat from his head, leaving a ring through his thick, wooly hair. His smile was bright: white teeth set against dark skin. *The moon reflected against the night sky,* Pearl thought.

"How do, Pearl?"

"Waitin' on you," she answered coyly, wishing she had something pretty to wear instead of the old, hand-me-down shift. She pushed the napkin-wrapped biscuit toward him.

"Thank ya."

Their fingers brushed.

"Come set a spell. I know you be tired," Pearl said, hearing the tremor in her voice, the shudder in her body.

Joshua took her hand, easing Pearl down next to him. Shoulder to shoulder they sat on the flat rock. Nothing moved, not even the sweat from their brow. Everything seemed to be waiting for some secret sign.

Gingerly, Pearl touched Joshua's hard thighs and felt the muscles knot beneath her long, persuasive fingertips. "Piano fingers" Joshua often called them. She pressed a bit harder, keeping her gaze fixed on the water trickling over the rocks. A gentle moan, no louder than the rustle of a breeze pushed past his lips.

A fat, green frog sat on the lap of a leaf, its big, black eyes stared at the couple—waiting. It didn't make a sound. Didn't move.

Above them the clouds stood still—at attention almost—the bands of blazing orange and gold hung majestically across the horizon. Waiting. Pearl's breath came in short bursts that she tried to hold in her chest.

Joshua took her hand and pulled her to her feet. He led her to the cove of trees by the river. *Yes,* Pearl thought, *the memory of that first time was as fresh as if it had happened yesterday.*

She knew it was wrong, being unwed and all. Knew she had sinned. Didn't matter none that for the time Joshua lay between her thighs the fire stopped burning. Naw, that didn't matter none. She'd sinned. Sinned. And she would spend the rest of her life making it up. She didn't want that kind of burden for her child, that kind of guilt.

But she also knew that the fire was a powerful thing. Make you forget what was right, bring younguns into the world too soon, and shame on your house. Naw, she didn't want that for her Cora. So she prayed. Prayed instead of talked.

"Now who be daydreamin'?" Lucinda asked, stirring Pearl from her past.

"Humph," Pearl snorted. "I'm just waitin' on an answer from this chile of mine." She eyed Cora hard.

Cora swallowed, wished they would leave her be. She folded the clothes a bit faster. Kept her eyes on her work. "I was just thinkin' 'bout . . . my solo for Sunday is all. Don't know all the words just yet."

Pearl watched the lie take shape, stand tall and proud between her and Cora, fill the room, suck up the air. She felt a tightness in her chest and wanted to shake her daughter, stamp that fire out. But she knew how powerful it was, how hot it could burn.

"Never knowed you to be worried 'bout singin', Cora chile," Lucinda, said. She opened a jar of stewed fruit and took a whiff.

"Ain't worried." *Least that part wasn't no lie,* Cora thought. "Just thinkin' is all."

"Little mo' work and less thinkin,' and we kin get don wit this," Pearl said. Her eyes cut to the side, watching Cora. The lie eased back and left the room.

Cora kept the rest of her thoughts tucked away, far in the back of her mind where they couldn't be seen. Weren't nobody she could talk to about her feelings and confusion. She'd keep them to herself. Mama would never understand.

"Whew," Lucinda lamented, wiping her plump, wood brown face with her hand. "Near suppertime by the hang of the sun."

The three women looked toward the west window. The ball of light was a blinding orange, the heavens a startling blue. The men would be coming home from the fields directly, and those who were lucky enough ta work in town would soon be headin' home.

"Tomorrow's another day," Pearl announced. "God willin'."

The three women quickly sealed up what boxes and bags they could, brushed off their dresses with swipes of their hands, and headed outside.

The air was still thick with heat that stuck to the skin and tugged the air from your lungs. Half naked children ran barefoot up and down the hard-packed earth and crisp, green grass, squealing in childish delight.

Cora smiled, remembering her own carefree days frolicking up and down the roads of Rudell. What would her children look like? she wondered, stepping down from the church steps. Would they be wild and wooly haired, long and thin, deep brown or black as berries? Unconsciously, she pressed her hand to her flat stomach, imagining it full with child. She could almost see the smile of manly pride on David's face for having done the deed.

She blinked. Her heart fluttered. What was she doin'? Her thoughts scared her. David hadn't done no more than give her a kind look, hold her hand, and help her into his fancy car. Here she was thinkin' . . . Her face burned with shame, and she lowered her head to keep from revealing the lust on her mind.

"Evening, ladies."

Cora's head snapped up, and she almost missed her step. She grabbed hold of the wooden rail. She'd conjured him up sure enough, she thought, as her heart took off on a wild gallop. A sensation of excitement and fear ran through her. Could he see in her eyes what was on her mind?

David approached, stretching out his hand to assist Lucinda, then Pearl, down the steps.

"Thank ya, Doctor," the women said, in near unison.

He tipped his straw hat, raising his gaze to meet Cora's, who still stood on the step, framed like a portrait by the arch of the church door.

David extended his hand to Cora. Tentatively, she reached out and placed her hand in his, taking slow, measured steps until her feet touched the ground.

"Looking very pretty today, Cora," he said, for only her ears.

Heat crept up from her neck to flush her cheeks. She favored him with a small smile, thankful for her dark skin. "Thank ya," she answered, a bit breathless.

Pearl and Lucinda stood like sentinels waiting for the two young people as they approached.

"Finished yo' day's work mighty early, Doctor," Pearl questioned more than asked.

"That's a good thing, ma'am. It means there's not a lot of sick folk in Rudell." He glanced at Cora then to Pearl. "So I figured I'd stop by, see if you ladies need a ride home. Know you must be tired."

"Well, that would be right nice of ya, Doctor," Lucinda answered enthusiastically. Her dark eyes widened in delight as they ran over the shiny black car.

"Y'all go on. I need the exercise," Pearl said.

"I couldn't do that, Mrs. Harvey. Wouldn't be right."

Pearl waved her hand in dismissal. "I been walkin' all this long time. One mo' day ain't gon' make no difference."

"Aw, come on, Pearl," Lucinda insisted. "I always wanted to try out one of these things." Her eyes gleamed as she ran her hand along the hood.

"Naw, I—"

"Come on, Mama," Cora pleaded. She wanted her to see what a good driver David was, what a gentleman. She wanted the neighbors to run out on the road and see her and her mama getting out of a fancy automobile. She hooked her arm through Pearl's and gently tugged her toward the car.

Pearl wanted to dig her heels into the earth, grow roots, and just stay right there. She wanted to scream for them to leave her be. Her heart was beating so fast she could hardly breathe. Truth was, she'd never been in one of them contraptions. And she was scared, plain and simple.

"Mama," Cora said in alarm, "you shakin'." She wrapped her arm around Pearl's stiff, narrow shoulders. "What's wrong? You got a chill? Comin' down with somethin'?"

Now she really felt the fool, Pearl thought, with mounting horror, feeling the tremors creeping up and down her body.

David approached, his voice low and soothing. "Mrs. Harvey, why don't you sit up front with me. Where it's safe."

Pearl's round eyes rounded some more.

Gently, David touched her arm and felt the clamminess of her skin. "Why don't you get Ms. Lucinda settled, Cora, and I'll take care of your mama here."

He looked down into Pearl's panic-stricken face. "If that's all right with you, Mrs. Harvey?" he gently asked.

Pearl's mouth was so dry, she couldn't speak. But there was something about the kind way he looked at her, the soft touch and lullabye voice that gradually slowed the racing of her heart. She gave two short nods.

David's smile bathed her in sunshine, pushing the chill aside. "Good, then. Now," he said patiently, as if explaining to a small child, "let me help you up in the seat. That's right," he encouraged, as she eased into the seat and sat with her long, thin body in one knot.

David hurried around to the driver's side, while Cora and Lucinda settled down in the back.

Pearl let out a short yelp when the car bucked, seeming to shake itself loose, before David eased it down the rutted lane. All the while that they drove from the church, David kept up a steady stream of chatter, pointing out rocks, houses, trees, and such that Pearl had seen all her life, but suddenly looked at through new eyes. David's tone was like a soothing massage after a hard day's work. Slowly, Pearl felt the tightness ease in her frame. She even dared to stretch her neck to get a better look at a family of brown-and-white jackrabbits sitting along the side of the road, watching them with big, button eyes and twitches of their noses. *What must they be thinkin'?* Pearl silently questioned. *We must sho' nuff be a sight.*

Pearl found herself smiling and even loosened the hold she had on her knees. They'd finally stopped shaking. She gave a quick, tentative wave to Deacon Earl's nephews playing on the porch and puffed her chest with pride when their mouths opened in awe.

David slid a glance at Pearl's profile. The tautness across her cheeks and the bright light of terror that had lit her eyes were gone. He relaxed in his seat and the familiar feeling of satisfaction after tending to a patient settled over him. Healing didn't always mean mending bones, breaking fevers, applying salves, and delivering babies. Sometimes, what needed healing more than the body was what the eyes couldn't see—the mind and the spirit. When he could experience that kind of healing, be part of the process, now that was doctoring.

David slowed to a stop, jumped out, and helped Lucinda from her seat and to her front door.

"You's a nice boy," Lucinda commented, when they reached her door, which was hung with one hinge at the top, leaving the door at an angle.

"Thank you, ma'am." He lifted the door by the knob and pushed it open.

"Whew," Lucinda puffed, the sudden slap of hot, damp air robbing her of breath. She stepped inside her neat home, a far cry from the crumbling picture it made outside.

David took a quick look around. The furnishings were sparse but finely carved. The waning sunlight bounced off the polished spindle legs of the kitchen chairs. Fresh floral-patterned curtains hung in the windows, and the long, wooden couch overflowed with pillows of the same fabric.

A frown descended over David's face and was quickly replaced with wonder. The entire house smelled clean, hand-scrubbed clean. Not the kind of smell he was used to in most colored homes he'd visited. They usually smelled of worry, fear, sickness, and despair. All as potent as the scents of fried chicken, roasted potatoes, collards seasoned in fat back, and moonshine cooked in the shed, that had all soaked into the walls and bedding, clinging to everything they touched.

Lucinda studied him steadily. Her narrow eyes drew to slits. "You best treat that gal good. You hear me, boy?" she admonished, wagging a finger near his nose.

David jerked back from her sudden assault. Before he could respond, Lucinda laced into him like a thief caught with the goods. "Cora be a good girl. You understand me?" She peered hard into his face, her mouth set in a permanent pucker, until he nodded in agreement. She snapped her head. "Good. She may look like a woman, but Cora still a chile in some ways," she said, her voice softening from its previous hard edge. "Don't know nothin' much 'bout nothin', specially mens." She angled her chin toward the door. "The good reverend and the missus keep her close to them. Too close, ifn you ask me. But ya didn't ask me, did ya?"

David opened his mouth to speak, but Lucinda paid him no mind. "Not good. Chile got ta learn ta stand on her own. They ain't always gon' be there to protect her from the world." She placed her hands on her hips and peered up at him. "You a smart fella, doctor and all. You care fo' Cora?"

"I—"

" 'Cause ifn you do, you do right by her," she said, cutting him off again. "You's the first man her kin let come anywhere near that chile." She angled her head. "Reckon that makes you somebody special." Her statement was almost a challenge.

This time David didn't attempt to respond. He didn't see the point.

"Well, does it?" she demanded, and David flinched in surprise.

"I—"

"You just make sho' you take good care of that girl," she puffed, moving toward the table and sitting down heavily. "She's special, too. She's like my own daughter—if I'd ever had one." She mumbled the last part.

"Yes, ma'am. I—"

"You best to be gettin' on and take them ladies home," she ordered, as if he was planning to stay awhile. She got up and began puttering around the small kitchen, setting pans on the black, potbellied stove.

With nothing else to be said, David made his move to leave.

"You a right handsome fella. Good bones and coloring," Lucinda said, stopping him in his tracks. "You and Cora could sho' nuff make some fine younguns."

David felt his face heat. "I guess I should be going," he stuttered.

Lucinda turned from the stove and pointed a warning finger in David's direction. "Don't forget what I said 'bout Cora, hear."

"I won't, ma'am—"

"Well, whatchu still standin' there fo'?" She flung her arm toward the door. "Get!"

David bobbed his head, knowing by now that it was pointless to answer. He slipped out of the door and hurried to the car.

"Miss Lucinda is certainly an interesting woman," he commented, as they pulled off.

Pearl and Cora simply looked at each other with identical knowing glances and laughed.

By the time they pulled up in front of the Harvey's home, Pearl had set aside all her fears, and Cora was proud as a peacock.

They'd passed Maybelle and Sassy as the two sat on Sassy's porch, and Cora couldn't stop herself from hollering out the open window and waving. The breach in ladylike manners was worth the open-mouthed looks she got from her friends and the cutting look from her mother.

"That was a right fine ride, Doctor," Pearl said, as he held her hand and helped her alight from the car.

"Glad you enjoyed it. I'd be happy to run you—and Miss Cora—into town from time to time." He looked at Cora and was gratified with a brilliant smile. His heart tumbled in his chest.

"I just might like that," Pearl said. "Evenin', now." She turned and headed toward the house, then stopped and called over her shoulder. "We still have supper to fix, Cora," she said. Her way of telling her daughter not to linger.

Cora's gaze followed her mother, who'd purposely left the door ajar.

"I'd better go."

David took a quick look toward the house, then clasped Cora's hand. "It was good seeing you today, Cora. I—couldn't wait till Saturday." He smiled and she noticed the dimple again.

Her pulse raced. She lowered her gaze. "I'm glad you stopped by," she said softly. "Lookin' forward to Saturday."

"Me, too."

"Co-ra!" her mother called in two long syllables from the doorway.

Cora snatched her hand from David's grasp, and she suddenly felt cold all over.

"Go on. I'll see you Saturday."

"Bye . . ."

Cora ran toward the steps, and she and Pearl waved in unison as he drove away.

"He seems like a nice enuf fella," Pearl commented, closing the door. "Fancy car and all. Must do well fo' hisself." She walked toward the kitchen.

Cora didn't reply. Her mind was already ticking off the hours until she would see him again.

▲ ▲ ▲

Friday was more of the days before. From early in the morning when the sun was barely peeking through the tree branches and casting its golden rays across the ripples of water, Cora and Pearl were in the church packing supplies for the needy.

Pearl hadn't spoken again about David or made reference to the ride home. But Cora could feel her mother's questions like someone's breath on the back of your neck, tingling whispering, reminding you of its presence.

Why doesn't she say something? Cora inwardly fumed, shoving a child's dress into a burlap sack. Couldn't her mama tell how nervous she was about her coming outing with David, how she could hardly sleep? Couldn't she see all the feelings tumbling 'round inside her with no direction?

Was praying enough? Cora worried. Mama seemed to think it was the answer to everything. Maybe it was and she just wasn't praying hard enough.

She snatched a glance at her mother.

Pearl Harvey was the same as Cora's first recollection of her mother. She still had those bright eyes, snappy eyes that could be warm and loving, then with a blink, put the fear of God in you. That "mama look."

Cora loved her mother's voice, too, the throaty, soothing tone of it. Her mama's voice reminded her of a warm bath—a treat. She was still slender, her back straight, her fingers nimble. But for all that stayed the same, there were things about her mama that had changed, things Cora missed.

Mama had stopped creeping into her room late at night to "steal a kiss from my baby." She'd stopped sitting on the edge of her bed telling her tales of growing up in Mississippi. Cora wasn't sure why those visits had stopped. At first she reckoned it was because Mama finally saw her as growing up, not "a baby girl" no more. And with that she felt a mixture of pride and sadness. Pride that she was a woman, as such. And sadness because she felt like she'd lost a friend. Right about now, she wished she had her friend back.

Pearl fretted all night about Cora and her first outing with the doctor. Seeing the two of them together, the looks that passed between them only increased her worry. She'd prayed long and hard to find the words to talk to her child, who was no longer a child but a woman.

She watched Cora now. Watched how her once long, lanky body had rounded into soft curves that couldn't be disguised beneath the full slip and simple dress. Her once awkward movements were now smooth, almost seductive.

Cora had her build and face, but Cora's eyes were darker, more expressive, her mouth fuller and inviting. There was an energy beneath Cora's serene demeanor, a sharp mind and an endless curiosity. No, Cora was no longer her baby, and one day she'd be a married woman with a family of her own.

Pearl sighed. No one had ever talked to her about loving, what that meant, what it could do to your mind and body. All her mama had ever told her was, "Don't let no boy get up under yo' skirts. We got too many mouths to feed as is." But she never told her about the fire that could flare up at any minute and burn you up with its heat. Make you sin. Leave you with a stain on your soul.

"Cora," Pearl said suddenly, needing to get it out before she couldn't.

"Yes, mama?" Cora turned questioning eyes on her mother, hopeful eyes.

Pearl cleared her throat. "I was thinkin' 'bout tomorrow." Pearl kept folding clothes.

"Yes, ma'am."

"I was thinkin' that maybe if I took the hem out of the pretty blue dress you could wear that to the picture show. "You always did look right pretty in that."

Cora felt her throat tighten with emotion. "Thank you, Mama. That would be nice."

"He gon' come pick you up, right?"

"Yes, Mama." Cora waited expectantly.

Pearl nodded. "You . . . like the boy, Cora?"

Cora swallowed. "I 'spose."

Pearl finally faced her daughter, and when she did she saw all the same questions and the same fears she'd had when she and Joshua were courting reflected in Cora's luminous eyes.

"It means a lot . . . when you take up with someone," Pearl hedged, feeling her way.

Cora inched closer, needing to catch every word dropped from her mother's lips. She waited, almost holding her breath.

"I knows how hard it kin get when yo' . . . feelin's start buddin'. Make ya feel funny inside like ya want to laugh all the time, even when nothin's funny."

Cora smiled. "That's how you felt with Daddy?" she asked softly.

Pearl briefly looked away. "Yeah, I did. Still do," she added, casting a look at her daughter. Pearl smiled. "Still do."

Cora sighed dreamily and sat down, looking up at her mother's soft expression. "That's why y'all got married, 'cause of that funny feelin'?"

Pearl nodded again.

Cora thought it over for a minute. "That's how I feel, too, Mama. Funny inside like my stomach is doing a dance. And my heart starts racing when I think about him," she went on eagerly, spilling all she'd bottled up inside like a dam that had burst.

"When I started seein' him in town, lookin' polished, I never thought he'd pay me no never mind." She giggled and covered her mouth. "Then I smiled at him." She gave her mother that mischievous look she often wore when she was a little girl and had been caught playing in her mother's things. "And he smiled right back, Mama!" Her voice lowered. "But I think he was scared of Daddy and wouldn't say anything." She giggled again.

Pearl held back a smile, knowing that Joshua was all bark and no bite. He was the most gentle, giving man she'd ever known. But he knew when to use his dark looks and hefty body to put the fear in you.

Cora's look grew pensive. A frown creased her brow. "You think me and David will be like you and Daddy?"

Pearl flinched.

"I mean . . . get married and all?"

"That's not up to me. It's up to the Lawd. If it's meant to be, it will. If you two love each other, it will." Pearl swallowed. "Now, I want you to listen to me, Cora." She took a seat on the pew next to her daughter. "Sometimes feelin's . . . kin get out of hand. Make you do thangs befo' it's time, befo' you's ready."

Cora nodded vigorously. "Did you and Daddy wait?"

Pearl's stomach rushed to her throat. She could barely look Cora in the eyes as the lie eased like dewdrops across her lips and sat there sparkling in the morning light. "Yes." It was a whisper.

Cora stared at her mother, memorizing the strained look that stretched the skin across her cheeks, the eyes that wouldn't settle down and the fingers that wouldn't be still.

"What . . . I'm sayin' is, no matter how powerful them feelin's get," Pearl said, with an adamant toss of her head, "you got ta control them till the time is right. Till you's married. Don't lay down fo' no man who ain't yo' husband, Cora. Lawd don't look down with favor on that. It's a sin. A powerful sin. What goes on between a man and a woman should be blessed by the Lawd." She paused a moment. "You . . . understand what I'm tellin' you, chile?"

"Yes, Mama."

"Good. David seems like a gentleman, and he'll treat you like a lady as long as you act like one."

"Yes, ma'am." Cora stared at the floor as Pearl pushed out a long, relieved breath, slapped her right thigh, and stood. "We best be gettin' busy fo' Sister Lucinda gets back and starts ta yakin' 'bout how lazy we are."

Cora stood as well and, without warning, wrapped her mother in her arms. She was just as tall as Pearl now, and her soft words hummed like a hymn in Pearl's ears. "I love you, Mama. Thank you."

Pearl gently patted her back like a baby after feeding. "I love you, too, sugah. Always know that." And as she held her daughter close, she could only pray that Cora would heed to her warning.

▲ ▲ ▲

Cora was jumpy as a rabbit on the run. She paced to and fro, peeking out of her bedroom window, then ducking from sight when she saw someone pass. She smoothed her unwrinkled dress, the one her mother had fixed. She patted her hair and put more cream on her hands, rubbing them nervously together. With every sound, she jumped, thinking it was David pulling up. And her heart sank to her belly each time it wasn't. "He ain't comin'," she concluded aloud, letting the curtain fall back in place. "He ain't comin', and I'm gon' be the fool."

She'd bragged all week to Maybelle and Sassy about going to the picture show. And even though Maybelle had Little Jake and Sassy had Harold Jr. as steady beaus, they couldn't claim to have ever gone any further than Joe's or out to the river. They were just as excited for her as she was, even if they were a little bit jealous. Cora had to beg them not to embarrass her by sitting on her porch when he arrived. With great reluctance and much moaning, they'd finally agreed, making her swear she'd share every detail when she returned.

Cora plopped down heavily on the bed and folded her arms. Now what would she tell them? Her eyes began to fill until the tears hung for a moment on her lashes before running down her cheeks.

"Co-ra!" her father called from downstairs.

She sniffed hard and swiped at her tears when she heard her father's heavy footfalls on the stairs.

"Yes, Daddy," she answered weakly.

Her father was standing in her open doorway. "What's wrong, chile? he asked, his voice full of concern when he noticed her watery eyes and trembling bottom lip. He came into the room, his height and bulk taking up much of the small space.

"Just got the sniffles is all," she said.

Joshua's eyes narrowed suspiciously. "Well, that young man's downstairs waitin' on ya. Should I tell him you sick?"

Cora's eyes widened in alarm. Her hand flew to her chest. "He's here?"

"Hmmm." Joshua held onto his smile. "Guess you thought he weren't comin'. That's enuf worry to bring on the sniffles."

Father and daughter shared a quick, secret look. Cora lowered her head. "Could you tell him I'll be down directly?"

Joshua turned, leaving Cora to gather herself together.

Several moments later she appeared in the doorway of the kitchen to see her mother and David chatting like old friends.

David sprang up from his seat when Pearl's gaze veered toward the doorway. A wide smile stretched his full mouth, revealing even, white teeth.

"Hello, Cora."

"Hi," she answered.

"The doctor, here, just delivered Tess Hawkins's baby," Pearl announced, as if she was the proud parent. "She had another boy."

"That's why I was late," David said, feeling the need to explain.

The tight expression on Cora's face began to soften.

"How many does that make?" Joshua asked, joining in the conversation.

"Six," Pearl answered, a bit awestruck as she tried to imagine herself as a mother of six.

"Guess I need to get ready for another baptism in a few weeks. Lord works in mysterious ways," Joshua said, almost to himself. "We lost Frank

Willis and now we have Tess's new boy." The thought spread through the room like a rumor, momentarily catching each one by surprise as rumors often do.

Joshua was the first to speak, stirring them from their reverie. "You two best be gettin' on. Be time for Cora to come home fo' y'all leave."

"Yes, sir," David responded, quick as lightning. "Are you ready, Cora?"

Cora quickly glanced at her mother and father, who both gave slight nods of assent.

"I'm ready."

David stepped up to her and hooked her arm through his. "I'll have her back early," he assured them as the young couple moved toward the door and out.

Pearl and Joshua stood in the arch of the doorway, watching in silence as the car pulled away, each caught in their own memories of a younger time.

"Our little girl is growin' up," Joshua said, as though mystified by some sudden transformation.

Pearl remained silent.

▲ ▲ ▲

"I didn't worry you too much when I didn't arrive at noon, did I?" David turned onto the main road leading to Jackson.

Cora momentarily thought of the anguish she'd felt, the million explanations she'd been planning to give Maybelle and Sassy. "No, I was busy . . . reading and didn't notice until Daddy said you were downstairs."

"Oh." He'd hoped she'd be a bit more concerned, worried about him at least a little. His manly pride dropped a notch.

Cora folded her gloved hands on her lap and took in the view. Row after row of bright green land and towering magnolia trees spread out beneath a spotless, pale blue sky. Mockingbirds flew overhead, hopping from tree to tree in what looked like a game of tag. The air was filled with the sounds of childish laughter and squeals of delight. In the distance, she caught a glimpse of the rickety boats that crept along the Left Hand River, its passengers in search of supper, while wood ducks toddled along the banks.

Cora sat back in her seat and relaxed.

"You like fishing, Cora?"

"I love to fish," she said with enthusiasm, her eyes shining. "Been fishin' since I was big enough to hold a pole and not get pulled in the water. Caught more black bass than I can count." She laughed.

"You?" he said, his voice rising a notch in pleasant surprise.

Cora planted her hand on her hip. "Yes. Whatchu think, all I can do is sing? Matter-o'-fact, I know I could catch more fish than you with one hand tied behind my back!"

David tossed his head back and laughed. "Now that's a challenge." He squinted his eyes in thought. "Hmmm, maybe we could spend the day fishing next week Saturday. How about that?"

Cora angled her head provocatively. "I hope you're up to it, Dr. Mackey," she tossed back, pleased with herself.

"We'll just have to see now, won't we?"

"Yes, we will."

They drove along for the next mile or so in silence, easy in each other's company.

"You been to many picture shows?" Cora asked, as they drew closer to Jackson, believing David to be worldly about everything.

"This will be my first." He turned and looked at her.

Cora's surprised smile was like a moonbeam, a bright slice against dark skin. "Then this be a special day, huh?" she asked, with almost child-like awe.

"It certainly is."

Cora's heart beat a little faster and that funny feeling kicked up again in her stomach.

▲ ▲ ▲

Shortly after, they arrived in the center of Jackson, and David found a space to park about a street away from the theater. The line to the ticket booth ran for the entire block. Everyone was out in all their finery to see *The Jazz Singer*, the first talking movie, starring Al Jolson. The level of excitement rose like waves, nearly visible in its intensity as the waiting moviegoers moved forward inch by inch.

By the time David and Cora faced the weathered face of the ticket clerk, Cora could barely contain herself. Unconsciously, she squeezed David's arm.

"Two, please," David said, repeating the request he'd heard others make.

The blue-veined woman glared at the couple. "Colored section is full up. Come back some other time," she spat.

"But—"

"Move along. Next!"

A uniformed officer approached when David didn't budge. "You heard.

Ain't no more room fo' no coloreds. Don't make me have ta run you in."
His pale gray eyes slithered up and down Cora's body like the tongue of a
rattlesnake.

Suddenly, David wasn't standing in the center of Jackson, Mississippi,
on a beautiful Saturday afternoon wanting to get into the picture show. He
wasn't a grown man with a doctor's education and a business of his own.
He was a little boy who was ignored and told to get on about his business,
patted on the head like a pet dog, invisible, while his brother lay dying in
his mother's arms.

His full nostrils flared as he sucked in air, and twin lights illuminated
his dark eyes with a hellish fire. Cora felt the muscles of his arm bulge,
saw his fist clench. She felt the pulse of mounting fear build in her chest.

The grumbling from the crowd grew louder as they complained about
the delay.

David thought about how helpless he'd felt that morning, how powerless
he felt now. He knew, without a doubt, that even the slightest move on his
part could get them both killed, or worse.

Once again, he could do nothing for the person he cared about, simply
because he was colored. Invisible. Yet he couldn't move.

"You hear me, boy?" The officer eased his club from its hook on his belt.

Terror ran in currents through Cora's veins. She felt the air around them
grow hotter, closer, as the angry crowd began to shout obscenities. So she
did what she'd seen her father do on many occasions with white folks. She
smiled sweetly and lifted her chin just a notch.

"Why, officer, had we only knowed there was no mo' seats for colored,
we would have never bothered to stand on this long line in the hot sun."
She fanned herself with her gloved hand. "Maybe a sign in the glass would
be a help in the future. Good day, now." Subtly she tugged David's arm.
"Oh, by the way, Officer, is there a nice place in this beautiful town of
yours that could offer us here a cool drink?" She smiled sweetly.

The officer looked at Cora for a long, dark moment, imagining what
that soft, brown body looked like beneath all the frill. She was young and
ripe, sho nuff, he reckoned, his thoughts on a railcar straight to his bed.

"Officer?" Cora queried sweetly.

A line of sweat rolled down David's brow. His jaw rocked slowly from
left to right. Cora's fingers dug into his arm.

The officer blinked his gray eyes and cleared his throat, hoping no one
had witnessed the lust that he knew hovered in his eyes.

" 'Bout a half mile down. If you stay on this street, you can't miss it."

"Why thank ya, Officer. That's right kind of ya."

Somehow David felt his feet move and heard the soft whisper of Cora's guiding voice. "Just keep walkin' to the car. We gon be there in a minute. Look straight ahead."

Cora felt her entire body quake with relief when they'd gotten securely in the car and begun to move slowly down the street. She didn't want to imagine what could have happened to them, what could have happened if the hate that was brewing inside David had exploded.

They drove down the street in absolute silence until they were well away from what was becoming an angry mob.

David's fingers gripped the wheel so hard that they began to hurt, the pain ricocheting up his arms until they, too, throbbed. "I'm . . . sorry, Cora," he said, in a flat, ridged voice. "Didn't want to put you through something like that."

She swallowed. "It weren't your fault." She stared straight ahead, not wanting to see the shame she knew would be in David's eyes.

"I guess I should take you home."

Cora released a breath. "Don't feel like going home," she said, pushing a lightness into her voice. "This is my first outing, and I expect to be out." She nodded her head with a snap.

David turned to her and saw the understanding, the hope in her eyes, and he knew he couldn't let her down again. "Well, all right then. What would you like to do?"

"Walk along the river. Get ta know you better."

David smiled. "To the river it is then." He paused a beat. The car hit a bump and bounced, then settled back down. "You was something else back there."

She felt the warmth of his words spread through her. "I learned it from my daddy," she said proudly, and knew that Joshua would be proud, too.

And with that, they put the incident behind them, vowing in a silent pact never to discuss it again.

▲ ▲ ▲

There were still a few boats to be seen floating along the river when they arrived. David parked the car beneath a blanket of trees, took Cora's hand, and guided her down a pebble-strewn path to the water's edge.

"Don't want you to sit on the grass and mess up that pretty dress."

Cora stood still and turned her body so that she faced him. She looked up into his questioning eyes. "You really think it's pretty?"

David swallowed. She was so close, he could count her silky lashes. And there was a soft scent about her, innocent almost, that floated around him like a cloud. He couldn't think.

Cora tilted her head to the side. "Well?"

"Y—es. Very pretty," he mumbled.

Cora stared at him for a moment. Her heart was racing in time with the thoughts in her head. She raised her chin a bit higher. "What does it feel like to be kissed?" she asked, with more boldness than she'd felt when she'd stood up to the officer.

David's eyes momentarily widened, then seemed to darken their rich brown color.

"It feels like all sorts of things, Cora," he said gently, still holding her hand. "Depends on who it's with."

She pressed her lips together for a moment before she spoke again. "What . . . do you think it would feel like . . . with us?"

David felt his heart slam against his chest. Quickly, instinctively, his eyes darted around them, then settled on Cora's determined expression. "I suppose . . . we'd have to find out."

His gaze held her there, and the world around them seemed to recede into the background. There was nothing but the two of them standing on a rise of earth, beneath the embrace of trees and the sound of rippling water.

Slowly, almost too slowly, Cora thought, David lowered his head. The muscles in her stomach quivered. Then like the brush of a feather she felt his lips against hers, soft, tender. Her head grew light and a shuddering gasp pushed through her closed mouth, parting the lips.

She felt David's strong body tremble and something, a sound deep and gutteral, something she'd never heard before, rumbled in his throat. Cora was suddenly against his body, the length of him, his arm wrapped securely around her narrow waist, binding her to him. Her back arched when he pressed for a deeper, lingering kiss.

David had not kissed many women, had been intimate with even fewer. But he knew that Cora was different. She made him feel things about and inside himself he'd never felt before. Ever since that first day, whenever he thought of her there was a happiness that bloomed inside him like a budding rose. When he was in her company, he felt strong and weak at the same time. And her smile, that smile could melt away all that was wrong in his life. And now this. This kiss. This pulse that beat inside him like a drum, leaving him shaken, but wanting more. Wanting Cora.

The fire was everywhere now, Cora realized, as the kiss took on a life of its own. It burned her insides, scalded her thoughts until they were all frayed at the edges. The feeling, that funny feeling in her stomach, had grown and spread to her chest, rushed down her legs and arms until she was certain she would fall if he let her go now.

Then, suddenly, her eyes flew open when she felt a wetness slide between her thighs in concert with the hard knots that her untouched nipples had become as they pressed against his chest.

David's large hands ran along her sides. "Cora," he whispered, against her mouth.

Was this what the girls whispered about? Was this what Mama was so fearful of? This feeling that took you out of your body, making it want to be a part of someone else's? But how?

Cora wrenched herself free of David's hold. When he looked at her, her eyes were wild. Her chest heaved in and out as if she'd been chased. Her face was flushed and loose strands of hair hung seductively around her face.

"What . . . is it, Cora?"

David stepped toward her. Cora eased back. "I—I should go home." She swallowed.

David reached out to her. "Cora, don't be afraid. I would never hurt you. I would never do anything you didn't want me to. Never, Cora. Never."

Her lips quivered as she stood there trying to catch her breath and her thoughts. The wetness was sticky now.

Oh, Lawd, Cora thought. What if it was her monthly? She would die of embarrassment. She pressed her thighs together.

"Cora, it's all right. Please, tell me what's wrong."

"I—I think it may be . . . my time. I should go home." She bit down on her bottom lip.

David looked at her with a puzzled expression. Then realization dawned on him. "Cora." He took her hand. His voice gentled. "Is this your usual time?"

She thought about it for a moment and realized that her time had passed less than a week earlier. "No," she answered weakly.

"Oh, Cora." He gathered her in his arms. "What happened to you is only natural," he cooed in her ear. "It's the way a woman readies herself for a man."

She craned her neck to look up at him. Her eyes were wide with questions.

David nodded slowly and smiled. "In time, Cora. In time. When we're ready."

Beat by beat her heart slowed to its regular rhythm. She rested her head against his chest. David stroked her hair.

"I—I liked how it felt," she said, that childlike wonder replaced with the awareness of a budding woman.

David smiled and kissed the top of her head, feeling her heart beat in harmony with his.

▲ ▲ ▲

When David and Cora pulled to a stop in front of Cora's house, her mother and father were sitting on the bench swing taking in the light breeze that blew in from the river. Joshua's arm was draped across Pearl's shoulder, and they were so involved with each other they didn't notice Cora and David until they were standing on the porch steps.

"Evening, Mrs. Harvey, Reverend."

Joshua stood, took a quick but all encompassing look at his daughter, then stuck out his hand to David. "Evenin'."

"How was the picture show?" Pearl asked.

Cora and David glanced at each other.

"I'll tell you 'bout it later," Cora said.

"Weren't no trouble, was there?" Joshua pressed, knowing something was wrong.

David stepped forward. "No, sir, there wasn't." He turned to Cora. "Thanks to your daughter here. You raised her up real good," he said, gazing at Cora with a smile of pride.

Joshua looked from David to Cora and back again. Satisfied with what he saw and was told, he nodded slowly. Cora would tell him later.

Pearl stood. "The church is havin' a picnic in a couple of weeks or so. It's the annual e-vent," she added, hanging onto the "e" before letting go of the rest. "Be nice ifn you joined us, Doctor."

"I'd like that very much, ma'am. Thank you for asking."

"Be a good thing fo' you to meet some of the peoples from this side of the river," Joshua added. His right brow arched in challenge.

"Yes, sir." He looked around from one to the other. "Well I, uh, guess I should be getting on."

Joshua and Pearl didn't move a hair.

David turned to Cora. "Night, Cora."

"Night. See you Saturday, for fishin', right?"

"Before sunup, for sure."

Cora grinned. She stepped up on the porch with her parents. "Night, then . . . David."

▲ ▲ ▲

For the next two weeks, David spent all his free time with Cora. Whenever there was a break in his schedule, he sought her out. They went for long walks in the woods, fished early in the morning, sat under the stars at night and shared their hopes and dreams.

Cora was eager to feel those feelings again, those feelings from that night by the river. And every time she could, she'd steal David away for a secret kiss. She'd discovered that a soft look or a gentle touch from her would make David moan and ask for "just one more kiss, Cora." If she pressed her body up against his and wrapped her arms tightlike 'round his neck, she could feel his manhood throb against her thighs. The wetness there didn't bring fear to her heart no more. She looked forward to it. Looked forward to all the things that would bring it on.

One day, she thought wistfully, watching David's profile in the sunrise as they sat on a flat rock fishing for bass, she was going to know what it all felt like—what that fire was that kept her up at night when she thought of him. She smiled to herself. Soon. Soon.

Four

‑‑‑‑wwwwwww‑‑‑‑

"You and that doctor spendin' a lotta time together," Pearl said to Cora, with the hint of a question in her soft, southern tone.

Cora continued packing the picnic baskets with the cakes and breads she'd baked all week. "Yessum." She picked up the bowl of collards and wrapped it in a towel. "He's good comp'ny."

"Hmm." Pearl peeked at her daughter searching for any hint of change, any sign. "Then I reckon y'all gettin' serious 'bout each other."

Cora glanced up and swallowed, her eyes wide, not sure what kind of answer her mother wanted. At times, her mama acted like her growing relationship with David was the best thing that could have happened. At other times, it was almost as if she was afraid of it, afraid for her, and wanted Cora to have no part of it.

Cora tugged in a breath. She looked her mother right in the eye. "Yes, Mama, we's serious." There, she'd said it.

"I see." Pearl nodded, her lips working but no words coming out.

Cora held her breath, waiting, for what she wasn't sure. "We ain't done nothin', Mama. We ain't," she assured. Her simple response was definite and final.

Pearl stared deep into her daughter's steady gaze, beyond their dark depths and into her soul. "All right then," Pearl said on a gust of air. "We best be gettin' on over to the picnic. Daddy been gone with the mens for a while now."

"Don't know why the mens have to go so early, no how. 'Specially since they don't do none of the cookin'."

Pearl chuckled. "That's why they kin get there early."
Cora laughed and shook her head in agreement.

▲ ▲ ▲

When Cora and Pearl arrived, loaded down with bags and baskets, all before them the vibrant green grass was transformed into a sea of waving color and shape. Children in every size and hue ran like wild things across the grass, leaping over mothers and fathers squatted on patchwork blankets, who shouted orders to behave that were lost on the early morning breeze.

For the most part, the men sat in huddled groups, their resonant tones like drumbeats to the ear. Joshua sat in a circle surrounded by several dozen men of Rudell, most of them from his congregation at First Baptist. His voice was low but filled with its usual fire.

"Ya'll heard 'bout the lynchin' in Natchez. Young boy no more than twelve," Joshua said solemnly.

"Yeah. Said he bumped into some white woman," Flem added, with the bitter bile of disgust in his voice.

Fleming Potter, better known as Flem to his friends, had been a part of Rudell for near fifteen years. Like Joshua, his parents had been slaves. As a young boy, he'd seen his father whipped by the master, his mother raped by the master's son, yet they still were able to hold their heads up and do the best they could for their ten children. Flem knew the meaning of freedom and family and living under the heel of those who meant you no good. He had no love for his oppressors, but at the same time he understood his place in the world and the best way to get around the injustices that were heaped upon them. Next to Deacon Earl, Joshua depended on Flem for his clear thinking, loyalty, and strong back. Folks listened to Flem, looked up to him. That was a good thing 'cause Joshua knew, deep in his heart, that there would have to be someone to take his place one day.

"They say thangs done got better for us coloreds," Joshua said.

"Negroes is what they call us now," Flem joked, and the men joined in the laughter.

"Whatever we's called, it ain't called 'equal,' " Joshua stated.

"Got that right," said Hutch, Flem's no-count brother. The men nodded and hummed in agreement.

"Everywhere we look, everythang we hear, some more Negroes done come to harm, burned, jailed, or lynched. Riots goin' on in Kansas and in Little Rock. In Memphis, the mayor refused the demands made by the group callin' theyselves the West Tennessee Civic and Political League, who wanted him to hire colored policemen and firemen and to get rid of the laws that keeps Negroes outta white parks," Joshua stated.

"We ain't got none of that here in Mississippi neither, Reverend," spouted Hutch.

"But thangs is changin' all 'round us," Flem said, in his slow, but steady baritone. "Folks up North, the National Association fo' the Advancement of Coloreds is fightin' for us, the NAACP. The workers is travelin' all over tryin' to get coloreds to vote, go to schools with white folks, and such."

The men looked from one to the other, mumbling their opinions and objections, some louder than others.

Joshua held up his hand and the gathering fell silent. His usual booming voice dropped a notch so that the men had to crane their necks to get close enough to catch every word.

"I been in touch with one of those workers. I done met with him a week gone Wednesday in Biloxi." Joshua looked from one to the other, holding them transfixed. "I told him 'bout the Willis boy, that folks done disappeared from this part of Rudell. Told him 'bout Sheriff Moss and how he lock up the colored men for nothin', keepin' them in those filthy cells fo' weeks. Told him 'bout the sharecroppers and how they ain't never gon' be free." He paused for a moment. "Told him 'bout the night riders and they visits to this part of town."

Deep gasps of alarm mixed with fear rounded the group.

"Just listen to what the reverend has to say," Flem counseled, turning this way and that to catch every man's eye.

By degrees the group quieted.

"He want to come down here and help us," Joshua said.

"Help us do what? Get killed?" Hutch demanded, nodding his head as others began to agree.

Slowly Joshua rose to his full six-foot height, his dark features like ominous clouds hovering over the land. He breathed in deeply, needing to be sure of the words that came next, because once they did, there was no turning back. His meeting with the worker from the NAACP had put more fire to his heart than he'd ever thought possible. All these years his vision had only been Rudell and his congregation, making it strong. But there was more to the world than his congregation, more in the world who needed someone to look up to, to lean on. If he was to truly be a man of the people, a Christian man, he had to be a man for all people, not just here in Rudell. He had to stand for more than just First Baptist. Wasn't that *his* dream, what he'd promised Pearl when he'd asked for her hand?

"What I'm gon' ask y'all ain't easy," Joshua began . . .

▲ ▲ ▲

As David listened to the discussion, his own fears began to climb. What the men were planning was dangerous. He'd heard the stories of the workers. He'd heard the good they were trying to do. But he also knew of the losses of life because of them.

Yet he couldn't help but admire the control that Joshua had over the men, the power of persuasion. These men were loyal to the reverend, loyal enough to risk everything, simply because he asked it of them and knew that he was willing to give the same if not more. This man was a leader, their leader.

Whatever false impressions he'd had about what the church and its power represented, what it meant to these people, were wiped from his mind. All around him were symbols of hope, from the woman who brought her last bag of vegetables to contribute to the feast, to the old men who stoked the fires with fingers that could barely bend from the pain. Still they came, one and all; with a little or a lot, they came. Gave what they could little afford to give, but gave anyway. Now he understood what Cora meant. Maybe this was a part of his life that he'd been missing all along but had refused to allow it to enter his heart, his spirit. This was strength.

When David looked again, he saw that the men were dispersing. Joshua was by his side. He put his hand on David's shoulder. "Glad you could make it, Doctor."

"Thanks for the invite, Reverend."

Joshua herded David toward the blanket where the women sat. "I knowed you heard some things while ago. Men things."

"Yessir."

"It stays that way. Ain't nothin' fo' these womens to hear. Understand? They worry too much, get in the way. We got much work to do, young man." He solidly patted David's broad shoulders. "But you stay out of it, hear?"

"But I want to help, if I could."

Joshua stopped walking and faced David. His eyes looked weary, his voice bore the weight of all the souls under his care. "You kin help me by lookin' after Cora." He nodded slowly, letting the words settle. "That's what you kin do."

David's chest tightened and a sudden unexplainable chill ran up his spine in the midst of the incredible heat.

$\mathcal{F}$ive

~~~~~~~~~~~~~

The September sun hung like a blazing orange umbrella across the expanse of shimmering blue river, turning its sinuous waves into beacons of bronze and gold. The comforting twitter of the mockingbirds, the answering caw of swooping crows, rustling footsteps of scurrying jackrabbits and big-eyed raccoons filled the early evening air, the only sounds for miles around.

Cora and David sat shoulder to shoulder, hip to hip on the riverbank, fishing poles poised and ready for the first bite, easy in their silence.

These quiet Saturday outings had become a ritual for the young couple during the past two months of their courtship. Folks of Rudell had grown accustomed to seeing them together on the riverbank and by silent agreement would leave them be.

The women of Rudell saw their younger selves in Cora, those early days of budding love and womanhood and quietly rejoiced in it, able through her to relive those days of carefree joy. They'd whisper woman secrets to her after choir rehearsal about special baths and oils to use to entice a man. They slipped family recipes into her apron pockets during the long hours at the church. They saved scraps of ribbon for her long hair to press into her hand if they passed her in the street and always reminded her of how grown up and pretty she was looking since she'd took up with that nice Dr. Mackey.

The men took pride in their roles as elders to David, passing along to him the secret ways of men and women and what would be expected of him as a husband and provider. They saw nothing wrong with pulling him to the side when he was on his way to visit a patient to tell him "something you best know" or waving down his car and spending up to an hour reminiscing with him about their own courtship with wives living or dead. In David they saw all they hoped their own sons and grandsons would become one day, and they wanted to be a part of that process.

For Cora and David it was a time of wonder and discovery of each other, a time of emotional upheavals, and rising passions.

David thought about it all now, thought about the late-night conversation with Joshua beneath the stars as they sat on Joshua's front porch following one of Pearl's belly-filling meals.

"What be yo' plans for my daughter?" Joshua abruptly asked about a week earlier as he puffed mightily on his sweet-smelling pipe.

David pushed a small stone with the tip of his boot. He always knew this question was going to come, when had been his only concern. "Well, sir, I'd like to make Cora my wife."

"Hmmm," Joshua hummed, as if he was thinking it over. He blew out a cloud of smoke into the air.

"With your permission, of course," David quickly added.

Joshua slanted him a look and chuckled softly. "Son, there was a time I didn't think much of ya," Joshua proudly confessed. "Ain't think someone like you was good fo' Cora." He paused and gazed thoughtfully up at the moving puffs of cotton ball clouds then stared David hard in the eye—a manish look. "But ya make her happy, son. You's steady and I believes you really cares fo' my daughter."

"I do, sir. I love Cora."

Joshua was quiet. "There's gon' be times when yo' love will be tested, tested by thangs stronger than you. Gon' be times when you gon' have ta sacrifice fo' that love."

"Yes, sir." David nodded in eager agreement.

"It's gon' test yo' soul, test what you made of as a man."

David frowned, studied the somber expression on Joshua's dark features, searched the world-weary eyes that saw images and experiences beyond his reach. In the months that he'd come to know Joshua, he'd learned that Joshua's wisdom, his view of the world, intelligence, and insight into people could never be learned between the pages of a book. That was why the townspeople of Rudell looked up to him, respected him. Joshua Harvey was a simple man of simple ways with unshakable beliefs by which he lived. He was one of them, one who spoke their language, knew and lived their struggles. Joshua was the wisest man he'd ever met, and each day he observed the quiet power that his wisdom yielded. David understood that hidden beneath the folds of his simple truths were lessons to last a lifetime.

Slowly, what appeared to be painfully, Joshua pushed himself to his feet. He looked toward the horizon into tomorrow.

"Gon' be rough days ahead," Joshua uttered almost to himself. "I done see it in my dreams." He swiveled his head toward David. "You best be ready, fo' yo'self and Cora." He moved toward the door, opening it, the unoiled hinges moaning in protest. " 'Night, now." He stepped inside, leaving David to digest his words.

Those words had taken on life within David, growing like a fetus in the womb. The desire to act, to do something quickly gained in strength with every passing day. He'd sat in on the hushed conversations at Joe's about the NAACP worker who was scheduled to arrive in Rudell the following week. Joshua had taken on the responsibility of gathering the men together to prepare them for the worker's arrival and what this Floyd Howell had to say. The meeting was set for later that night in the field behind Deacon Earl's meager farm.

David had his reservations about the presence of the northerner in their midst. There'd been terrible tales of retribution put on colored folks who tried to change the southern way of life, gain rights and privileges denied them. Yet he understood that in order to make changes, there had to be sacrifice.

He glanced at Cora, his beautiful, sweet Cora, and realized that as long as he had the breath of life he would give whatever was necessary to make a better life for her, to make her happy.

"Be 'bout time to head back," Cora said quietly, her eyes focused on the water. "Meetin' startin' soon."

"I believe so."

She snapped her head in his direction. "You scared?"

The question didn't surprise him. Over the months that they'd spent time together, Cora had learned to read his mood, see things in his eyes that his lips would not say.

Slowly David nodded. "Yes, I 'spose so, Cora."

Cora set her pole down and folded her hands on her lap, her expression tight and pensive. "Daddy say we gots to stand up fo' ourselves. Get a fair shake. He say the Lawd will look over us, protect us. He'll make a way."

"Hmm," he hummed, preferring not to comment when it came to the ways of the Lord.

"I believe He will," Cora said with assurance. We tryin' to do a good thing here in Rudell."

That's what colored folks are trying to do all over the country, but that didn't stop them from getting killed, David thought. But he kept that comment to himself as well. No need to worry Cora.

Cora tossed her line back in the water with a light, perfect flick of her slender wrist. Her touch was so light, the water barely moved. She pondered the possibility of a new way of life. Maybe if they got some changes down here in Mississippi, more jobs, better pay, decent places to live, and not have to be feared to be out after dark, she wouldn't have to leave and go North. She could stay in Rudell.

For several moments they sat in the cooling blanket of silence, each wrapped in the vision of their own new world.

"Cora." He said her name as reverently as a prayer.

"Yes?" She gazed at his profile with wide, questioning eyes.

"You . . . still plan to leave Rudell?"

Her heart stumbled, it felt, in her chest. "I . . . want somethin' mo' than this. Mo' than church singin'," she answered, without answering fully.

"Would it matter if I asked you not to go, Cora?" He turned to her then, a silent plea in his eyes—questioning—waiting.

Her throat was suddenly bone dry. Her heart thumped. "To choose. That what you askin' me, David?" Fear of his answer wove its way through her question, chilling her in the soft glow of the setting sun.

"I'm asking you to marry me, Cora. Make a life with me here, in Rudell."

How long had she waited for this moment, dreamed of it since she was a little girl on her daddy's knee? And now that it was here, picturesque, just like in her dreams, she had no answer. To give it would mean letting go of everything she'd ever hoped for. To let it go, would mean losing the man she loved. How could she choose?

Suddenly, David frowned. Slowly he stood and looked over his shoulder to where the colored homes of Rudell rested.

The acrid smell of burning wood floated like unsettled haints across the darkening sky.

"Something's burning," he said, with a terrible urgency in his voice that rose the hairs on Cora's arms.

Cora jumped up, sniffing the air.

David grabbed her hand, fishing poles forgotten. "Come on."

They ran through the woods, across rocks, and uneven rolls of earth, around century-old trees and water-filled ditches. The closer they came, the more powerful was the smell. And the noise. Shouts of, "Fire!" could be heard in the distance. Screams of terror in the night.

They burst out of the woods, and the flames could be seen leaping into the sky. From every shack and shanty they ran, ran down the road to the Harvey house, the only illumination in the darkness. Into the night millions of red-and-gold cinders like the dance of fireflies scattered across the wind.

Cora couldn't breathe. Dread sucked the air from her lungs. Before her, flames more brilliant than the rising sun engulfed her home, licking the walls, the roof, the porch with fiery lashes of its hungry tongue. The angry fist of heat gave a mighty shove, knocking the stunned observers back on their heels.

Cora broke free of David's hold, trying to push her way past the knot of bodies who tossed useless pails and cups of water on the blaze. But she seemed to have no strength in her arms and legs; she couldn't seem to move them. No one saw her, heard her screams. She was invisible.

Hands were suddenly on her, strange hands, strong hands, soft and crippled hands, holding her back from the inferno, clawing at her.

Why couldn't she move? she wondered in a confused haze. Where was Mama and Daddy? Her eyes wildly searched the maddening crowd, searched the faces for Mama and Daddy.

Mouths moved, talking to her, she imagined, but she couldn't make out the words, couldn't hear what was said. It was as if she watched everything from behind a foggy, glass window. So she ignored the voices, the hands.

She had to get to the house, get Mama and Daddy out, she chanted to herself as she broke free of the grasping hands and arms and ran headlong toward the burning building. Then all at once the wind screamed—a keening, agonized wail, tortured, it seemed, by the intense heat.

David shouted her name above the melee, pushed his way to her. He scooped her up into his arms, snatching her out of the grasp that would have claimed her as its own, just as the roof collapsed in finality.

Six

—∿∿∿∿∿∿—

Dreams. Dark, shadowed dreams. She was running, but couldn't see in front of her. Thick, black clouds hampered her vision. Voices. Voices cried out to her, calling her name. But she couldn't find them. She couldn't.

Terror rose from the darkness like a living thing, reached out and grabbed her. She ran but couldn't get away. Terror wrapped itself around her and squeezed. She gasped, struggled for breath, and her lungs filled with the stench of smoke that burned her nostrils and teared her eyes.

The grip grew tighter, pulling her away, away from the voices.

"No!" Cora's eyes flew open. Her body covered in a thin film of sweat, quaked as though dipped in ice. Frantically she looked around, her heart and head hammering wildly. Where was she? Was this heaven?

Slowly, she began to focus, the room cleared, *Ms. Lucinda's room.* Her bottom lip trembled as the floodgates of memory flew open. This wasn't heaven, and she wasn't home. She'd never be able to go home again. All at once the images of a night she'd never forget loomed large before her. Cora covered her face in her hands and cried.

▲ ▲ ▲

She didn't know how long she'd sat there, sat in the middle of this strange bed, in this unfamiliar room, in these clothes that weren't hers, until the lilt of hushed women's voices drifted to her from another part of the four-room house.

60

"Po' chile," said one voice, the sound of a pot clattering against the stove following her declaration.

"Town ain't gon' be the same without the good reverend and Pearl, no sir," said another voice.

"That boy been by here to see her every day. Them two girlfriends of hers, too. She won't talk, won't eat. Just sleeps," lamented Lucinda. "Near a week now."

"Hmm, umm," the women chorused. "Po' chile," they repeated.

"Ain't nothin' we kin do fo' the good reverend and Pearl, God rest they souls," came Lucinda's no-nonsense voice, "but we got a responsibility to look after that chile in there. Help her through this as best we kin."

Cora lowered her head, feeling her eyes fill again, but no tears would fall. She was empty. Of everything. She hugged her bottom lip with her teeth, curled her aching body into a tight ball, and tumbled into a fitful sleep.

When she opened her eyes again, night had fallen. She tried to peer into the darkness, squeeze her eyes to make out the odd shapes. Where was the dresser with her nightgowns, undies, and stockings? Her head swiveled toward the window. Those weren't her curtains.

Panicked, she leaned over the side of the four-poster bed, sweeping her hand beneath it in search of her secret box. Slowly, she sat up, wrapped her arms around her body, and rocked back and forth.

▲ ▲ ▲

Lucinda stood at the foot of the bed. Her usual robust face was drawn tight with concern as she watched Cora's sleeping form.

She silently worried, ticking off the days in her head. Cora still hadn't eaten, refused to drink, wouldn't talk. She just stared and the emptiness in her eyes simply broke Lucinda's heart. Cora had shut the door on the world and locked herself inside.

Lucinda understood grief, understood that it took time to pass. And a loss like the one Cora suffered might take the rest of her life to mend. But what worried her most was Cora's refusal to live. Lawd knows Lucinda couldn't have that on her hands.

She pushed out a breath of determination, crossed the room, and sat on the side of the bed, dipping it almost to the floor with her weight. "Chile," she called softly. "Cora." Gently she shook her shoulder and was shocked to feel the bone so close to the skin. "Cora . . ."

Why wouldn't they leave her be? Couldn't they see she only wanted to be left alone? She tried to shake the heavy hand from her shoulder, but she didn't have the strength.

"Cora," Lucinda shook her a bit harder. "Now you listen to me, chile, 'cause I knows you kin hear me. You kin either get up and get outta those days old clothes yo'self or I kin do it fo' ya. Up to you."

Cora groaned in protest and curled into a tighter knot.

"You don't leave me no choice," Lucinda huffed.

She scooped Cora up as easily as if she was no more than a loaf of bread, cradled her thinning body against her own meaty flesh, and carried her out into the kitchen where she'd prepared a bath in a huge, wooden tub.

For a brief moment the gazes of the two women connected, and Lucinda felt a chill all the way to her soul. Cora's expressionless face had aged in a matter of days what it takes years of trouble to do. It was like the light had been cut out behind her eyes. Dark half-moons hung beneath her bottom lashes and her cheeks had hollowed, giving her a starved appearance. The corners of her mouth turned down at the edges with a kind of hopelessness that comes from heartache. With a gentleness born of love for another, Lucinda slowly undressed Cora and placed her into the soothing, scented water, talking in soft, cooing tones as she ran the bathing sponge along Cora's limbs.

"I know it be hard, chile," she whispered. "Know what it be like to lose yo' folks. Happened to me, sho' nuff." Lucinda shook her head as the memories threatened to overtake her. "But the Lawd makes a way, Cora. Yo' daddy and mama believed that. And they wouldn't want you to do this to yo'self, Cora, chile."

Cora flinched, blinked rapidly to halt an onset of tears. She pressed her lips stoically together and stared into nothingness.

"You keep yo' mama and daddy alive in here." She pointed to Cora's heart. "And in here." She touched Cora's brow. "But to do that, Cora, you gotta live." She paused. "I know I ain't yo' mama, but I love ya just like you was my own. Come back to me, chile. It's gon' be all right."

Cora's lips trembled and the first tears of healing tumbled from her closed eyes and mixed with the cleansing water.

▲ ▲ ▲

With Lucinda's tender care and gentle persistence, Cora slowly began to spend at least an hour a day out of bed. During those brief spells, Lucinda would get her to drink a bowl of soup or eat a biscuit.

At night Lucinda would sit Cora between her thighs and brush and comb her thick hair, just like she had done when Cora was a little girl.

It was a ritual that Cora began to look forward to in the ensuing days. The soothing sensation of Lucinda's firm but gentle fingers took her outside of herself, relaxed her mind and body. And Lucinda always had a story to tell. Whether it was truth or a lie, Cora could never tell. But it didn't matter. Just the sound of the voice kept her anchored, reminded her that she was still connected to something, to someone.

"That young man been here ta see you agin," Lucinda said, twirling a thick sheet of hair into a smooth braid.

Cora didn't respond.

"He's real anxious 'bout you. Least let him see you all right. He worryin' himself sick."

Cora pressed her lips together, breathing deeply through her nose.

"I invited him to come by tomorrow after breakfast."

Cora snapped her head around, and the comb went sailing across the floor. The first flash of light glistened in her dark eyes. "How could you do that?"

Lucinda tucked in a smile. "Do you some good to see a face besides this old, fat one. 'Specially a handsome face like the doctor." She chuckled deeply.

"I . . . ain't ready to see him!"

"Well, you get ready. You cain't put him off forever, Cora. Ain't right."

Cora jumped up and paced the wood plank floor, her bare feet hitting the wood in an uneven rhythm.

"What's right 'bout anything?" Cora snapped. "Is it right that I ain't got my mama and daddy?" Her voice rose in pitch. "Is it right I ain't got no home, no clothes—" her voice cracked "—no nothin'!"

Lucinda remained silent, letting Cora hurl around the room all the thoughts that she'd kept locked inside, growing like a sickness. That's what was eating her alive—the bitterness and pain that she'd latched onto. The only way she'd ever find her way back to herself was to get it out of her.

Cora's chest heaved. Her eyes snapped with fire. "I was with him, Ms. Lucinda." Her voice trembled. "Down by the river."

Lucinda folded her hands on her lap. "Go on, chile. Tell me what happened," she encouraged softly.

"Mama . . . always told me to be a lady. Don't let my feelin's make me . . . do nothin' wit David fo' I was married." She swallowed. Her eyes darted around the room. "Said the Lawd didn't look down with favor ifn we did."

"Whatchu sayin', baby?"

"I—we didn't do nothin' . . . not really." Her wide eyes begged Lucinda to believe her. "But . . ." She gave Lucinda her back. "I let him touch me . . . sometimes . . . under my skirt." Her voice choked. "Couldn't help it, Ms. Lucinda. And it scared me sometimes 'cause the feelin' was so powerful."

"Chile, ain't nothin' wrong wit how you feel 'bout that boy."

"That's why the Lawd took them away," she said, almost to herself, ignoring Lucinda's sage words. " 'Cause of what me and David did."

Lucinda pushed herself up from the bed with a huff. She snatched Cora by the shoulders and turned her around, shocked to see the agony and guilt hovering in the girl's eyes.

"Now, you listen here. Our God is a good God, a fair God. You cain't think fo' one minute that yo' feelings fo' David is what kilt yo' folks," she said, with all the conviction she could summon from her soul. "That was a horrible accident. Nothin' else," she added, although the rumors were running wild that the night riders were behind it. Cora didn't need to know that. She had enough on her head.

Lucinda searched Cora's eyes, hoping to see acceptance there, but what she saw was the answer. "That's why you don't want to see David, 'cause he remind you of that night, remind you of some wrong you think you done?"

Cora slowly bobbed her head and covered her face with her hands in shame.

Lucinda wrapped her arms around Cora's fragile frame and hugged her against her ample bosom. "Lovin's not a sin, Cora. But love comes with a heap of responsibilities. It's about thinkin' of the person you love above yo'self." Slowly Lucinda released her, holding her at arm's length. "If you love David, even a little bit, you gotta think 'bout his feelin's, too." She paused a moment. "Talk to him, Cora. Tell him how you feel 'bout everythin'. He'll understand. David's a good, decent man. Don't forget that."

▲ ▲ ▲

The past few weeks had been the most miserable David could remember living. He felt so alone and disconnected from the world without Cora being a daily part of his life. Even his patients commented on how he'd changed and was no longer the smiling, full of confidence young man he'd been.

"How you gon' make me feel better, lookin' all down in the mouth yo'self?" old Mrs. Harris asked when he'd given her a new salve for her swollen joints.

He'd tried to laugh it off by saying he was tired. But Mrs. Harris had seen that look before, seen it in her own eyes when her husband would leave for weeks at a time to find work.

It was rumored that Stella Harris had crossed over one hundred years and was on the way back again. She'd forgotten more than most folks of Rudell would ever know in a lifetime. Her near berry black face reminded David of a sun-dried grape, wrinkled and sweet.

"Ya need to just march yo'self on over to Sister Carver's house, take that chile, Cora, by the hand and tell her what you want." She snapped her steely gray head for emphasis. "Just grief that's taking her away from herself. Grief make you forget everything else in the world 'cept feelin' bad."

David was humbled into silence by her openness.

"You do want her, don't ya?"

David cleared his throat. "Yes, ma'am."

"Then tell her," she insisted, with a shake of her curled finger. "Fo' it be too late."

"Yes, ma'am," he'd promised, after tucking her in.

After that incident he'd tried to cover his feelings better, not wear his sadness on his sleeve. He may have been able to fool the rest of the folks of Rudell, but he couldn't hide it from his mother. She'd noticed the change in him, too.

"You gon' just set there starin' out the window, son?" Betty Jean asked one morning, as she held up a yard of fabric for a dress she was making.

David stirred himself out of his malaise and forced a smile. "Just looking at the seasons changing is all. It'll be Christmas in a few more weeks," he mumbled.

Betty Jean watched his strained profile. "Think you'll be seein' Cora for Christmas? Maybe she would like to spend it here with us . . . since . . ." She didn't finish her sentence; she didn't have to.

David lowered his head. "Don't really know, Mama. Cora still won't see me."

Betty Jean crossed the floor of the small kitchen and stood behind her son. Gently she patted his back. "Healing takes time, son. For some it takes longer than others. Cora's tryin' to heal, put things together in her head."

David turned and looked up into his mother's knowing eyes. "But I want to help her. She won't let me."

Betty Jean released a slow breath. She gazed out the window, watching the flow of colored people moving about their day, dressed in fine clothes, some even driving cars. There was a time when this part of Rudell was out of her reach, those days when they lived in a shack in the woods and no doctor would take care of her dying son. Now she made the clothes the colored and white women wore, and her son was the colored doctor. Funny how life turns around.

"Cora has to help herself, David, before she can let anyone else help her. She has to search inside herself for a reason to go on, a place to put the memories."

"Like you did with Cleve?"

Betty Jean pressed her lips together in a tight line and slowly nodded her head, continuing to stare out the window, seeing a time that had stained her entire life forever.

David thought about all of that now as he drove along the road leading to Ms. Lucinda's house. Maybe there wasn't anything he could do for Cora until she was ready. But there was a part of him that needed to see her, hear her voice. Sometimes the feeling was so strong it was like a physical pain that twisted his insides, kept him awake at night, sent him to the river in the morning.

Still he believed that if she saw him, and he had a chance to talk with her, he could somehow make things better, make things like they were between them.

When he pulled to a stop on the dirt road outside Lucinda's house, Lucinda was on the tilted porch rocking in her chair. His first thought was that she'd been sitting in wait to warn him that Cora had changed her mind and didn't want to see him. But when he saw her welcoming wave and broad smile, the queasiness in his stomach slowly settled.

" 'Morning, Miss Lucinda." He took off his hat as he gingerly walked up the rickety steps.

" 'Morning. Had breakfast yet?"

"Yes, ma'am."

She looked him up and down, then nodded in approval. "Don't expect much," she said. "She's not the same girl you knew a few weeks gone." Her small, brown eyes held his in a firm grip. "You gon' have ta take yo' time with Cora."

"Yes, ma'am. I will."

"Go on in then. She in the kitchen."

David held his hat and his heart in his hands as he stepped through the one-hinged front door, not knowing what to expect.

Cora was seated with her back turned, staring out the window, when he entered the sunny kitchen. "Hello, Cora," he said quietly, so as not to startle her.

She only turned her head and looked upon him with a quiet sadness in her eyes. Her voice barely reached him across the room. "Good to see you agin', David." She turned back toward the window.

Tentatively, David crossed the room and pulled out a chair from beneath the table and sat down. "How are you, Cora?" He wanted to touch her, brush that loose strand of hair away from her face, wipe away the sadness that had etched fine lines around her eyes.

She didn't answer.

"I—I've missed you."

Cora lowered her head. How could she tell him she hadn't wanted to think about him, that thoughts and images of him only made her feel pain? And yet, she'd missed him, too.

With hesitation he reached out and covered her hand with his. A sudden sensation of warmth shot through him, like a man left out in the cold and finally allowed to sit near the fire. "Cora, maybe you didn't need to see me, maybe you didn't want to see me. But I needed to see you, needed to know you were all right." He gulped. "I'll go if you want me to. I'll stay if you let me. Just don't shut me out, Cora. Please."

She turned to him, took him in with her eyes. He was still so handsome. His dark, sharp features still keen, his eyes soft and warm. But it was his gentleness that still touched her deep in her heart.

Cora pressed his hand to her cheek, held it there, needing to feel him close to her. Her heart seemed to swell in her chest, rising to her throat and beating like the frantic wings of a trapped bird. "I—I missed you, too," she admitted over a choked sob.

"Oh, Cora." He moved closer, gathered her to him, and held her gently against his chest. His eyes drifted close as he inhaled the soft scent of her, tired to absorb her into his veins.

"They're gone," she whispered.

"I know, sugah. I know," he said, his voice as gentle as a breeze. "But it's gonna be all right. I promise you that. Whatever it takes." He stroked her back. "I love you, Cora. I love you so much it about makes me crazy. And when you hurt, I hurt, too. We can get through this together. If you let me."

It would be so easy to give into him, just let David take over so she wouldn't have to think, wouldn't have to do nothing but just be. And she was so tired. So tired. Yes, it would be easier that way.

"Whatever you want," she mumbled against his chest.

David eased back and stared down into her eyes. "You sure? You mean that?"

Cora nodded.

He grazed his thumb along the side of her face. "Then today is a new beginning. We can start over. Try to move forward."

She nodded again.

"We can be happy again, Cora. *You* can be happy again. It's gonna take time, but I swear, I'll be with you every step of the way. As long as you let me."

"Awright," she agreed, with all the conviction she could muster.

▲ ▲ ▲

David came to see her every day after that. As soon as he finished seeing his patients, he came to Lucinda's house to sit with Cora. He'd tell her of his day, share the wild tales of the townsfolk and their illnesses, real or imagined.

Cora didn't say much during those visits, but she smiled a bit more and would nod her head at all the right spots. She still refused to go back to the river. But David didn't care as long as he could be with her. That was all that mattered.

Christmas was in two more weeks, and David had searched high and low for his gift to Cora. He was certain enough time had passed and she was getting better day by day. Things were going to work out, he was certain of it.

Lucinda had finally convinced Cora to accompany her into town, saying there was no way she could tote everything herself. She had a wheel barrel full of preserved fruits and baked breads that she sold every year to Joe's for the holidays. Of course she kept her own supply for the congregation of First Baptist.

Reluctantly, Cora had agreed to go, her first outing since that night. In the months since the loss of her parents, she hadn't seen anyone other than Lucinda, David, and occasionally Sassy and Maybelle, who'd both eventually stopped coming by, unable to deal with Cora's somber moods. Lucinda had begged her to come back to church, but Cora had refused. She couldn't walk into that church knowing that her father was no longer the reverend, that the sermon would be preached by Deacon Earl or Deacon Flem. She couldn't sing in the choir and look out into the congregation and not see her mama's face. She just couldn't do it. At least not yet, maybe never. Maybe some day.

But since Miss Lucinda had been so good to her, mending her back to physical if not emotional health, she gave in and went with her into town.

Cora was thankful that when they walked into Joe's ice cream shop and general store, it was empty save for Joe, Miss Lucinda, and herself.

After an agonizing few minutes of condolences and unanswerable ques-

tions put to her by Joe, Cora was able to ease away, while Lucinda bois-
terously haggled over the price of her goods for sale.

Joe's scratchy transistor radio sat on the counter, squawking out "Creole
Love Song," by Duke Ellington. Cora instinctively hummed along as she
gravitated to the back of the store, where the racks of magazines were kept.
Most of them were always months old by the time they reached Rudell,
but they still held their magic. Some of the newspapers were dropped off
by folks passing through town or sent by former residents who'd been lucky
enough to get out. Deacon Earl's niece Margaret, who'd moved to Chicago
about a year earlier, regularly mailed a copy of the *Chicago Defender,* which
kept Rudell aware of what went on outside of their little town.

Cora picked up a copy of a Wanamaker catalog and flipped through the
pages, looking at the latest women's fashions and imaged herself in finger
waves and a dress of crepe de chine instead of braids and dresses of plain
cotton. How long had it been since she'd sat in her bed and stared at the
beautiful pages under the moonlight wishing for all the world that it could
be her in the lovely dresses on the arm of a handsome, wealthy man? Or
singing those forbidden songs to a crowd that hung on her every word?

She bypassed a tattered copy of *Colored Citizens* and picked up a copy
of the *Chicago Defender* that falteringly mouthed a short article about Josephine Baker, who'd just appeared at the Savoy Ballroom to a standing-
room-only crowd. Her heart beat a bit faster. The article went on to read
how the colored population was growing, and business and entertainment
was booming for coloreds on the Southside. Wasn't Deacon Earl always
bragging about how his niece Margaret was doing so well?

Thoughtfully, Cora returned the paper to its place, as something old and
familiar began to tingle with life inside her.

▲ ▲ ▲

"Now I ain't ask much of ya since you been here, Cora," Lucinda chided,
"but you gon' go ta church on Christmas Eve ifn I have to drag ya by that
pretty hair of yours."

They'd argued back and forth all day, but Cora finally realized this was
a fight she could never win. She was pretty sure that if she defied Miss
Lucinda she would be good at her word and drag her by her braids right
down the road to the church. With great reluctance Cora put on her one
good dress, a donation from the women of the church, combed her hair,
and followed Miss Lucinda out the door.

When they arrived, the small, white church was already full with folks ready to give thanks and praise. Her throat grew tight with emotion as she looked down the aisle and saw Deacon Earl standing at the pulpit.

Mumbled whispers rippled through the room as all eyes turned on her from the left and right side of the church while she slowly made her way down the aisle to a seat in the front pew.

Deacon Earl smiled, nodding his balding head, as he sent up a silent prayer of thanks. This was a special day. The prodigal daughter had returned to the flock.

Lucinda held onto Cora's hand throughout the entire service. Cora wasn't sure if it was because Lucinda was afraid that she'd get up and run out or to give her comfort as the deacon spoke passionately of healing and new beginnings. For whatever the reason, Cora was grateful, especially when Deacon Flem asked that Cora come and join the choir for the final hymn.

"Go on, chile," Lucinda urged in a hushed whisper. "Do yo' mama and daddy proud."

Cora looked around the room at all the familiar faces, faces with hope and love, faces she'd grown up knowing and loving in return. She turned to the back of the church, and men, women, and children were standing five deep, and among the expectant congregation was David. A rush of hot air shot through her chest. A gentle smile of encouragement moved like a ray of hope across his face.

She turned to Lucinda. "Go on, chile, go on now."

On trembling knees Cora stood and a solemn hush fell over the packed room. She made her way to the front of the assembled choir and each of the members reached out to touch her in welcome. She turned to face the congregation.

Cora took a deep, steadying breath, raised her eyes toward the heavens, and let the words ascend from her soul. Like a haunting whisper they began, building in strength and power, cascading over the assembly in wave after wave of emotion denied.

" 'Just a little talk with Jesus, tell him all 'bout your troubles, just a little talk with Jesus, He will make it right . . .' "

She'd forgotten how much she loved to sing, forgotten how good it made her feel inside. Her voice became her prayer and she spilled out the trouble in her heart, opened her spirit, and let the answers come in. When she walked out the church door that Christmas Eve of 1927, embraced and kissed by her family, she knew what she must do.

Seven

~~~~~~~~~~

David was waiting for her and Lucinda outside of the church. He waited patiently as the congregation gathered around Cora, welcoming her back to the fold and telling her how much she'd been missed. Finally, she made her way to where David stood by his car. His tender smile greeted her.

"That was beautiful, Cora." He rubbed her shoulder.

"Thank you."

"Can I take you and Miss Lucinda home?"

Cora gazed over her shoulder and saw Lucinda engaged in conversation and knew they'd be there for hours if they waited for her.

"I think Miss Lucinda is gon' be here fo' a while. Let me tell her I'm leavin'."

Cora returned shortly, with Lucinda's approval, and she and David drove off to the smiles and waves of the First Baptist congregation.

"I know how hard that must have been for you in there, Cora," David said, as they bumped and chugged along the uneven road.

"Hardest thing I ever did," she admitted. She turned to David as realization settled around her like a comforting arm. "At first, I did it fo' my folks, make 'em proud, like Miss Lucinda said. But then as the words came from me I knew I was doin' it fo' me." She pressed her hand to her chest, and her eyes sparkled with a happiness David hadn't seen in far too long.

"It's a start, Cora. The healing. It's not always going to be easy. But it's a start, and I want you to know I'm with you, no matter how hard it gets."

She reached out and caressed his hand. "Thank ya, David."

"I want to do it, Cora."

71

He eased the car to a stop in front of Lucinda's house. His heart started hammering in his chest. He turned to her, the light of the full moon reflected in his anxious eyes. David took both her hands in his. "I want to be with you, Cora, every day of my life. That hasn't changed these past months. My feelin's for you have only grown stronger."

He fumbled in his pocket and pulled out a small, black box. "I want to take care of you, Cora." He flipped the box open and a thin gold band lay nestled on a bed of cotton. "I don't ever want you to be alone or hurt again. Marry me, Cora," he said in a hushed urgency. "Be my wife."

Cora gazed down at the precious gift being offered to her, the unbroken circle that would bind them until eternity, watched it sparkle in the night light, a beacon to the future. Tentatively she stretched her fingers toward the circle of light, and suddenly she was filled with a sense of total clarity and peace.

Cora closed the box, covered it with her hand, and looked across at David. "I love you, David Mackey. You know I do. First man I ever loved 'sides my daddy." She swallowed. "I want to marry you mo' than anythang—but I cain't."

"Why?" he asked on a breath that was squeezed out of the pain in his chest. "Tell me why?"

Cora studied her fingers for a long moment, lining up the thoughts in her head. Lawd knows the last person she wanted to hurt was David. But if she married him, she'd hurt him more later than anything he could feel now.

" 'Member when we talked 'bout dreams?" she asked softly. "I still have mine. I thought they up and died with my folks, but they didn't," she said, in a tone filled with the awe of discovery. "You got yo' dream, David. You the doctor you always wanted to be. You ain't invisible no mo'." She grabbed his hands that were cold even in the warmth of the night. "That's how I been feelin' these months—invisible. I'd lost my dream." She pulled in a long breath. "If I stays here in Rudell, my dream will die, and part of me will, too. I want to go North, make a new life." She hesitated. "Come with me. Come with me to Chicago. They says life is better there fo' coloreds." Her voice grew with insistence. "We could have a good life. You kin tend to the sick or work in a hospital, and I kin find a job singin' in one of them clubs," she hurried on, totally taken with the idea. "Maybe even make a record, be on the radio—"

"Cora—" His voice was so low, she forced herself to hear it. Her eyes snapped to attention.

"You know I can't leave Rudell, Cora. Leave these people. What would they do for a doctor? How many of them would die 'cause the white doctor won't treat them?"

"They, they could get a doctor from Alligator. Or, or sometime old Doc Hubbard don't mind treatin' coloreds."

"As long as he doesn't have to touch them," he said, the bitterness burning his tongue. He turned fully toward her, his gazed fixed and imploring. "Cora, you don't have to go North to be happy. Everyone here loves you. I love you. You can do all the singing you want—in the church. Doesn't that mean anything to you?"

Cora stiffened her back and looked him square in the eye. "Don't what I want mean anythang?" Her heart was running like a scared rabbit. She'd always given in, all her life, done what was expected of her. It was her time now. She saw her mama and daddy's faces. Mama was fretting, but only mildly so. Daddy was smiling and nodding. They may have wanted different things for her, but she knew deep in her heart that they both wanted her to be happy most of all.

"You cain't leave, and I cain't stay," she said quietly.

David nodded sharply, too hurt, too confused to do more. His world had suddenly stopped spinning. Everything around him stood still. There were no night sounds or the gentle ripple of the river rolling over rocks and pebbles. There was nothing but a stillness that echoed over and again. *"I cain't stay. I cain't stay."*

He pressed the box into her hand and closed her fingers over it. "I—I want you to keep this." He swallowed over the knot in his throat. "I want you to remember that no matter where you are, or what you do, that I love you, Cora. And—if—whenever you're ready, if you ever change your mind—I'm here—waiting for you."

Cora's eyes filled and a single tear of hope, regret, and the fear of an uncertain but exciting future slid down her cheek.

▲ ▲ ▲

The only thing David could do for the next few weeks leading to Cora's departure from Rudell was to stay away, as much as it pained him to do so. He knew that if he went to see her he'd beg her to stay, to reconsider this decision of hers. And he knew it wouldn't be right, be fair to Cora. As much as it hurt him to know that she was leaving Rudell and him, he understood what having a dream and wanting it to come true was like. He knew the fire that burned inside, and there was nothing to put it out but to go after what you wanted. He also knew that if he pressed her, she would eventually give in and both of them would regret it in the years to come. Cora deserved her chance and he loved her enough to be sure she got it.

Now the day had arrived. All night he'd lain awake praying for a miracle. But as the sun rose majestically across the horizon, he knew this prayer had not been answered.

The members of First Baptist had gotten together and raised nearly two hundred dollars for Cora's trip and money to live on, according to Miss Lucinda, who made it a point to keep David informed. Even his mother had taken time away from her regular customers to sew two dresses for Cora, patterned after the latest styles she'd copied from a Montgomery Ward catalog. David tucked the dress box on the backseat of his car and drove to the railroad station.

When he arrived at the open-air station, that was no more than a stall as big as an outhouse for the ticket seller, he immediately spotted Deacon Earl, Flem, Miss Lucinda, Maybelle, and Sassy, standing along the lines of the tracks among the eager gathering of travelers and impatient greeters. And there in the center was Cora.

Her starched white blouse and pencil-thin, black skirt were simple but elegant on Cora. Her straight back was turned to him, and the single, thick braid rested between her shoulder blades. She carried a dark jacket over the crook of her arm. A cardboard suitcase sat at her feet.

He stood there watching the scene in front of him, and for the first time since he'd known Cora, he felt like the outsider. Surrounding her were the people who'd known her all her life and she in return. He, on the other hand, only represented a year in her life. He didn't belong here. He shouldn't have come.

David is here. She could feel him sure as she could feel her own heartbeat. She'd prayed that he would come. That she'd see him again. Her prayer had been answered. She snapped her head across her shoulder and all at once the crazy bumble bees that had been buzzing like wild in her stomach began to settle down. She was instantly filled with that familiar warmth as her heart rushed to her throat.

Letting go of the security of Miss Lucinda's hand, all she could see in front of her was David. The weary mother who shouted for her five children to stop running, the wrinkled old man who coughed and smoked his pipe, the newlyweds who hugged and kissed all disappeared. He stood there, among them all, tall and straight, his smooth, dark skin tight across the sharp cheeks that she loved to run her fingers across. He looked like he could pose for one of those fashion magazines. But of course no colored man would ever be in a fashion magazine.

He wore her favorite blue suit and sparkling white shirt with his straw hat. The realization tightened her throat, bringing tears to her eyes. He only wore it on special occasions. She walked toward him as if pulled by a magnet, and everything around her melted into the background. All she saw was him. She'd remember him, this moment, just like this, she promised herself, stopping a mere foot in front of him. *Just like this.*

He wanted to touch her, hold her tight against him, lift up her tiny body and run away with her. Love her gentle and slow, fill her with child so she'd never leave him. Everything in him screamed in silent pain.

"I—brought you something from my mama." He gulped and tried to control the rapid racing of his heart. "She—wanted you to have something nice—for your—trip."

Cora's eyes stayed locked on him, memorizing every detail, every line of his face, the sweep of his dark brows, the curve of his mouth.

"Thank ya. Tell yo' mama thanks fo' me," she whispered, on a strained breath of air.

Was that the only reason he'd come? she wanted to ask, but didn't. She couldn't bare it if he said yes. Did he miss her as much as she'd missed him? She hadn't seen him since Christmas Eve, and it had been so hard, so hard and lonely without him. Worst than she'd imagined. But she knew that if she'd broken down and seen him, he'd somehow convince her to stay—and she couldn't do that. But what if he asked her now, at this moment?

The rumble of the train rapidly approached, closed the distance, vibrated like a chill beneath their feet. *Ask me now, the train's coming.* She breathed faster.

Stay with me, Cora, he urged in his head, hoping she would hear his silent plea.

Anxious faces peered down the track, moved closer. *It was coming.*

"Come with me," she said suddenly. She clasped his arm in a fierce grip. "I got enough money fo' the both of us." Her lilting voice carried a note of escalating urgency as the train drew nearer. She pressed closer.

David's eyes darted down the railroad track. Black smoke billowed in the air. He stared into her imploring eyes, imagining his days and maybe the rest of his life without her. He reached out and cupped her cheek in his hand. "This is your time, Cora," he said quietly, "your dream. You have to take it."

The huge iron machine, swirling its smoke and dust around them, screeched to a grinding halt. The smell of burning coal assaulted her nose, filled her lungs.

Cora glanced quickly over her shoulder to where Miss Lucinda and the others began to approach, moving through the ragtag crowd.

Passengers poured out of the opened doors, tumbling onto the dirt platform, welcomed by shouts of greeting and tears of joy, becoming tangled in the web of travelers who would replace them on the train.

"All aboard!"

A terrible excitement raced through her veins, mixed with a deep sadness, as she witnessed the array of emotions on the faces that rushed by her, the curious ones that peered out of the sooty windows.

How long had they been gone? How long would they stay? She wanted to ask them what they had seen, what the world was like. Was it what she imagined and heard? Had they found their dream? Was hers really at the end of the line or right here in Rudell? But no one saw her. No one stopped. Couldn't they see the questions in her eyes, feel the terror in her soul?

"I guess this is good-bye," David said, fighting the shudder that closed his throat.

He wasn't going to ask her to stay, was he? She was leaving, wasn't she?

"All aboard!"

"You must wanna miss that train, chile," Deacon Earl said, appearing at her side.

She looked around, witnessed the love, worry, and doubt reflected in their eyes, burning the images into her mind.

"First thang you do is find a good Baptist Church," Miss Lucinda sniffed. "You gon' need one out there. Heap a sinners in the cities."

That's just what Mama would have said, Cora thought, a soft smile touching her lips. "I will."

"Margaret gon' meet you at the station," Deacon Earl assured her. "Don't you worry none. And you tell that niece of mine she need to come on home and visit."

"Yessir," Cora mumbled.

Flem put his hand on Cora's right shoulder, his voice was low and measured. "Chicago ain't like Rudell, Cora. You gon' be in a whole new world, a faster life. You ain't gon' have folks who care 'bout ya to look after ya no mo'. You gon' have ta do that yo'self. Just don't forget what you learnt here, that we's here if you need us."

Cora listened to the reassuring voice, the wise words, and was reminded of her father. It was what he would have said to her if he'd stood in the same spot.

Sassy and Maybelle each gave her a hug and promised to answer her letters.

Wisely, one by one, they moved away, leaving Cora and David.

"Don't forget what I said, Cora. If you ever change your mind . . ."

Cora drew in a long breath, stretched up, and placed a tender kiss on his lips, not caring what the others thought, needing to kiss him that one last time, stop him before he said more. She looked down and reached between the buttons of her blouse with her white gloved hand and pulled out the ring that hung on her mother's thin, gold chain. "I'll remember," she whispered, fingering the ring, then spun away and ran for the open door before she changed her mind.

Flem helped her up the three steps and passed up her suitcase.

"Thank ya, everybody. I'ma make y'all proud."

"We knows, sugah," Lucinda warbled, no longer attempting to hide her tears.

David ran over just as the train began to chug. "Here," he raised the box with the dresses to her. "I love you," he mouthed.

The train began to move.

"I'll write. Every day."

What was she doing? she asked herself in a fleeting instant of terror.

Flem, Earl, Lucinda, Sassy, Maybelle, and David all waved as the train eased down the track.

The departing whistle pieced the air, jolted her. Her heart raced. She squeezed the ring between her fingers. If she jumped now before the train sped up, she'd probably only get a few scratches and scrapes. The ground below her feet began to blur.

She looked back to where she'd been. The station, the people, Rudell were getting smaller, fading like a promise unfulfilled. In a few more minutes she wouldn't be able to see them at all. She wouldn't be able to see them.

"Ticket," the conductor shouted near her ear.

Through tear-filled eyes, she fumbled in her purse and with shaky fingers handed him her ticket.

"You need to go set in the colored car," the red-faced man in the dark blue uniform instructed with a wave of his hand.

"Yessir," Cora nodded.

Cora rocked from side to side, her suitcase bumping against her hip as she held the dress box to her chest and made her way to the back of the train, past unfamiliar faces and pairs of eyes that didn't see her. *She was invisible.* She clasped the gold ring in her hand and found an empty seat, stared out the window, recognizing nothing.

And the journey to a new world, a new life began.

CHICAGO

Eight

—wwwwww—

Cora couldn't believe it, that she was finally doing it, leaving for the North and all the wonderful sights and sounds she imagined awaited her there. The horrible scene at the railroad station still had a vice grip on her, but she fought it down. It would be no good for her to cry and moan all the way to Chicago. She refused to be pitiful. Papa always told her that there was nothing worse than a pitiful woman.

Desperately she tried to sleep, but it was nearly impossible with the low roar of voices around her, the bothersome noise of babies wailing, the foul stench of old cigarette smoke, mixed with the raw odor of bodies pressed together like dried fruit in a jar. Still, there was something comforting about the rolling and rocking of the train, the rhythm of the massive metal beast as it hurtled along the tracks. If she couldn't rest her eyes, she'd use them to watch the passengers, their odd gestures of using their hands to talk, their fancy clothes that looked to cost too much, and their almost indifferent way of being with one another, nothing like the way the folks acted back home. They talked at each other not to each other as people did in the Delta. Nobody seemed to pay each other no never mind. Just kept talking. So strange.

Eventually Cora did drop off for a spell, lulled by the lullaby of the locomotive. When she stirred from the awkward slumber, her body slowly unfolding from its curled up, pretzel fashion on the hard seat, Cora's eyes widened like two half dollars as she pressed her face shamelessly against the glass to drink in more of the sight. She couldn't be sure that her eyes weren't playing tricks on her; maybe she was imagining things. *Lawd, it was really snow.*

Watching the snow gave her a slight chill and she drew her thin jacket around her shoulders. The snow was sure pretty to look at, but the cold was another matter. It felt like the cold came right through the glass into her body. Please, Lawd, don't let Chicago be this cold. How could anybody stand it? How could she stand it?

She curled up a bit tighter in her seat and looked around at the montage of weary faces. Where had the gleam in the eyes gone, the excitement of the voices? Chicago couldn't be too much farther. It just couldn't. She closed her eyes and tried to sleep. Sleep would help her forget the hunger pangs in her stomach.

▲   ▲   ▲

"Chicago! Union Station! Five minutes!" the conductor shouted, moving from car to car.

Cora roused herself from an uncomfortable sleep and gazed through half-closed lids at the towering plumes of concrete and glass that had mysteriously replaced the blankets of snow. She sat straight up in her seat. "Oh, Lawd," she said on a long, hushed breath of amazement.

A sensation of excitement began to build in the tiny car, moving from one to the next like storm clouds moving across the fields. Cora clutched the dress box close to her chest, patted her braid that had come undone, and worried what city girl Margaret would think of her rumpled condition.

She was here, actually here in Chicago! In a few minutes she would walk off this stuffy, smelly train. Oh, Lawd, she was really here. Her stomach twitched and she held her breath as the train screeched to a halt. Mechanically, almost dazed, she followed the other passengers out of the car into a mammoth vault of humanity. Panic suddenly seized her limbs, locking her in place. People, hundreds, maybe thousands, swarmed like honey bees around her, moving at a dizzying pace. Slowly she craned her neck up, up to the arched ceiling that looked like it touched heaven. Her mouth dropped open at the sight of the powerful pillars, brilliant lights, and stained-glass windows. Everything was big, too big. Yet there didn't seem to be enough space for all the people. People everywhere she turned.

The aroma of foods she couldn't name clawed at her innards from places unseen, reminding her of how hungry she was. Her stomach grumbled loudly. She looked quickly around, embarrassed, but no one noticed or cared.

"Papers! Get your papers! *Chicago Daily Tribune.* Get your paper!" a young white boy shouted, holding a newspaper high over his head. "Herbert Hoover leading in the polls for president! Get your paper. Read all about it."

" 'Scuse me, Miss, you know how to get to State Street from here?" a colored woman with a little boy asked her. The little boy with big, brown eyes looked up at her hopefully.

Cora shook her head numbly.

The woman sucked her teeth and snatched the boy by the hand and moved on.

White folks were everywhere. Mixed right in with the coloreds. Nothing like Rudell.

Cora was shoved from left to right, bumped from front to back, but she still couldn't move. The world seemed to be spinning wildly around her.

"Shoe shine. Get yo' shoes shined," a jolly-looking colored man singsonged from a stand along one wall. Next to him was a fat woman selling hot dogs, which was right along side of a glass-covered shop with all manner of folks sitting down at tables covered in white cloths.

There were shops to buy food, clothes, shoes; everything a person could want was right here. But where were the houses? The sky? Weren't there no grass or trees in Chicago? And the noise. It was deafening and it seemed to echo against the enormous walls of concrete, ringing in her ears. The roar and rumble of trains coming in and out of the station pouring out more people continued in an endless cycle.

Her head felt light, just like before a fainting spell from the heat. She gulped in a lungful of air and shut her eyes.

"You must be Cora."

Cora's eyes snapped open.

"Look just like your mama," a brash voice announced. A wide smile took up her whole face.

She blinked, taking in Margaret in one long gaze. Margaret Holmes was nothing like she'd imagined at all. She looked just like all the other womens who clicked around on those narrow heels and held their bodies in a state of agitation, like everything was moving too slow and they wanted to get on with things.

Her mouth was as red as one of Flem's apples from his tree, and shiny, too, set against her dark skin, like somebody had colored it and just slapped it on her face. She was dressed real sharp with a long, gray wool coat and what looked like a dead raccoon wrapped around her neck with a little hat to match.

Oh, Lawd.

"Well, come on now. We need to get going. I have to be to work in a couple of hours." She started marching off, narrow hips swaying, head held high. Her red high-heeled shoes click-clicking against the hard surface.

Cora scurried to keep Margaret in sight between the bodies that cut them off without a second thought, without an excuse me.

Where was Margaret taking her? Hopefully her house was close. She wanted to get away from all these mannerless folks, set down a spell, and try to collect herself. She clutched the box tighter and got a good grip on her suitcase.

They pushed their way through the people, around the stalls that were set up to sell everything to attract the eye, around the paperboys, and the shoe-shine man, the train conductors announcing the arrival and departure of the trains, around the noise. The noise.

Finally, they climbed a set of stairs that opened to a long row of gold-and-glass doors that spun around in a circle when you pushed them. Maybe it was some kind of strange Chicago ride, like when the carnival would come to town.

"Come on," Margaret tossed over her shoulder, as she pushed through the revolving door.

Cora stood there for a minute, tried to time the swinging and stepped in, her box and suitcase jamming the door. She was stuck in between two pieces of glass. She pushed and tugged, and all at once the door swung free and she was practically tossed on the other side, to be slapped in the face with a backhand of frigid air.

Margaret stood there howling with laughter, her head tossed back, mouth opened wide, wide enough to reveal gold caps on her back teeth.

Cora stood there bewildered, shivering, and embarrassed, her dress box crushed and the dresses falling out from the ruined sides. Her mouth trembled. She wanted to cry.

"You about as country as they come." Margaret hee-hawed. "We gonna have to get you citified right quick. Come on, honey, the trolley's coming." This time she took Cora's arm and herded her down the crowded street.

Margaret was walking so fast, Cora could barely take in the wondrous sights, the almost frightening scenes. The first thought that came to her mind was the Tower of Babel from the Bible. Chaos for as far as the eye could see. Under her feet was the same hard surface, covered in a thin, dirty coat of snow. The buildings really did reach heaven, pierced the clouds with their pointy tops. She looked behind her. The station was quickly disappearing into the background. A whole world under the ground, she realized in amazement, and still there were more people.

The sound of bells ringing in the chilly air drew Cora's attention.

"Here it comes," Margaret said, craning her neck down the street.

A trolley car! A real live trolley car was coming right at them, just like she'd seen in the pictures. Wait till she wrote the folks back home.

After a lot of jostling, Margaret and Cora managed to squeeze in.

"Hang on," Margaret warned. "Don't want to lose you. Uncle Earl would kill me sure enough." She laughed that raucous laugh of hers.

Cora hung onto one of the poles for dear life as the wind whipped around her face and snuck up under her thin clothes. The buildings, the people, cars, animals went flashing by in a series of color and sound. It was too much to take in, to digest. She was near giddy with excitement, like a child who had toys for the first time and didn't know what to play with first.

"This is us," Margaret announced, pulling a cord over her head, which sounded the bell.

They hopped down from the trolley, stepped over muddy puddles and short hills of dirty snow, and trudged up a sloping street with houses so crammed together they looked like one long building, with black, iron, winding steps running down the front from top to bottom.

"Hey, Sonny." Margaret waved to a young man across the street in a pin-stripped suit and no overcoat. He was leaning against a shiny black car smoking a cigarette with his hat tipped low down over his right eye.

"Looking good, Margie. Who's that you got witchu?"

"Friend. And you just leave her be, Sonny Carter."

"You know I only got eyes for you, Margie," he grinned, flashing a gold front tooth.

Margie click-clicked down the street. "Don't pay Sonny no attention. He don't mean no harm. He talks like that to everybody."

Cora sidestepped a group of about six raggedy brown children who were throwing dirty snow at each other.

"One of you little ragamuffins hit me with some of that nasty snow, I'm gonna tell your mama," Margaret warned, narrowing her tiny eyes to look more threatening. "You hear me, Joe Willie?"

"Yes, ma'am," he said, darting by her.

"Damn kids. Mamas don't pay them one bit of attention. Out in the streets all times of night into one set of mischief or the other," Margaret fussed. "Hey, Liz," Margaret beamed at a young woman with a protruding belly. The woman named Liz gingerly walked down the steps to the street.

"Hey, girl. What you know good?"

"This here is my friend from back home, Cora Harvey. She's gonna be staying with me for a while." She turned proudly to Cora as if she'd just introduced the queen of England. "Cora, this here is Liz Cooper, lives upstairs from me. Ready to have her very first baby. Ain't that right, Liz?"

Liz nodded shyly and protectively patted her belly. "Nice to meet you, Cora."

Cora stuck out her hand. "Please ta meet you, too."

"Need anything, just holler up the stairs; I'm home all day."

"Thank, ya," Cora said.

"See ya later, Liz."

"Working tonight?"

"Of course. Got to keep myself looking good," she said, punctuating it with that laugh that echoed up and down the street.

Margaret led the way up the stoop and opened the front door, which opened onto a dim hallway that smelled like something old and damp. One bare lightbulb hung from the middle of the long ceiling, casting more shadows than light.

"I'm up on the third floor." Margaret started up the steps, which creaked and groaned beneath her feet. Cora followed, holding onto the banister, letting her eyes roam along the thick, wooden walls and secret-looking doorways that did little to contain the aromas of stewed red cabbage, fried chicken, and pork chops. Cora's stomach grumbled loudly. Music from some unseen place followed them up the stairs, accompanied by sounds of hand clapping and feet stomping against the wood floors.

"Whew. Here we are." Margaret fumbled around in her purse, pulled out a key, and opened the narrow door, one of four on the long hallway.

"Come on in. Make yourself at home." Margaret pulled off her coat and tossed it on top of another mountain of discarded clothes.

Make myself at home? Cora looked around in dismay. Stockings hung from the doors, shoes were scattered on the dull, wood floor, dishes overflowed in a tiny sink tucked off to the side of the two-room apartment.

"Well," Margaret breathed, startling Cora by walking up behind her. "Guess we gonna have to find you some space." She laughed loudly. "You don't have to be too particular when you live alone." She grinned slyly. " 'Cept those nights when my sugar pie comes over." She winked. "You'll get to meet him." She planted her hand on her hip and angled her head. "Maybe I can get him to introduce you to one of his friends."

"Naw, that's fine. I gots me a fella back home. He—"

Margaret waved her hand in dismissal. "You know how far Rudell is from Chicago, girl! You best to find you a fella." She poked Cora in the side. "Keep you warm on these cold winter nights." She laughed again. "I wish I could stay and help you get settled, but I got to get to work. Mr. Morgan don't like it when I'm late."

"Who—who's Mr. Morgan?"

Margaret spun around and grinned. "Mr. Morgan is the wealthiest, most powerful Negro in Chicago. He owns damn near everything. At least everything that Mr. Capone don't own."

"Who's Mr. Capone?"

"Humph. Believe me, you don't need to know about him. He runs all the bootlegging and numbers in Chicago. Trying to move in on the Southside, too, but Mr. Morgan has a lock on it."

Cora gaped at her in bewilderment.

Margaret waved her hand again. "Never mind."

She sashayed into the next room and reappeared a few minutes later in a skintight, black, strapless dress that barely contained her heavy breasts. Her feet were encased in matching spike heels, and her mouth looked redder than before. She grabbed her coat from the heap on the floor and, with a wave, was gone.

Cora turned around in a slow circle, taking in the chaos and confusion, which seemed to be all that Chicago was about. She grabbed the ring that hung around her neck and pressed it tightly between her fingers. What had she done?

Nine

—〰〰〰—

The sound of the front door being messed with stirred Cora out of her exhausted slumber. She jumped up with a start, looked around trying to figure out where she was. Her eyes began to focus. A dim, grayish light peeked in through the window. Slowly her heart returned to its natural rhythm. *Chicago. Margaret's house.* She rubbed her eyes, just as Margaret stumbled through the door.

The small front room was immediately filled with the smell of cigarette smoke and liquor. "Ssh," Margaret slurred. "Didn't mean to wake you." She pulled off her heels and dropped them in the middle of the floor. Then, for several moments, she stood in the center of the front room with a curious look on her face. She gazed around, thinking maybe she'd tumbled into the wrong apartment.

Margaret planted her hands on her narrow hips and reared back. "Well, look what you done to the place," she said in awe. Slowly she walked around. The dishes were washed and stacked, papers that had been piled on the table were neatly stowed away, the clothes that had grown to monstrous proportions had been folded and put in a box next to what she recognized as her couch that was now Cora's bed.

"I'll be damned." She strutted into her bedroom and found the same neat order. The bed was made with clean sheets, clothes and shoes tucked away in the closet. Her dresser with its array of nail polishes and lipsticks had been organized and dusted. "I'll be damned," she mumbled again. And if she didn't know better she'd swear the place even smelled different. Clean, like back home.

"I hope you don't mind, I straightened up a bit," Cora said sleepily, stepping into the bedroom.

Margaret spun around, nearly losing her balance. "Mind! Chile, where you been all my life?" She laughed uproariously, slapping her thigh. She marched back out into the front room. "So this is what the place really looks like. Just wait til Jimmy sees this. Always said the only reason he wouldn't settle down and marry me is 'cause I don't know how to take care of a house like a real wife." She beamed as proud as if she'd done it herself.

"Jimmy?"

"My sugar pie."

"Oh." Cora rubbed her eyes. "What time is it?"

"Going on six." Margaret yawned loudly. "I need to lay down for a few so I can get ready to go to work."

"You just came in from work, didn't you?"

Margaret turned away and began taking off her dress. "Don't you worry about it, okay," she snapped. She faced Cora, standing there in her slip. "A girl has to do what she got to do to get along in this world." She pointed her finger at Cora. "And if you intend to make it, you best learn that quick, or you might as well pack up your little suitcase and go on back to the Delta!"

Margaret plopped down on the bed, stretched out, and was asleep in minutes.

Cora stood in the doorway, dumbfounded. What had she done to upset Margaret so? She didn't want to make no trouble. But how was she ever going to know anything if she didn't ask?

She returned to her makeshift bed on the couch and tried to return back to sleep. She'd hoped that Margaret would show her around, help her find a job. But how could she if she worked morning and night? Was she going to be stuck in these two chilly rooms, in this strange place, for good? She sniffed and pulled up the thin blanket over her shoulders.

She squeezed her eyes shut. Flem was right. This wasn't Rudell, and the only person she could depend on was herself. She had to make it. She had to find a way. She took a deep breath. She couldn't tell them that she'd failed. She just couldn't.

▲ ▲ ▲

When Cora awoke again, the tiny apartment was silent. She could hear the wind tapping against the window, making every effort to get inside. Cora shivered. Wrapping the blanket around her shoulders, she tiptoed toward Margaret's bedroom. It was empty. Margaret's discarded clothing lay in a heap on the floor. Instinctively, Cora picked up the flimsy pieces and hung them in the closet, then straightened out the bed.

"These floors could use a good scrubbing," she said aloud, looking at the dull, stained wood.

She went into the kitchen area, searching around for a scrub brush and some brown soap, realizing in short order that those were items that Margaret knew little about.

A timid knock on the door drew her attention. She frowned and crossed the room. She dared not open the door like back home, not after the warnings that the folks in Rudell had given her.

"Who is it?"

"Cora, it's me, Liz."

Cora cracked open the door. "Mornin'." She beamed, happy to see a familiar face. "Come on in."

"Wow," Liz gasped, when she looked around. "Look at this place. It never looked this good even when Margie is expecting Jimmy to stop by."

Cora covered her mouth and giggled. "Same thing Margaret said."

"Well, you've been busy. Have you had breakfast?"

"Uh, naw. I'm not really hungry," she lied, and hoped her stomach wouldn't tell the real tale.

"I was fixing some eggs and bacon, more than I could eat—even for two," she added with a smile. "You're welcome to share a table with me."

"That's right kind of ya, but—"

Liz folded her hands across her bulging belly. "I ain't taking no for an answer." She placed a hand on Cora's shoulders. "Listen," she said gently, "I know what it's like being in a strange place with no friends. I thought I'd go plum crazy when I first came here from Georgia. Margie was there for me, and I feel obliged to do the same for you. Now come on. Throw on some clothes and come upstairs. I'm in the apartment marked 4C." She turned away and waddled off, closing the door gently behind her.

Cora stood there for several minutes, the expression of Liz's kindness warming her chilled body. For that brief moment, it almost felt like home.

▲ ▲ ▲

"If you gonna go out in the street in this weather you need more than that little piece of jacket I saw you with yesterday," Liz warned, as she washed up the breakfast dishes.

"It's all I got for now. I'll be fine."

"I'm sure I can find something for ya." She turned from the sink. "I used to be your size before all this." She laughed and patted her stomach, leaving a damp handprint on her pale blue dress.

"That would be right nice of ya. I'll take good care of it, and I promise to bring it back same as I got it once I gets me a job and get on my feet."

Liz waved her hand. "Don't worry yourself none. What are friends for?"

Cora smiled. *Friends.* "Thank ya," she mumbled.

Liz hummed an old Negro spiritual, " 'I don't feel in no ways tired. . . .' "

Cora closed her eyes, absorbing the melody, letting it fill her, and without realizing it, her melodious voice resounded throughout the room, sweet and powerful as it captured the essence of strength and endurance with every word, every turn of phrase.

Liz absently put down her dishcloth, dumbstruck by the beauty of Cora's singing. Her skin prickled as the perfect pitch notes sent chills rushing along her spine. Reverently she placed her hands across her stomach as if the words, having the power of prayer, would bless the life growing inside her.

Slowly, Cora opened her eyes as the spiritual drew to an end. She lowered her gaze, embarrassed, suddenly realizing what she had done. "Sorry," she mumbled, and tried to smile. "Guess I just forgot myself."

"That—was beautiful," Liz uttered in a hushed voice. "You always sing like that?"

Cora shrugged. "I 'spose. That's what folks back home says."

"The folks back home is right. Girl you kin sing!" Liz crossed the short space and took a seat at the neat, round table opposite Cora. She covered her hand with her own. "There's plenty places for a voice like that here in Chicago. Margie knows a ton a folks down at that club where she works." Her dark eyes gleamed with excitement.

Cora's eyes widened. "She does."

Liz nodded vigorously. "And she is good friends with that Richard Morgan fella. Word is he and Bessie Smith tight like this." She crossed her fingers.

"You lyin', *the* Bessie Smith?" Cora pressed her hand to her chest. "I'd do just 'bout anything to meet her, just one time."

"Shucks," Liz flicked her wrist. "Tell Margie to take you on down to the club. Everytime Bessie's in town she hangs out at the Lincoln Garden Café. Hottest night spot in Chicago," Liz affirmed, smiling broadly.

Cora gazed off in the distance, imagining herself meeting the great Bessie

Smith, better still, letting Bessie hear her voice and tellin' her how won-derful she was and that she could sing right along with her. Her breathing picked up its pace. She'd hear her voice on the radio; they'd hear it back in Rudell. Her face would be in all the colored papers. Then she could have some money, a real life. And then . . . maybe David would join her . . .

Liz waved her hand back and forth in front of Cora's face.

Cora blinked and felt her face heat. "Sorry," she mumbled. "Just thinkin' is all."

Liz smiled indulgently. "I knows. Felt the same way when I came here from Georgia." She sighed heavily, propped her elbows on the table, and rested her chin in her palm.

Cora pushed her own thoughts aside and focused on Liz's sudden som-ber expression. "What happened?"

"Humph. I had big ideas," Liz said dreamily. "Thought I was gonna find gold on the streets." She chuckled bitterly. "Found a no-good man instead, who made a heap of promises he couldn't keep."

"Oh. . . ." For a moment she was confused. "He, you and him . . ." She looked down at Liz's stomach.

"Naw, run off as soon as I told him 'bout the baby." Her voice trembled. "But it's all right though. I kin take care of both of us."

All the lessons her mother had drummed into her head beat their way back to the surface. If she'd let her nature take over with David, much as she'd wanted to, she could be in the same predicament as Liz. Although she knew *her* David would never run off. He loved her. But she would be somebody's mama, somebody's wife, and she still wasn't sure who *she* was yet.

She looked kindly upon Liz, who stared off to a past she could never reclaim.

"It's gon' be all right, Liz. I'll help ya anyway I kin."

Liz pressed her trembling lips together and forced a shaky smile. "Thanks." She pushed out a breath and slapped her palm on the tabletop. "Let me find you that coat, so we can go out for a spell."

▲   ▲   ▲

"Hey, Lizzie, you gonna introduce me to your friend?" Sonny greeted Liz as soon as she and Cora stepped out on the stoop. He was in the same spot as yesterday; and if he hadn't changed his suit, Cora would have believed he'd been there all night.

"She don't need to meet the likes of you, Sonny Carter!" Liz shouted back. She grabbed Cora by the arm and steered her down the block. "Stay as far away from Sonny Carter as you can," she said under her breath, sidestepping an old woman pushing a shopping cart.

Cora twisted her head to look behind her, and Sonny was blowing kisses. She turned quickly around. "Who is he, anyway?"

"He thinks he's a pimp."

"A what?"

"Pimp, you know. A man who uses women to make money."

Cora frowned, then realization hit her. She drew in a shocked breath. "Oh." She looked over her shoulder again, but Sonny was engaged in a very close conversation with a woman with lips redder than Margaret's and hips enough for two. She tucked the blue, wool coat tighter around her. Bootleggers, number runners, pimps. Her head spun. There was all sorts of devilment in Chicago. Maybe Ms. Lucinda was right. She needed to find a good Baptist Church straightaway.

As they moved down the long, winding block, from almost every window hung laundry flapping in the chilly breeze, everything from men's under-things to bedsheets. Folks stood out on the iron landings that zigzagged across the fronts of buildings and shouted back and forth across the street to each other. The infamous voices of Alberta Hunter and Ida Cox could be heard singing the blues from the scratchy radios that sat in windowsills. Children tumbled and wrestled in the wet snow; cars honked their horns. Things sure were different in Chicago. There seemed to be a secret song playing, a rhythm that only these people could hear. It was in everything they did. The way their heels pop-popped against the ground, the melody of their talk, the flash of their dress. It was in the air they breathed, in the laughter that sang out loud and free. In the flick of a wrist, the turn of a smile. And Cora felt out of step. She wanted to hear the music, too.

Liz took Cora to meet Willie, the owner of the vegetable market and Stu, who ran the meat and fish market, who both kindly gave her a sample of everything if she promised to come back. Cora promised she would, and tucked her brown paper–wrapped treasures under her arm. Maybe she'd fix up some fish and greens for dinner and surprise Margaret when she got home. Whenever that was.

"You must be tired with all this walkin'," Cora said, after about an hour of wandering in and out of the stores.

"I don't get out much. And sure don't have much company. I'm enjoying it." She turned to Cora and smiled. "How you like things so far?"

"Takes a lot of gettin' use to, I guess. Never seen so much of everything before."

Liz laughed. "Same way I felt when I got here. You ain't seen nothin' till you go to some of the clubs. Now that's something for the eye."

Cora gazed at Liz's profile. "You . . . think Margaret would bring me down?"

"Sure. She the one who took me." Then her jovial voice changed to one of regret. "That's where I met Hank." They turned a corner and headed back up their street. "Just don't you let none of these slick-talkin' city boys trick you into nothin', Cora. You got dreams, girl, and real talent." She exhaled, her voice as hollow as time long gone. "Don't let this city take it from ya, hear?"

Cora nodded slowly and wondered what Liz's dreams had been. Was Margaret living hers, and what did she do all day then half the night? Well, if Margaret was the key to her meeting the people who could change her life, then it was only a matter of time before she found out, and it was much sooner than she thought.

Ten

———\~\~\~\~\~\~\~\~———

Cora'd been in Chicago more than a month, and she'd seen no more than she had the first day Liz took her on a tour of the neighborhood. She saw Margaret even less.

Margaret floated in and out at all kinds of hours, passed out and went to sleep then got up and was gone again, never saying more than a hello and good-bye. She was either too tired or too busy to talk. One night she brought Jimmy home in the wee hours, and Cora did all she could to keep from screaming as she listened to their moans, grunting, and the squeaks of the old brass bed. She buried her head under the blanket and said a silent prayer for Margaret's sin-ridden soul. If her Uncle Earl knew how Margaret was carrying on, he'd drag her straight back to Rudell.

Day after day she cleaned, cooked, and scrubbed, trying to do something for her keep. Margaret became so accustomed to coming home to a clean house and a hot meal; she acted like it was her due and plum forgot all about, "Thank you, Cora, for doing such a fine job." Not that she was looking for any "thank you," but one every now and again would have been nice.

Sighing wearily, Cora sat at the table, beneath the dim light, and reread the letter she'd received that morning from David.

Dearest Cora,
I hope you are well in your new surroundings. I think about you every day and miss you terribly. Everyone in town asks about you. They all await news of your new life. I long to see you. Miss Lucinda sends her

love and so do Sassy and Maybelle. They promise to write soon. Please let
me hear from you so that I know you are well.
All my love,
David

Cora fingered the thin, gold band. What could she say to David? She
couldn't very well tell him the truth.

She folded the letter, tucked it back in the envelope, and slipped it
between her two good dresses that she kept in the box beneath the couch.
She'd write when she had news to share.

Cora looked around at her "new surroundings" and a wave of sadness
built and settled in her chest. This was not what she had expected. Not
what she'd dreamed for herself. All she did from sunup to sundown was
clean and cook and pick up behind Margaret, who paid her no never mind.
Her one friend was Liz; and with her time growing near, she didn't come
downstairs for visits as often. She was all alone. Cora lowered her head
onto her arms and cried, and that's how Margaret found her.

"You look like you're tired, girl," Margaret announced, as she switched
through the door, shutting it with a thud behind her.

Cora's head snapped up. Quickly she wiped the tears from her eyes.
"Just restin' a spell."

"Well, you need some excitement in your life. All work and no play will
make Cora a dull country gal." She laughed loudly, flashing her big teeth
that were smudged with red lipstick. Cora cringed.

"Come on, sugah. Me and you are gonna hit the town tonight." Margaret
waved her hands over her head and wiggled her hips. She switched to a
jerky hand-and-foot motion. "Can you Charleston?"

"What?"

"Charleston." She put on a short show, arms flailing, legs twisting, head
tossed back in euphoria. "It's the rage," she said, a bit breathless. She ran
over and pulled open a cupboard and took out a phonograph machine,
wound it up, and put on a record. Sharp toots of horns in a frenetic,
scratchy beat filled the tiny room. Margaret reached out and pulled Cora
from her seat. "Come on, I'll show you. It's easy."

Cora tried valiantly to keep up with the twists and turns until she had
some semblance of the dance.

"Loosen up, chile," Margaret said, working up a sweat. "Whoever heard
of a colored gal with no rhythm. That's it, shake those hips." Margaret
kicked her legs higher, swung her arms faster.

This is totally decadent, Cora thought as she slowly got the hang of it, letting herself become one with the music. But she was loving every minute of it, she realized wickedly, and promised herself to say an extra prayer before bed. She moved a bit faster, twisted her hips in a way she didn't know she could. The music filled her, lifted her spirit in a way church singing never did. Her insides smiled, keeping in step with the new beat.

The music wound down and the two dropped into chairs, legs and arms stretched out in front of them. Cora tossed her head back, giggling like a little girl, fanning her face with short waves of her hand.

"Whew! Not bad," Margaret complimented. "Now if we can just do something with that sorry hairdo, put some color on your face, and find you something flashy to wear, you'll turn every head in the joint tonight."

Cora's head snapped up so fast she grew dizzy. Her eyes widened in alarm. Dancing in the house was bad enough. But makeup, new hairdo, flashy clothes. *Oh, Lawd.*

"Come on, girl." Margaret snatched Cora's hand and jerked her from the chair, dragging her into the bedroom. "We'll fix you up so fine, you won't recognize yourself."

Cora was so stunned she couldn't speak, as Margaret pushed her into a chair in front of the dressing table and turned her away from the mirror.

Margaret planted her hands on her hips and looked Cora up and down, then smiled from one side of her mouth. "I know just the thing . . ."

Cora closed her eyes and sent up a quick prayer that she wouldn't be too awful by the time Margaret got finished with her. She winced as Margaret combed and brushed her long hair and put some sort of pomade in the front then lined it with metal clips that gripped her scalp, and curled the long ends with strips of brown paper bags. Heaven help her, she silently implored.

Then Margaret applied a white cream all over Cora's face and wiped it clean with a tissue, before applying rouge to her cheeks and a thick coat of ruby red lipstick to her mouth. One by one Margaret removed the metal clips from Cora's hair and dropped them on the dresser, followed by the strips of paper bag.

She stood back and beamed with pleasure at her handiwork. "Take a look. Take a look," she urged eagerly.

Tentatively, Cora slowly turned around in the chair to face the mirror, not sure what to expect when she gazed upon her reflection. When she met her face in the looking glass, a gasp of dismay rushed up her throat, but good manners kept it from pushing out.

She leaned closer. This couldn't be her. In a daze she raised her hand to her head, running her fingers along the rows of shiny black waves that crowned the front of her head. She puckered her lips. She'd never seen anything so red in all her natural life.

Cora swallowed, breathing faster. She looked just like one of those women in the magazines. Just like 'em. She was going to hell sho' nuff. But what scared her most of all, what brought an exhilarating terror to her heart, was that she liked it. Maybe just a little, but she liked it. She no longer looked like the little girl from the Delta, but a grown woman. A city woman. Cora straightened her shoulders. A city woman.

Margaret picked out her favorite navy blue dress with the short, cap sleeves—something simple, she assured Cora, a pair of silk nylons—Cora's first pair—and what Margaret considered a conservative pair of heels. "Don't want you stumbling around and breaking your neck," she laughed, as Cora wobbled around the apartment.

"Just look at you," Margaret said, bobbing her head from side to side. "You gonna catch every man's eye in the place."

Cora stopped her pacing. The ring, hanging on the thin, gold chain sat cushioned between her breasts like a watchful eye. Her heart beat against the tiny circle of light. "I ain't lookin' for no man," she said, quiet but firm. "I gots me a fella."

"You won't have to look, sugah, they're gonna be looking at you." Margaret laughed loud and long and marched off into her room to get ready.

Cora sat down on her makeshift bed, worry lines wrinkling her brow. Maybe she should just stay home. Let Margaret go have her fun. She felt like a fool with all this makeup on and a dress so tight she could hardly breathe.

Thoughtfully, she smoothed the cool, dark blue fabric. She'd never had nothing this silky next to her skin before. She stretched out her legs and watched the shimmer of the stockings against her warm brown flesh, still feeling the tingle of energy running through them.

She sighed. It would be downright rude to have Margaret go through all this trouble and then leave her to go out alone. It was the only nice thing she'd done for her since the day she picked her up from the station. Cora wasn't raised up to be rude.

Cora peeked around the doorway into the bedroom and saw Margaret wiggle into a shiny, bright green dress. Margaret needed watching anyhow.

Eleven

~~~~~~~~~~~~~~

Cora concentrated extra hard on keeping her balance on the thin heels as she and Margaret click-clicked from the cab to the club.

Loud music and bubbling, tumbling laughter rolled out of the swinging doors, filling the sharp night air with an electric beat that pumped through your veins, doubled your step, swayed your hips. Bright lights shone like a hundred stars from the wide windows that framed the glittering, colorful, black, brown, and tan faces inside.

She was really here. A real live nightclub in Chicago. Her pulse quickened in time with the music.

"Come on, girl," Margaret urged, hooking her arm through Cora's. "Since I'm off tonight, I can introduce you around to the important people." She laughed, tossed her head back with a flourish, and pulled open the door.

Cora followed close behind and stepped into a dazzling, almost blinding world. None of her most vivid imaginings could compare to what was spread out before her. Never in her life had she seen so many fancy-looking colored people. Not even in their Sunday go-to-meeting best did the towns-folk of Rudell ever sparkle like this.

Slick-haired men, clothed in black tuxedos with snow white shirts, dark blue and brown pin-striped suits, with pants creased sharp enough to slice through baked bread.

Jewelry flashed on the necks, wrists, and in the ears of the glamorous women, with finger-wave hairdos cut close to the scalp, their lush bodies covered in slinky, slinky gowns. Cigarette smoke hung in the perfumed air, giving the entire scene a feel of unreality.

A ten-piece band, led by trumpeter King Oliver, were on a raised platform in the center of the tightly packed space, surrounded by round, rectangular, and square-shaped tables, covered in red linen and topped with white candles, and plates of pigs' feet, black-eyed peas, and seasoned collards. King Oliver was just announcing the return of somebody named Louis Armstrong on clarinet, and the audience roared its deafening approval. *He must be somebody special.* Cora thought.

The music, scents, sounds of hand-clapping, finger-popping, and fast-talking conversation swirled around her at a dizzying speed. Everywhere she turned there was something new and wonderful to see. Then there were the scenes that brought stains of embarrassment to her cheeks: the couples that danced belly to belly; large, dark hands cupping soft, round backsides; long, wet kisses; tongues that glided over succulent red lips; and deep whispers in gold-studded ears. Cora pressed her hands to her chest in alarm. *This was the devil's playground sho' 'nuff.*

Margaret was immediately kissed, hugged, and greeted by an assortment of men and women, whom she dutifully introduced to Cora, who just as quickly forgot all their names. She did her best to keep up with the rapid-fire conversation that was a curious mixture of southern drawl and city slang, creating a unique language with a rhythm all its own.

Margaret clasped Cora's hand, then pointed with the other. "There's Richard Morgan over there," she shouted over the din. She pulled Cora through the densely packed bodies, winding around the tables and gyrating couples on the dance floor, until they reached Richard's six-foot table.

The leather couch that lined one side was filled from end to end with dazzlingly beautiful women, their bodies bursting like ripened fruit from their dresses. Cora looked away from their shame and tugged the collar of her dress closer to her chin. On either end sat two thick-bodied men with dark, probing looks carved onto their threatening features.

The tabletop was covered with opened bottles of unlabeled liquor, ranging in color from dark amber to crystal clear. Overflowing ashtrays, plates, some half full, others the remains barely recognizable, filled up the rest of the space.

And in the center of it all sat Richard Morgan, like a king among his subjects. His darker than midnight tuxedo spread across his wide shoulders set against a white, silk, broadcloth shirt and a black bow tie, perfectly knotted. He raised a glass to his lips and a brilliant flash of light sparkled from the diamond ring on his pinky and a matching bracelet on his wrist.

It was almost as if he sensed her standing there, like an animal on the scent of its prey. He slowly rotated his head in her direction. Her breath caught and held in her throat. She suddenly felt warm from the inside out when Richard's black eyes, made darker by the shade of his thick lashes, rested on her face.

His close-cut, black, waved hair, with sprinkles of gray at the temples, shone like the ripples of the Left Hand River under the moonlight. His skin reminded her of cherry wood that had been polished to a smooth-to-the touch shine. His lips and nose were full, powerful, set between prominent cheekbones. His eyes, frightening in their intensity, locked onto Cora, seemed to root around inside her, quickening her breath. A slow, smug smile raised the left corner of his thinly moustached mouth. He saluted her with his raised glass.

"I see you brought company tonight, Margie, girl. Who's this pretty young thing?" He took a sip from his glass, his gaze never wavering from Cora's stricken face.

Margaret angled her body provocatively to the side, hand customarily on her hip. "This here is Cora. Cora Harvey, from Mississippi. She stayin' at my place for a spell, till she gets a job and a place of her own." She opened her purse and pulled out a cigarette. One of the men struck a match. Margaret bent low to accept his offer before blowing a cloud of smoke to mix with the rest in the air.

"That right," Richard commented, in what Cora concluded sounded like a rugged whisper that could cut through the darkness. He gave some kind of hand signal and everyone on his right side slid out of their seats and stood—waiting.

Richard patted the empty space next to him. "Have a seat, little Cora."

Cora glanced from one face to the other, gauging the expressions that ranged from sullen to outright fury. She threw pleading eyes on Margaret, who nudged her toward the empty spot on the couch.

"Thank ya," she mumbled, and took the vacant seat.

"Come on a bit closer," Richard invited, draping an arm around Cora's shoulder and easing her flush against his side. "I don't bite." He chuckled. Everyone at the table laughed at the joke she didn't get.

The raw power of his aftershave shot straight to her head, invaded her body. She studied the plates on the table and tried to keep from shivering.

"What can I get you to drink? Eat? Whatever you want, little Cora." He grinned and the gold rimming his front tooth flashed for an instant in the dim light.

"I—I don't—some water would be fine," she mumbled, not sure where to look or what to do. She folded her hands in her lap and suddenly wished she'd stayed at home.

Richard poured her a glass of water from a pitcher on the table as he spoke. "Where you from in Mississippi?" He handed her the glass.

"Thank you," she whispered, and brought the glass to her lips, hoping to drench the dryness of her throat. "Rudell."

"Just outside of Alligator, ain't it?"

Cora's features softened a bit. Surprise put some of the light back in her eyes. "Yessir," she nodded. "It is."

Richard slowly stroked his mustache. "Went through there once, about ten years ago. Quick trip. On my way to Clarksdale." He laughed, a deep from the belly laugh. Sobering slowly he turned to her. "Rudell ain't no place for a girl like you. I can see that. What do you plan to do with yourself in Chicago?" He signaled to one of a half-dozen cigarette girls, who wiggled their way around the club with a tray of cigarettes strapped around their necks. He asked for a pack and gave the girl a whole five-dollar bill. Cora forced her mouth not to drop open.

"So you were going to tell me about your plans." He angled his body so that he could focus all of his attention on Cora. His fingers tucked her hair behind her ear and a rush of something unspeakable flowed through her. Her skin prickled.

Self-consciously she patted her hair and inched away. "I—I want to sing." She gulped down the dryness in her mouth and imagined how ridiculous she sounded.

"Sing, huh? Can you sing, little Cora? Little bitty thing like you."

The women at the table giggled and snickered, feeling vindicated by her shaming.

Richard's head did a slow sweep along the table, the storm cloud of his brows hovered threateningly over his dark eyes, which seemed to flash lightning, striking each of them into an abrupt silence. He raised his chin sharply, and one by one the women rose from their seats and dispersed into the crowd. Richard never uttered a word.

"Rudeness is one thing I don't tolerate," he said, in that rasp, deepened by his anger, "even from a pretty woman." He took another sip from his glass.

Cora wasn't sure what she'd just seen. The only man she'd ever known who could make folks bend to his will with just a look was her daddy. And this man was nothing like her daddy. Richard Morgan was the sound you couldn't make out at night, what you knew was in the shadows but couldn't see, the creak in the stairs, that feeling that comes upon you sudden like a chill and you don't know why—clothed and polished in the shape of a man.

Margaret seemed not to notice a thing, paid no attention to how scared she was, up under this man with the fancy clothes and sparkling jewels, hair that glimmered in the light. The man who sat too close and touched her too often, too familiar. Margaret was too busy with one of the men who anchored the table, engaged in close and animated conversation, to notice a thing.

"So, little Cora, you want to sing."

"Yessir." She nodded over the drumbeat of her heart and focused on the tabletop.

"The name is Richard, little Cora." He stroked her hair again. "Where have you sung before?"

"Uh, just in the church choir back home." She wanted to run, duck beneath the light that shone from his eyes illuminating her soul. But she couldn't move, held in place by the sheer magnetism of the man. All she could do was hold herself tight and pray that she didn't burst with pure humiliation.

He suddenly laughed and his teeth sparkled like ivory against his skin. Cora felt compelled to defend herself. She didn't want to be seen as some country gal who didn't know nothing about the big world. She arched her chin and straightened her shoulders. "I done heard all of Bessie Smith's music and Alberta Hunter, and Ida Cox, too."

"Is that right." He chuckled some more. "Well, little Cora, me and Bessie are good friends. Friends since our days in Alabama." He peered deeper into her soul, saw her yearnings, and held it up in front of her. He leaned back, sensing her discomfort at his nearness. "How would you like to meet her?"

Cora swallowed, studied her hands while bobbing her head. "I would. I sure would."

"Maybe I can arrange that for you." He eased a bit closer again. "In the meantime, what are you doing about a job?"

Cora shifted her gaze to the glasses lining the table. "I don't have a job . . . just yet," she said softly.

"You could work here if you want. I could fix that for you, too." He shrugged. "I have a few friends. I'm sure they'd be willing to help you out. Margaret could teach you the ropes."

Cora glanced quickly around at all the flash and splash, the sparkle and city slick, the fast talk and faster walk, the music that ran up and down making a body jerk, jump and grind, fingers pop.

"That's right nice of you, Mr. Richard, sir. But . . . I ain't sure this is the place for me." She wrapped her hands around her glass.

Richard chuckled. Fine, young innocent thing was little Cora. Innocent and pure as new snow. But it wouldn't be long. Chicago would change all that. It changed everything and everyone. He took a long, slow drag on his cigarette then crushed it out in the overflowing ashtray.

"You think about it, little Cora. When you're ready, you come to me. 'Scuse me now, I have some business to tend to." He lifted her hand and brought it to his lips.

Cora's entire body tensed.

"Anything you want," he said, staring into her guileless, brown eyes, "is on the house tonight. My compliments." He stood and eased away, giving Margaret a wink on his way out.

▲ ▲ ▲

The sun was on its way up over the tips of brick buildings that sliced across the cloudless sky in an uneven pattern of gray and brown.

The energy was still at this hour, taking its rest. Tender almost in its touch against the skin, so unlike what it would be in a few hours when eyes and mouths opened, bodies stretched, feet clapped against the cold, wood floors, and babies awoke for their first feeding of the day.

Cora and Margaret tiptoed up the stairs that creaked and groaned in protest, their bodies as weary as the steps that held them. Margaret eased open the door to her apartment and immediately stepped out of her shoes, leaving them exactly where they stood at two right angles. Cora was tempted to do the same, but instead returned hers to the bottom floor of Margaret's overcrowded closet.

"So what did you think of Mr. Morgan?" Margaret asked, over a loud yawn, stepping out of her dress and leaving it in a shimmering pool on the floor.

"He seem nice enough," Cora replied, believing it was the right thing to say since Margaret thought so much of him. After all, he had offered her a job and a chance to meet Bessie Smith. But the real truth was, Richard Morgan frightened her and, at the same time, fascinated her. He could be alternatingly charming and threatening in less than an eye blink. Richard Morgan was nothing like the men back home.

Absently she fingered the ring that hung from her neck, bringing warm images of David to her mind. She still hadn't answered his letters, which came every week like clockwork. She kept them all tucked away in a box beneath the couch. Maybe soon she'd have something to tell him.

"He sure thinks a lot of you," Margaret mumbled, as she sprawled across the bed. "Talked 'bout you all night." She yawned and pulled the spread up over her shoulders. "Take you to work with me tomorrow night . . ." Her voice drifted off.

"Tomorrow? I ain't said yes," she protested weakly.

Soft snores filled the room. Cora stood there for several moments. Realizing it was pointless to talk to Margaret, she went to her own bed and wrestled with indecision for the rest of the night.

▲ ▲ ▲

When Cora awoke the following morning hoping to catch Margaret, she found Margaret's bed rumpled and empty. By rote she straightened the bedcovers and hung up Margaret's discarded clothing.

All through her near sleepless night, she saw visions of herself trapped between the smoke-filled air, perfumed and bejeweled bodies, hearing a language she didn't understand, surrounded by large-handed men who groped, grabbed, and touched, and women who seemed to love it.

More than once her eyes flew open, thinking that some strange hands were exploring her body. And the face that loomed before her was Richard Morgan's.

Her skin crawled and she felt her body involuntarily cringe each time she recalled the previous night as she went about her morning chores.

How could Margaret work there, night after night? Had she been so blinded by the allure of the fast life, drinks, food, and money overflowing that she'd forgotten everything she'd been raised to become back in Rudell?

Cora sat down at the small kitchen table and stared out of the window, unable to see anything of beauty beyond the dark brick buildings and billowing clothes hung from makeshift lines. That's how she was beginning to feel about her dream, her reason for coming this long way from home. It felt like everything was blowing away, and if she wasn't the clip that held fast, all that she wanted for herself would be tugged away, disappearing like morning dew.

There had to be something else she could do to earn her keep other than working in that club. There just had to be. Papa and Mama would stand up in their shallow graves if they could have seen her last night. She couldn't disgrace their memory that way, or herself.

Maybe she could ask Liz to help her find work, although she wasn't too sure how Liz managed to take care of her own self. But after she fixed herself a cup of strong black coffee, she'd go upstairs and ask Liz, anyway.

▲ ▲ ▲

Liz moved slow as a shackled bear around the tiny kitchen. *Won't be too long before she drops that baby.* Cora thought, and wondered if the daddy would ever turn up.

"Ain't much for colored folks to do," Liz puffed, as she took a seat and put her swollen legs up on a vacant chair. "Most folks work in the factories, the speakeasies, or clubs. Some get lucky and have their own business. Usually run them on their own 'cause they can't afford to pay nobody." She tenderly massaged her protruding stomach. "But the best jobs are in the clubs. Pay's good. Only thing to worry about are the raids by that I-talian fella Capone. Gets it in his head every now and again to bust in the clubs and threaten folks with guns, break up things, and such. But he don't fool with Mr. Morgan too much. Ain't been no trouble over there in quite sometime." Liz nodded wisely.

Cora flinched at the thought. Guns. "Maybe I could get a job in a factory."

Liz screwed up her puffy face as if she was in pain. "Believe me, Cora, you don't want to do that if you don't have to. They treat colored like they was back on the plantations."

"I got to do somethin', Liz. I'm going plum crazy boxed up in here. I ain't come all this way to set at home pickin' up after Margaret and fixin' meals for her and that Jimmy fella."

Liz rested her chin on her palms. "It ain't so bad at the club. I worked there till this happened." She glanced down at her stomach.

Cora's eyes grew wide. "You? I would never believe it."

Liz smiled ruefully. "Once you get used to things and how folks with a bit of change act, it ain't so bad."

Cora shook her head, remembering the sinful scenes she'd witnessed, and wondered if Margaret let strange men rub up against her and hem her up in corners.

"And didn't Mr. Morgan say he'd introduce you to Bessie Smith? How you gon' mess up a chance like that? This ain't Mississippi, Cora. You best get used to that. Folks don't act the same or think the same."

"I know, but . . ."

"If Mr. Morgan says he can do it, he will. Everybody knows he's good at his word." She lowered her voice as if she was afraid the cracks in the wall would overhear her confession and spread it out into the street. "Truth is, I wouldn't be able to make it, keep a roof over my head, if it wasn't for him."

Cora frowned, confused. "Whatchu saying?"

Liz blew out a breath. "When he found out that Hank left me high and dry, he promised that he would help me out. Sends money every month for the rent and food, with change left for me to buy little things for myself and the baby. Don't nobody know what he's doing for me 'cept you, Cora."

Cora sat in stunned silence. That's the way folks back home treated each other. She would never expect that from the people up North, who were always too busy, or too tired, to even say "how do" when they passed you on the street. Maybe Richard Morgan wasn't so bad, even if he did have some wicked ways. Still, working in the nightclub was a whole different story. She'd have to think of something else. She had to.

Twelve

~~~~~~~~~~~~~

For the next six weeks Cora walked the streets looking for work. Day after day she came home tired and disappointed, feet swollen, legs and head throbbing, despair weighing down her heart.

She'd heard, "Sorry, no jobs," so often it rang like an evil echo in her head. Then at night she'd have to listen to Margaret tell her that Richard had asked about her, wanted to know when she was coming back, that his offer was still good. And she'd get up in the morning and start all over again.

Cora stared into the remains of her cold cup of coffee, watching some of the loose grains float to the surface, swim around with no direction, no connection to anything or each other.

A tear fell, stirred the grains, causing a momentary ripple before disappearing. This was what her life had become. One among many, no different, no better, nothing special. Back home she was hugged and kissed. Everyone knew her face, lived for Sunday mornings to hear her sing. She was the preacher's daughter, the love of Pearl's life. And even after they were both brutally snatched away from her, she was still loved, still special. But not here.

Here was too many, too noisy, too crowded, too busy. There was neither time nor reason to make her feel special and loved. In this swarming gray city, without grass and rivers or sounds of night, and sunrises you couldn't see straight out of your window, there was no one to care about Cora Harvey.

You ain't gon' have folks to look after ya no mo', she heard Flem whisper in her ear. *You gon' have ta do that yo'self. Just don't forget what you learnt here, that we's here when you need us.*

She wanted to go home, go back to the comforting arms, to a place where she fit and wouldn't disappear like the tears in her cup. But she couldn't. Her pride, that stubborn pride she'd inherited from her daddy, wouldn't let her. How could she go back? She hadn't kept her promise— she hadn't made them proud. She'd failed them and herself. She wasn't just any ole' gal from the Delta. She was Cora Harvey, the reverend's daughter, the survivor with the Harvey name. Her father had done battle with the devil every day. Loss his life, and Mama too, just to make things better for all colored folks. They didn't back down, turn tail, and run. Neither would she.

Cora pushed herself up from the table, her soft, pale yellow cotton gown clinging to her body, and took the cup to the sink, pouring the remains down the drain. She watched them disappear. That would not happen to her. No, sir.

She tugged in a breath of resolve, turned and gazed out the window. Spring was coming. You could see it in the way the sun hit the buildings, lasted longer at the end of a day, the way the birds were beginning to return, setting out on the black iron railings and budding tree branches— waiting.

A time for change and new beginnings. Maybe it was time she did, too. Shed some of her old ways for new ones. She was a woman now, not that little gal from Rudell. She had to start acting like one. It would be summer before you knew it.

Cora started washing the few dishes in earnest and completed her daily household chores in no time. By noon, the laundry was hand washed and hanging to dry on backs of chairs, knobs, tops of doors, and windowsills throughout the sunny kitchen. She'd cut up some scallions, a green pepper, the last tomato, and three tiny white potatoes to mix with the small piece of beef she had simmering on the stove. *It almost smells like home,* she thought wistfully. *Almost.*

With the house in order and supper underway, Cora went to the couch and pulled out the long, battered box from underneath. Setting the box on her lap, she opened the crushed top and had a momentary sensation of being trapped between two doors. She shook her head and opened the box to look at the two dresses that David's mother had made for her.

A pang of melancholy stabbed at her heart. *David.* For the most part she tried not to think about him, tried not to see his dark, handsome face, the light of his smile, the touch of his hand. Tried to forget their walks through the woods, fishing at the river, rides in his car, their fevered kisses. If she did, she'd pack everything up and take the next train back home. So she didn't. She pushed him to the back of her thoughts just like she'd pushed this box under the couch.

Slowly, almost reverently, she lifted one of the fine dresses out of the thin paper that wrapped around it. It was soft beige, so soft it almost looked white, made from two layers of silk covered in chiffon. A low-hung sash, like the ones she saw the women wear, was attached, making the dress flow in a soft sweep just below her knees. On the bottom layer of the dress, Betty Jean had hand-sewn circular rows in a darker beige that looked like a sunburst.

She brought the exquisite dress to her face, closed her eyes, and pressed it gently against her cheek, experiencing the soft feel of it. *In a dress like this,* she thought, *I'll look just like all the other womens who come out after the sun sets. I won't be different.* Sometimes you had to take the chance of being a lamb among the wolves. That's what her daddy would've said.

▲ ▲ ▲

When Margaret stepped out of her room later that evening, ready for the night, she was stopped in her high heels to see that Cora was dressed to go out.

She put a well-placed hand on her narrow hip, looked Cora up and down. A slow, wicked smile slid across her red-tinted mouth. "It's about damn time," she declared, then slapped her thigh. "Get your coat and let's go!"

When they arrived, the club was in full swing. Margaret took Cora to the back and introduced her to the other girls who waited tables, checked coats, and hawked cigarettes.

"Cora is a good friend of mine," Margaret announced, so treat her decent. She's still green, needs to learn the ropes."

"You ever work a club before?" a woman named Rose asked. Rose was the color of flour, skin so pale you could just about see through it. Only way you could tell she was colored was by the wide set of her nostrils and thick, full lips.

Cora shook her head no. "But I'm willing to learn."

"Good," Rose declared and lit a cigarette. "We can use all the help we can around here. These men keep us busy." She laughed and the whole room joined in on the joke. Cora remained silent, offering only a weak smile in response.

"Come on then," Rose instructed. "You can work with me tonight. One of my girls took sick." Before Cora could protest, Rose took her by the hand and pulled her out into the crowded room.

"First thing," Rose said, standing along the side of the club to get a good look, "you clear all the tables of used plates and ashtrays and such. You can do that, can't you?"

Cora swallowed and nodded her head.

"When you collect more than you can carry, take everything back there." She tossed her head over her shoulder. "That's the kitchen." She blew out a puff of smoke and coughed.

Cora nodded.

"We gets paid at the end of the week. You responsible for your own tips."

"Tips?"

"Yeah. If a customer thinks you did a good job, or asks a special favor of you, they'll give you something extra for yourself. We can keep all our own tips. Money's good, sugah, if you know how to work it." She winked at Cora. "Just be nice and smile a lot." She reared back and gave Cora the once over. "Girl looking like you will make plenty of money. You get started on that side of the room. Go on, now." Rose shoved her lightly in the back and hurried off in the opposite direction.

Cora's heart was beating so fast she could hardly breathe. She stood there in the midst of laughing mouths and shimmying bodies and the low-down rhythm of the King Oliver band playing the blues.

"Don't just stand there," Margaret shouted, suddenly behind her.

Cora turned with a start, for the first time actually thankful to see Margaret's face.

"Come on, girl. Somebody liable to think you a piece of furniture you keep standing there." She sashayed away.

Cora tucked in a lungful of smoky air and tentatively began to move to the other side of the room. She kept her head bowed as she asked for an excuse me to remove the dirty dishes from the table. No one seemed to notice her one way or the other, she realized, with some degree of relief as she moved to the next table.

Every now and again she let her eyes rise from the floor to scan the room, see if she could pick Margaret or at least Rose out of the crowd. That's when she saw Richard Morgan come through the door with a heavyset, sassy-looking woman on his arm, who pranced proud in a wide head-dress full of feathers and a floor-length feathered boa tossed casually around her neck. Folks practically fell over themselves trying to see to what Richard needed, but more so for the woman who commanded everyone's attention. An electric buzz hummed through the room. Heads began to turn in Richard and the woman's direction. Whispers grew to a fevered pitch, until they sounded like swarming bees.

"Wonder if she's gonna sing tonight," Cora heard one man ask another.

"That Bessie sure can wail," replied the other.

"That's not all I heard she can do," the man laughed nastily. "Plenty of stories about that one."

"Why you think she sing so good? Done lived it is why. Every bit of it, the way I hear things."

That was Bessie? Bessie Smith? Coming right at her, Cora realized. It was really her, with the gay, deep laugh and smile for everyone. The one with the voice that got down under your skin and shook everything underneath, made the flesh rise in tiny, little bumps.

Bessie strutted, she didn't walk, flinging that boa like it was a fan and everyone she passed reached out to touch her, get a bit of what it was she had—magic that lit up the room like a sudden bolt of lightning. They wanted a kiss, a hug, just a look their way.

"You gonna sing tonight, Bessie?" someone shouted.

"You got to sing for us, Bessie, liven this place up," came another request.

Bessie tossed her head back and laughed. "I came to be entertained this night, y'all. What you got good?"

The band swung into the song that had made her famous, "Down Hearted Blues," and the crowd roared and stomped its approval.

That could be me one day. It could, Cora thought. *All those folks yelling and calling for me, loving me and what I do. I could be just like Bessie Smith, maybe bigger. I could, know I could.*

Richard leaned down and whispered something in Bessie's ear. She laughed and slapped him playfully on the shoulder as he slipped his arm around her waist and ushered her toward his table, right near where Cora was standing.

Cora opened her mouth to say hello, and they walked right past her, like she wasn't there, didn't see her invisible self. Richard didn't even stop, with every eye in the house on him and Bessie. Bessie Smith.

Her throat knotted, she could feel her cheeks flaming as she stood there looking the fool with an armful of dirty plates and her mouth open and frozen—Hello, Ms. Smith, I'm Cora Harvey, stuck on her tongue like the taste of bad food.

Somebody shoved into her from behind and she lost her grip on the dishes. They crashed to the floor. Seemed like the whole world grew silent. Still. Couldn't hear nothing but the sound of those dishes smashing against the shining wood floor, echoing over and again. Shattered pieces of white mixed with the remnants of chewed collards, laid there, exposed, for all to see. Runaway peas with black eyes stared back at her, and greasy ribs with the sticky, spicy, homemade sauce spread out in a dark brown circle at her feet.

She couldn't move. Just kept staring at the mess at her feet, spreading, getting wider, just like her humiliation, until it took up her whole self. That's all she was.

"Don't just stand there, girl," Rose shouted. "Here." She shoved a soiled towel into Cora's hand. "Hurry and get this mess up fo' somebody falls in it." She whirled away.

With her chest tight and tears burning her eyes, clouding her vision, Cora bent down and began gathering up the broken pieces, the wasted food.

"I'll help with that," a male voice said, quickly collecting the shards of white china.

Cora dared to look up into the face of a waiter. "Mr. Morgan said for me to take care of that, and for you to come sit with him and Miss Smith."

Cora blinked. "What?"

"I'll do this, Miss. Mr. Morgan said for you to come to his table. Don't just everybody get invited to his table. You must be somebody special," the young man said, with a slight tone of awe in his voice. "What's your name?"

"Cora. Cora Harvey."

He nodded, as if agreeing that, yes, that was her name, and continued with his work.

Unsteadily, Cora got up, glanced quickly around, then smoothed out her dress and patted her hair. Stiffening her shoulders she walked over to Richard's table, clasping her hands in front of her.

"Evenin'," Cora said, so low she could barely be heard over the music.

Richard glanced up and a sincere smile of welcome spread across his smooth, handsome features. "Cora, I thought you'd never come back. Have a seat and join us."

Maybe he really hadn't seen her earlier, she reasoned, and wasn't just ignoring her. Cora bobbed her head and tentatively took a seat at the end of the table.

He put his hand around a young, brown-skinned man's shoulder. "This is my nephew, Lionel Hampton." Lionel stuck his hand out for Cora to shake. "Lionel's going to be big one day, wait and see. Best drummer this side of the Mississippi. Ain't that right, son?" The young man simply grinned in response. "I've been telling Bessie here all about you, little Cora," he segued, by way of introduction.

Cora's face burned. She tugged on her bottom lip with her teeth.

Bessie filled a glass almost to the top with the dark amber liquid and took a long swallow. "Aaaah," she expelled, as if she'd just sunk into a hot bath after a long, hard day. She turned her dark, laughing eyes on Cora. "Richard says you can sing. Is that true?"

"Yes, ma'am. I reckon so."

"Either you can or you cain't. Which is it?"

Cora swallowed. "I—can."

Bessie took another gulp of her drink. "That's better." She wagged a finger at Cora. "Don't never back down from what you believe." She refilled her glass. "Maybe I'll get a chance to hear you one day. Come on by to-morrow night about this time so we can have a chance to talk. Let me hear fo' myself if you's as good as Richard says you is." She leaned toward Cora and lowered her voice. "Show you how to knock a man out with one good punch if he gets out of hand, drink your liquor straight, and hit a high note without battin' an eye." She reared back, hooted with laughter, and slapped her palm on the table, rattling the glasses. "Got to be tough in this business lest you wind up a floor mat."

"Folks know Bessie's not one to be fooled with," Richard said. "But once you got her as a friend, she's yours for life."

Bessie waved off his comment with a short smile and a slap on his thigh, then turned her attention back to Cora. "You be sure to stop by tomorrow night and set a spell, hear."

Cora wouldn't let all that appalling talk about fistfights with men even settle in her mind. All she heard was that Bessie Smith was asking to meet with her. "Yes, ma'am. I'll be here." Cora started to get up.

"Good to see you again, little Cora," Richard said, saluting her with his glass and a wink.

"Yessir." She hurried off, found the ladies' room, and locked herself in one of the stalls. Perspiration ran down her back and tickled her under-arms. She took long, deep breaths to keep from passing right out and pressed her head against the cool, wood door. She wasn't sure what she had expected from Bessie Smith. Didn't know what it would feel like to actually see her up close, hear her talk. It all felt like a dream, but a dream come true. Tomorrow would be her big day, the one she'd lived and waited for all her life. After tomorrow she was going to set down and finally write a letter to David. She would sho' nuff have something to tell. Yessir.

The rest of her night was a blur. She did as she was told, worked the tables and picked up people's leftovers. When she and Margaret dragged themselves home near sunup, she realized she'd made nearly ten dollars in tips. She stashed it away in the knotted handkerchief where she kept the money the First Baptist Church had raised for her. Most of it was gone now. In the months she'd been in Chicago, she'd had to use it to buy food, help with the bills, and purchase a few personal items for herself. Now she could start adding to it.

She looked at the damp bills, remembering how she'd had to tuck them into her bra while she worked, how the men looked at her with hungry, heavily lidded eyes when she did it, how dirty she felt. Rose had been the one to tell her that's how things were done, and it was that or lift her dress to tuck the money into her stockings. She pushed those troubling thoughts aside and returned the handkerchief with the money to her suitcase.

As she lay down on the couch, she prayed long and hard for guidance, for forgiveness for being in the company of so many sinners. But this was her load to bear, her river to cross, and once she got to the other side, all that she'd wished for would await her.

Cora shut her eyes. She had to believe that, had to. Because if she didn't, she'd never be able to go back there, no matter what the rewards. But as she fell into an exhausted sleep a single question filtered through her thoughts: How much was she willing to sacrifice of herself, of her beliefs, in pursuit of her dreams?

▲ ▲ ▲

Picking up behind others came easy for Cora at the Lincoln Gardens Café, after having done so much of it since she'd been living with Margaret, she thought, as she carried another armload of dishes to the kitchen. For the most part the workers seemed nice enough, although they didn't pay her much attention. The hardest thing for her to deal with was watching the men grope and grab at the women and the women laughing at it. How could they? What kind of women were they? Drinking and smoking was bad enough, but that . . .

She pushed through the door of the kitchen and back into the tangled web of the densely packed room. She looked in-between bodies and over heads to see if she could spot Richard and Miss Bessie. Neither of them were at his table. A lump of disappointment anchored in her stomach. Half the night before and all day she'd waited for tonight. *Please let her come,* she silently prayed. *Please.*

"Hey, Cora," the young male waiter from the other night called out, "they need you in the back."

She looked at the man, perplexed. "Where?"

"Back there," he said, pointing to a corridor with a door at the end.

She looked down the dimly lit walkway, hesitant.

"Hurry up, they need refills." He wiped his shiny, brown face with a dingy hand towel and shoved it into the pocket of his black pants.

"But I—"

He was already busy serving another table.

Cora took a breath and tentatively walked toward the door. Timidly she knocked but couldn't hear if anyone responded over the music of the band and raised voices in conversation lifting higher and higher to be heard. She'd never in her life entered a room without permission. She glanced over her shoulder, then turned the knob and stepped inside.

A single lightbulb illuminated the room, throwing shadows against the dark walls, which were in fact the outlines of bodies surrounding a table. Cigar and cigarette smoke hung in the air like a fog. Deep, guttural voices hummed in the room. Half-full bottles of liquor lined the floor. The stench of alcohol rushed to her head in the confined space, turning her stomach. Stacks of money sat in piles on the table.

Cora stood there not sure what to do, what she'd walked in on. She stepped back, feeling her way to the door with her hands.

"Hey, sugah," a heavyset man in a black derby said over a thick cigar that hung in the corner of his mouth.

One by one the men at the table turned in her direction. Something resembling smiles turned up their mouths.

Her breath ran in and out of her chest. She tried to catch it, but it was too fast, too much in a hurry to get away.

"Come on over here in the light so we can get a better look at you," the man in the derby instructed.

Her limbs trembled as she took one step forward, then stopped.

"Pretty little thing," a man with a gleaming bald head announced. A round of appreciative chuckles bubbled from their throats.

"They said you . . . needed refills . . ."

"You can start by taking these bottles out of here," a high yellow man said, as he shuffled a deck of cards.

"You must be new, but you sure ain't friendly." The man in the derby stood and approached her, nearly pinning her against the door. His protruding belly and the heat of his stale breath pressed against her.

Cora stepped back. He reached out and stroked her cheek. "You suppose to make us happy. Ain't that why they sent you?"

She turned her face away. "I—I," she swallowed down the fear that was building like a summer storm in her chest. "I just came to—"

He ran his hands along her hips, pulled them up against him.

She jerked, scorched. "Please—don't . . ." Her voice sounded like a baby's.

"Oh, come on, sugah, give Daddy some." He cupped her right breast and squeezed. The other men laughed uproariously, egging him on.

"Show her a good time, John."

"She's just shy."

"We about to change all that," the man named John announced proudly.

Cora tried to push him off of her, get out of the door, but she was wedged against it, barring her own exit.

"Help me! Somebody help me!"

John tried to raise her dress, while he pressed his wet mouth against her neck. A terrible tremor shook her body. Her head spun, the fear gripping her by the throat until she couldn't breathe. She gasped for air. She'd heard stories of rape, horrid stories whispered among the women of the church, stories of how night riders would rape a women right in front of her husband and children, or drag a colored woman off the road on her way home from work and have his way with her, then leave her for dead. But not her own kind. Lawd, not her own kind.

Cora screamed again, twisted her body, flayed her arms, struggled to get free.

"Aw, leave the girl alone, John, and come on back and play," the high yellow man said. "You done had your fun."

"Yeah, come on," two others chorused. "You're holding up the game."

John laughed, swayed away from Cora, and grinned down into her terror-stricken face. "You sure are one pretty little thing." He staggered a bit and returned to his seat.

Instantly Cora pulled open the door and ran blindly down the hallway, tears streaming down her face. Everything was a blur as she bumped and pushed against bodies trying to find the door, a way out. Hands were everywhere. She swatted at them, tried to brush off the lips against her neck.

Where was the door? Everything was spinning, spinning. She needed to find Mr. Morgan, tell him what happened. He needed to know. Someone needed to know.

Cora pushed through a door, out into the misty rain. She turned around in a circle not knowing where she was, the rain obscuring her vision. Her body shook uncontrollably.

The sounds of muffled moans reached out to her in the distance, from farther down in what looked like an alley. Oh, Lawd, she'd come out the back way. She tried to see.

Shadows, hulking shadows, were leaning over a huddled mass on the ground, kicking and pounding it. She covered her mouth to stifle a gasp of alarm, not alert anyone to her presence. Too late.

A figure stepped out of the shadow, his face illuminated by the light of his cigarette and the half moon. Cora's stomach rose and fell. Richard Morgan stared back at her, and in that instant she saw evil.

Cora ran and ran, out into the teeming street, into the night, terror on her heels, tapping her on the shoulder. She hailed a cab and jumped in.

"Where to, lady?"

Sobs wracked her tiny body. She couldn't stop shaking. "Home," she whimpered. "Please take me home . . ."

She couldn't recall what address she gave the man, but when the driver pulled up in front of Margaret's apartment building, a surge of total despair erupted like a geyser and the tears flowed again. This wasn't home and it never would be.

Thirteen

Margaret paced back and forth in front of her, water streaming off her face and hair, her dress stuck to her body. Angry fists of rain pounded against the window demanding to get inside.

"Are you crazy, girl!" she shouted. "Runnin' out of there like some scared ass rabbit! I been out in that rain looking for you for hours."

How long had she been sitting here, knotted up in a ball? She couldn't tell. Images of that man, his mouth and foul breath wrapped around her and squeezed, drawing her tighter.

"I could lose my job because of you." She sneezed loudly. "You have any idea what you done? You know you can't go back there. Not after this," she went on and on. "Everybody's talking about you—and me, wondering why I'd bring a silly thing like you to work at the club. It's for women, real women, not some backwoods infant!"

She wanted to get up and scrub, scrub the dirt off her body, from her mind. Wash away the scene in the alley, the look of pure calm on Richard's face as he watched that man get beaten. But she couldn't move. If she did, she was sure she'd fall apart.

Margaret sneezed again, followed by a cough. "Let me tell you one thing, sister, don't think for one damn minute that you just gonna lay up here on me. No, sir. If you can't handle it, take your sorry ass back to the Delta where you belong." She stomped off toward her room and slammed the door.

Sorry ass . . . little backwoods infant . . . for real women . . . The accusations raced around in her head. She drew herself tighter.

▲ ▲ ▲

At some point she'd drifted off to a haunting sleep. She was running, running through dark alleys, in and out of doors that led nowhere. She could feel the terror of something behind her, reaching out to grab her, making her run—faster, faster.

It was the sound of silence that actually woke her up. Wearily she twisted her neck to look out the window. The rain had stopped, leaving behind a dull morning, hampered more so by the tall buildings that blocked the sun.

She sat up and pulled the thin blanket around her shoulders. During her wretched sleep, she'd awakened with a decision. She was going home, back where she belonged, just like Margaret said. This wasn't the life for her. It wasn't a life at all, not the one she'd hoped for. Her mama had been right all along. Maybe she'd understood the wicked ways of the world better than her daddy.

What hurt her most, she thought, as she packed up her few possessions, *was that Margaret never asked what happened, didn't seem to care, didn't want to know how scared she was or if she was hurt.* Is that the kind of woman Margaret had become living here in this place? Would *she* be the same if she stayed?

As was her habit, she cleaned and scrubbed, rooted around in the icebox for something to prepare for supper. When Margaret got in from wherever it was she went during the day, she'd tell her she was going back home. She'd thank her for her hospitality and she would go back home—where she belonged—out of Margaret's way. She'd put all this behind her and go on with her life in Rudell. Maybe marry David, if he would still have her.

When Margaret came in around five, her usual time, she was more subdued than ever. She barely spoke and her eyes were runny and red. She kept wiping her nose with the back of her hand.

Cora tried to offer her something to eat, said they needed to talk, but Margaret refused both, saying that she needed to lay down for a while, get the ache out of her bones.

Cora sat in the other room, listening to Margaret's heavy breathing and thick cough for the few hours that she slept. Still, like clockwork, Margaret roused herself, got up at her regular time of eight o'clock, somehow managed to get dressed, and walked out, without a backward glance at Cora.

We'll talk when she gets home tonight, Cora thought, as she stared at the closed door.

But when Margaret returned, it wasn't alone. A sharp banging on the front door stirred Cora out of her malaise several hours later. Cautiously she opened the door and stood in opened-mouthed shock to see Rose struggling to hold Margaret up. Cora rushed to help, half-carrying, half-dragging Margaret into the house. She could feel the heat radiating off Margaret's body like flames from a hearth.

"What's wrong with her?" Cora puffed, as they lay Margaret across her bed. Cora placed her hand across Margaret's forehead. It was dry and steamy to the touch.

"Got sick at work. Almost passed out. Richard put us in a cab so I could bring her home. She's burning up."

"What we gon' do? Maybe she needs a doctor."

"I got to get back to work. The cab is waiting for me downstairs."

Cora's eyes widened in alarm. She'd never taken care of a sick person in her life. "You just gon' leave me here with her like this? What if she gets worse?"

"Maybe if she hadn't been running around in the rain looking for you, she wouldn't be sick. I got to go." Rose shut the door solidly behind her.

Margaret moaned.

Cora didn't know what to do first. She tried to think. Cool rags. Yes. Cool rags. Ain't that what David said his mother did for his brother, Cleve? She dashed in the kitchen and ran a pan of cold water, grabbed a rag from the pile of clean clothes, and returned to Margaret's bedroom. But as she stood over Margaret, listening to her labored breathing, she remembered what else David had told her. His brother, Cleve, had died. She shook her head wildly and worked faster.

Cora tenderly undressed Margaret, leaving her in her slip. All through the night, she pressed the cool cloth against Margaret's fevered brow, dipped the rag again, and stroked her limbs.

Every now and again Margaret's eyes would flutter open; she'd let out a rattling cough and drift back off to sleep. But Cora wouldn't budge. She kept talking, telling her she'd be fine. Kept pressing that cool rag against her body, refilling the pan dozens of times with cold water.

By the time the sun began to crest, Cora's eyes were gritty with fatigue, her arms stiff from rubbing and wiping. Margaret was finally resting comfortably, the fever not as high as it was. But Cora was so tired she couldn't be sure if it was truth or wishful thinking.

She just needed to lay down for a minute, close her eyes for a minute. Just a minute. She tiptoed into her quarters and stretched out on the couch.

The instant her head touched down on the cushion, she heard Margaret's hoarse voice call out to her.

Cora jumped up, her head spinning, and ran into the room. "Margaret. You okay? What is it?"

Margaret opened her eyes and tried unsuccessfully to smile. She coughed deep and long then finally caught her breath. "I needs you to do something for me."

"Sure, anything. What is it?"

"I need you to . . ." She coughed. "I need you to go down to Stu's."

Cora frowned. "The vegetable man?"

Margaret wheezed and nodded. "He should be open by now. Tell him you need to use his phone."

"To call a doctor?" Cora asked hopeful.

"No. You need to call . . ." She coughed again, gulped in some air. "Mr. Clark, my boss. Tell him I'm awful sick and that you my cousin and will take my place."

Cora reared back. "Take yo' place? Where? Doin' what?"

Margaret swallowed. She grabbed Cora's arm and stared hard into her eyes. "I work . . . as a maid . . . at the Rutherfords'." She breathed deeply. "Wealthy white family on the Northside."

A maid. White family. Margaret. She couldn't be hearing right. Girl must be delirious with fever.

"You just sick is all, Margaret. Imagining things. You get some rest." She patted Margaret's shoulder.

"No! You listen." She gripped Cora's arm tighter. "I can't lose my job." She coughed, louder this time. "You hear. I can't. I need you to call Mr. Clark so you can take my place. I don't show up, he'll fire me for sure."

Cora stared into Margaret's pleading eyes and all at once she realized that Margaret wasn't imagining things. She was for real.

"Ain't there nobody else you can send?"

"I'll let you keep half my wages. It's just cooking, cleaning, and laundry. That's all. Most times you have the house to yourself."

"Margaret—"

"What have I ever asked of you since you been here? Nothing. Just this one time. One time." Another fit of coughing shook her body. She gulped in some air. "I'll be fine in a few days," she panted. "Then I can go back."

"But . . . Okay. Just for a day or two until you get better. And when you do, I'm going home. Back to Rudell."

Margaret nodded. "The number for Mr. Clark is in my purse." She swallowed. "Hurry, 'cause it's getting late. I can tell by the sun."

▲ ▲ ▲

Cora clutched the piece of paper with the Rutherfords' address in her hand as she rode in the back of the crosstown colored bus with all the other colored folks on their way to some job or the other.

As she peered out of the window, she watched the scenery before her slowly transform from the leaning gray buildings with the ugly black railings to two-story houses with a bit of land around them. A few trees dotted the concrete earth. Along the route, one by one the coloreds got off with their brown-bagged lunches and thick shoes, making their way to the homes of their employers.

Cora sat up straighter, pressing her face closer to the window, trying to see her street. *It must be soon,* she thought, *mostly all of the coloreds have gotten off.* The houses were getting farther apart, bigger, brighter, with wide patches of green grass out front. Shiny automobiles lined the street. Finely dressed white men and women walked the street at a casual pace, not like back in the crush of the city. The sun even seemed to shine brighter on this side of town. She haltingly read Margaret's scrawl, sure she'd missed her stop.

Nervously, she got up and edged up to the front by the driver.

" 'Scuse me, sir. I, uh, was lookin' for Hopson Lane."

"Last stop, Miss. Coming up." He turned and looked at Cora's wide eyes. "You must be new. Don't remember seeing you on my route."

"Yessir. I'm working fo' . . . my cousin, Margaret."

The colored driver's face lit up like a lamp. "Margaret. Well, I'll be. You a relative of hers, huh? That Margaret is something else, ain't she? Always good for a laugh. She ain't sick is she? Don't remember her missing a day's work in near three years."

Three years. "Yes, she's feeling poorly. Said I should take her place . . . at the Rutherfords'."

"Yep, that would be the place. Pretty nice . . . for white folks," he said, lowering his voice. "Hear they treat us pretty good at that big old house. Plenty of money. Plenty," he emphasized. "They usually throw a huge party over the holidays; any white person worth their salt shows up."

Cora sat down eager to hear more about her soon-to-be employers. "What . . . do they do?"

"The husband is some sort of stock man working his way into pol-o-tics, way I hear it. Don't know what the wife does 'cept spend his money." He laughed at his own joke.

Cora slowly processed the information.

"Well, Miss, here's your stop. That's the Rutherford place right there." He pointed out the three-story home with the winding lawn that sat alone and stately on the street.

Cora blinked, snatched a quick look at the driver, and got up. "Thank you, sir."

He tipped his brimmed hat. "You have a good day. And tell your cousin that Horace said hello."

Cora stepped down off the bus. "I will."

The bus rumbled off, leaving Cora standing on the quiet, tree-lined street. Looking up and down the street, she noticed a few colored women in starched black uniforms with white aprons pushing baby strollers, their bundled charges stretching little white hands into the air, already claiming all around them. There was one colored woman loaded down with brown paper bags in each arm, having already made her daily trip to the grocer. There were two old, gray-haired, colored men, bent almost in half with age, one hauling garbage, the other raking the grass.

Cora clutched her purse to her chest and cautiously walked down the paved lane, embraced on either side by towering willows, up the three white marble steps to the front door. An enormous brass knocker sat squarely in the center of the intricately carved door, daring her to use it, while two black marble lions sat stony eyed on both sides guarding the entrance.

Hesitantly she raised the knocker then let it drop against the door. She held her breath. She hadn't never knocked on a white person's door in all her natural life, neither had she ever been invited. Since she'd come to Chicago, she'd done a whole heap of things she would have never dreamed of, nor wanted to.

She snatched a look over her shoulder. But the few folks on the street were all tending to their own business. She turned back to the door. It was getting near seven o'clock, the time Margaret said she was to be at work. She took a breath and raised the knocker once more, just as the door was pulled open.

Cora immediately straightened, barely containing a yelp of surprise.

A woman, whiter than the snow she'd seen on the ground, whiter than anything she'd ever known, stood in front of her, with gleaming, fiery hair that was cut close and tight to her scalp. Tiny freckles dotted her skinny nose and her sharp cheeks. Her mouth was a thin, red line, her eyes the softest-looking blue she'd ever seen, like a blanket for a baby boy. She was tall and slender, at least a head above Cora, who dared to slowly raise her gaze.

"Yes?" the woman asked, in a questioning tone.

" 'Mornin' ma'am. I'm Cora Harvey. Came in the place of . . . my cousin . . . Margaret." Cora gulped, watched the stern expression of the woman slowly relax.

She looked Cora up and down and then again as if inspecting something for sale. "Mr. Clark rang us up and advised my husband that Margaret had taken ill." She paused, looked Cora over again. "I hope it's nothing too serious," she said, in the clipped accent that Cora couldn't place. She didn't sound nothing like the white folks back home.

"Since this is your first day, I'll excuse you. But from now on remember that the help uses the side door." She paused. "Well, come in then. You're already five minutes late. I guess you know as much about cleaning and cooking as any other Negro."

Cora lowered her gaze and inwardly flinched. The woman stepped aside to let her enter. "Follow me."

The woman walked quickly ahead of her, barely giving Cora time to take in the incredible sights in the enormous house. Cora snapped her head back and forth, nearly gaping at the huge window with velvet drapes, mahogany mantles over deep fireplaces. The wood floors shined so bright she could see her reflection. Nothing like the hand-scrubbed floors back home. They passed a room, whose door was partially opened, and she noticed a grand piano set in the middle of the floor. People had pianos in their own homes? she wondered in amazement.

"My husband, Mr. Rutherford, had an early business meeting and has already left for the morning." She pushed through a swinging door that opened onto the kitchen. "Your uniform is in that closet." She looked Cora over again. "I suppose it will fit. If not it will just have to do, won't it?"

She paced the room as she talked, crossing her arms beneath her breasts. "Each day the three bathrooms upstairs need to be scrubbed—thoroughly. The linens on all the beds are changed, the halls mopped, and the banisters, mantels, and tables dusted. Once a week the drapes are taken down and outside to be cleaned. I expect an immaculate kitchen, Sadie—"

"It—it's Cora, ma'am, Cora Harvey."

Lizbeth Rutherford's blue eyes snapped in surprise as if she'd found her husband locked in the arms of a Negro woman. "What did you say?"

"I—I was just sayin' my name is Cora, not Sadie, ma'am."

Lizbeth looked completely confused. "Does it really matter, as long as the work gets done and you get paid at the end of the week?" She continued her pacing, dismissing Cora's interjection as if she hadn't heard it. "Lunch is served promptly at one. And dinner at five. You can leave as soon as dinner is served. The girl, whatshername, who comes in the evenings will clean up." She turned and smiled benevolently. "Now that we have that all out of the way, you can get started. It's much easier to start upstairs and work your way down. You'll find the linens in the hall closet on the second floor." She folded her hands in front of her. "Any questions?"

"No, ma'am."

"Good." She turned to leave, then stopped. "I'll be expecting you to do a good job and not try to slip any of the silver in your purse." She laughed, a sound that reminded Cora of a whinnying horse. Before she could protest, Mrs. Rutherford had left the room.

Cora stood in the center of the spacious kitchen more humiliated than she'd ever been in her life. Fighting back a surge of tears, Cora put her purse on the counter and changed into the uniform that hugged her rounded body tighter than she would have liked. She found the brushes, soaps, and brooms in the same closet with the uniform. Putting them all in a bucket she went upstairs to the bathroom. Down on her hands and knees, scrubbing the white, tiled floors and cleaning the porcelain toilets, her first day as the housemaid for the Rutherfords began.

Fourteen

~~~~~~~~~~~~~~~~~~~~

Lizbeth Rutherford moved imperiously through her Lake Shore mansion, touching, sniffing, inspecting Cora's handiwork. She lifted pot tops and opened oven doors, approving the roasted chicken and steamed vegetables.

Cora stood stone still, eyes downcast as she pressed her lips together to keep from screaming in outrage. Is this what all colored folks had to endure up North under the rule of the white man as well? Sure, she'd heard tales of colored help catching heck in the Big House down home, folklore about slavery, seen the effects of separate but unequal. Sure, she knew that colored folks wasn't looked on as human beings like whites, but she'd never had to deal with it up close—continually—never had to be subjected to the ridicule and humiliation—every day.

Was this the real world her daddy wanted her to see, and her mama wanted to keep her away from? She didn't know what was worse, living in a fantasy or stepping into this degrading truth.

Lizbeth spun around, her pale cheeks flushed with what Cora assumed was pleasure. She clapped her hands together and held them. "You did a splendid job. Absolutely splendid." Her thin mouth stretched into a wide smile, displaying perfect, off-white teeth. A diamond broach sparkled against the soft, green fabric of her dress. She approached Cora, lowering her voice. "You work much better than your cousin, I must say. Margaret is a wonderful Negro girl, but sometimes"—her brow arched pointedly—"she can be a bit . . . careless in her duties. You, my dear, are a jewel. I suppose it runs on your side of the family."

For an instant Cora's lowered gaze rose with defiance and slapped the beguiling look off Lizbeth's pale countenance.

Momentarily flustered, Lizbeth fingered her broach, the corners of her mouth flickered like a bulb going bad, before she recovered and forced a smile, uncertain if she'd just been offended or not.

"Well, my dear, I'll see you tomorrow morning at seven sharp. Unless, of course, dear Margaret is feeling better."

"Yes, ma'am," Cora mumbled, wanting to escape this woman and the clawing perfume that followed her around like a trained pup.

"Very good then. You can see yourself out." She turned to leave then stopped. "Oh, and by the way, don't forget to use the side door in the morning. I'd hate to have the neighbors start to gossip."

Cora stood there, humiliated, smacked as surely as by the woman's hand. She felt the sting on her cheek, on the right side and the left. She steeled herself against the painful flurry of insults that had greeted her the moment she'd set foot in this place. But she couldn't let it break her spirit. Her ancestors had gone through more than she cared to think about. As Jesus said from the cross: "Father, forgive them, for they know not what they do." Sadly, she shook her head, sorrier now for Lizbeth Rutherford than she would ever be for herself.

Gathering up her cleaning tools, she was returning them to the closet when she felt the presence of someone in the room. Images of the night before flashed in her head. She turned with a start, the broom clasped tightly in her hand.

William Rutherford stood in the doorway, an engaging smile on his tanned face. He was tall, slender, thin almost, in a rugged sort of way. Even in his finely tailored, navy, pin-striped suit and sparkling white shirt, his manner was casual and open. His hair was dark black like a crow and combed away from his wide forehead and thick, black brows. But what was most striking about him, hypnotizing almost, were his startling green eyes, the rich color of jade. And they sparkled just like the stone.

"Well, hello. I don't think I've seen you before. Has my wife, Lizbeth, finally run Margaret off with all her nagging?" Laughter danced in his gaze, settled around his mouth, and eased the knot in her stomach.

Slowly Cora felt herself relax, but she didn't let go of the broom. "Margaret took sick. I'm . . . her cousin, Cora."

His thick brows knitted. "She's not too bad off, I hope."

"Not sure, sir. She was feelin' mighty low, fever and all."

"Oh, dear. Please give her my regards. She's such a lovely girl." He looked

Cora over. "Well, pleasure to meet you, Cora. Perhaps we'll see each other again."

"Yessir," she said softly.

William turned and walked out, leaving Cora curiously unsettled.

▲ ▲ ▲

When she got off the bus and walked the two long blocks to Margaret's building, Sonny waylaid her.

"Hey, Sugah." He blocked her path.

"Evenin', Sonny. Now let me pass. I'm really tired." She tried to walk around him.

"They took Margaret."

"What?"

"Jimmy and Rose came and took her to the colored hospital early this afternoon."

Cora pushed past him and ran up the stairs, all the way to Liz's place. She banged on the door, her heart racing with dread.

Moments later she heard Liz's heavy footsteps padding to the door.

"What happened to Margaret?" Cora practically screamed.

"Come on in, girl. I went down to check on her like you asked me to, and she was crazy with fever. Went down to Stu's and called Jimmy over at the paper—the *Chicago Defender,* where he works. He came straightaway, brought Rose with him. Drove off in his automobile. Said he was taking her to Cook County."

Cora rolled her eyes around the room, covered her mouth with her fist, her distress mounting. "How bad is she?"

"Pretty bad," Liz said solemnly. "I ain't heard nothin' since they left, but I seen enough pneumonia to know that's what's got hold of Margie."

"Pneumonia!"

Liz bobbed her head.

"Oh, Lawd. I was plannin' on goin' back home. How can I go now if she's low sick?"

"Guess you can if you have to." Liz let her statement hang in the air then rub gently against Cora's Christian conscience.

Cora released a long sigh. She was trapped between those doors again. She sat down heavily in a chair and covered her face with her hands.

▲ ▲ ▲

The next day Cora returned to her work routine at the Rutherfords' and faithfully rushed home to catch the last hour of visiting at the hospital. The doctors said Margaret was completely worn out from the physical strain of working two jobs and getting so little rest. It was easy for a simple soaking to turn from a little cold to the more serious pneumonia that had attacked both of her lungs. It would be awhile before she was on her feet again.

Awhile turned into eight weeks, and when Margaret finally came home, she was thin as a bean pole and still weak. She'd break into fits of coughing at the drop of a hat. So Cora cared for and cleaned up after the Rutherfords during the day and did the same for Margaret at night. She'd stopped paying much attention to Missus Rutherford and her bossy, uppity ways and lived for the kind words of Mr. Rutherford.

He let her borrow books to read. All kinds of books about the world, places she'd only heard about, and volumes of poetry by a woman named Elizabeth Barrett Browning and a New York writer, Langston Hughes, who wrote about a man called Simple. She liked those best and would sit curled on her couch-bed late into the night absorbing every word. Sometimes she'd read to Margaret, since she'd never learned how. Often Mr. Rutherford would let her browse through his enormous library and pick anything she liked if she promised to tell him all about it when she finished. One of her favorite books was *Wuthering Heights*. She read about the doomed lovers, Heathcliff and Catherine, time and again.

The summer was over by the time Margaret was up on her feet, but she still wasn't strong enough to go back to work. So it was up to Cora to take care of them both, which she did without complaint. And slowly, like the seasons that were changing around her, Cora began to accept her new life, let it become a part of her.

And then she received a letter from David.

Fifteen

The letter was on the table when she came in from work. For a moment she could only stare at it, not sure if she wanted to read what was inside.

It had been months since she'd written David, hadn't done so since she let him know she'd met Bessie Smith, which seemed like a lifetime ago. She'd left out everything else, too ashamed to tell him what had almost happened to her. And as the weeks turned into months, it got easier not to say anything, easier to have him and everyone back home in Rudell believe that she was living her dream, walking to that rhythm in her heart.

"You gonna open that or what?" Margaret asked, appearing in the doorway of her bedroom, clothed in her customary frayed bathrobe and house shoes.

Cora glanced once at Margaret then back to the envelope. Instinctively she clasped the ring that still hung from her neck. She reached for the letter, took it to her little corner on the couch, and opened it.

Dearest Cora,

It has been many months since I heard word from you. I hope and pray that you are well. I suppose that your new and exciting life and new friends in Chicago take up a lot of your time. And I'm happy for you. It's what you always wanted. We all listen to the radio at Joe's, hoping to hear a recording from you. I'm sure it will be someday soon.

Cora, I understand how important your new life is to you and the dreams that you set for yourself. And that's why this will be my last letter.

Her heart banged in her chest, her eyes rereading the words, praying that they weren't true. Not true.

Her hands trembled as she read on.

> *I don't want to interfere, Cora, or make you feel obligated to me in any way. Know that I will always love you, but it's best this way. Be happy, Cora, and be well.*
> *I remain,*
> *David*

She crushed the letter in her fist as if she could wrench the words from the page, crumble them into fine dust, make them go away as if they didn't exist. But they did. They did.

Her neck arched as her eyes squeezed shut, and a silent cry of anguish trapped itself in her throat, ringing in her head.

The last tie to her past had been severed. Chopped down like wood for a fire. She had nothing now. No link to the past, no path to the future. Trapped between the doors of her own making.

"How are things back home?" Margaret asked, appearing again.

Cora opened her eyes, stopped her tears of loss, and stared at Margaret head on.

"Everything's just fine," she lied. She'd gotten good at that, too. Lying.

▲ ▲ ▲

Cora stared out the bus window watching the few, last-minute stragglers hurry home to friends and family. Bright-colored lights twinkled from the windows of the houses, casting a rainbow of color across the drifts of snow. It had snowed for three days, in some places as high as her knees, with wind bitter cold enough to snap you in half. She was lucky to catch this bus that was probably the last one for the night. Had Missus Rutherford had any kind of heart, Cora would have been gone long ago.

"If you value your job, you'll be here to serve Christmas Eve dinner," snapped a flustered Lizbeth, when Cora asked for the night off.

Liz and her new baby, Corine, Margie, Jimmy, and Rose had planned a little party for the holidays at the house, since it wasn't wise for Margie to be out in bad weather. She continued to have bouts of chest-rattling coughing and wheezing, would grow weak with too much activity.

Cora had thought of going to the Mister but realized it would do no good. The Missus had full run of the house.

"I leave all these household headaches to Lizzie," he'd confessed one afternoon as he sipped his customary cup of afternoon tea in the study. "I'd prefer to deal with those bank hounds any day." He laughed.

He'd turned to her suddenly then. "What do you plan to do with your life, Cora? You're much too pretty and smart to be a maid forever." He sipped his tea, observing her downcast expression over the rim.

Cora fidgeted with the dust cloth in her hands. "I—don't really know, sir. Things didn't turn out much like I planned."

"Hmm." He nodded sagely. "Well, Cora, take this bit of advice. Changes in plans are merely temporary obstacles to distract you from your goals. If you let them, they will, and set you on a completely different course."

"It certainly has done that, sir," she said, over a tentative smile.

"You'll be just fine." He opened his newspaper, and Cora understood that their brief talk was over.

Later, on the bus ride home, Cora sighed and stared out the window then looked down at the small, square box wrapped in red paper with gold ribbon. Mr. Rutherford had slipped it to her as she was leaving. "Something just for you," he'd whispered. "Enjoy it and have a Merry Christmas, Cora."

While she'd stood outside praying for a bus, her curiosity got the best of her and she carefully peeled away the wrapping. It was an autographed copy of short stories by Langston Hughes. She ran her gloved hand over the smooth surface. This was the very first book she could call her own.

She wiped her hand against the moist windowpane and pressed the gift to her chest. This would be her first Christmas away from home. The first holiday of her life without her parents, without her friends gathered round her. The first Christmas she wasn't singing in church.

So much had happened to her since she'd left home. She smiled sadly as she spotted a couple laughing and throwing snow at each other. Her heart seemed to shift with emptiness. So much had changed. She had changed. On this very day, one year ago, David had asked her to be his wife. She lifted the ring from the pillow of her breasts and watched it shine in her hand.

If she had the chance to do it again, would she have said yes? As much as she loved David, and still did, her life away from Rudell had given her something she wasn't sure she'd ever get in Rudell—character. If she'd stayed, she would have forever been coddled, pampered, and cared for by everyone as well as David, who would have believed it his duty to protect her. No. If she had the chance, she would have done things the same way. As hard, confusing, painful, and often mysterious as this life in the city could be, she couldn't imagine not having lived it. When she left home, she was a simple, soft beige. Now she was the rainbow, a larger, more complete person.

▲ ▲ ▲

Bone tired, she said a Merry Christmas to the bus driver and trudged through the drifts of snow to Margaret's house, longing for a hot soak and a good night's sleep.

When she opened the door, she leaped back in pure fright when Margie, Jimmy, Liz, and Rose all yelled, "Merry Christmas!"

"You didn't think we could party without you, little country gal," Margaret teased, her smile big and her eyes reflecting an uncharacteristic warmth.

Cora glanced from one joyous face to the other, the lively decorations that filled the house, the scents of pine, baked ham, thick macaroni and cheese casserole, snap peas, and sweet peach cobbler hung in the air, wrapping around her like a warm blanket.

Margaret walked to her, putting her arm lovingly around Cora's shoulder. "I know I been giving you a fit since you been here, and it may seem like I don't appreciate all you done for me. But if you hadn't been here, I don't know what would have happened to me."

Cora could hardly believe what she was hearing. Margaret was the toughest woman she'd ever met. Her compliments, if any, were rare. She knew how difficult this was for Margaret, and because of that, it meant so much more.

"We all 'preciate everything you done, Cora," Liz added, hugging a sleepy Corine to her chest. "You been my friend and I hope I been yours. I know how hard it is leavin' home and comin' to a strange place. But you got family here now."

Cora sniffed loudly, emotion rising within her unchecked.

"Before everybody starts balling," Jimmy interrupted, "we have an announcement to make." He draped his long arm around Margaret's shoulder. His red-bone complexion, sprinkled with wet-sand-colored freckles, the same shade as his kinky hair, seemed to glow from within. "I finally broke down and asked Margie to marry me." She beamed and he kissed her cheek. "And she actually said yes."

Everyone oohed and ahhed at the tiny stone on Margaret's proud finger and shared kisses and hugs.

"Merry Christmas, everybody!" Rose shouted, handing out cups of hot apple cider laced with cinnamon.

As Cora gazed at all the shining faces, listened to the laughter, and felt the warmth, she truly understood that family was more than just blood, it was people who cared about each other, sacrificed for one another.

She sipped her spicy cider and joined in the Charleston line. And now that Margaret and Jimmy were getting married, she'd truly be on her own. She kicked her legs higher and let out a hoot of laughter. It was a challenge she was ready to face.

Sixteen

⁓⌇⌇⌇⌇⌇⌇⁓

Margaret and Jimmy had a small wedding in the little storefront Baptist Church in the spring of 1929 and left the same night to start their new life in New York.

It was odd having the place herself, not having to pick up after Margaret and put up with all her odd comings and goings. But she missed her, at least a little bit, although she still had Liz and Corine, who was getting bigger by the day.

Since Margaret's wedding, Cora had started going back to church again and was even thinking of joining the small storefront choir. She didn't want to neglect her voice, her blessed gift. Maybe in time.

She opened the window to the kitchen, hoping that a breeze would want to come in and rest with her a minute. The heat had been unbearable for more than a week. At times like this, back home, they'd go down to the Left Hand River and dip their bare feet into the cold, running water. Or sit under the shade of the towering pines and cast their fishing lines, hoping for a bite.

Was that what David was doing right now, sitting by the river like they used to do? Did he still remember her? Could he see her face in his dreams like she did his? Would his love for her die?

It had taken all of her willpower to keep from writing, asking him not to let her out of his heart. So many times she'd wanted to write and tell him the truth of her life and that it was nothing like she'd thought it would be. But she wanted him to be proud of her, not know that her leaving him had only led her to becoming a lowly maid. She couldn't bear to see the disappointment in his eyes.

136

So she'd tried to find a way to do better for more than a year. She'd tried to tuck thoughts of David away. And she'd failed time and again at both things.

His handsome face came to her like a welcome spirit at night. Sometimes in just the gentle rustle of the cover, or the sound of crickets, the twinkle of stars, the tickle at the back of her neck, the glow of the moon. At times his presence was so strong, she'd jump out of her sleep and stare wide-eyed into the darkness, sniffing the air for his scent. But he was never there—only in her mind and still in her heart.

Liz had been badgering her to write David, at least to let him know she was all right, even if she refused to admit that she still loved him. She'd run out of excuses and they'd started sounding false to her own ears. It was days like today, hot, steamy Saturdays with the sun beating down, the heat snakes slithering through the air, and the desire to run along the river, that her longing for him grew.

She gently cupped the gold band in her palm. Yes, she would write him. A simple letter to let him know he was still in her thoughts, in her heart.

▲ ▲ ▲

It was nearly three weeks before she heard from David. Every day she'd hurry home, hoping that there would be an envelope with his familiar scrawl in the mailbox. And each day she was disappointed. Maybe he was married by now. Sassy and Maybelle were both hitched and had moved to New Orleans with their husbands.

She couldn't blame David though, she concluded, taking slow, measured steps up to her apartment one evening. After all, she'd moved on with her life and couldn't expect him to do less.

When she opened the apartment door, the sight of an envelope shoved under her door caught her attention. It couldn't be a note from that nasty landlord, Mr. Bernstein. His rent was all paid up.

Bending, she picked it up and turned it over. The blood rushed to her head. As quick as the heat would allow, she tore the envelope open and hurried to her spot on the couch.

Dearest Cora,
My whole world was immediately brighter when I came home and found your letter.

She sucked in a breath of joyous relief and read on.

Please accept my apologies for taking so long to respond. The town seemed to have a sudden overflow of babies that needed bringing into the world.

I'm glad to know you are doing well and that you kept the ring.

Cora, this past year has been the most difficult one in my life. I thought it would be easy to cut my ties to you and forget everything I felt. But I cannot. I believe I will always love you, Cora Harvey, and I believe in my heart that we will be together.

I hope that we can continue to write and see where it takes us. Miss Lucinda sends her love and longs to see you as I do.

I look to hear from you soon.

David.

Cora read the letter again and once more before she went to sleep. As she closed her eyes, she could almost feel David's arms around her, his lips brushing her cheek. She'd write him first thing in the morning.

In her letter she told David of Margie's wedding and her newfound freedom in her own place. She never mentioned her job as a maid at the Rutherfords'. She also didn't mention what was being called the St. Valentine's Day Massacre that had folks running scared. Word had it that Al Capone had set it up to get rid of his competition. Papers said the Justice Department was bringing in somebody named Eliot Ness to try to get rid of the crime and gangs in Chicago. David didn't need to know all that. It was months ago anyhow. And he would just worry about her. Instead, she wrote about the excitement and rush of big city life. . . .

I do miss the river, though. Especially at night, the nights we'd walk along the banks and talk in a hush to keep from stirring the critters.

I think of you, too. Often. And sometimes I wish real hard that you could leave Rudell and join me here. I know there's plenty of work for colored doctors in Chicago. We even got our own hospital. They cared for Margie when she took sick with pneumonia.

But I know you cain't leave. They depending on you and all. I was thinking of comin' home for a visit. For the holidays. Just for a spell. Not too sure right now, but I'll write and tell you for certain.

Thank ya fo' not forgettin' 'bout me, David.

Love, your Cora.

For the rest of that blistering summer of '29, Cora and David tentatively rekindled their love, at least on paper, and moved into a quiet state of unspoken anticipation as the days moved swiftly toward fall.

Cora was dusting the bookcases in the library one afternoon in late October when Mr. Rutherford came in early from work.

Soon as she laid eyes on him, she knew something was wrong. It was in the tight set of his narrow face. The way his eyes were squeezed tight into thin slits, like he was fighting off some kind of pain. He'd always had a word for her when he came in, asked her about her day, but he said nothing. Walked right by her like she was a haint—invisible—and went to the bar.

She moved silently around the room, wanting to hurry and finished her work, move away from his dark mood. When she stole a look at his hard profile as he sat in the high-backed wing chair, she thought about her trip to work that morning.

There was a tension in the air that morning, like back home when everybody sat 'round waiting for the bad news to come in from the woods after somebody's daddy, mama, daughter, or son had vanished without a trace. Everywhere she looked that morning, white folks were huddled in tight knots talking in low voices with scared rabbit looks on their pale faces.

Everybody on the bus ride to work was whispering and jawing about a big crash. She didn't know what that meant except it felt like powerful trouble. 'Specially if white folks was scared. Folks was talkin' 'bout losing everything, jobs, homes, how all the money in the banks wasn't worth nothing, that hard times were coming. Hard times.

When she peered out the bus window, folks were running out of their homes waving newspapers over their heads and shouting words she couldn't hear. So she concerned herself with doing a mental list of the tasks ahead of her for the day.

She'd let herself in the side door of the Rutherford home and started on her day, thankful that the missus was away visiting relatives somewhere farther up North. While she cleaned and scrubbed and put on the dinner meal for Mr. Rutherford, she'd totally pushed aside that raw feeling of unease she'd had earlier. Until now.

Mumbling to himself, William reached for the phone, dialed a number with great haste, and began talking a mile a minute. She tried to hear what he was saying, but it only came to her in snatches of enraged chatter.

"Stuart, what do you mean I should have seen this coming? Hell, nobody saw this coming. . . . It has nothing to do with what Hoover did with the farmers and farm relief legislation. . . . Wheat and cotton prices have been erratic for months. You told me to invest in those stocks, that they would level out, that the market would become stable. . . . No . . . no . . . that's not what you said, Stuart. You told me to get the money for the investments any way I could. Damnit, man, I mortgaged my home, borrowed from brokers, from banks, sold my liberty bonds. I have nothing left, nothing!"

With that, Mr. Rutherford slammed the phone against the cradle so hard that it leaped free into the air. There was a growing air of desperation about him as he shoved his hands into his pockets and paced the floor. He kept talking to himself while he moved over to the table where the forbidden liquor was hidden. After all, this was still Prohibition and any manner of alcoholic beverage was outlawed, although it was found in the homes of rich folks and at the speakeasies. Frantically, he twisted the top off a bottle of illegal home brew, poured the potent, clear liquid into a tall glass, and downed it in a single gulp. He repeated this process again and again until he felt the spirits dull his senses but not his frustration and pain. Still not content with his intoxication, he pushed the glass away and drank directly from the bottle, still mumbling that he had nothing left, that he was financially ruined.

"What's wrong, Mr. Rutherford?" Cora asked, after she summoned up enough gumption to open her mouth. She sensed that whatever was the trouble, it shook him up something awful.

His back was to her when he whirled around, still holding the bottle by its neck. She saw something in his drawn, pale face that had never been there before. "You know what's wrong? You know what's wrong? I'm broke. I've lost everything. . . . That's what's wrong."

The tone of his voice startled Cora, who backed away from him. She thought about leaving the room, maybe leaving the house, because he seemed not himself. Feeling uneasy by his drunkenness, she turned to walk toward the hall and the kitchen, where she would feel safer. But Mr. Rutherford stopped her by cutting off her exit and grabbing her arm. She jerked it, trying to free herself, but his grip was strong.

"Cora, don't be so skittish," he slurred. "I'm not going to hurt you, wouldn't hurt you for the world. You know something, darling? I never noticed what a nice little figure you got under that uniform."

Cora looked at him with a pained expression. "I don't know what's wrong with you, but you ain't yourself. You ain't yourself at all. Whatever it is, I'm powerfully sorry for you . . . whatever it is."

Without warning, Mr. Rutherford suddenly slapped her hard across her face, temporarily blinding her with a white flash, and she fell with a loud thud to the hardwood floor. He stood over her, towering and angry. His words came in a rapid flood, full of rage and lust. "I don't need any nigger pity," he growled. "None of your nigger sympathy. I'll show you what I need . . . show you what I need. . . ."

His hands seized her around the shoulders, hoisted her up bodily, and slung her across the room toward a couch. She missed it, landing only partially on its length, but he was quickly upon her, pushing and pulling her struggling frame onto the expensive furniture. One of his long, bony hands covered her throat, cutting off her ability to scream, while his other hand worked feverishly under her dress. She pleaded desperately with him in a tiny, wheezing voice, "Please, Mr. Rutherford, don't do this, please." His face, with its almost demon look and liquor breath was close to hers, but he seemed unable to hear her. He kept repeating, "I'll show you what I need, nigger bitch . . . show you what I need."

She felt her panties being torn away and his fingers probing her down there. Her fists pounded solidly against his head and shoulders, yet nothing seemed to do any good. She heard someone scream, scream, scream, from far away, as something tore her apart between her legs, ripping her soft flesh like a pair of hot scissors. He grinded and bucked against her savagely, one of his hands harshly clutched a fistful of her hair, grinding and bucking, until he suddenly quivered, shaking the full length of his body as if being struck by lightning. *I'll show you what I need, nigger bitch.* Finally, he stood up, zipped up his pants, unable to look at her ravaged body sprawled before him, to face what he had done.

"Get up and clean yourself," Mr. Rutherford said in a lifeless voice, walking toward the table for yet another drink. He sloshed the liquid over the glass, spilling it over his hands and onto the smooth wood, then took a long swallow before stumbling out of the room and into the street, leaving Cora alone with the horror and shame of what had been done to her.

Seventeen

~~~~~~~~~~

Cora didn't know how she left that house, pieced together her tattered uniform or took the long, excruciating bus ride that sent shockwaves of pain jettisoning through her body each time it hit a bump or made a short stop.

Voices were swarming around her like angry bees, curious faces staring, fingers pointing. She didn't know why, couldn't make out the words or understand the fearful looks directed at her. All she could see was green, jade green and vile, burning into her soul, ripping out her heart, violating her body.

Back home she mechanically filled a tub with boiling water and thick, brown soap. What remained of her clothes she shed, bundling them in a ragged heap before placing them in the metal pail and setting them on fire. She watched the flames leap into the air, the smoke billow, filling the small kitchen. Why was there a fire? she wondered through a haze of green film.

Bewildered, she turned to the tub, watching the steam rise and beckon to her. Numbly she walked into the bedroom and stood in front of the mirror that hung behind the door.

Dried salt from what she supposed were tears ran in a multitude of white lines down her cheeks, giving her an almost clownish appearance. Her thick, black hair stood out from her head in a wild frenzy. Absently she tried to pat it back in place and noticed the dark almost purple bruises that ringed her neck like a chain. The bruising didn't end there but dotted her brown skin and seemed to grow larger and multiply even as she stood there, until they reached the dark patch between her thighs and were replaced with dried blood and sticky, white fluid that still ran in drips out of her.

She blinked, confused, wondering how she could have let herself get in such a state. Stumbling through that green haze that would not leave her be, she returned to the tub, wincing as she raised her legs to get in.

The steam, sensing her anguish, gathered around her; the water like the warm hand of an old friend took her in. She sank into it, became one with it, allowed it to hold her up—the cleansing water—kept her from falling, the blessed water. But even as she blindly scrubbed her skin raw, howled like a wounded animal, the world obscured by the tears that ran in a continuous stream, she knew she'd never be clean again.

It was October 30, 1929.

▲   ▲   ▲

It would be good to get back to Rudell, get rid of the chill that seemed to be forever in her bones. Return to a world that was slow and familiar, find a way to put that night in the past, leave it in Chicago.

Cora stared out of the train window, watching the landscape change shape and color before her eyes. Going back the same way she'd come. Having lost more than she'd ever gained. Had she been punished? Was this God's way of telling her she wanted more than she should have and for that there was a price to pay? She'd left a man she loved in search of a dream she'd never found. Maybe Mama had been right.

Still, it had been a hard decision to finally decide to return. She'd pondered on it for weeks. But with the world in chaos after the crash, the hardest thing for a colored person to find was a job. Fortunately, she'd saved some of her money, enough for a train ticket home, and enough left over to make a start, find a place to stay.

She hadn't told anyone what happened to her, what Mr. Rutherford had done. Not even Liz, who stopped by every day with Corine to share a meal or just to talk. She couldn't. It was too horrible, too ugly. To speak of it would make it real, and that she couldn't bear. Liz asked her more than once what was wrong, that she seemed different somehow. But Cora would wave off her concerns as simply worry about making ends meet. Yet many times she'd caught Liz staring at her as if she could see behind the lie. She had to get away before it slipped out, stood before her pointing a finger at her dishonor.

All the way to Rudell she prayed that no would notice that it hovered around her like a shadow, reminding her that she was spoiled, damaged, dirty. But maybe if she smiled just right, remembered all the names and faces, went back to the church, nobody need never know.

She returned to Rudell to welcome arms, tight hugs, and wet kisses. She visited First Baptist, but declined to sing, said she wanted to wait a spell. She went into town and bought ice cream at Joe's, no magazines though. She settled herself into the routine of Miss Lucinda's household and her fussy ways. But best of all, she was with David again.

She'd been back almost two weeks, and she and David had spent all their free time together. It was almost as if nothing had changed between them. Almost.

"It's good to have you back home, Cora," David uttered in a low voice as they sat across the table from each other in Miss Lucinda's kitchen. He held her hands in his.

Cora's gaze flittered like a butterfly around the room, looking for some safe place to land, her conscience making it hard to look him in the eye. "It feels good to be back." That much was true.

"You're not going to hurry back after the holidays, are you? You'll stay a while, won't you?"

She swallowed, forced a smile. "I plan to stay . . . for a spell." She looked around. "Miss Lucinda could use my help to get things together for the church for Christmas." That was a good reason, wasn't it?

He clasped her hand a bit tighter and stared into her eyes. "Have Christmas Eve dinner with me at my house."

Cora lowered her head. "I—wouldn't want to impose on your family. I—"

He cupped her face. "You are family, my family. Don't you know that by now?"

Her eyes widened in a joyous wonder.

"You mean everything to me, Cora. Being apart from you all this time only made me realize that I could never stop loving you. Never. With you gone I lost my best friend, the other side of myself. The only person I could trust with my thoughts, my feelin's, my heart." He took a breath. "And now you're back."

Each word was like a slice through her soul, shredding her to bits inside. How many nights had they sat together along the riverbank, walked together through the woods, sat together in the church under the eyes of the Lord, and she wanted to tell him what had happened, what had been done to her. She wanted to tell him of the nightmares, the pain, the terror that never seemed to leave her. She wanted to curl up in his arms, burrow her way under his skin, and let his love make the hurt go away, ease her sorrow. But she couldn't tell him. She couldn't utter the words of disgrace. She couldn't bare to see the look of pity turn to disgust in his eyes, linger there for all to see. That would kill her sure enough. So she said nothing, and prayed on her knees that his love would somehow heal her.

She tentatively touched his face, his handsome, strong face. Ran her finger along the line of his jaw, studied the new creases around his eyes, the darkness of his skin. "I'd be honored to share Christmas Eve dinner with you and your family."

▲ ▲ ▲

Betty Jean Mackey had prepared a feast fit for kings. All manner of meats, vegetables, and desserts lined the table from end to end. Even Miss Lucinda was impressed after finally giving in to Cora and David's insistence that she join them.

After cleaning up the dishes and storing the food, David and Cora took Miss Lucinda home and got her settled for the night.

The young couple sat out on the porch steps beneath a blanket of a million twinkling stars. Cora pulled her sweater a bit tighter around her shoulders, gazing out upon the tranquil beauty of this little corner of the world. If she closed her eyes and thought really hard, she could almost believe that nothing had changed, that she was the same girl who'd left Rudell two years earlier. At moments like this she almost felt good, whole again.

"Have you thought about . . . how long you're going to stay, Cora?"

She turned toward him, saw the look of hesitation and hope in his eyes. She looked down, saw the ringlet flash of gold sparkle on her chest. "I . . . was thinkin' . . . maybe I would stay on for a while longer."

David pressed his lips together as if trying to stall the words that danced on his tongue. "Cora—" he took her hand—"I know how you feel about staying here and all." He swallowed. "I know you want bigger things for your life." He reached toward her neck and lifted the chain from around it, stared down at the ring. He unfastened the chain and slid the ring off, placed it in the palm of his hand, and squeezed his fingers around it. "But I was hoping . . . that you might reconsider . . ."

Her heart began to race, and her breath stopped and started.

David opened his hand. "Marry me, Cora. Take this ring and wear it on your finger. We can make a good life together. I promise you that. Whatever it takes to make you happy, as long as you say yes."

Cora looked deep into David's eyes and knew that what he promised could be true. He would protect her, love her, keep her safe. Nothing bad would ever happen to her again. If she let him, his love *could* heal her, push the past firmly behind her. She could make a life with him, be a good wife, and maybe a mother one day. And if she worked really hard no one need never know.

"I tried to find my dream in a place where there ain't none to be had," she said softly. "I looked for happiness and what I discovered was that everything I really wanted was right here all along. I 'spose I needed to do that, get it out of me, to be able to come to this place, this day." She looked down for an instant then directly at him. "If you'll have me, I'd be honored to be yo' wife. And I'll work everyday of my life to make you happy. I swear I will."

David kissed her long and slow, and as he held her soft body against his, he realized that his prayers were finally answered.

▲ ▲ ▲

On January 1, 1930, Cora Harvey and David Mackey stood under the roof of First Baptist Church before man and God and pledged their love and fidelity.

Cora and David moved easily into married life, taking each day they were together as a blessing, making up for lost time. Cora learned to cook his favorite meals, and David learned the fine art of foot massage that would soothe her at the end of her work day at the local market.

Day by day their love grew and Cora often wondered why she'd ever left Rudell, ever thought she could find her happiness elsewhere when her happiness had been right there waiting for her in David.

They didn't have much money, but they made the best of the little they had, going fishing on Saturday mornings, holding hands in church on Sundays, and loving each other every day of the week. Cora was David's world. He lived and breathed for her smile and couldn't have been happier when she told him she was carrying his child.

Seemed like everyone in Rudell was happy about Cora and David's baby, as if the child's birth would somehow be their gift for the loss of their beloved Joshua and Pearl. They teased her about her rapidly growing belly, and with each passing day, the fear inside Cora bloomed with the growth of the child she carried. She prayed, she cried in the dark, she begged for the worst not to be true. Many a night she'd turn to her loving husband, the truth burning her lips, but she could not make them speak. She could only hope.

On July 30, 1930, Cora Mackey gave birth to her daughter, Emma, six months after her marriage. Two days later, David did the hardest, most painful thing in his life, he moved out, leaving Cora and baby Emma in the little rented house by the Left Hand River.

.

BOOK II

Emma

Eighteen

~~~~~~~~~~~~

EIGHTEEN YEARS LATER

Emma came down the stairs from her room, her long, silky black hair cascading in a tumble of waves around her shoulders. She walked into the kitchen and glared at her mother's back.

How I hate her, she thought malevolently, *with her thick, black work shoes, dry hands, and forever pitiful look in her eyes.* Every day she watched from the window as Cora plodded home from working in the home of some white family, she cringed in shame. Why did Cora have to be her mother? She was so sorry to behold with her frayed cotton dresses washed so much they'd lost all color and shape. Was she ever happy, ever pretty? She never smiled, never had a spark in her eyes. She just worked and walked around like a ghost. Never had much to say to her either. Never really hugged or kissed her like she'd seen other mamas do, like she was ashamed of her or something. She was the one who should be ashamed. Ashamed that people whispered behind her back, stopped talking when she entered a room, called her daughter half-breed and other names she wouldn't repeat. She couldn't count the days she'd run home in tears, bury her face in her mother's lap, and ask why everybody hated her so much. Why none of the children wanted to be her friend. Why they called her a bastard. Why she wouldn't tell her where her father was.

And her mama would just sit there, still as stone, and absently pat her back, tell her not to worry herself about those people. *They was just evil.* And that her daddy had moved on, that's all to it. And when she'd look up into her mama's face, Cora would almost flinch as if she'd looked into the eyes of the devil himself, and Emma would wonder what she'd done wrong. Finally she stopped seeking comfort from Cora and just tucked away the hurt, the insults, the ridicule inside herself, until it started eating away at her soul, bit by bit, until she was all hollow inside and nothing could hurt her, nothing could touch her. She created her own world, lived in her own space where nothing and no one mattered but *her.*

Emma learned early that Cora had no real capacity to give her love but would give her things instead when she cried or became sullen. So Emma may not have had her mother's heart, but she made her pay for her loneliness in this tiny, ugly town that wouldn't accept her. Emma had a closet full of the finest clothes that she demanded her mother buy from the catalogs. By the age of ten, she refused to go to school in the hand-sewn clothes that Cora sat up long into the night making for her after she'd worked from sunup on her hands and knees. But Emma didn't care. Her bedroom was fit for a princess, with frilly curtains and lace doilies for her dresser that was crammed with silky underthings. And she flaunted her finery in the ugly, black faces of the schoolchildren of Rudell, which only pushed them farther away, made them whisper all the more. But Emma didn't care. She'd never learned how.

Looking at her mother now, stirring stew in the pot, seeing her slumped shoulders and swollen ankles, the resentment built up inside her like a boiling cauldron of water pushing the top off trying to get out.

"I'm hungry!" she snapped, wishing she could shake some life into Cora.

"Supper be ready soon," Cora said, almost to herself in the broken English that Emma detested and worked hard to rid herself of.

Emma heaved a breath. "I'm going for a walk." She turned and stomped out, slamming the door behind her. She stalked off toward the river, her rage building like gathering thunderclouds. Her smooth, black brows set against her porcelain skin hinged together in a tight line. Her green eyes glistened and filled as she took deep, gulping breaths of air. Why did she always feel this way, so angry and lonely? There was no one to share her thoughts, answer her questions about herself, tell her how to be happy.

Emma sought out her favorite place, the flat rock just beyond the riverbank, and sat down. One day she'd get away from this place, she vowed, staring out across the gentle ripple of the water. She'd get away and make a new life and forget all about this terrible place and all the people in it.

The sound of a car coming down the uneven road drew her attention. She craned her long, milky neck to see who was coming.

The car drew closer and came to a stop. A white man, dressed in a good-looking blue suit with a black fedora cocked over his eyes stepped out of the car. Instantly, Emma was on guard as a rush of fear scurried along her limbs. White folks didn't come to these parts, and when they did it usually meant trouble. She sat perfectly still.

"Excuse me, ma'am." He politely tipped his hat.

Emma blinked in confusion. *Ma'am.* "Ye-yessir."

"I was hoping you might direct me toward the highway. I was on my way to Biloxi for the night and got turned around somehow." He laughed lightly.

Slowly Cora stood. "If you stay on this road, you'll see a fork. Stay to the left and you'll find the highway."

He smiled gratefully. "Thank you, Miss. Last place I want to be is lost in these woods after dark." He looked around nervously and chuckled. He gazed at her for a moment, angled his head to the side. "Pretty thing like you needs to be getting home, too. You know how these Negroes are, see a pretty, white woman—" He let his voice drift off, but his meaning was clear. "Hate to see anything happen to you. I'd be happy to give you a lift into town."

Emma tried to make sense of what this white man was saying to her. *White woman. Pretty, white woman.* She couldn't respond.

He stepped closer and took off his hat; his sandy, brown hair glistened in the waning light. He was almost tall, slender in a rangy sort of way and young, no older than her, she guessed.

"Miss, are you all right?"

Emma snapped to attention. Her mouth trembled into a smile. "Yes. Fine, sir." She bobbed her head.

"Name's Hamilton. Elliot Hamilton."

"Emma. Ma—McKay." Her heart sounded like thunder.

"Pleasure, Miss McKay." He stuck out his hand, which she tentatively shook. "The offer is still open."

"Offer?"

"For the ride—into town. Are you sure you're all right, Miss. You look flushed."

Cora touched her check. "No, I'm fine. Just the heat." She looked straight at him, just to see if she could. No slap came, no flurry of curses, just a curious smile. "Thank you for the offer. But I'll be fine. I—I'm waiting— on a friend."

Elliot looked around, then checked his gold watch. "I'd wait with you, just to be certain you stay safe until your friend arrives, but I really need to be moving on."

Her chest heaved in and out. "It's fine. Really. Thank you."

He put his hat back on and slid his fingers along the brim. "You be careful out here."

Emma nodded.

He turned then stopped. "I guess you hear this all the time, but—you sure do have the prettiest green eyes I've ever seen."

Emma felt her face heat. She arched her chin just a bit but wanted to hide her face, so unaccustomed was she to compliments. "Thank you—Mr. Hamilton."

He tipped his hat. "My pleasure." He returned to his car and drove off.

Emma watched the car until it disappeared in a cloud of dust. Her knees began to wobble, and her entire body trembled. She reached behind her for the rock and lowered herself down.

Her thoughts tumbled over each other like a cascade of rocks kicked from the top of a hillside. She raised a shaky hand to her face, ran it over the smooth skin. She touched her hair, stuck her hands out in front of her, and stared at them. She gazed down the road where the white man had gone. And for the first time in her eighteen years of life, she felt the inklings of hope.

▲ ▲ ▲

Cora sat at the kitchen table picking over the food she'd prepared. The last rays of light streamed through the window and danced merrily across her hand-scrubbed floors. The windows sparkled from her vinegar and water washing. The corners of the house remained dustfree from the constant turn of the broom she gave them. Clean, hand-washed sheets billowed like sails on the line in the back. The vegetable garden popped with tomatoes, cabbage, and snap peas.

She shut her eyes. This was the home she'd dreamed of, the one she thought she would share with David for the rest of their lives. Her chest tightened. When she thought of him, as she did nearly every day of her life, it was with a sadness that drowned her, snuffed out her energy like a candle that had been doused. To this day she could almost see the look of shock, horror, and disappointment on his face when he pulled Emma from her body.

"I can see the baby's head, Cora, sweetheart. Come on, push. Take a deep breath and push."

Cora drew in all her strength and bared down, sweat popping from her brow, muscles strained to near breaking. She screamed as the pain ripped through her.

"It's okay, sweetheart," David soothed, wiping her brow with a damp cloth. "Soon. It'll be over soon. I promise. Just took us by surprise and all, coming two months early."

Another pain seized her and she clawed his hand. Two months early floated through her head. *Oh, God, oh, God—please, please, please—no.*

The fear had grown over the months as her belly bloomed too quick. But she'd pushed the awful possibility to the back of her mind. Everyone said she was just "carrying' big" for a tiny girl and she believed them, needed to believe them. And David was so happy, so proud. He'd fixed up a room just for the baby, repaired the front steps so she wouldn't trip, and waited on her hand and foot, reminded her every day how much he loved her.

Cora gripped David's shirt. "David," she sputtered, gasping for breath. "The baby . . . it's . . . it may—Augggh!"

Her head slapped back against the pillows as her body arched, her parted thighs trembled, the scream spilled out into the air, as she pushed Emma into the world.

The sound of the baby's newborn cries followed. She tried to sit up, but she was too weak. She could just make out David's back as he tended to the baby. He didn't utter a word as he worked, and the terror in her mounted in a steady upward spiral until it pounded against her temples.

"David," she whispered. "David."

Shortly he stood over her, holding the baby wrapped in a clean white sheet. Dark, straight black hair peeked out from the top.

Cora looked up at her husband, her breath standing still in her chest. All time seemed suspended, holding them there in this telling moment.

His mouth, the mouth that had kissed away her pain, hushed away her fears, was set in a hard, untouchable line. The eyes, warm and brown, were lifeless and filled with tears that ran unchecked down his face. The skin of his face that she joyed in touching shuddered; his nostrils flared as if he'd been running. He stood like an executioner above her, dark, ominous, the last thing she would see before her life was cut short.

She watched his throat work up and down, but the words remained trapped there, unspeakable. And maybe it was best that they were. His face and dead eyes said it all.

David placed the baby on her breasts, turned and walked away.

Trembling, Cora looked down at the life she'd brought into the world.

A tiny, perfect face, a shade darker than the sheet, with rosy cheeks and pink, delicate lips, lay wrapped in her arms.

Her head spun and the room moved in and out at a dizzying speed. She felt faint. "Oh, Lawd, Lawd," she cried weakly.

Tiny little hands pushed up toward its face, which wrinkled up ready to let out another wail. The dark lashes fluttered, the near transparent lids lifted, and brilliant, jade green eyes gazed back at her, damning her for all time.

▲ ▲ ▲

She didn't know where David went, and he didn't return for two torturous days. When he did come back, Cora wouldn't have recognized him except for his height and distinctive walk. His face was haggard and seemed to sag around the edges. The whites of his eyes were red, the lids swollen. His clothes were wrinkled and soiled as if he'd slept in the woods. And the smell of liquor hovered around him like a halo.

He wouldn't look at her as he moved soundlessly through the house. Wouldn't come near the baby, wouldn't respond when she tried to talk to him. He packed his things, left an envelope with money, and walked out.

Cora stared at the door now, just as she'd done that night eighteen years ago, still hoping that he would change his mind and come home, that somehow she'd find the words to explain. But neither thing ever happened.

She tried to love Emma, but every time she looked at her face she saw those vile, green eyes glaring down at her, felt her womanhood being stolen from her, her body invaded. So she did the best she could, she gave Emma whatever she wanted. Everything but her love—God forgive her—everything but her love.

Once word got out and spread brushfire quick through Rudell, the townspeople turned their backs on her like she carried the plague. The women turned up their noses, and the men snickered and made cutting remarks about her virtue. When she went to church, the one place that had been her salvation, the parishioners moved aside when she came in with Emma. Whispers behind hand-covered mouths, eyes that stared at her with pinched, judgmental expressions on loveless faces told the tale. She never went back.

Miss Lucinda would stop by on occasion, never uttering a word about the baby or how it got to be white. And all Cora could do was move through her house, through the town, with her head lowered in shame.

David had moved away, taking his mother with him, leaving the town without a doctor or a dressmaker, which made them resent Cora all the more.

Over the years the whispers lessened, but the rumor, which turned to town folklore, remained, discussed, she was sure, over dinner tables and in the shops in town.

Deacon Earl and Flem were long gone now, laid to rest in the field behind the church. All who remained was Miss Lucinda, the one soul in the world with whom she had any connection, even though what plagued her most she could never share, and it hindered the close relationship they'd once enjoyed. So all she had was Miss Lucinda and her daughter, who she'd failed to love.

The banging of the front door snapped Cora from her mental wanderings. She looked up from her cold bowl of stew as Emma sauntered into the kitchen.

"Yo' supper be on the stove, Emma, gettin' cold."

"I'm not hungry," Emma tossed back. "I'm going to my room." She whirled away and ran up the stairs.

Secure in her room, she stood in front of her mirror and slowly took off her clothes. Inch by inch she examined her body in the reflection with new eyes: the smooth pink-and-white skin, firm breasts with round, pink nipples, tight, flat stomach and narrow waist, the patch of hair that was as silky as the hair on her head, tapering down to long legs and thin ankles. Her excitement mounted. A slow smile crept across her face and brightened her eyes. With a toss of her head she stared boldly back at herself. "Yes. Yes. Yes," she uttered, in a tremulous whisper.

Nineteen

~~~~~~~~~~~~~

"I'm not feeling very well today, Miss Holly," Emma said in a mealy voice to accentuate her plight.

Florene Holly, owner of the one clothing shop in Rudell, looked askance at Emma. There was plenty to do with the fall season quickly approaching, and she didn't take kindly to anyone who couldn't hold up their end of the job. But, she had to admit, since Emma started working there after school a year earlier, she hadn't missed a day. Fact was, she felt kind of sorry for her. Florence supposed it was real hard on her looking like a white woman in the middle of a midnight black town. There was all manner of rumors about Emma's mama, Cora, and how she got to have Emma in the first place, and how she made a horse's ass out of the good doctor then sent him packing. She never saw the child with a friend, never saw her with a young man or a smile on her face. Sad. Sad. Sad. But with so much heaped on her thin shoulders, Emma kept a regalness about her like she didn't have a care in the world.

Florence eyed Emma's wan expression once more. "All right. Go on home." She wagged a finger at her. "But it will be double the work tomorrow."

"Yes, ma'am. Thank you." Emma took her suit jacket from the hook behind the stockroom door and hurried out, slipping it over her pristine white blouse.

As she strolled casually along the dusty streets of Rudell—just in case Ms. Holly was peeking from the doorway—Emma could feel the rush of adrenaline that tried to push her into a run toward the edge of town. But she breathed slow and deep to stem the urge. Her small change purse contained enough coins for her to entertain herself once she reached her destination.

She followed the rows of businesses, past Joe's, past the dry goods shop, past the shoe repair and the schoolhouse until she reached the edge of town. Looking right, then left, she kept going around the bend toward the river and then across the plank-board bridge that separated the colored section of Rudell from the white.

For more than a week since she'd met the white man at the river, a plan had been forming in her mind. Today was the day. A test. She couldn't fail. Failure could cost her her life or worse.

After about a mile or so walk, Emma emerged from the woods and found herself on the crest of a hill looking down at the collection of neat houses and smooth roads, cars moving easily along the paths.

Hardly able to breathe, Emma moved forward, down the streets, passing two white women who paid her no notice as they chatted about their day, briefly glancing at her with faint smiles. Shutting her eyes briefly she continued on, walking passed the fenced-in homes with well-dressed children playing in yards budding with flowers and neat lanes of grass. She moved on, head held at just the right angle of assurance, her flowing hair caressing proud shoulders. Her step grew a bit quicker as she passed the houses and approached the town.

Shiny black cars moved up and down the dirt roads. There were beauty shops, a doctor's office with a sign in the window saying no appointment needed, a clothing store just for women, a fish market, a small theater, a post office, and a bank—a real place to put your money other than a mason jar or under a straw mattress. Everything was clean. All the faces were open, smiling, laughter floated along the air. Such a contrast to the harsh lines carved on black faces, the bent and weary bodies, the sense of futility, and the dusty, paveless roads she was used to. There was an aura of happiness here that she'd never felt in her part of Rudell. Even the air smelled different. There was hope and confidence in this air.

Two white men approached and that built-in fear took hold, lowered her gaze, and shortened her step. Her heart raced in fear of discovery. This was no twilight by the river, shaded by the open hands of trees. It was the bright light of day, a cloudless day in the white section of Rudell.

She could always claim to be looking for work if she was stopped, she quickly reasoned, as the men drew closer.

Her body heated with all the hurt, ridicule, loneliness, questions, rage, and fears that lived with her every day of her life. And it all fueled her, raised her eyes in salute, and curved the corners of her red mouth.

Both men smiled broadly, tipping their hats. One stopped. "And how are you this fine afternoon, Miss?"

"Why, fine, thank you, sir." She held her breath.

"You look a bit lost. Maybe I can direct you?"

"Well . . . I was just looking for a place to get a cool drink."

"Smitty's is right down the street on your right," the second man offered, giving her a long, appreciative look.

"Thank you both."

The men nodded and continued down the street.

Emma's heart beat so hard and fast her head began to spin. She pulled in a long, deep breath, willing her body to stop its shuddering. Suddenly aware that she hadn't moved, Emma continued down Loren Street to Smitty's.

When she stepped inside, no one turned to stare, no one came to shove her out or hurl curses at her. She walked toward the counter and took a seat, her pulse racing at an unnatural rhythm.

"What can I get for you, Miss?" the shopkeeper asked, wiping the space in front of her with a clean, white towel.

Emma cleared her throat. "A seltzer water would be fine."

"Comin' right up."

Cautiously, Emma gazed around the small establishment that served as diner and local gathering place. Three of the six tables were occupied, two men sat alone, the balance was a mixture of women and children.

"Here you are, ma'am."

"How much do I owe you?"

"Five cents."

Emma bit down on her bottom lip and pulled a nickel from her purse. The shopkeeper took his pay and went to serve another customer.

Emma breathed slow and easy, kept her back straight, her knees together, and her feet planted firmly on the floor. All the signs of a lady.

When she finished her glass of seltzer, she calmly rose, again thanked the shopkeeper, and stepped out into the settling down afternoon.

A smile bloomed like a young bud inside her as she strolled by one white face after another and none took any special notice, other than a fleeting smile, a bob of a head, or a tip of a hat.

Emma walked toward the edge of the town proper; past the neat, fenced-in houses with the cut grass and blooming flowers; past the children with golden hair and sparkling eyes; past the shiny cars that sat in perfect rows on smooth streets—onto the woods, across the bridge, back to the other side of Rudell.

When she gazed out across the expanse of sloping, leaning, aching beaverboard shacks, eyed the chickens running in the yards with the ragged brown children, stared into the vacant eyes of those who understood hard times, she knew this was a world she was no longer a part of and maybe never was. Perhaps they all were content to want no more than the square patch of land beneath their feet. But she had discovered her ticket out, and she intended to use it.

▲ ▲ ▲

Cora didn't know where Emma went in the afternoons when she finished work. Almost every day for weeks she'd return near dark, say she wasn't hungry, and close herself up in her room.

More than once Cora inquired of her whereabouts, and Emma would quietly inform her, in that superior tone of hers—as if she was the mother and Cora the child—"I was out walking," she would say. "No need for you to concern yourself with me."

But Cora was concerned, although she had long ago accepted that part of her that couldn't show it. She couldn't expect Emma to share her life, her thoughts, and dreams with her now. Cora had put a seal on that part of their lives, more to protect herself and her heart than to hurt Emma. Although it did. She believed that the less they spoke, the fewer questions Emma asked about her life, the less chance there would ever be about revealing that dark corner of shame that lived in her soul. The shame that stained her, ruined her marriage, broke the spirit of the man she loved, turned the town and church against her—that stood before her day in and out with those green eyes that begged for answers she could not give, that reminded her of all the things she wanted to forget.

So many nights she lay awake wanting to love Emma, show her the love her parents had given her. But she couldn't, and she hated herself for it. Emma didn't ask for this life. It was thrust upon her. Each night for eighteen years she'd prayed for answers, prayed for a path to right the wrongs. At times she could almost feel her heart soften, her spirit open, when she'd stand in the doorway of Emma's room and watch her sleep.

Emma really was quite beautiful. She had Cora's slight body frame, but she was taller. Her features were close to her grandmother Pearl. Emma even had some of Pearl's ways, the cut of an eye in warning, the curve of her mouth on the rare occasion when she smiled. Sometimes in the velvet embrace of night, Cora would kneel by Emma's bedside and tenderly stroke her hair, brush a feather of a kiss on her butter soft cheek, and ask her forgiveness in a silent whisper. One day maybe she'd be able to face her child and ask her in the light of day. Maybe.

▲ ▲ ▲

Cora was washing the dinner plate in the sink when Emma came in.

"Evenin' Mama."

"Where you been, chile? You off work hours ago." Cora wiped her hands on the dish towel.

"Walking. That's all."

There was a flush to Emma's face, a glow beneath her pale skin. Those green eyes sparkled in delight. Her child actually looked happy. Happy.

Cora stepped cautiously forward, almost afraid to break the magic spell. "I saved supper for you."

"Thank you." Emma put her purse on the table and sauntered toward the stove, lifting pot covers and sniffing the contents.

In the blink of an eye, Emma *was* Lizbeth Rutherford examining her cooking skills her first day in that house. Cora's stomach rose then settled. She grabbed the edge of the kitchen table for support as a wave of nausea rolled through her stomach.

"Smells good. I'll wash up and fix a plate."

Cora nodded absently as Emma breezed by her and went to the sink.

Emma thought of the letter she had tucked away in her purse as she watched the water slide over her hands. It had come as she was leaving for work. It was postmarked "New York City." Emma knew she shouldn't have opened it. Knew it was wrong. But she also knew that her mother would never tell her, never salve her curiosity. Cora didn't share anything with her. She'd grown to accept that, accept the secrets, the distance and differences between them, but it was eating her alive day by day. So she'd opened the letter and read it, then read it again.

Dear Cora,

I know it's been years since we've seen each other. I hope this letter finds its way to you. With my Uncle Earl having passed, I didn't know who to ask for your address. I took a chance on sending it general delivery. Unless

Rudell has changed, there ain't many people to choose from to get this letter.

I know you must be wondering why I'm writing now. Well, I ran into Mr. Rutherford. I know you remember him. And he recognized me right off. First thing he asked me was about you: Had I heard from you? Where were you? He said one day you just run off from the job without a word and never came back.

That sounded so strange to me. Not the Cora that I remember. What happened? Why did you leave?

I told him I hadn't seen or heard from you in nearly twenty years, since I left Chicago. I supposed you were just fine. And I sure hope you are.

Funny, I should bump into him after all this time, but come to find out he's running for some political office. Ain't that something? I sent the newspaper article telling all about it. Nice picture, too.

Me and Jimmy are doing fine. We have three kids, a boy and two girls. Jimmy actually made an honest woman out of me. Can you believe it? If you ever come to New York, be sure to look me up.
Your friend,
Margaret

Emma had almost memorized the letter. Every detail. What role did these people play in her mother's life? What happened to her in Chicago that made her leave? Who was Margaret and Mr. Rutherford?

These questioned tumbled around in her head all day. They followed her to work, whispered in her ear as she pranced through the white section of Rudell, held her hand on the way home, and tugged at her skirt, demanding answers.

Emma sat at the table and gazed down at her plate of fresh collard greens, sweet corn bread, buttered yams, and a single slice of cured ham. A tall glass of sweet tea stood to the side.

Cora took a seat, folded her hands in front of her, and studied her daughter's averted face. For an instant she wanted to reach out and stroke away the lines of worry that ran between her sleek brows, tell her that whatever the trouble, it would be all right. For a moment she wanted to be a real mama to her daughter.

Emma's gaze suddenly snapped up. "Who's Mr. Rutherford, Mama?"

Again the lines from the letter came to Emma: *What happened? Why did you leave?* She watched her mother's discomfort, the uneasiness of her gaze, the sudden fear that came to her weary eyes. The older woman, for some reason, lowered her face, choosing to stare at the supper on the table rather than at her daughter's bold expression. The girl wanted answers to questions that she had denied even asking herself all these years. Who's Mr. Rutherford? How did Emma know about him? What did she know about him? Or the trouble she had back in Chicago what seemed a lifetime ago? *No, not now.* Cora understood this day would come, but she didn't know what she would do or say when her daughter started digging into her past and the secret that had forced her to return to Rudell in shame.

"Who's Mr. Rutherford, Mama?" Emma repeated, this time with something demanding in her words. It was no longer a question but an ultimatum. She wanted to know everything, she wanted the truth.

"He's jus' a white man I worked fo' when I was up North," Cora forced herself to say the words with as little emotion as possible. She didn't want to give away anything in her voice, in her words, in her expression.

"For a long time I've wanted to ask you what brought you back here," her daughter said, putting a fist under her chin, her stare strong and unwavering. "Just why did you leave Chicago? Did your leaving have to do with Mr. Rutherford? Answer me, Mama. You owe me this much. You owe me the truth."

Cora took a deep breath, leaned back, and said her piece. "I don't owe you nothin', girl. I left there and that's that. I've raised you the best way I could, given you everythang you ever wanted, ain't ever denied you nothin', and here you is, speakin' to me like you's the mother and I's the child."

Emma refused to give ground. "Who's Mr. Rutherford? And what does he have to do with you coming back to Rudell? Why are you getting upset unless there's something you're hiding?"

"I don't have to hide nothin' from you," Cora said, in a low voice, a voice seething with barely restrained anger. "How do you know 'bout Mr. Rutherford anyhow? Who told you 'bout him?"

For an instant the momentum of the exchange shifted, with Emma now on the defensive. She dared not reveal the intercepted letter from Margaret or its contents. To do so would give her mother the upper hand and that would be the end of the conversation, and there was so much she needed to know, so many questions she wanted to ask. Emma sat there, matching her mother's unblinking stare with her own, weighing her next move.

"I asked you a question, girl," Cora said, with even more force behind her words. "You answer me. Jus' how you come to know 'bout Mr. Rutherford?"

Emma straightened up in her chair and sent a trembling hand through her long, black hair. "I just know about him, that's all. Who is he? What did he do to you? Is he why you left Chicago in such a hurry?"

Cora swallowed hard, pursed her thick lips, and stood up. "Are you gon' eat yo' supper or what?" There was no way she was gon' to tell her daughter 'bout what happened that horrible night, how that white man had forced himself upon her and stole her dreams and innocence, changing her life forever. This was a part of her long, hard life that she refused to share with anyone, a dark, tormented episode that she would take with her to the grave.

As Cora moved to leave the room, her daughter got up and followed, dogging the older woman's every step. She was almost hysterical with impatience and frustration. "Mama, answer me," Emma shouted, totally forgetting herself or their customary familial role. Cora was no longer her mother but just another person, just another woman she needed some answers from.

Suddenly Cora whirled and seized her daughter by the arm, startling Emma. "I don't have ta tell you a damn thing, girl. It's none of yo' business what happened, and that's all I'm ever gon' say 'bout that ag'in in my life."

The fury of her mother's response completely caught Emma off guard, stopping her aggressive inquisition in its tracks, shrinking her resolve and replacing them with fear and bewilderment. She had never seen her mother so angry. She knew she had hit a nerve. There was something in her mother's secret past having to do with Mr. Rutherford and her working for him. Maybe this white man was her missing, unmentioned father. All these thoughts flooded into Emma's confused mind and then vanished like timid frost under the glare of the sun. She ran to her room, threw herself across her bed, and cried herself into a troubled sleep.

In the days that followed, Emma and Cora were two bowstrings pulled to their limits, ready to snap in half. They remained silent, wary partners in the tiny house that seemed to grow smaller each day. The roof became the lid that kept everything and everyone beneath it on a slow simmer. The contents boiled and bubbled. Everything that had been wrong between mother and daughter was laid open, lanced like a festering wound; and the poison, no longer contained, seeped out infecting them both.

Each night that Emma came in, Cora wanted to reach out to her and explain, tell her the truth, the entire story. Tell her how hard it had been, how lonely. She wanted her to know that she had tried to love her in the only way she knew how. But still, she could not form the words even at the cost of losing her daughter for good.

▲ ▲ ▲

The sun made a show of closing its act for the day, fanning out across the horizon in a huge, multicolored umbrella, spreading its brilliant orange and gold rays across the crests of the rolling hills and valleys to settle into a shimmer along the river. But Cora didn't notice. She couldn't. Every muscle, every limb ached. Her eyelashes pulsed each time she blinked. Each footfall up the creaky wood steps shot vibrations of agony through her weary limbs. She felt as if she was on the threshold of seeing her centennial year instead of her thirty-seventh.

Slowly she turned the knob on the door, hoping by some miracle that Emma had prepared dinner. But the instant she stepped through the door and smelled nothing but the cloying summer heat, she knew her last wish for the day had been wasted.

She pushed out a long breath, crossed the small, front room, and put her purse on the hall table.

"Emma! Emma, I'm home."

Her call was met by silence as it had been for weeks. But this was different. "Emma." Cora walked farther into the house to the foot of the stairs, an eerie sensation like a black cat crossing your path sent a sudden chill running through her. The muscles of her stomach tightened.

There was a time when Emma was always the first one home, if for no other reason than to tell her how much she resented the fact that her mother spent her days on her hands and knees cleaning other people's dirt, to find a way to humiliate her.

Cora didn't want to go up those stairs. She knew what she was going to find. Nothing. But she must. She must put closure to at least one thing in her life.

One by one she climbed the stairs, the squeaking sound of air being pushed out with every step. The closer she came to the top, the more she accepted the outcome.

She walked into Emma's room, with its pristine white walls and lace curtains that shuddered from the hot breeze that sneaked up on them and tiptoed through the open window. Cora took a breath of resolve, her world-weary eyes slowly panning the spotless room.

There was no need to check the closet or the drawers. She was sure they'd be empty of all the clothes she'd sweated and scraped enough money together for so that Emma could buy them from the catalogs.

Languidly, Cora turned away, walking toward her room across the hall.

She sat on the edge of the bed, pressed the toes of her right foot against the heels of her left, and pushed off her thick-soled black shoes. Then she repeated the process on the other side. With effort she raised her swollen legs up onto the bed and stretched out, crossing her hands over her stomach.

For several moments she stared at the crack that ran the length of the ceiling. She should be happy that Emma was gone. Finally. Now the futility of their existence together as mother and daughter could come to a close. Her struggle to make something be that never could was over. She could finally stop trying to make up to Emma—with things—for bringing her into the world, for not being smart enough, pretty enough, rich enough, light enough. Cora closed her eyes and wept, in relief or soul-wrenching sorrow, she couldn't be sure.

▲ ▲ ▲

Free. She was finally free. Free of that dismal place where everyone turned their noses up at her, whispered about her and her mother behind their backs. Free of watching her mother drag herself home, beaten as surely as if she'd been whipped—day after day. She pulled the newspaper clipping from her purse, memorizing the face of William Rutherford. Her expression as she turned to stare out of the train window grew hardened and resolute as the town of Rudell grew smaller.

Twenty

When Emma emerged from the womb of Pennsylvania Station in New York City, it was with the pain and exhilaration of a newborn. Except for Emma it was a rebirth, a starting over, putting her other life behind her.

She deeply inhaled the scents of mustard-coated hot dogs, salted pretzels, roasted nuts, shoe-shine polish, expensive cigars and filter-tipped cigarettes, perfumes and colognes. She picked up the beat of the rapid tap-tap step that left no room to falter. She absorbed the energy, let it flow through her veins. She welcomed the rush, the push and shove, the jangle of voices that sang out in strange languages and accents she couldn't place, the bright lights, and the roar of trains.

"Where are you heading, Miss?"

Emma turned with a start, the momentary terror of being found out caught in her throat, sat there and swelled, making it impossible for her to speak.

A smiling, red-faced young man, with a red-boxed hat and red vest stood before her.

Emma blinked, a shaky smile forming around her scarlet lips.

"Can I help you with your bag, Miss?"

Her smile curved into a firm, ripe fruit. "You certainly may," she replied in her best woman-of-the-world voice.

"Will you be needing a taxi, Miss, or is someone meeting you out front?"

"I will be needing a taxi," she said, feeling giddy with the excitement of her secret plain enough for all eyes to see. But they couldn't. They couldn't. She almost laughed as she trailed behind him in short, quick steps, winding their way like a needle and thread through the rainbow fabric of people.

Emma stepped outside, into the balmy chaotic air of New York City. Buildings towered toward the heavens, creating an imperfect picture of majesty. The shrill sound of the red cap's whistle penetrated the honking horns, the sounds of shots when cars backfired, spitting their fumes into the already crowded air. A yellow, checkered taxi squealed to a stop at the curb.

The young man quickly rounded the back of the taxi and deposited Emma's one suitcase into the trunk.

She'd overheard in conversations at Smitty's that everybody in the big cities up North expected a tip for every little thing they did, some change for doing the smallest kindness.

Emma stood back a moment as if she was inspecting the vehicle, the driver, and the handling of her bag. What she really observed was a couple getting into a cab behind her. The man took two coins from his suit jacket and gave them to his red cap, then helped his wife into the car.

Emma nodded her regal head of cascading onyx hair in approval and gave her young man two quarters for his troubles.

"Thank you, Miss," he said profusely, making Emma wonder if she'd done too much. "Thank you." He hurried off to find another customer.

Emma smiled tightly and slid across the cool, leather seats.

"Where to, Miss?" the driver asked, around the smelly stub of a thick, brown cigar jammed into the corner of his thickly mustached mouth.

Where to? She hadn't planned on where she would stay. Somehow she'd lost the envelope with Margaret's address and had no other person to turn to. She glanced nervously out of the window, then at the back of the driver's head.

"I was hoping you'd be kind enough to offer a few suggestions. Something . . . not too . . . expensive, but clean and safe." She swallowed down the lump in her throat.

He curved his leonine head across his shoulders and looked at her with tight blue eyes.

"There's a coupla hotels in midtown. Single rooms. Lotta newcomers stay there until they get settled."

Emma grabbed hold of her runaway breathing. "I—I'm expecting my fiancé to join me in a few days," she said, sensing that she didn't want this man to think she was totally alone and defenseless.

"Then one of those hotels I'm telling you about should work out for you. Until your, uh, fiancé gets here, that is."

She waved her hand nonchalantly. "We'll work that all out later when Hamilton arrives." She tucked in her smile, thinking how appropriate that she should choose his name, the man from the river who'd inadvertently opened the door to her freedom.

He slowly turned back around and eased the taxi into the flow of midday traffic.

Before she had time to digest all of the delicacies of the city, they were coming to a stop in front of an ominous-looking brown building on a long street of buildings that looked almost identical, so tall they cut off all the light on the narrow street. The only illumination was the rows of aluminum garbage cans that lined the block.

There was a dimly lighted sign above the entrance door: HOTEL ARMS.

This can't be right, she thought. She leaned forward and peered out of the window; then panic clenched her belly. This man must have figured out that she was a Negro, and this is the place where she should stay. She didn't know if she should vehemently complain or prepare a flurry of excuses when he demanded to know why she'd tried to fool him.

Just then a white man, finely dressed, opened the door of the hotel and stood on the top step surveying his world, then trotted down the three steps. On his way down, a white woman with glistening blonde hair and a tightly fitting suit with wide, padded shoulders went up the stairs, past him, and inside.

"That'll be a dollar and five cents, Miss," the driver said, sounding annoyed.

Emma counted out the money and handed it to the driver, who only grunted in response before getting out of the car to retrieve her bag from the trunk. By the time she got out, he'd deposited her bag on the curb and was pulling off.

With much trepidation Emma climbed the steps and pushed through the door. A wizened man of about seventy, she guessed, with bushy, white brows, sitting behind what served as a counter, asked gruffly, "How many?"

"I need one room, please."

"Five dollars a week payable in advance." He held out his hand across the scarred wooden counter.

Emma gave him the money, and he replaced it with a key. "Fifth floor, number three. No loud noise and the bathroom is at the end of the hall."

Emma climbed the five flights of stairs, listening to the voices of men and women seeping from beneath the slits in the doors, inhaled the scents of burned food and old sweat. She made her way down the narrow hall to the door marked three.

That night, lying across the lumpy, stale mattress with flickering, colored lights bouncing in and out of her window, the sounds of banging and shouting closing in around her, Emma only smiled.

This is merely temporary, she thought, not at all disturbed by her surroundings. Before long she would live the life she was destined to live. Of that she was certain.

Twenty-one

~~~~~~~~~~~~

Each morning Emma was up before the sun, her years of early rising in Mississippi were paying off, combined with her discovery that the other tenants on her floor didn't rise for the day before seven. Knowing that, she generally had full and private use of the public bathroom.

She didn't mingle with any of the occupants in the building, only barely acknowledging the few she passed going in and out or on the stairs and hallways. She wanted to keep it that way, or at least that's what she told herself was true. In reality, Emma didn't know how to make friends, hadn't developed the skills of making small talk, sharing her thoughts and feelings with another person. For the most part, she'd grown up and lived her days alone, her only company being herself and her determination to get as far away from the people and environment that had shunned her.

But when she watched other women laughing and talking with each other, shopping in stores together, sharing a sandwich during lunch, or the couples who held hands and gazed into each other's eyes with hope, fulfillment, and love, she wondered what that was like, what it felt like to truly be a part of someone else's life, cared for.

Maybe that kind of life wasn't meant for someone like her. It wasn't something she should hope for, dream about. So instead she turned any ability to feel into a commitment to acquire all she believed was due her, that she had been denied. Did her mother miss her, think about her at all? Was she glad to be rid of her?

Emma shook off the sudden sting of the questions, the emotions that the thoughts evoked. She pushed back the pang of sadness that reverberated inside her. There was no time and no place in her life for weak moments, wishing for things that could never be. She raised her coffee cup to her lips and snapped open the newspaper.

Emma began each day with an early morning visit to the local diner for a short breakfast of one egg over easy, two slices of toast—lightly buttered—and two cups of coffee, extra sweet.

Old Henry, as all the customers called the owner, knew her order before she said a word and routinely had her coffee waiting when she arrived promptly at seven o'clock. Henry took a special liking to Emma. She so much reminded him of his own daughter: beautiful and aloof. But he didn't believe that Emma's aloofness was a result of breeding or temperament, but more because she simply didn't know any other way to be. Loneliness was written all over her proud bearing. So he tried in his own way to be a friend to the young woman, probably the only one she had he guessed.

Emma sipped her coffee and scanned the paper. Although she'd saved some money, she knew she couldn't live off of it forever. At some point she had to find a job and a place of her own.

Most of the jobs she'd seen were either for secretaries or salesgirls, neither of which appealed to her. She wanted to work some place where she had the greatest opportunity to meet people with potential, people who could further her objectives.

Running her finger down the want ads, she noticed a position available for an office assistant at a real estate office in midtown Manhattan.

Emma's eyes widened with hope as she slowly replaced the cup in its chipped saucer. *"No experience necessary. Will train. Immediate hire."*

The wheels began to turn. This was just what she was looking for. People who came to real estate offices were those who wanted to buy homes, rent apartments, find locations for business. People with money, potential, and possible connections.

Emma circled the ad and closed the newspaper. She checked the clock on the wall. It was only seven-thirty. If she left now, she'd arrive long before the start of business. She'd be the first one there. The only one they'd need to see.

"Not hungry today, Emma?" Old Henry asked, noticing her half-eaten plate of food as he refilled her cup.

Emma looked up. "I found the job I've been looking for, Old Henry."

Henry chuckled deep in his throat, his barrel chest rising and falling beneath his stained, white T-shirt. "Beautiful woman like you shouldn't have a need to work. Some man will snatch you right up before you know it."

Emma zeroed in on his once handsome face, sagging now in layers from age and one drink too many.

"That may be true, but until that day comes, I intend to be able to take care of myself," she said, with the confidence built on having to stand alone. "Have something to call mine."

"I wish you a lot of luck, Emma. But, if you don't mind, I'd like to share some advice with you."

Emma straightened in her seat. "What's that?"

"Men like women they can take care of, that depend on them—as men." His brow arched. "Know what I mean?"

Emma pursed her lips, letting his words roll around in her head. All her life the women she'd seen worked just as hard as the men. It was expected, a part of life. But this wasn't the world she'd grown up in; she had to remember that.

"I'll keep that in mind, Old Henry," she said thoughtfully. She slowly rose from the stool at the counter. "I certainly will." She picked up her purse, paid for her breakfast, and tucked the newspaper under her arm.

"Good luck," he called out, as she pushed through the door.

Emma walked down Forty-sixth Street toward Broadway. The city was slowly coming to life as shopkeepers opened their doors for business, delivery trucks rumbled down the streets, and people began to come out from behind closed doors. She took extra notice of who walked the streets, hailed a cab, and hurried about the start of the day. Men. Mostly men.

She frowned. The few women she did see were pushing baby strollers, or Negro women on their way to clean someone's home or office.

That wouldn't be her, she determined, picking up her pace as she headed farther uptown. Not her. She hadn't come this far to go back to what she'd left. Her future awaited her, only blocks away.

▲   ▲   ▲

When she arrived at Meridian Real Estate, a middle-aged man was just unlocking the front door.

"Excuse me," Emma said.

The man turned and looked Emma up and down over a pair of half-framed glasses. "Yes?" he asked with suspicion.

"My name is Emma McKay," she said clearly, having decided that Mackey sounded much too country. "I saw the ad in the paper and I've come to apply for the position." She folded her hands in front of her and held her breath.

He stared at her for another minute, slipping the lock and key in his suit pocket. "What would a pretty young girl like you want with a job like this?"

Emma cleared her throat. "Well, sir, I want to pay my own way, and I can do the job."

"How do you know that? I haven't told you want it entails."

"I'm a quick learner," she replied, completely unflustered.

He stared up at her for a long minute. "Come in," he finally mumbled.

▲ ▲ ▲

Within the hour, Emma was an employee of Meridian Real Estate. She was to replace the young man who'd gone off to join the army. Mr. Meridian barely explained her responsibilities as he flitted about the small, two-desk office like a firefly.

"You'll answer the phones, keep the client files, and . . . if I see that you're learning the business, I may let you take a client or two out for a visit to see a house or apartment. You will be here at eight o'clock sharp, and your day isn't over until the last client has been served." He looked her over and smiled. "A pretty face like yours may be just the thing we need to bring in some business."

"Yes, sir," she replied to all of his instructions, while she tried to remember the location of all the information he threw at her in a torrent.

He stood in front of her, his small, brown eyes and bulbous nose just reaching her chest. She could look directly down on the shiny bald spot in the center of his head. "Married?"

"No, sir."

"Engaged?" he asked, in a gruff mumble.

"No, sir."

"Good. Then you won't be running off anytime soon." With that, he turned away and busied himself at his desk. "Well, get to work," he ordered, when he realized she was still standing there.

Emma stood there, her face impassive.

Mr. Meridian peered over the top of his glasses. "Problem, Ms. McKay?"

"Well, sir. You didn't discuss my pay."

He pulled his glasses off and sat them down on the cluttered desk. He worked his thin lips in and out as if the words were stuck on his tongue. "Forty dollars a week"—he wagged a finger at her in warning—"and not a penny more."

She swallowed, nodded politely, and took her seat. Forty dollars! That was three times the amount she made working for Ms. Florene. A small fortune. Before long, she would have everything she wanted. Almost everything. But that would come in time. All in good time.

As the hot, summer months moved into fall, Emma adjusted comfortably into her new job, becoming capable in her duties. Her boss watched her silently, quietly monitoring her progress, pleased that he had made a good choice this time. Not like the others. Before long Mr. Meridian was leaving her alone to run the office. And just as he predicted, business had picked up since her arrival. However, Emma wasn't quite sure if it was her presence or the fact that every Monday morning Mr. Meridian made her stand outside the office. She handed out leaflets to everyone who passed Meridian Real Estate explaining that a person's dream home was just on the other side of Meridian's door. He'd even sent her out with a young couple in search of their first apartment after only a month on the job. A real coup.

While the weeks added up, so did her bank account, which she'd proudly opened with her first week's pay. Before long, she'd be able to move out of that dingy one-room into a livable apartment of her own. Very soon.

One day in late October, just before closing, Emma was once again alone in the office. She was busy filing away the day's paperwork when the bell over the door jingled.

When she turned, for the first time in her young life, something stirred deep within her. A sudden rush of heat flowed through her veins, and her heart beat a bit faster. Michael Travanti, her future, stood in front of her.

Twenty-two

—\wwwww—

"May I help you?" Emma asked calmly over the rapid thudding of her heart.

Michael, dressed in full army uniform, swept his cap from his head, uncovering inky black hair that glistened beneath the overhead lights. Even the standard buzz cut looked appealing on him. He was of medium height, not much taller than Emma, but his ramrod straight, regal bearing gave him the appearance of a towering knight—strong and invincible. His uniform coat spread snuggly across his shoulders, the sharp creases in his slacks, even and severe, fell just above highly polished black boots. One couldn't help but admire the angular structure of Michael's patrician face. Perhaps not considered classically handsome by many, there was a warmth and pleasantness about his Roman nose, rugged, square jaw, prominent cheeks, wide mouth, and warm olive complexion. What set him apart, for Emma, was his striking Mediterranean blue eyes that seemed to take in everything around him and savor it.

"I hope so," Michael replied, stepping farther inside.

Emma pushed the file drawer closed and moved behind her desk, for some reason needing to put a physical barrier between them. She stretched out her hand, indicating an empty chair. Noticing her hands were shaking, she folded them on top of the desk and linked her fingers tightly together.

Michael placed his cap on his lap. "I've been commissioned to New York, and I'd rather have my own place than live on the base." He smiled, revealing an even row of sparkling white teeth and an almost lopsided grin that snatched Emma's breath away.

"Did you have any place in particular in mind?" she asked, upon her recovery.

Michael leaned forward. "You're from the South, aren't you?"

Her face heated, the air catching in the pockets of her lungs.

"I can tell a southern belle a mile away." There was that grin again. "There's something different about southern women. They're softer, real ladies. Real genteel." He pressed his lips together. "Hmm. Mississippi, I bet."

The alarms rang in her head. She wasn't sure how much she should admit to him. Where would it all lead? But there was an honest openness about him that she couldn't resist. Yet she clearly understood that she must distance herself as far away from her past as possible. She swallowed hard before answering him.

"Biloxi."

"I knew it," he said, slapping his knee. "I've never been there, but I hear it's pretty nice."

She nodded, smiling tightly. "Have you thought about where you'd like to start looking?" Emma questioned, needing to turn the corner, move away from her and the dark road she kept behind her.

Michael leaned casually back in the chair. "That's what I was hoping you could help me with. What do you suggest?"

"We have a few rentals in the downtown area that might suit you." She paused a beat. "Is this for you and your family?"

He grinned again. "Just me. I haven't found anyone willing to put up with me yet." He looked long and intently into her eyes until she felt the heat snaking its way up once more from the bottom of her stomach to stain her cheeks. She was the first to look away.

Was it relief she felt, slowing the race of her heart? And if so, why relief? Why should it matter if he was single or not? But somehow it did.

"What about you?" he asked in return. "Husband, kids?"

She shook her head. "No. There's no one."

"What about your folks in Biloxi?"

"I have no one," she repeated, and the admittance of the half-truth filled her with a weight of unexpected sadness. Her gaze drifted away from the curiosity that played with the lights in his eyes.

"I—I'm sorry. I didn't mean to pry," Michael said, seeing the sadness take its place between them, blocking him from reaching out to her. He wanted to push it out of the way, make it step down, as he watched the feeling gather in strength, envelop her, making Emma one with it. He shoved words at it, forcing it to take heed, get out of his way.

"My friends say I talk too much. It's a bad habit I have. I hope you won't hold it against me."

Her smile momentarily faltered, then held. "It's fine. Really. It was a long time ago. I've gotten used to it." A vision of her mother's soft, brown face with its tender, sorrowful eyes loomed before her. She willed it away. "I could take you to see one of the vacancies now, if you like."

"I have nothing but time. I'm at your mercy. Drag me where you will," he added dramatically, and that made Emma smile.

She stood, surprised to find her legs a bit unsteady, as if she'd run for a very long time and suddenly stopped.

"What should I call you?"

"Oh, I'm sorry. My name is Emma McKay. But Emma is fine."

"Emma." He rolled the name around on his tongue, sampling the texture and flavor of it like a fine wine. He smiled at her, his blue eyes sparkling. "I like the sound of it. Simple and solid. Emma," he said again, storing it away. "I'm ready when you are. And you can call me Michael. Travanti to my commanding officer."

She gave a short nod of her head. "I'll just get my coat and lock the door; then we can go."

She was happy for the momentary distraction of locking up for the evening. It gave her a chance to try to clear her thoughts, put these new emotions in some sort of perspective. And in the midst of her swirling emotions, she realized she was also happy that she was wearing her new gray suit and brand-new wool coat with the real fur collar.

Certainly she'd grown slowly accustomed to being accepted and viewed as a white woman, she thought, locking one file cabinet and then the next. She no longer had to question whether it would be appropriate to walk into a store, a restaurant, a bank, or an office. She didn't get those suspicious or condescending looks anymore. She sat where she wanted on a bus, in the company of white men and women, held a job no Negro woman would ever get. She was given keys of admittance wherever she went, and it wasn't to clean, or cook, or mend for someone else. And because they "believed" she looked like them, she *was* one of them.

She turned from the coat rack, and Michael darted around the desk to help her with her coat. In doing so his fingers brushed across her neck. A gasp rushed up to her throat, seeming to want to outrace the sudden tremor that ran along her spine. She turned, the air still jammed in her throat. He was staring at her. Not in a leering manner that made her uncomfortable, but in a way that somehow softened the angles of his face, gentled his mouth, and darkened his eyes with an inviting warmth. No one, not even her mother, had ever looked at her that way, as if there was more to their observation of her than pity, shame, and ridicule.

"I, uh," he glanced down at his shoes, then at her. "This may sound very forward, Emma, but—and I hope you don't mind me saying this—but you're quite beautiful." He pulled in a chestful of air, then chuckled self-consciously. "I don't think I've ever said that to a woman I just met—or at all," he admitted. He twisted his cap in his hands nervously.

Emma couldn't move, seemed to forget how to breathe. No one had ever called her beautiful. No one. Except that man that day by the river, but it was near dark and she was never certain if he meant what he said. *Beautiful.* Her eyes suddenly burned and filled. She began to button her coat.

"I'm sorry if I embarrassed you. I told you everyone says I talk too much. And I spend a lot of time apologizing."

"It's"—she swallowed—"I . . ." Emma didn't know where to look. "It's a first for me, too," she admitted, barely above a whisper.

For several breaths, they both stood facing each other, an unspoken, unexpected crossing of boundaries had taken place, surprising them with its lightening flash of intensity.

"We'd better go," Emma said finally.

Michael followed her out, mindlessly sat next to her on the crosstown bus, intermittently stealing short, reassuring glances at her, reminding himself that she was real. There was an aura of mystery about Emma Mc-Kay, something just out of reach: the way she held her head high, her back straight, looking neither right nor left, an invisible blockade between her and the world, protecting her from what, he didn't know. Yet in total conflict with this cool, almost icy aloofness, there rested a need, a longing, that lay beyond her shimmering green eyes, just at the edges of her mouth, something he believed had never been filled. To look at Emma McKay, one immediately saw a beautiful, almost delicate flower, heart-breaking loveliness combined with a naïveté sheathed in steely determination that radiated from the center of her being. And all together, she was irresistible.

▲　▲　▲

They disembarked at Twenty-seventh Street and went into the third building from the corner. It was a simple railroad apartment with one bedroom, a utility kitchen, small living area, and bath.

Michael off-handedly checked cabinets, beneath the sinks, window frames, and door locks. He took his time with his inspection, meticulously searching for every defect or flaw.

Upon completing his military inspection, he smiled and turned to face her. "I'll take it."

"You will?"

"This will suit me fine." He crossed the room from the kitchen to close the distance even more, standing directly in front of her. "Will you visit me sometime?"

Emma was stunned. Is that what he expected? She moved back a step. Was it proper for a lady to visit a man in his home? That's not how things were done back home. No young lady visited a man, even a suitor, without a chaperone. She was confused for a moment. She didn't know. Had no experience with such things.

"I'm sorry. There I go again with my big mouth," he quickly apologized, when he saw the stricken look on Emma's face. He didn't want to appear overly aggressive or forward. "I should never have asked you anything like that. Please forgive me."

Emma shoved her hands into her pockets and stared at the floor. "It's all right."

"No, really. I'm sorry. My intentions are perfectly honorable. I should have asked you to dinner first." He grinned as she looked up in wide-eyed surprise.

"Dinner?"

"Yes, Emma McKay. Would you do me the honor of having dinner with me?" He swept his hat from his head and bowed low as if in the presence of royalty.

Emma giggled, actually giggled, the lighthearted sound of it foreign to her ears. "I—I don't think . . ."

"Please say yes, Emma," he pleaded in a low, deep tone that settled down in the pit of her stomach and sent a deliciously intoxicating wave of sensation pulsing through her.

She'd never been asked to dinner, to be a part of anything. It was something she'd only imagined when she saw couples through the restaurant glass, laughing over a cup of coffee, a plate of food. Only imagined what it would be like to have her chair pulled out for her, her hand held firm and gentle in a man's secure grasp. She'd seen it, wondered about it, but never believed it would ever be a part of her reality.

"Say yes, Emma." He continued his effort to woo her to join him for a meal.

"Yes," she gushed. "I'd like that."

And so it began, that first night in early November, in an empty apartment on Twenty-seventh Street in 1949. The start of a romance that surprised them with its power, its durability, its joys.

▲ ▲ ▲

Michael met Emma after work each evening and took her to picture shows, dinner, or maybe just a walk along the brightly lit avenues. He bought her flowers, boxes of chocolates, embroidered handkerchiefs with her initials. He was the gardener tending to a field that had been left fallow. His tenderness, laughter, and easy way of giving showered down upon the parched wasteland of Emma's soul, spreading its nurturing waters until she bloomed, day by day. His touch clipped the thorns from her heart that kept people at bay. His smile was the sunshine that strengthened her belief that she was worthy. Now over the weeks that tumbled toward the holidays, Emma actually looked forward to spending it with someone who mattered to her.

Still, even as Michael watched and was part of the magical transformation, there was a part of Emma that he was unable to touch, parts of her life she was unwilling to share, like her family, her friends, her past. It was almost as if Emma McKay hadn't existed before he met her.

▲ ▲ ▲

As was still her custom, Emma rose with the sun and had her breakfast at the diner with Old Henry.

"You're looking brighter and brighter, Miss Emma," Old Henry commented, as he wiped down the counter and placed her coffee cup in front of her.

Emma smiled politely. "Thank you."

"There's a glow to your cheeks and a sparkle in your eyes these days." He leaned close enough for Emma to see the fine pores on his cheeks. He lowered his voice even though they were the only two people in the diner. "I think you found yourself a young man. That's one sure thing to put some color in a lady's cheeks."

Was her happiness that obvious, she wondered, feeling her face flame with embarrassment.

"You just make sure he treats you good. You deserve it." He turned back toward the grill, cracked two eggs, and let them drop onto the sizzling surface.

Deserve it. Deserve to be treated good. Until she met Michael, she'd always felt that what she deserved were *things:* new clothes, shoes, a seat on a bus, a good job, a window seat in a restaurant, to walk down any street and not be scorned for who her mother was and the color of her own skin in the wrong place. Those were the things she thought she deserved because they replaced the one thing she knew she'd never have or wasn't worthy of receiving, the love of another.

Now, under Michael's tender care, she'd gradually begun to believe that she could feel genuine happiness, and that perhaps she was worth someone's time and attention. Yes. She did deserve to be treated well—finally.

The paperboy brought in a stack of the *Daily News,* bound tightly in white cord, and deposited them on the counter with a thud.

"Hey there, Billy."

"Mornin', Mr. Henry, sir. Mornin', Miss Emma," the young, colored boy greeted them.

"Good morning, Billy." She smiled briefly at him. His young, shining brown face and large, round eyes beneath a cap of crinkly, black hair reminded her of the children back home in the Delta. For an instant, a pang of melancholy settled within her, gentle as a feather, nothing heavy, but just enough to stir the embers of memory.

At times, the early hours before dawn, or the evening in that instant between dark and light, she'd long for home, the familiar, the comfort of kinfolk. The beat and rhythm of country-flavored voices that could dull the aches, send the spirit soaring, weave a tale, and set you straight. The voices that flowed like a river, sounded like music to the trained ear, the laughter that was as hearty and rich as the soul, still coursed through her veins. At times she missed that music, the rhythm, the smell of rich, tossed earth, the aroma of fat back simmering in a pot of freshly picked greens, chicken fried until it was golden in a vat of sizzling, seasoned grease.

Car horns, sirens, and fumes replaced the twitter of birds, the hoot of the owls, and the scent of green grass and pine. Concrete, glass, and steel threatened to rob all that was pure and natural in her, but that would never happen. The Delta would always occupy the center of her being, of who she was.

Yes, there was a part of herself that would always be tied to those memories, a part of her that would need to drink of who she really was, feel the need to be among the familiar. She could, from time to time, walk through that colored world, brush up against brown and black skin, inhale the richness of their scent, listen to the lyrical cadence of their voices, take what she needed to replenish and then return. But she also understood that these very same things that she revered in the deepest recesses of her being had never and would never accept her, even as she cried out for them to do so.

Emma blinked and lightly shook her head, scattering the thoughts and images. When she glanced beside her, the paper was tucked next to her plate.

Staring back at her from the front page of the *News,* waving to the crowd, was William Rutherford at a fund-raising dinner at the Waldorf-Astoria for his run for Senate. There was a better picture of him this time, clearer than the previous grainy one. Emma slowly raised the paper and read the article prominently displayed on page three.

She still had the wrinkled article that Margaret had mailed to her mother. She'd kept it with her, tucked away in the corner of her wallet. Each night before she went to sleep, she read it again, spread it out on the wobbly dresser top, and stared at his face, then hers, in the mirror. She'd hear her mother's words of denial that William Rutherford was only a man she'd worked for over a short time. Just another man. She'd hear the words of denial accompanied by the pained and guilty look in her mother's eyes, and her stomach would roll, its acid rising to her throat and burning her tongue, threatening to expel everything in it. Her head would grow light and her legs weak, as wave upon wave of sickness would sweep through her.

However, the sickness became less overwhelming with time, slowly replaced with the raw bitterness of revenge for what had been done to her. She stared nightly at the smug, patronizing expression on Rutherford's face. Even the cold, severe line of his lipless mouth said: here was a man in control, a powerful, white man who never knew the meaning of lack, defeat, surrender, guilt, or the word, "sorry." She'd see Rutherford beg and plead for forgiveness. He'd pay for every night of suffering she had endured. She embraced her hatred—that familiar emotion—holding it close like a tender lover, letting it suckle at her bosom, a nagging child who needed constant attention.

Emma knew where he lived with his wife, Lizbeth, the pencil-thin, white woman who stood next to him in the new article. She'd simply looked the address up in the directory. They resided in a sprawling high rise on the Upper West Side of Manhattan, facing Central Park.

On several occasions she'd taken the train to Seventy-second Street and walked along the side of the park, wondering if she'd see him come from his building, walking with his wife, and what she would do if he did.

She'd grown bold one Saturday afternoon and entered his building. She walked directly up to the blue-suited, gold-buttoned doorman and asked quite plainly for William Rutherford.

"I'm sorry, Miss, but Mr. Rutherford and his wife are on holiday. Would you care to leave your name and a message?"

Her pulse pounded in her ears. She raised her chin a notch. "Yes. Please tell him that his daughter, Emma, stopped by, and I'll call again."

"Did you say daughter, Miss?" asked the bewildered man. Having known and worked for the Rutherfords for more than a decade, he'd never known them to mention a daughter.

Emma arched her thin, right brow, her mouth tilting downward in distaste. "I wasn't aware that my father allowed the hired help to involve themselves in the business of the family," she said, in the imperious tone she'd heard white men and women use on common laborers or anyone they considered an inferior.

"I—I'm sorry, Miss. It's just that . . ."

She held up her gloved hand to stop him. "Do pass along my message."

Emma spun away, dizzy with the thrill of what she had done. She basked in the glow of the thought of his panic once her message was conveyed. Briskly she walked down the tree-lined street, her legs shaky, her heart ready to burst from her chest, down a street that didn't smell of fumes, garbage, and unfulfilled dreams. It smelled of money, success, realities that were born of dreams come true. This was her world, a world denied her by the color of her mother's skin. But no more. She would get what was rightfully hers. And she would get her revenge.

She had even taken to calling his home periodically—never at the same time—just needing to hear the voices that lived behind those ornate concrete walls. Once she'd actually gotten *him* on the line when she'd called in the middle of the day. She'd thought she was prepared, had steeled herself against any sort of emotion, but she hadn't.

The deep, almost gentle rustle of his voice stunned her, sealed her lips tightly over the words that tried to force their way along the ridged path of her tongue and through the barrier of her clenched teeth.

"Hello? Hello?" Slowly she replaced the receiver, the echo of Rutherford's voice ringing in her ears.

Then another voice, a familiar, friendly voice brought her back to the cocoon of the diner. "Want me to refill that for you, Miss Emma?"

With the spell of memory broken, Emma blinked, looked up at Old Henry in momentary confusion. "Pardon me?"

"You want a refill?" he asked again, looking at her curiously. She nodded. "You sure was looking at that story hard. Somebody you know?" He replenished her coffee.

Emma's heart began to thunder. "No."

Old Henry turned the paper around to read the front page. He chuckled. "William Rutherford. Plenty rich. He's sure to buy his way into the congress. I don't trust none of 'em. Living in big, fancy houses, with fancy cars, people waiting on them hand and foot. What do they know about what hard-working people really need?" He turned the paper back around. "I hear it's near one hundred dollars to get into one of those shindigs."

Emma's eyes momentarily flashed. "Really?"

"So I hear," he said, turning back to the grill.

Emma read the rest of the article. There was another fund-raiser scheduled for the following month, a Christmas ball at the Plaza Hotel.

One hundred dollars, she thought. And she would be there.

Twenty-three

~~~~~~~~~~~

Christmas was less than three weeks away. The holiday in New York City brought out a never-ending army of shoppers, filling the brightly decorated streets, cluttering the stores in search of gifts. Even the number of cars on the thoroughfares seemed to multiply and often their horns sounded well into the night. It was like nothing Emma had ever seen before. And something else Emma had never witnessed before lay spread out before her one day when she awoke—a brilliant white blanket of snow. Tiny white crystals trickled down from puffy clouds, looking like miniature diamonds against the still darkened sky.

Emma rubbed her hand in a circle against the steam-coated window, giving her a better view of this brand-new world. She'd never seen anything like it before and wondered what it felt like against her skin.

Quickly she dressed in her heaviest wool coat, wrapped a scarf around her head, and went out into the street. Turning her face up to the sky, she giggled as the wet flakes fluttered across her cheeks, hung on her eyelids. She laughed mightily when she discovered she could see the warm plumes of her breath against the frigid air. An old, dark woman walking past her stopped and smiled at her with a subtle hint of remembrance of a time when she was young and first experienced the wonders of winter. For Emma, it was a glorious moment, much like a toddler taking that first step or a young girl discovering the sensation of a first kiss, the revelation, the newness of it. She felt the exhilaration of the experience, a time of new beginnings and self-affirmation. It was times like these that rewarded her decision to leave Rudell to find her place in the

187

world, to seize her time before life made her decisions for her. There was no turning back now.

Emma looked around her, beyond the rows of buildings, to what lay on the other side of her corner of the universe. She inhaled the crisp, clean air. Her new journey was underway and everything seemed possible; everything was within her grasp. All she had to do was reach out and take it. And she would.

▲ ▲ ▲

"I had no idea you were interested in politics, Em," Michael commented, as they walked toward his newly purchased car, a shiny silver Ford coupe, at the end of Emma's workday.

"There are a lot of things I'm interested in. Politics happens to be one of them," she said, slipping her arm through his.

Michael kissed her cheek. "You constantly amaze me, Emma McKay. One day I think I know all about you, and the very next day I feel I know so little."

"I'm really quite easy to understand. I want to expand my world, my life, whatever that takes," she said, with an edge of gutsy determination that Michael had never heard in her voice before. "I don't believe in letting fate rule your life. Sometimes you have to take matters into your own hands."

He looked at her curiously. "What does this ball have to do with taking matters into your own hands? How will it expand your life?"

"It's the people you meet in this world that lay the path for change, Michael." She stared him in the eye. "You and I are a perfect example of that."

He was thoughtful for a moment, taking in what she said. "You have changed my life. I'll admit that." He stopped and turned her into his arms. "Until I met you, Emma, I never thought of having anyone in my life, someone special to share my thoughts and dreams with." He caressed her lovely face. "That's all changed."

"Has it?" she asked in wonder.

"Emma, I love you. You're the most genuine, self-assured woman I've ever met. You're beautiful, intelligent, and inquisitive. The times we spend together are the best times of my life. My family"—his probing gaze rose then lowered and settled on her face once more—"they want what they want for me. They strongly believe in tradition and the old way of doing things. They want to control my life and everything in it. That was the main reason why I joined the army—to get away from them."

"You never told me that." She was briefly stunned by his admission.

"I know. I should have. I want you to know everything about me. No secrets. Especially if we're going to spend the rest of our lives together." His declaration hung in the air.

"Michael?"

"Marry me, Emma. I know this seems too quick, but I've never been more sure of anything in my life," he said urgently, grasping her shoulders.

A flood of thoughts and emotions went cascading through Emma. *Love, Marriage.* Fear, excitement, and joy mingled and took hold of her, filling her until she was sure she'd burst. No one had ever said they loved her. It possessed an incredible sweetness that went beyond words of explanation. It was all she'd ever wanted—love—pure and simple love. And now she had it. However, she was dizzy with doubt. If she married him, she would forever have to live her life as a white woman, live in a world of pretense. She'd planned this, lived this in her mind. But now that it was presented to her so easily, so effortlessly, ready for the taking, her hands trembled as she gingerly reached out to seize it. And once she did, once she took this other world into the palm of her hand and closed her fingers around it, there would be no chance to second-guess herself, to reconsider her choice. This lie, this masquerade, forged of love and opportunity, would become her life forever and ever.

Her heart raced. Emma wanted to run, run back to the Delta and Rudell. But she knew there was no place for her there. There never had been. A white woman among the coloreds. An outsider. A freak. Although no one had ever been openly disdainful to her, the harsh truth of what she was showed in their wary stares and polite tolerance of her presence. She looked into Michael's eyes, saw into his heart. Her place was here, where she was accepted for who she was, what she appeared to be. She knew she could be whoever he wanted her to be—that and more.

"Yes," she whispered, and everything around her seemed to settle. The wind that blew around them stilled, the snow that fell hung watchfully in the air, dancing around the crescent moon. Silence echoed along the darkened New York streets. The knot that curled inside her unwound. "Yes. I'll marry you."

Michael smiled as if he'd been given the greatest gift. He cupped her chin, tilting it upward until his mouth covered hers, breathing new warmth and possibility through her body. "You won't regret this, Emma. I'll make you happy, and everything you've ever dreamed of will be yours. You'll see. I swear to you."

Yet even as she listened to his words, reveled in his love, she believed that the only person who could guarantee her happiness was herself. She wouldn't rest until she had it all. And then maybe she could finally put the past and all its ugliness behind her and give Michael the love he had so readily given her.

▲ ▲ ▲

When Emma and Michael walked along the street toward the Plaza Hotel, she was surprised at the size of the crowd standing near the entrance, divided into two large groups held behind barricades. Michael watched her face, enjoying its shifting expressions of wonder and delight, while her eyes darted from one thing to the next. A squad of policemen separated the surging onlookers from the arriving dignitaries and celebrities as they stepped from their long, black cars onto the red carpet leading into the grand hotel. Photographers gathered like a flock of crows at the curb, snapping pictures of every person who looked important. Three uniformed peacekeepers rode on well-behaved horses around the fringes of the throng. Emma stopped and marveled at the spectacle of the event, listening at people shout out the names of various actors and actresses, sports figures, radio personalities, and politicians hurrying their way into the landmark building. She heard a woman yell, "Oh, God, there's Robert Montgomery, Robert Taylor, and Ronald Reagan." Another voice cried out, "The Duke, John Wayne, just got out of his car, and he's taller than I thought."

Emma was only momentarily distracted by the star-gazing, flashing cameras, crowd noise, and general mayhem because she was there on a mission. She needed to find Rutherford, to face him and hear the truth from his lips. Finally, she'd know everything that been concealed and kept from her.

▲ ▲ ▲

Easing to the front of the walkway, she watched the hotel security staff and police officers scrutinize the identification of every person permitted to enter the premises, no entry without proper clearance. There were no exceptions. After all, William Rutherford, the newspapers said, was an up-and-coming political. Tonight was his big, long-awaited announcement party and fund-raiser for the prized New York congressional seat.

"Do we have tickets for this thing?" Michael asked, wondering what they were doing at the hotel. "Do you know somebody in there?"

"Yes, I have connections," Emma said, laughing. "And no, we don't have tickets."

"How are we going to get in?" Michael quizzed her. They were dressed with sufficient style to enter the hotel and to attend the gala. But Michael was certain proper attire was not enough to get them beyond the front door.

Emma motioned for Michael to follow her, waving her hand like a plotting conspirator, and walked through the crowd to a catering truck where several men were unloading large trays of pastries and appetizers and hurrying into the side door—the unguarded door.

Emma strutted nonchalantly behind the delivery men, with Michael at her heels. She heard him whisper in her ear, "Emma, you're nuts. What are you doing?" She replied in a soft voice, "Just follow me and I'll explain everything later."

They walked into the chaotic kitchen where countless cooks, waiters, and waitresses scurried about oblivious to the new faces. Emma and Michael continued walking toward the door marked EXIT, periodically peeking at the array of foods to be offered as if they were inspecting the wares. The other side of the kitchen door opened upon a maze of corridors; Emma and Michael casually slipped out among the hotel's rich guests.

"Where are you going now?" Michael asked, holding his date by her waist.

"Upstairs. I've got to see a man about a secret," she joked.

"Huh?"

"No, really, I've got to see an old friend of the family, and he's only in town tonight," Emma lied, one of several she'd tell before the night was over. In order to live her new life, she would have to be quick on her feet with both responses and cover-ups. One slip and it was back to her old colored misery or, worst yet, Rudell.

Michael ran behind her, both strangely worried and excited. This was yet another Emma that had revealed herself, and he wasn't quite sure what to make of her. Would their married life be just as filled with surprises? "Emma, are you sure you're not a private eye or something?" he teased her, just before she stopped in front of a bank of elevators. She turned and gave him a quick peck on the lips, her eyes sparkling with mischief.

He watched her take in the full sweep and splendor of the hotel, and she was, for a moment, awestruck by its magnificence. Massive crystal chandeliers hung in perfectly placed order from towering, ornate ceilings. The marble floors reflected the glitter of the stiff-gowned women and tuxedoed, blue-blooded men gathered to do Rutherford homage. Slender white tapers placed throughout the spacious ballroom gave the entire space a fairy-tale appeal, their fluttering flames bouncing off the eggshell white walls.

Emma took a step, then sauntered toward the enormous dining room. There were another clot of security men, Rutherford aides, and city policemen near the entrance. From where she stood, she could see hundreds of circular tables covered in white linen with brilliant red poinsettias dotting the room. Bejeweled women with diamonds at their throats, ears, and wrists floated like angels up and down the spiral staircase, assuring themselves of being seen. Men stood in small herds, tossing back drinks, smoking cigars and cigarettes, while discussing the future of world politics, closing market prices, the Russians' activities in Berlin, and the Cold War.

Two more Rutherford staffers stood next to them near the elevator. They were discussing his appearance before the guests, an upcoming campaign stop the following day at a meeting of war veterans, and an evening press conference. Finally, the elevator came. Suddenly Emma turned to Michael, her hand pressing against his chest. "Wait for me. I'll be right back." Before he could protest, Emma stepped on with the two men and another couple and the doors slid shut. When the elevator came to their floor, the staffers exited and Emma followed.

Emma proceeded a half step behind the duo, who were too engrossed in their own conversation to pay her much attention. They continued down the plush hallway with its deep, red carpet and turned left at the end of a private corridor that opened onto a half-circular room where small knots of elegantly dressed men and women were gathered. Negro waiters soundlessly replenished drinks and whisked away empty platters. Here the voices were hushed, intense. None of the frivolity of the floor below. This was William Rutherford's inner circle. Among them stood William Rutherford, surrounded by those who would make him king.

She knew it was him as soon as she saw him. She'd studied his picture, matched it to the face she saw every day in the mirror. He was no longer a grainy, black-and-white image, flat and one-dimensional, he was flesh. Her flesh. Her breath stopped and started; the blood rushed to her head.

He stood there, proud and handsome, laughing with that big smile that surely won the hearts of many. There was an undeniable charisma about him. One that forced you to take notice, seduced you, drew you closer almost against your will. And then it seemed as if he sensed a new presence, and his gaze shifted suddenly in her direction.

All the air rushed from her lungs. Brilliant jade green eyes, *her* eyes, stared back at her. The resemblance was extraordinary, the connection in the genes sure and definite. If there was ever any doubt in her mind, it was gone.

William Rutherford examined her in a quick, sweeping glance, summing her up expertly. The corner of his mouth lifted in an absent smile. He nodded his head in a short acknowledgment, a brief frown darkening his smooth countenance, before turning back to his coterie of advisers and aides.

Emma drew in a deep breath of resolve and moved forward, feeling almost as if this was someone else's dream and she a mere observer floating through it. Everything around her took on a sense of unreality, filtered and viewed through a scrim. Like the historic waters of the Red Sea, the battalion of men bracketing Rutherford stepped gallantly aside as she stood before them, exhibiting an assured pose that left no doubt she belonged in this elite circle.

"Good evening, Mr. Rutherford," Emma said, in a terse greeting. She gripped her beaded purse in her hands.

Ever the aristocratic gentleman, Rutherford tilted his head to the right side and regarded her with a dispassionate glance. "You . . . look oddly familiar. Have we met?"

"I'm sure you're thinking of my mother . . . Cora Harvey, at the time. She cleaned your house, cooked your meals." Her voice rose in both pitch and tenor, emotion warring with reason as the long-awaited confrontation of her dreams unfolded rapidly before her eyes. "Picked up after you and your wife. Do you remember her now?"

One of his aides moved swiftly and expertly to Rutherford's side, cupped Emma's elbow, and whispered harshly in her ear. "Let's go, Miss. We won't have a scene."

Emma didn't move; she couldn't. It was not going the way she imagined. She stared Rutherford directly in the eye, saw his pupils widen in alarm, watched his face turn a dangerous crimson, stopping at the line of his thick, salt-and-pepper hair. "I'm Emma."

She stepped a bit closer, lowered her voice an octave, then leaned toward him with her face just inches from his. "The resemblance is shocking . . . isn't it . . . Dad?"

"Get her out of here," blustered Rutherford, his face suddenly drawn and flushed. "She's obviously drunk and on the wrong floor."

A tense silence followed. All eyes were on the promising congressional hopeful, waiting to see how he would handle such a potentially scandalous crisis. Mindful of his surroundings and his unflappable reputation, Rutherford chuckled and flashed his high-voltage smile. "Sorry, young lady. Wrong party."

On cue, the group chuckled nervously at their host's clever response, feeling it break the tension of the moment. But the gravity of the young woman's accusation was on all their faces. Just who the hell was she? Was what she said true? The staffers and others stole glances at each other. Those out of range of the initial confrontation tried to move closer and pick up what tidbits they could.

Despite the cool, detached demeanor of the man, Emma saw something in his eyes that let her know that he not only recognized her but was deathly afraid of the huge uproar she could cause. While she had been a New Yorker only a short time, she understood the damage that any one of the ten newspapers in the city, especially the tabloids, could inflict on a reputation or a career. Rutherford was no fool. He had a great deal to lose.

"There's plenty of press downstairs," Emma said, her tone taking on a threatening edge as her inner fury mounted. He wasn't going to toss her aside like so much garbage. She wouldn't let him. She wasn't Cora, her mother. "Since you're not interested in what I have to say, I'm sure the newspaper people will hang on my every word."

She snatched her arm away from his aide.

Rutherford held up his hand to halt any further outbursts. "Take her to my suite," he whispered from the side of his mouth. "I'll be right there."

Emma glared at him triumphantly and followed the aide out of the room, which had slipped into an uneasy silence.

Rutherford faced his audience, his expression open and affable as if nothing out of the ordinary had transpired. "Please, everyone, I apologize for the intrusion. Everything has been taken care of. Sometimes we have to handle these crackpots with kid gloves." He raised his glass of white wine in salute. "Drink up. This is a party, remember."

Rutherford smoothly mingled with his guests, passing a joke here, a scrap of information there. Heartily he patted his supporters on the back, kissed the cheeks and hands of their companions. Allowing a decent amount of time to pass, and feeling a sense of normalcy had returned, he excused himself, using the ruse that he must prepare for his upcoming speech in the ballroom. He hurried down the corridor to his penthouse suite, followed by two of his staffers.

Upon entering the lavish, eight-room suite, with its floor-to-ceiling windows that looked out upon the incomparable skyline of New York City, Rutherford spotted Emma standing before them, gazing out at the twinkling lights and multitude of stars. For an instant she looked fragile, vulnerable, and tiny almost, set against the enormity of the teeming city. But as he quickly discovered, this breathtakingly beautiful young woman was anything but weak and vulnerable. As much as he hated to admit it, he had to admire the guts it must have taken to walk into that room and confront him. It was the kind of thing he could see himself doing and had done on many an occasion. There was no place in the world for the faint of heart, the indecisive. You must go after what you wanted. No one was going to give you anything for free and without a fight. He'd learned that when he'd lost practically everything during the Depression. He'd earned his redemption in the business world and now in politics, and he'd be damned if he'd let some backwoods Negro upstart take that away from him.

"Leave us alone," Rutherford grumbled, shutting the door behind him.

The one staffer who'd stood sentry duty until Rutherford's arrival looked cautiously from him to Emma then reluctantly followed his colleagues. "We'll be right outside the door," the hired hand uttered under his breath as he passed Rutherford on his way out.

Slowly Emma turned from the window, raised her chin in battle-ready challenge.

"How dare you come here and toss around accusations," he growled, wanting to immediately take the offensive. "You speak of things you know nothing about."

Emma looked around with a hunger in her eyes at all that should rightfully be hers: the expensive furniture, plush carpet, the full-length, mink coat that was casually tossed across the couch, crystal glasses that glittered like diamonds along the ornate bar. Emma crossed the room and boldly poured herself a glass of wine. She took a sip, fortifying herself.

"Are you saying you don't know my mother?"

"I don't know what you're talking about," he insisted weakly.

"I have a letter."

His green eyes flashed. "What letter?"

Emma opened her purse and pulled it out, holding it with her fingertips, taunting him, thankful that it was only the envelope she'd lost. "The letter from Margaret. She worked for you, too. Remember her?"

His jaw clenched. "What do you want?"

"I want what you owe me."

"I don't owe you a damned thing."

"Did you at least care for my mother, even a little bit?"

Her question threw him off guard. He turned his back to her.

"I want to know. Did you care for my mother!" she shouted, her body suddenly trembling. She wanted to hear the truth.

At night he could still see her terrified face, tears streaming down her cheeks, hear her pleading with him not to do it. "Please, Mr. Rutherford, please," she'd begged him. But he wasn't listening. It was as if some monster had taken over his mind and all he wanted was to exact revenge, hurt someone or something, and she happened to be there. All these years, he'd tried to push that day out of his mind, pretend it never happened, but it haunted him day and night. And now the result of his recklessness stood before him, demanding retribution, wanting answers he could never give, would never give.

"I don't think you realize who you're dealing with, Emma, or whatever your name is. This is no game." He spun to face her. "Get out. Get out now before I have you arrested for harassment. I've given you as much time as I intend."

"Fine," she responded lightly, crossing the room to the door. "I'll go. I suppose I'll just have my chat with those hungry reporters downstairs." She opened the door.

Rutherford pushed it closed. "What the hell do you want?" he ground out.

They stood inches apart, powerful adversaries, father and daughter, bound by blood and will. Neither was ready to surrender, to back down.

"I want . . . enough money to take care of myself for a very long time."

"How do I know that if I pay you you won't come back?"

"You don't. All you'll have is my word."

"And I should take the word of a blackmailer. There're laws for people like you."

"Then call the police."

He stared into her face, the resemblance to his younger self completely unnerving him. "How much?" he finally relented. "How much will it take for me to be rid of you?"

"Two hundred thousand dollars. In small bills," she added, having heard that line in more than one motion picture.

He tossed his head back and laughed. "You're crazy."

"We'll just have to see, won't we?" She put her hand on the knob.

"All right. All right. But on my terms."

"What are they?" she challenged.

"He thought for a moment. I have this suite for one more day. Be here tomorrow at four o'clock, by yourself. I'll have your money for you. And then you go away. I don't ever want to see or hear from you again."

Emma pressed her lips together, her nostrils flaring as she tugged in air. Without another word, she pulled open the door and stood face-to-face with Lizbeth Rutherford.

Lizbeth's pale eyes widened in surprise then tightened in alarm when she looked upon the face that so completely resembled her husband's. She'd been the one who'd received the message from the doorman that Mr. Rutherford's daughter, Emma, had stopped by for a visit. He'd passed it off as some sort of crank, and over time she'd forgotten about it. But it was true; it always had been. Her eyes darted to her beloved husband's pained expression that said it all, just as Emma brushed by her and hurried down the hallway. She watched the young woman walk proudly and defiantly through the group of well-wishers, staffers, and guests gathered along the corridor.

Twenty-four

"You owe me an explanation, Emma," Michael demanded, as he helped her into her coat on the ground floor of the hotel. "I've been worried sick, pacing the floors down here like some sort of idiot, and you're off doing who knows what."

Emma slipped on her leather gloves, her mind still racing from the scene she'd just left. She barely heard Michael's complaint. What occupied her thoughts now was that it was done, contact had been made. Rutherford was going to pay up, and all her dreams would come true.

"Emma! I'm talking to you," he hissed through his teeth, mindful of the posh crowd. "Tell me what's going on. Whatever it is, I can handle it. I'm a big boy."

"Let's just go, Michael. I'll tell you all about it. I promise."

They found a small café several blocks away from the hotel. Emma ordered coffee, Michael started with a frosty mug of beer. He sipped it as he waited for Emma to explain what she had been doing at the hotel.

"You want to tell me what the hell is going on with you, Em. You sneak us into some star-studded gala, say you have to visit a friend of the family, then you disappear for more than an hour." His eyes blazed into a dark, stormy blue that penetrated her weak shield of deceptive calm, ready to explode. "Where were you?"

"I told you. I went to see a friend of the family." She tried to look him in the eye but couldn't. She concentrated on the menu.

"What family friend? Who is it?"

"Does it matter?" she tossed back over the top of the menu, using it almost as a defense against him.

"Yes. This time it does, Emma. We're planning on building a life together. How is that possible if we start it off with secrets between us?" He paused a beat. "You're acting like this 'family friend' is an old lover you don't want me to know anything about. Is that it, Em?"

She reached across the table and for the first time since she'd returned she was able to look him in the eye. "No, Michael. It's nothing like that at all."

"Then tell me what it is."

She swallowed, concocting her alibi as fast as humanly possible. "It wasn't a family friend at all," she confessed, lowering her head in shame. Then she looked up and stared him straight in the eye. "You're really going to think I'm mad."

"What is it, for heaven's sake?"

She blew out a breath. "I sneaked up to William Rutherford's suite, just to see if I could. Just to see what it was like," she admitted sheepishly. "I didn't think I'd ever get the chance again," she rushed on, caught up in her own fairy tale. "And . . . if I got caught . . . I didn't want to be embarrassed in front of you. I couldn't bear it." She lowered her gaze, feeling her mouth suddenly become parched.

For a moment Michael simply stared at her in astonishment, then abruptly burst into a fit of laughter. "Emma, Emma," he sputtered, "you are absolutely the most unpredictable, totally incredible woman I've ever met." He shook his head in delight. "I just know our life together is going to be full of surprises."

Emma smiled in relief, the half-truth of her lie moved easily into place between them, settled itself comfortably at the table, weaving itself permanently into the fabric of their relationship, forever and ever.

▲ ▲ ▲

Since the first day Emma began work at Meridian Real Estate, she had never been late or absent. So Mr. Meridian had no qualms about letting her leave early. She'd been a dependable employee; and as reluctant as he may have been about her capabilities in the beginning, he had no doubt that hiring Emma McKay had been the wisest decision he'd made.

Emma took the crosstown bus, then hailed a cab to the hotel. All the while on the short trip, her mind was racing as quickly as her pulse. What would he say? Suppose this was all a setup on his part, and he'd have his henchmen drag her off somewhere never to be seen or heard from again. She should have told someone where she was going, she thought, twisting and untwisting her hands as the taxi veered in and out of the late-afternoon traffic. But she couldn't very well do that either, could she?

"Two bucks, lady," the driver announced, as he squealed to a halt in front of the hotel. He peered up at the building's magnificence. "This place must cost a mint, huh?" he questioned. "Fancy pants rich folks living in the lap of luxury, and poor saps like me gotta scrimp and scrape for every nickel and dime." He glanced over his shoulder. "No offense, Miss, but ya gotta admit it's true."

Emma simply looked at him, too caught up in what lay ahead of her to concentrate on this grungy man's rantings. She pulled two single bills from her purse and handed them over, opened the door and slammed it, but not before she heard his last grumbling comment, "Nothin' worse than cheap rich folks!"

Emma's short heels clicked rhythmically against the pavement. She was a half hour early, but that's the way she'd planned it. The doorman pulled open the door and bid her a good afternoon. Emma barely nodded in response. She looked neither left nor right as she headed straight for the front desk.

"Would you ring Mr. Rutherford's room, please?"

"Who should I say is here, Miss?"

"Emma," she stated simply.

The concierge looked at her skeptically for a moment before picking up the phone. He spoke softly into the mouthpiece. "There's an . . . Emma here to see Mr. Rutherford. Yes, sir. Right away."

"You can go up. Penthouse floor."

"I know," she replied, making sure he understood that he was giving her no information she wasn't already privy to.

Emma crossed the same hallway she'd traversed less than twenty-four hours earlier and stood patiently in front of the elevator. Momentarily, the gold-plated doors soundlessly opened.

"Floor, Miss?" the elevator operator asked.

"Penthouse." She stared straight ahead, forcing her mind to stay clear, as the elevator slowly rose, the lighted floor dial ticking off the minutes to revelation.

The elevator opened onto the foyer of the penthouse suite. A Negro male servant greeted her at the door. "Mr. Rutherford is expecting you," he said quietly. "Please follow me."

Emma was escorted through the hushed cavern to a set of closed, white inlaid doors with gold doorknobs. The servant opened them, stepped aside as she walked past him, and quietly retired from sight. At first Emma thought she was alone, as she took in the palatial layout of what must be the study. Floor-to-ceiling bookcases lined one long wall, stacked from end to end with every manner of books, some appearing to be hundreds of years old.

In the center of the room was a wide mahogany desk that glimmered beneath the dimming sun streaming in from the bay window directly behind it. A gooseneck lamp, a marble paperweight, and a leather desk blotter were its only ornaments. Plush, overstuffed, brown leather furniture strategically dotted the glossy wood floors, surrounding an enormous Oriental rug of brilliant oranges and gold. The waning scent of cherry pipe tobacco hung in the air. On the far side of the room was a grilled fireplace, its warming flames dancing along the perfectly placed logs of wood, tossing abstract shadows along the walls and floors.

"You're early."

The well-modulated voice came from the recesses of the room. Emma turned toward the sound, momentarily startled.

Rutherford appeared like an apparition from behind a door she hadn't noticed upon her arrival. His dark suit elegantly covered his long, still lean body. He purposefully crossed the room in measured strides to stand behind his desk. He pulled open the drawer and extracted a brown envelope then dropped it with a thud on the desktop; the sound like an explosion reverberated throughout the high-ceilinged room.

Cautiously, Emma moved forward, back straight, head held proudly aloft. "I wanted to be sure you were here," she answered, in response to his comment, sounding bolder than she felt. She stood directly in front of him, the desk being the only thing separating them.

It was then she noticed his haggard appearance, nothing like the well-groomed, self-assured man of the night before, even clothed in what was obviously an expensive, handmade suit. His eyes were red-rimmed with half-moon shadows underscoring them, and there was a faint outline of stubble coating his angular jaw. The smooth control he'd previously exhibited was replaced with short, almost stilted movements, like a person forced to concentrate on every action.

Rutherford turned away under her scrutiny and recrossed the room to the bar. Pouring himself a tumbler of scotch, he drank it straight down, the brief shutting of his eyes being the only indication that the potent spirits had any effect on him.

"There's your money," he said stiffly. "Take it and go. Isn't that what you wanted?" He poured himself another drink, straight without ice.

"I want the truth," Emma said firmly. "I want answers."

Rutherford's eyes narrowed, becoming penetrating and steely. "You want money. You want to ruin my life, my reputation with your lies and accusations. If that money will make you go away, then so be it." He tossed down the drink.

"Ruin *your* life?" she stammered incredulously. "*Your* life? Do you have any idea how you've ruined *my* life?" She stepped closer. "Look at me. Take a good look at me. What do you see?" Her glare pinned him in place. "A woman who has spent all of her life not knowing where she belonged, not fitting in, having everyone around her whispering things about me—my mother. Do you know what it feels like not to know who you are—*why* you are? Do you know what it feels like to have your own mother look at you with emptiness and shame—the one person in the world who is supposed to love you without question?" Tears of anguish and desolation rolled in steady streams down her pale face. "Look at me, damn you to hell! This is what you've done." She pounded her finger at her chest. "You've ruined *my* life!" Her entire body trembled with rage.

He seemed to crumble before her tear-filled eyes, the solid seams of his righteousness splitting open under her razor-sharp assault. His throat worked up and down, the words trapped there for almost two decades, never uttered, had congealed into a knot of remorse that was more devastating than anything he'd ever endured. But to admit that was something he was incapable of doing, standing before this woman who longed to find some part of herself that would somehow validate who she was. To confess to what he had done would make the nightmare of that day a reality, a reality he still couldn't acknowledge even now. There was no forgiveness or absolution for his depraved deed. And he accepted that. As long as he kept it tucked inside, he could somehow face the day and go out into the world with his mask intact. The worst thing, he understood, was to confess to oneself that there was a corruption, an illness of the soul, that enabled you to become everything you detested in others.

Yet here she stood. The product of a warped, heinous episode in his life. A young woman who needed more than he could ever hope to give. A young woman who, under any other circumstances, he would open his arms, his heart, his home to. A woman he would be proud to call daughter. But he couldn't. They both knew that. So all he could hope to give her was the money, make a small down payment on his redemption, and perhaps things would somehow be right. Truthfully, he knew nothing would ever be right.

"Your payment should be answer enough," he uttered, his tone hard and controlled. For the first time since her arrival, he looked directly into her eyes, hoping to convey with a single glance what he couldn't say with words.

Emma pressed her lips together, drew herself up, and took the damning envelope from the desk. Without another word or a backward glance, she walked stiffly toward the door.

As he watched his daughter walk away and out of his life, his final words reached out and wrapped around her. "I never meant . . . to hurt your mother. Never."

Emma's step faltered then settled. Her head raised a notch and her shoulders straightened. For the beat of a heart, she stood there, let his words reach down to that dark, tortured place in her soul, and finally there was light. She dropped the envelope at her feet, opened the door, and walked out.

Twenty-five

~~~~~~~~~~

For days after her meeting with Rutherford, Emma was withdrawn, almost sullen, so unlike the vivacious, fun-loving woman Michael had come to know. And there seemed nothing he could do or say to rescue her from the place where she'd vanished deep inside herself. Nothing he did had any lasting effect on her gray mood. Even her favorite Godiva chocolates had barely raised a smile. Tickets to a Broadway play brought a momentary light to her eyes, and then it was gone. Admittedly, when they'd first met and started courting, Emma had been reserved and cautious. But over time he'd seen the changes in her, seen her bloom into the exquisite flower he'd grown to love.

Having moved out of the rooming house, she was now living in a neat, one-bedroom apartment in downtown Manhattan. As he watched her move soundlessly through the kitchen, preparing their dinner, he was overcome by the sadness that radiated from her like body heat. She was hurting and he didn't know why, and because of that he was hurting, too.

"Em," he said, easing up behind her and pecking her with a gentle kiss on the back of her neck. "What's wrong, sweetheart? You haven't been yourself in days." He slipped his arms around her waist and pulled her close.

Emma let her body fold against him, allowing the comfort of his embrace to temporarily soothe her. She was deeply conflicted about what course to take with Michael. Didn't love mean openness and honesty? She desperately wanted to talk to Michael candidly, to expose the ugly truth of her secret, to tell him everything that had happened, who she really was, where she'd

come from, yet knowing that if she did, everything gained from her sacrifice, toil, and suffering would be quickly snatched from her. She'd be
tossed back into that nether world of gray, that limbo existence of Jim Crow,
where everything was defined in stark black and white. For all appearances,
she looked, spoke, and acted the part of a white woman. No one, no one,
had ever questioned that. It was a masquerade that held up under the
closest scrutiny. But inside, in her soul, she was a Negro and always would
be. She'd perfected the art of walking that thin color line and succeeded,
but at what cost? Instead of Rutherford's admission freeing her as she'd
momentarily felt it did, in truth, it trapped her in a void she'd never be
free of. She'd spent most of her life living with an inner rage at her mother
and the mystery man who was her father, only to discover that they were
both only humans—who'd made irreparable choices. And so had she.

Emma turned into Michael's embrace and rested her head on his chest.
Tenderly, he stroked her hair. "Talk to me, Em. Something's troubling you.
If we talk about it, maybe I can help."

She looked up into his eyes, saw the love there, felt it in the beat of his
heart. And she knew she could never tell him. Never. He believed too
deeply in her, trusted her, an unconditional trust she didn't deserve. But
she was unwilling to lose anything or anyone else.

"I know I've been acting out of sorts lately." She stroked his cheek fondly.
"I've just been worried, that's all."

"About what?"

She fumbled for an answer and found the truth. "I'm worried that I
won't be the wife you deserve."

"Em, how could you think that? You're perfect. Everything I've ever
wanted."

"But what about your family, Michael? I know that as much as you want
to rebel against them, what they think is important to you. What if I don't
measure up?"

He took her by the hand and led her to the couch. He was thoughtful
for a moment. "You're right. My family is important. But not more important to me than you are. Nothing is. When they meet you, I know they'll
love you as much as I do. Once we're married, I know they'll accept you
as part of the family."

"Are you sure?"

"Absolutely." Michael sounded so convinced that there could be no op-
position from anyone in his family. "Is that what's been bothering you?"

She nodded.

"Why don't we get married right away," he said suddenly. "We could go down to the justice of the peace and make this official."

"Just like that?"

"Why not? We love each other. We want to be together. There's nothing stopping us, Emma. Besides, I don't want you getting cold feet and running off on me."

She stared at him for a long, tortuous moment, saw all the promises of a real future swimming in his eyes. "All right. All right. Let's do it," she agreed, casting all doubt to the wind. "Let's do it."

▲ ▲ ▲

On January 15, 1950, Emma McKay married Michael Travanti, and the pact that would ultimately spring forth a new generation was sealed.

Twenty-six

A week after the impromptu wedding, Emma and Michael flew to Europe to meet his family, who were living in Milan. He'd taken a two-week leave from his position serving as a military liaison attached to a unit stationed at Fort Lee to enjoy his Italian honeymoon, and show his beautiful new wife the wonders of Europe.

Emma had never been so nervous in her life as when they pulled up in front of the Travanti family's sprawling villa on the outskirts of the old city. It was a majestic, two-story home, built of hand-polished stone, with a balcony that circled the entire structure and acres of surrounding land set against the Milan countryside. Sailboats could be seen on the nearby man-made lake. A few hundred yards away, the family vineyard, one of the most profitable in all of Milan, was situated near a large grove of trees.

"Well, darling, this is where I grew up," Michael announced.

"Michael, you never—"

He hopped out of the car to be met by one of the many servants, who profusely greeted him and took their bags from the car.

"*Signore* Michael! It is so good you are home," the man beamed as if Michael was his own prodigal son. He hugged him tightly, kissing him on both cheeks.

"*Graxie,* Paolo, *Graxie.* It's good to be back." He chuckled, patting the man solidly on the back. He rounded the car and opened Emma's door. "This is my wife, Emma." He stretched his hand to help her out.

Stunned, Emma slowly alighted from the car, trying to take it all in.

"*Signora.*" He inclined his head and smiled politely. "Welcome and congratulations." He turned back to Michael. "Your parents are in the garden waiting for you. I will take these bags upstairs. To your old room. Yes?"

"That will be fine, Paolo."

The man hurried away, waddling from left to right from the weight of the suitcases.

Michael glanced quickly at Emma and squeezed her hand reassuringly. "It'll be all right, I promise you," he whispered, as they made their way along the expansive, grass-covered grounds to the back of the house.

"But, Michael, you never said anything about your family . . . being . . ."

"Rich?" He smiled. "I didn't want to scare you off." He pecked her on the lips. "Come on. And don't look so frightened. They'll love you."

About a half-dozen occupied tables, topped with a rainbow of umbrellas and laden with an indescribable amount of food, greeted them upon their arrival. A small bandstand beneath a white canopy, now filled with white-tuxedoed musicians, had been constructed at the far side of the seating area. Bubbling laughter and rapid-fire conversation could be heard coming from the collection of guests seated amid the aroma of smoked sausages, sautéed shrimp with garlic, baked breads, pasta, pies, and flowing wine.

"Michael!" A statuesque, brunette beauty stood with open arms when she spotted him. She possessed dark, dancing eyes, with sweeping brows and a perfect sun-washed tan layering her warm, olive complexion.

With Emma in tow, Michael expertly mingled with the guests, speaking to familiar faces gathered at the tables. "Mama."

The woman who looked young enough to be his sister cupped his face in her slender hands and looked lovingly into his eyes, her smile as brilliant as the sun that shone above them. But upon closer inspection, Emma could make out the fine lines that touched her expressive eyes and outlined her mouth, giving her added character rather than diminishing her beauty.

"My son. You've finally come home." She drew him to her, smothering his face with countless kisses. Finally she stepped back and looked him over with the eyes of a mother inspecting her child before sending him out into the world. "You look thin. They work you too hard in that American army. You need to come home and work with your father, where you belong."

Michael chuckled. "You say that every time you see me, Mama."

She reared back in feigned surprise. "Because it's true." Her attention snapped to Emma. "And this is the Emma you wrote to me about?"

"Yes, Mama. This is Emma . . . my wife. Emma, my mother, *Signora* Marguarite Travanti," he said formerly.

"Pleased to finally meet you . . . Mrs. Travanti." Emma froze as the all-seeing eyes rode slowly up and down her body. Where only an instant earlier the rich mouth was turned up into a welcomed smile of greeting for her son, it was now a thin, tight red line of barely concealed suspicion, or perhaps it was her own conscience she saw in Marguarite's eyes.

Slowly, the hardened countenance of Marguarite began to ease and the smile returned, illuminating the dark clouds of her eyes. "Welcome to the family, Emma. If my son loves you as much as he says he does, we will love you, too. And you must call me Mama." She graciously stepped forward and embraced the terrified Emma in her arms, kissing her cheeks. Easing back, she stretched her arm dramatically across the gathering. "As you see, we have prepared a feast in honor of your wedding." Then her tone turned conspiratorial. "You know your papa is still upset that you married without his knowledge or permission. But I have talked to him on your behalf." She turned to Emma, gently taking her hand. "And once he sees the choice you have made, he will come around. I am sure of it."

"Where is Papa?"

"In the study. Being stubborn. Go inside. See him before too much time has passed."

"Thank you, Mama."

She patted his cheek. "Go, go. The party will wait for you and Emma."

Marguarite watched the young couple move through the gathering, greeting the guests and accepting their congratulations. Finally, she turned away, put on her most sociable face, and went back to playing hostess to her son's many reception guests.

The heavy drapes were drawn, enveloping the room in near darkness. A lone lamp was lit on the desktop, giving the room a haunting, sinister feel. Emma gripped Michael's hand tightly as they entered the patriarch's inner sanctum.

"Just relax," he whispered.

A shadow moved out of the high-backed, leather chair and stood to its full height. Emma could just make out the slowly moving figure in the dim room. He was stout, shorter than Michael, clothed in a dark suit, as if he'd returned from a funeral. The dank, pungent smell of cigar smoke hung in small clouds about the room.

"Papa, why are you sitting in the dark?" Michael pulled Emma closer. "I want you to meet Emma. Emma, this is my papa, Salvatore Travanti."

The man moved across the room without a word and sat behind the desk. Michael turned on the lamp, and the face became fully illuminated.

He had thick, graying hair, cut close to his head, with matching bushy brows and thin mustache. The resemblance between father and son was immediately clear. Although Michael obviously took his height from his mother, he had his father's strong Italian features. With an easy, deliberate manner, the man folded his thick fingers on the desk, ignoring the introduction.

"You come to me now after the deed is done. That is not the respect that your father is due, Michael," he said, in a thickly accented voice. "First you leave the family business, the business that I built for you, my son, and you run off to America. And now this."

"Aren't you going to at least ask me how I am, Papa? It's been more than a year."

"I see how you are," he grumbled, "an ungrateful, disrespectful son." He turned his heavily lidded eyes on this stranger, Emma. "How could you have married such a man who has no respect for family?" he demanded to know.

Emma opened her mouth, about to reply, then closed it.

"Papa," Michael interjected, "I have to live my own life. I told you that years ago. I'm an American citizen, born in the United States. This life you want me to live is not what I want. I do not have disrespect for the old ways, your ways, but this is a different time. Emma married me because she loves me, as I love her. I didn't come all this way to fight with you, Papa. I'm tired of fighting with you. Let's put our quarrel behind us. Emma's part of our family now."

He grumbled something under his breath. "Let me see this woman you love." He waved his hand in a short, abrupt motion. "Step closer," he instructed Emma, which she did. His eyes shrunk to two slits as he studied her carefully from head to toe. "Hmmm." He opened a box and pulled out a fat cigar, ran the tip through his mouth, then lit it, the smell wrinkling Emma's nose. He wagged a finger at her. "I hope your sons are not as disrespectful as this son of mine," he said in warning. "You treat my son good, yes?"

Emma swallowed down the dryness in her throat. "Yes, sir."

"Hmmm. Maybe something will become of him one day then."

Michael chuckled. "Maybe, Papa."

He waved them away. "Go. Go back to your party. Your mother is all excited. Do not deny her this happiness."

"Aren't you going to join us, Papa? This is a celebration. It won't be complete without you," Michael cajoled.

"I am not feeling well," he complained. "I think I'll sit here for a while."

Michael bit back a smile. "As soon as you're feeling better, will you come outside?"

"Hmmm," he grumbled again, blowing a cloud of blue smoke into the air.

Michael began to lead Emma out of the room, holding her confidently as a young lover would do.

"Where did you say you were from . . . Emma?"

"I'm from Mississippi, sir."

His eyes widened in alarm, thinking of all the things he'd heard of the brutal American South, where men cruelly spoke of the pope as the Antichrist and Catholics as pagans, and he quickly made the sign of the cross. *Holy Mother, protect my son.*

Michael shook his head sadly and took his bride to meet the rest of the family.

The celebration went on for hours, with countless toasts and well wishes, mostly directed at Michael. Emma was received with a detached, cool acceptance and wary looks. Most of them knew very little about Americans, so they considered her a foreigner and not worthy of the respect paid to one of their own. The music, food, and laughter continued unabated well into the night, and Emma felt the full weight of the tight scrutiny of the family guests, who closely watched her every move. All she wanted to do was to leave, to get away from these people who would never accept her or accept what Michael had done—married some American southern belle with no family name. If they knew the real truth . . . she shuddered at the thought.

Salvatore had yet to emerge, and when he did, it was as if a magical signal of silence had been given. By degrees, conversation diminished to fleeting whispers, the band stopped playing, and the wine momentarily ceased flowing. He stood in front of the bandstand where everyone could see him. He gazed around at the assemblage, until nothing could be heard but the water rippling in the distance.

Salvatore took a deep breath and stared hard at his son. Michael pulled Emma close. "My son Michael, my only son," he began, in a strong, clear voice, "has come home. He has brought with him a wife . . . from America." He paused for a long moment. "I want to welcome my son home . . . and welcome his wife, Emma, into the Travanti family." He reached for a glass of wine from a servant's tray and raised it above his head. *"Salute!"*

"Salute!" everyone shouted.

Marguarite beamed at her son. And Michael turned Emma into his arms and kissed her long and hard for all the world to see, to the hand clapping and shouts from her new family.

▲ ▲ ▲

Michael and Emma spent three days at his parents' home, enjoying long days of swimming, boating, and walking in the vineyard. They spent one day on a casual drive into Milan proper, the fashion capital of Italy. Emma was amazed at how well dressed everyone was, their poise, their undeniable sense of style. Marguarite insisted that Emma learn to cook Michael's favorite regional meals and kept her in the kitchen, where she quizzed her about her background and her family. Emma stuck to the story she'd given Michael that her parents were both dead, and she'd left Mississippi to make a better life for herself.

Salvatore, for the most part, kept his distance, greeting her pleasantly when they met in the garden and at mealtimes. His was a presence that need not be seen to be felt. Emma couldn't have been happier when they bid the family farewell and drove off toward the train station and onto Rome, London, and then Paris.

They spent the last days of their honeymoon touring the quaint shops of Paris, sitting in cafés for long nights of Pernod and chat, rising at noon, eating feather-light croissants, visiting the Eiffel Tower and world-famous *Courtier* houses, where Michael purchased expensive gowns, suits, and perfumes for his beautiful bride. They even had an opportunity to meet singer Josephine Baker during her cabaret performance at the famed *Folies Bergère*. At night they reveled in their love beneath the open window of their countryside chalet, just hours from the City of Lights. Emma was finally, truly happy.

Eventually, the couple returned to the United States to officially begin their new life as husband and wife. Emma worked during the day, eagerly awaiting its end so she could get home and fix Michael's favorite meals before settling down to a romantic evening. He spent his days at the local army offices and lavished all of his attention on his wife when he returned home. Emma embraced her new life and flourished in the role of wife and lover. Michael gave her a huge, monthly allowance to maintain their household and for her personal needs and insisted that she stop working, which of course she didn't. Although other aspects of her life had dramatically changed, some qualities remained intact in Emma, her strong will, her need for contact with the outside world, and her sense of independence. Though Michael mildly balked against it, he was proud of his wife and relented in his demands.

And no one could have been happier than Michael when Emma announced that she was pregnant. Nature had accomplished what he could not. Now she would have to stay home, and he could take care of her the way a man should.

Twenty-seven

———〰〰〰〰———

Emma wished she had someone to talk to, a friend, a confidante, someone with whom she could share her thoughts and fears. Although she'd met several of the wives of Michael's army buddies, she wouldn't consider them friends, and she generally kept her distance, being polite but never taking them into her confidence. At times she even wished she could talk to her mother, ask her what to expect, what being a mother would involve. But that, too, was impossible.

As she watched her body slowly change shape, become round and fuller, and the life within her move with abandon, she had moments of joy and wonder. But more often they were shadowed with doubts and "what ifs." Sometimes at night, she would lie awake staring up at the ceiling, quietly massaging her growing mound of a stomach. Other nights, she lay on her side, listening to Michael's gentle breathing and wishing that she'd told him the truth long ago. Now it was too late. It was those times that she would soothe herself with the knowledge that her father was white, she looked white, and she had married a white man. She lived, breathed, and existed in a white world. So it stood to reason that her child would be white as well.

As her time drew closer and her body heavy, Michael wanted to send for his mother to stay with them and look after Emma.

"I'm fine, Michael," she insisted, after days of the same conversation. The last thing she wanted was Michael's mother, with her all-seeing eyes, hovering around her, watching her every move.

"I don't like the idea of leaving you alone all day, Em, with the baby

due in a month. I know you and my mother will never be the best of
friends, but she could be a help."

"No! I don't want her here!" she shouted, on the verge of tears. Her
emotions seemed to always be on a constant seesaw. One minute she would
be elated, the next in a rage or ready to burst into tears. Her mood swings
were maddening to her, but she couldn't help it. "I can take care of myself.
And you're here at night," she said, willing herself to calm down.

Michael wrapped his arms around her and rested her head on his shoulder. "All right. All right. Don't get yourself all worked up. It's not good for
the baby."

She struggled to get up from the couch. "The baby, the baby. That's all
you ever think about, talk about anymore," she sniffed, her labored
breathing rushing in and out.

Michael came to her side. "That's not true, Emma, and you know it," he
said gently. "But of course, I'm concerned about the baby. This is one of
the most important things to happen to us." He turned her to face him. "I
just want everything to be all right, Emma. That's all." He stroked her
cheek. "Don't you?"

Her lip trembled. "Of course I do."

"Then we both want the same thing," he said, with a tender smile.

Emma glanced at him for a moment and was suddenly overcome with
her love for him. It filled her with an incredible sense of peace and com-
pleteness. She would do anything to keep it, to ensure that he would never
stop loving her, that this joy they shared with each other would never
change.

She pressed herself as close as her growing belly would allow against
him, letting his warmth and nearness settle her racing heart and jangled
nerves. Everything would be fine, she reasoned.

▲   ▲   ▲

One week into her ninth month, Michael came home early while she was
busy sorting through the box of baby clothes that had just been delivered
from the department store.

"Michael! What a surprise, sweetheart. What are you doing home so
early?" She neatly refolded the tiny garments and placed them back in
the box.

Michael stood in the doorway. "We need to talk, Em."

She looked up and her pulse raced when she saw the tense expression on his face. Her thoughts went wild, imagining the worst. He'd found out. Oh, God, he'd found out. "W-hat is it?"

He lowered his head, then reached into his suit jacket and extracted an envelope and handed it to her.

With shaky fingers, she opened the envelope and read the official government document. As her eyes raced over the neatly printed type, she almost bubbled over with relieved laughter. "They're sending you to France," she said weakly, the sudden relief making her mildly dizzy.

"Em, I'm so sorry." His voice shook. "I tried everything to get them to change their minds." He crossed the room and gathered her in his arms. "How can I leave you now? You can't travel with the baby only weeks away."

She shut her eyes and breathed slow and easy. "I'll be fine. I promise you. How long will you have to stay?"

"They don't know. As long as I'm needed. I fly out tomorrow morning. First to Berlin, then London, and finally Paris."

She arched her neck and looked up at him. "As soon as the baby comes and the doctors say it's okay, I'll come to you. We'll all be together. It'll be all right."

"I'll call you every night."

"I'll be here."

He kissed her long and slow. "I love you, Emma. So much."

"I love you, too, Michael," she whispered. And she did.

▲ ▲ ▲

As she stood in front of the window at the airport watching the plane roar down the runway, she was suddenly overcome with dread. She'd convinced Michael not to send for his mother, he was gone, she had no real friends. She was truly alone. Alone. She'd been so bold and brave telling him everything would be fine, and in the flurry of last-minute activity, there wasn't much time to dwell on what she would do when her time to deliver came. A sick sensation rolled through her. What *would* she do? How would she manage?

She turned away from the window and slowly lumbered toward the entrance. Day by day the pressure of the baby resting in her body grew heavier. Even with her meager knowledge of childbirth, she understood that her time was very near. She'd started having mild, gripping pains across the expanse of her lower waist when she awoke that morning, but had refrained from telling Michael. Especially since they didn't last and she'd attributed them to the added weight and the nervousness over his departure. She still had a few weeks before her due date, she assured herself, while moving laboriously toward the exit in the hope of quickly finding a taxi.

But as the day drew on, the pains returned in short bursts but more intense each time. By nightfall, she was pacing the floor in agony, sweat beading on her forehead, at times the pains nearly bending her in half.

"It's too soon, too soon," she kept mumbling in fear, as she struggled from the bed, to a chair, to the couch, and back again. During a momentary reprieve from the searing pains, she almost made her way to the door when another onslaught of torment slammed into her, bringing her to her knees. The only thing that kept her from falling to the floor was her grip on the knob as a flow of blood and water ran down her thighs.

Tears of terror and agony rolled down her cheeks. Her body shook as she curled into a fetal position on the cool, wood floor. She'd never make it to the hospital she realized through the dizzying pain. She tried to think how far away was the phone. *In the bedroom.* She squeezed her eyes shut as an unbelievable urge to bare down overwhelmed her. Something inside her seemed to rip, and she screamed in agony as the building pressure widened her. Through the haze of pain and fear, she realized that there was no one to help her, no one she could call. She was alone. She'd have to do this by herself. Drawing on her last reserves of strength, she managed to free herself of her undergarments and began the final ordeal of bringing her child into the world.

Hours later, weak with exhaustion, she looked down at the tiny little girl she'd wrapped in a clean sheet. When she stared at the perfect features, the wisps of curly, dark hair, and miniature fingers, she realized with complete desolation that everything she'd worked for, sacrificed for, was over. Forever.

Unless she could find a way out.

Twenty-eight

—⁓⁓⁓⁓⁓—

Dear, God, what was she going to do? On shaky legs, Emma moved unsteadily about the bedroom, holding onto the wall for support. Intermittently she snatched horrified glances at the baby curled in sleep on the bed. Her little, brown baby girl. Her Negro child. Her heart squeezed painfully in her chest. She shoved her fist to her mouth to keep from screaming. The room moved dangerously in and out. She had to think, but couldn't get her thoughts to stay focused. It was all too appalling. Her greatest nightmare had come true.

Maybe if she lay down, the dizziness would clear and she could figure something out. She made her way to the bed and gingerly stretched out next to the sleeping child.

When Emma next awoke, it was to the faint sound of crying. Confused, she opened her eyes, thinking that she had been dreaming about a crying child. But the crying was real, coming from right next to her. Her stomach rolled. It was no dream. The little bundle kicked and squalled, balling its fists in fury.

"Hush! You hush now," Emma implored, fearing that her neighbors might hear the damning whimpers.

Tenuously, she eased the baby near the warmth of her body and gently patted its back. It was the first time since she'd delivered her and wrapped her in the sheet that she'd actually touched her, and she was surprised to discover how delicate she felt, how soft and small. A sudden wave of maternal protectiveness flowed through Emma. Instinctively she wanted to hold and comfort this tiny creature. By degrees the baby quieted. The sobs turned to little mewling sounds. Emma smiled weakly, feeling she'd made some small accomplishment. But just as quickly as the baby had quieted, she started wailing again.

"What's wrong with you, chile?" she demanded, her agitation escalating again, and the old southern drawl that she'd worked so hard to discard, easily slipped back into place. The baby instinctively moved its mouth in a soft, sucking motion, turning its head toward Emma's body.

Emma jerked back in alarm. She looked down at the baby, seeing its helplessness, the purity of its innocence, and realized that this child was totally dependent upon her. It was an overwhelming sensation that momentarily humbled her.

"You're hungry?" she asked gently. "Hungry," she murmured, easing away her clothing and offering her swollen breast.

The baby tentatively suckled, then greedily drew in the nourishing fluids, between dozing and waking, and Emma began to feel something she didn't want to feel—a connection—a surge of warmth and tenderness.

While the baby nursed, Emma touched the soft, wiry, black curls, ran her fingertips along the cottony skin. She examined her fingers and was surprised when the infant wrapped its hand tightly around her pinky.

Emma suddenly felt full, her heart seeming to swell with a joy she'd never before experienced. This was her and Michael's daughter, what they had created out of their love.

"I don't want to love you," Emma whimpered. "I can't. Don't make me."

Momentarily satisfied, the baby drifted off to sleep.

When Emma was sure the baby was sleeping soundly, she eased from the bed and went into the bathroom, her steps slow and unsteady, the pains in her stomach curling her body. But she needed to clean herself, she needed to move away from this miracle so that she could think. She needed to rid herself of the traces of what happened from her body and her mind.

Standing under the beat of the steamy shower, Emma forced her thoughts away from the pink water swirling down the drain. She wished it was as easy to wash away everything that had happened, make it all disappear.

But things like that didn't happen, you made them happen. She closed her eyes and let the water run over her face, through her hair.

Her baby. A little girl. The weight she'd carried in her body for nine months, felt its twists and turns and long stretches, was finally here. She'd touched her beautiful skin, held her body against her, nourished her with milk from her breasts. All the things a mother would do. She was a mother.

She had a baby. A baby. The wonder of it sent a chill along her arms and down the curve of her back. And she was beautiful, perfect in every way—except one.

Emma's bottom lip trembled. She wouldn't let herself feel, wouldn't let herself fall in love with the child she had borne of love. She'd mastered the art of masking her emotions, pushing them out of her heart. She would do it now. What other choice did she have?

Emma turned off the shower, wrapped herself in a clean towel, and returned to the bedroom. The baby girl was still in a peaceful sleep, her small face, so much like her own, created a tender picture. For a moment, doubt froze her in place, made her second-guess herself.

Maybe she could leave, she thought, disappear with her baby and build a new life in another place. Her gaze slowly rose and her reflection in the dresser mirror stared back at her, the face of a white woman.

The baby stirred. Emma moved toward the bed and lifted her daughter. She briefly shut her eyes and held the baby to her breasts. Pushing out a breath of resolve, she took the baby to the bathroom and turned on the tub water.

While the water slowly rose, Emma unwrapped the baby, the cord still protruding from its navel, the lifeline that connected them. She wouldn't think about that. Couldn't allow herself the luxury of being distracted by sentiment. That connection was broken.

Emma knelt down by the side of the tub and lowered the baby toward the water. And then her daughter's eyes squinted open, jade green eyes, just like hers, gazed back at her. Emma's heart rocked in her chest as the baby's tiny fingers grasped a loose curl of her hair and held it. Her stomach seesawed. She couldn't do this. The baby whimpered.

The phone rang in the distance. Emma froze, suddenly terrified that somehow her heinous thoughts had been read by some unseen being. Her heart raced.

The phone rang again.

Michael! He would be calling to see how she was, let her know that he'd arrived safely. If she didn't answer, maybe he would worry and send someone to check on her.

Frantically, she listened to the insistent ringing that demanded her attention.

Torn by indecision, she finally wrapped the infant in the sheet and returned to the bedroom. The baby squirmed in her arms.

Emma picked up the phone.

"Hello?"

"Mrs. Travanti?"

"Yes."

"Is your husband Michael Travanti?"

"Yes . . ."

"This is General Jefferson, your husband's commanding officer."

Slowly Emma lowered herself to the bed. "Yes." Her heart rate began an upward spiral.

"Mrs. Travanti, I'm sorry to inform you that your husband, Michael Travanti, is being detained in East Berlin. His transport was stopped at Checkpoint Charlie. But the army assures you that we are at this very moment working on his release. We expect results in days."

Emma frowned in confusion. "Michael? Detained? What are you saying? What are you telling me?" Her voice rose to near hysteria.

"Please, Mrs. Travanti. Your husband, as far as we can determine, is fine. He's being held by East German authorities pending some questions."

"Why? What questions?" She was shaking all over. Only seconds ago she was prepared to drown her newborn baby to save her life and her marriage, and now it might all be taken from her anyway.

"That's all I'm free to tell you at this time."

"I want to talk to him. I—I have to talk to him," she stuttered.

"I'm sorry. That's impossible. We'll keep you informed as the situation develops. We'll have your husband out of there soon. Is there anything we can do for you, Mrs. Travanti?"

Emma stared at the pale green wall, the color she and Michael had spent days choosing. "No." Absently she hung up the phone.

The baby rooted around for her breasts. In a daze, Emma curled on her side, cradling the baby in her arm, and let her nurse.

They both dozed, comforted by the closeness of each other. Moments before sleep captured her, Emma realized what she must do. But she'd have to wait until dark. It would be safer then.

Twenty-nine

Emma went through all the drawers and hiding places where she knew Michael kept money. She had more than a thousand dollars and her bank book tucked away in her purse.

She glanced nervously around. She'd cleaned up the apartment as best she could, washed and dressed the baby, and took several aspirin for the residual pain from the delivery. A taxi was on the way.

She wouldn't allow herself to think beyond the immediate moment. That would only confuse things. One step at a time, she kept repeating. One step at a time.

The taxi blew its horn.

Emma wrapped the baby snuggly in a white wool blanket with satin trim. She had picked it out special to match the padded white snowsuit with the little green bunnies. Her throat suddenly tightened. Was she doing the right thing? Was there some other way she could fix all of this, make things right? She quickly covered the baby's face with the tip of the blanket, picked up the suitcase, filled with baby clothes and crept out, praying with every step that she wouldn't be seen.

▲ ▲ ▲

Once aloft, Emma stared out of the airplane window, watching the carefree puffs of clouds drift by. In a few more hours, this entire nightmare of her life would be behind her. She would forget it as if it had never happened, and Michael would be released and they would go on with their lives.

Everything would work out. It had to. She'd risked too much for it to be any other way. With that resolution ingrained in her heart and mind, she closed her eyes in sleep, her baby daughter held tightly against her.

Five hours later the plane landed in Jackson, Mississippi. Emma boarded a bus heading for Rudell. Her mother owed her, she reasoned, as the bus lumbered along the dirt-packed road, and it was finally time that she paid up. If her mother resisted, she would remind her of what her deception had cost her, of how she had suffered under the weight of her lies.

▲ ▲ ▲

When Emma arrived, the lights were out and there was no sign of life from inside the tiny house. Cora couldn't imagine who would be at her door at such an ungodly hour. The sun wasn't even peeking out yet. Wearily, she pulled herself out of her bed, even as the pounding on her front door grew more insistent.

"Comin', comin', Lordhammercy." She turned on the light and opened the front door. For a moment, she thought the incessant pounding at her door was a dream, that she was doing that walking in her sleep that she'd heard tell about. She couldn't say anything, just stared dumbfounded at the figure in front of her.

"Hello, Mama."

"Em—Emma," she stammered.

"It's me."

Cora's face slowly brightened, her eyes snapping with fire. "You don' come home, chile. Oh, Lawd, oh, Lawd." She covered her mouth to seal the cry that rushed to be heard. Her eyes filled with tears of joy, and she was sure her heart would leapfrog right out of her chest.

Cora peered closer in the dark. "That yo' baby?"

Emma nodded shyly, cradling the infant close to her.

Cora shook some sense into her head. "Come in, come in." She took the suitcase and ushered Emma and the baby into the house.

Emma placed the baby down on the tattered couch that was still covered by the handmade quilt to camouflage the worn spots from years of sitting. She turned to her mother, who still stood in the entrance to the room.

For a moment they took each other in, seeing all the changes, the things that remained the same. Emma was still strikingly beautiful, maybe more so. She looked tired, and the weight of the new baby showed on her face and the new curves of her body. But there was an added assurance in her eyes, a worldliness that hadn't been there when she'd left nearly three years ago. Three years—and there wasn't a day that God sent that Cora didn't think about her, wonder where she was, how she was. And now she was back, out of the blue, and with a baby. What did it all mean?

Cora had aged, Emma noticed right away. She could see it around her large, brown eyes and the new gray strands in her still-plaited head. She hadn't gained a pound. If anything, she seemed thinner. But what was most telling was the aura of serenity that radiated from her, as if she'd somehow managed to accept her life and herself and was at peace with it. That relentless sorrow that had curled her shoulders and turned down her full lips was gone, replaced by a calm that was as still as the morning around them. How did that happen? she wondered.

"Why don't you set on down and rest. You look tired," Cora said. "I'll fix you somethin' to eat," she added, not knowing what else to do. Food and drink always seemed to fill the gaps, and the preparation of it took your mind away from the things at hand.

Emma took off her coat and unwrapped the baby who began to kick when disturbed out of its warm cocoon. Emma rocked the child in her arms until she settled back into sleep, then lay her down on the couch between two pillows.

She looked slowly around the rooms where she'd spent nineteen years of her life. She was home. All the familiar things, things she'd needed to get away from, but in her heart never did. Listening to the soft chirp of the birds outside the window, the gentle rustle of the wind blowing the scent of rich earth and sweet green grass, she knew that this simple life would forever be a part of who she was no matter how far she ran.

Shortly, Cora returned with a tray of handmade biscuits and hot tea. She set it down on the large, wood table and took a seat in her favorite chair by the window.

"Thank you," Emma mumbled, but didn't touch the offering.

Cora stared at her daughter and took fleeting glances at the sleeping baby. "How old is it?" she finally asked, after the silence had taken on a heaviness.

"A day."

"Looks to be so," Cora said simply. "You done come a long ways?"

"New York."

Cora pressed her lips together. "You done come all this way with a day-old chile. Must be a reason."

Emma looked away, afraid that her intentions could be read on her face.

Cora pushed herself up from her favorite chair and crossed the room. Gently she picked the child up from the couch and cradled it in her arms and returned to her seat. She moved the light blanket away from the baby's face, and a soft glow illuminated her expression. "Looks like you, Em," she said in wonder. She slipped her finger between the child's closed fist and rocked in the chair. Slowly she looked up at her daughter. "Why you come back, Emma, after all this time?"

Emma drew herself together. "I'm married now, Mama, to a good man who loves me."

"I'm happy for you." Cora didn't look at Emma while she talked; only the baby seemed to hold her attention.

Emma swallowed. "I can't—let him see the baby."

Cora frowned in confusion. "Whatchu sayin'?" She stared at her daughter.

"I have a new life, Mama. A different life."

Cora's throat worked up and down. "A white life, ain't that right?"

"Yes," she snapped. "A white life!" She breathed hard. "A life that I'm happy with, that accepts me. A life that suits me just fine."

"But not yo' chile . . ." She let her knowing words hang in the air.

Emma snatched her glance away, unable to stare truth in the eye. "I won't give it up. I won't. I can't." She paused a moment. "I'm leaving her here," she said with finality.

Cora's mouth flickered. "I discovered long ago, Emma," she said in a faraway voice, "you cain't run from who you is, what you done. It gon' catch up to you, expose you to the world. Just like mine done. Just like yours done. You think leavin' this chile here gon' change that?"

"Keeping her will change everything. And I won't do it. I won't lose what I've gained." She glared at her mother. "You never understood. Never. You never understood what it was like to be me. Living in a world all by myself, where nobody gave a damn about me. Not even you." Cora flinched, and Emma relished her pain. "How dare you tell me about secrets and lies. Our whole life was nothing but one big lie." She whirled away. "I met him," she said, under her breath.

Cora's heart began to thunder. "Who?" she asked, not really wanting to hear any more.

Emma spun around, pinning her mother with her shame. "My father." She almost laughed out loud when she saw Emma's face twist in pain. "I look just like him, you know."

Suddenly she snatched up her coat and her purse. "When my husband arrives in Paris, I'm going to join him. I'm going to tell him whatever I need to tell him to make all of this," she pointed at the baby, "go away. And I'm never coming back. You don't have to worry about that." She moved toward the door, refusing to look at the baby one last time. Refusing to let her mother see the pain in her heart.

Cora sprung up from her seat. "Emma! Don't do this. You'll regret it."

Emma kept walking toward the door. "Tell her what you want. Tell her I'm dead. You've always been good at lies and deceit. I learned from you, Mama."

"Emma, Emma, please. Don't make the same mistakes I did."

"Here's your chance to fix those mistakes, Mama." She opened the door.

The baby whimpered and stirred.

Emma straightened her back and took a deep breath. "He . . . he said . . . he never meant to hurt you."

With that, Emma silently shut the door and was gone, and with each step she wanted to run back and ask her mother to love her, teach her how to love her child. She wanted to feel her baby's soft skin one more time, inhale the newness of her. But she couldn't do that. All she could do was hold onto the memory of what might have been.

Through tears and a wrenching pain in her soul, she made her way to the bus stop, putting this chapter of her life and as much distance as she could behind her.

Thirty

~~~~~~~~~~

"Whatchu gon' do?" Miss Lucinda asked, as she fussed over the baby while Cora nervously paced the floor.

After Emma abruptly left and Cora took a few minutes to collect herself, she wrapped up the baby like a birthday gift and headed straight for Miss Lucinda's house.

Over the years, after the initial shock of Emma's birth had wound down, Lucinda had remained a staunch friend, her only one. She'd never questioned or ridiculed her, but had always hovered in the background, assuring Cora that she had the strength and determination of her parents running through her veins and that blessing would sustain her. So, of course, faced with this latest crisis in her life, she turned to Lucinda for guidance and support.

Cora wrung her hands. "What kin I do? Don't look like I got much choice in the matter."

Lucinda pinned a fresh diaper on the baby and put on a clean undershirt. "Pretty little thing," she said.

Cora momentarily stopped her pacing. "Looks like . . . her grandfather," she blurted out.

Lucinda stood stock still. Never, in twenty years, had Cora uttered a word about Emma's daddy. She lifted the baby into her arms. "That right," she said, with all the calm she could muster. "Musta been a good-lookin' man." She kept her focus on the baby, instinctively understanding that Cora needed this time to find her way, to sort out what had just transpired.

"I—I worked for him when I was in Chicago." And then, like a dam that had split its seams, the words poured out of her in a rush.

More than three hours later, with the two friends facing each other, that final burden that had blackened Cora's soul was finally lifted. She felt as if she'd been given wings of flight. Tears of cleansing relief ran unchecked down Cora's still smooth skin, mirrored in Lucinda's own tears of sorrow.

"All these years," Lucinda began. "All these years you kept that kind of pain balled up inside you." She slowly shook her head, rocking the baby in her arms. "You coulda told me, chile. I woulda helped you."

"Shame is a powerful thang," Cora said softly. "It humbles you, cripples yo' spirit, makes you do and think thangs you never would have. Makes you scared to look at yo'self in the mirror. Scared to have others look in yo' eyes. That's what I been feelin' all this time. Shame. And I let it ruin my life, destroy my marriage, and my chile."

Slowly she rose from her seat. "I ain't gon' pass that shame along to my grandchild. The burden is too heavy to bear. It gon' stop here. Right now. I cain't go back and fix nothin' I already done. But I kin try to make the future better fo' that little one."

"Whatchu gon' tell her 'bout her mama?"

"For this one time I'm gon' do what Emma asked." She nodded her head in affirmation. "She my baby now. My responsibility."

Lucinda looked at her with skepticism about her decision, her conscience warring between right and wrong. But she realized, too, that Cora had taken a mighty step this morning. And maybe that should be enough.

Slowly, Lucinda nodded her head, and an unspoken agreement was reached.

▲ ▲ ▲

"What's the child's name?" Lucinda asked, several days later when Cora returned home from work. Lucinda had readily taken on the role of baby-sitter and old auntie, which gave her something to do with her days while helping Cora out in the process.

"Been thinkin' 'bout it. Guess we cain't keep callin' her 'baby girl' and 'chile' forever." She laughed lightly and plopped down in her favorite chair, releasing an exhausted breath.

"You right 'bout that." Lucinda picked up the baby and brought her over to Cora. The sweet smell of the infant floated around her, soothing the aches in her body like a warm massage. "Hey, sugah," Cora cooed tenderly. "You been a good girl fo' auntie?" The baby made a tiny, gurgling sound. The two women laughed. "Guess that means yes."

"You gon' have to get papers for the chile," Lucinda advised, as she washed her hands in the old pump sink.

"Don't know how."

"I knows a way."

Cora looked up. She knew that tone. Lucinda was up to something. Her eyebrow rose in question.

"From a doctor, that's how. Chile needs to be checked out anyhow, make sho' everythin' okay."

"What doctor gon' make up some papers?"

"David."

Cora's eyes snapped to attention. Her skin suddenly prickled. "No." She vehemently shook her head. And the baby, sensing her distress, began to cry. "Ssh, ssh," Cora stroked her fat cheeks and rocked her in her arms. "Hush now. Ain't nothin' for you to be frettin' 'bout. Yo' crazy auntie just got some wild ideas is all."

"Well, what else you gon' do? Chile cain't go through life wit no papers. Simple as that. And ya need somebody you kin trust."

"Trust! David wouldn't come nowhere near me. And I wouldn't blame him none. Not after all of what I put him through. Don't even know where he is," she added weakly.

"I do. Always knowed."

"What?"

"I always knowed. He right there in Alligator. Been there all along. Write to me every now and ag'in, too." She paused a beat. "Always ask after you."

Lucinda watched the waves of emotion swim across Cora's worn face: love, fear, regret, sadness.

"W-hat you tell him—'bout me?"

"That you doin' fine. Would do better wit him, but you fine just the same."

Cora got up and moved away. She didn't want the words to get hold of her, slip into her heart, and give her hope. She hadn't seen David in twenty years. Hadn't heard a word, and he'd been less than fifty miles away all the time. And he'd asked about her. Maybe he still cared just a little. She didn't want to hope. She didn't dare.

"You—think he'd do it—fix up her papers and all?" Her heart hammered.

"I 'spect he would."

"But—I—I could never ask him . . ."

"That's why I will." Lucinda nodded her head sharply. "It's 'bout time."

▲ ▲ ▲

David labored long and hard over Lucinda's request—near two weeks—thought about the right and wrong of it and what going back there, seeing Cora again, would do to him, what it would mean. She needed him. He had once promised that if she ever needed him, he'd be there for her. He never thought he'd live to see the day when Cora would ever need him again. That was what finally steered his mind to this moment.

Now, walking down the familiar path and seeing the old house standing in front of him, he had every right to turn away. What was behind that door he didn't need in his life. It was the only way he could keep from going crazy. His work kept him busy during the days; but at night, Cora's face continually haunted him, sure as a ghost. He'd see her pleading eyes, the curve of her mouth, as she asked him not to leave her. He'd remember the weight of her body against his. At times like that, he would get up in the night and walk until he was weak with exhaustion, then collapse into bed. Yet as much as he wanted to stay away from her, exorcise her from his dreams, his mind, his heart, he still needed to know that she was getting by, that she was all right. So he would write to Lucinda and wait with maddening impatience for the slow return of her reply.

And now here he stood, back in the place he never thought he'd leave, the place where he swore he'd never return, the place where his heart had always remained.

The door opened suddenly, and there she stood. His breath halted in his lungs just like that summer Sunday morning when she'd walked like a heavenly vision out of the front door of First Baptist Church. The sudden surge of raw feeling stung his eyes with memories that wouldn't die. Oh, God, he still loved her. Would always love her.

He still looked so uncertain, Cora realized the instant she saw him. The same sweet confusion on his face like that day when he first met her mama and papa. How she'd missed that look, which was so contrary to the determined and strong-willed man she'd grown to love.

Cora took a tentative step down, unsure if the thud she'd heard was her step or her heart.

David swallowed the dryness in his throat and slowly moved forward.

"David." "Cora." They spoke in unison, then laughed with nervous embarrassment.

Cora willed herself to be calm and slow the rapid racing of her heart. "Thank you fo' comin', David."

David gave a short bob of his head in polite acknowledgement.

"Come in—please." She moved aside as he walked past her, snatching his wide-brimmed hat from his head as he crossed the threshold.

Cora smiled with recollection as she followed him inside.

David looked around and it was as if he'd been thrown back in time. All at once the wonderful images of the days they'd shared there together came hurtling toward him in an unstoppable flood, and there was nothing he could do to halt them. He could almost hear the laughter in the walls, the hope that bloomed through the sunlit window, the passion and love that had pulsed as strongly as the beat of his heart. He could still see her standing at the stove fixing a meal, and he'd sneak in behind her, scoop her up, and spin around the room with her nestled in his arms until she become delirious with laughter. For a moment everything was as he remembered; nothing had changed.

He blinked and the reality of the situation enveloped him.

David's jaw involuntarily clenched from the tension. Feeling her presence behind him, he turned to face her, not knowing what he might see in her face.

"Kin I fix you somethin'? You hungry, thirsty?" She nervously folded and unfolded her shaky fingers.

"No. No, thanks. I just came for what I was called about, Cora. That's all."

Cora, stung by the chill of his response, pressed her lips tightly together and raised her chin. "She's in the bedroom." Cora walked up the stairs without another word and wondered how often David remembered the times they'd shared in this room, or if he remembered at all.

When she entered the bedroom with David close behind, the baby was wide awake, peddling her plump legs in the air. She was cooing softly to herself.

The baby had sprouted up like a potato bud in the three weeks that she'd been with Emma. She stayed awake for longer periods of time, looking curiously around with those same green eyes as her mother. Well, almost the same. The baby's were even more arresting, more striking being set against the rich sheen of her tea-colored skin. The tiny arms and legs were filling out, and Cora was certain it was because of the spoonful of pablum she fed her twice each day and the rich formula made of condensed milk and Karo syrup. Her cheeks were plump, with a little dimple on her chin, and her hair was growing like weeds in an untended garden, thick and black and full of spirals. Cora knew she was going to have her hands full getting a comb through it.

"She 'bout three weeks and two days by my count," Cora offered.

David stepped closer and sat on the side of the bed. He put his medical bag on the nightstand, opened it up, and put his instruments on the bed. Carefully, he placed his stethoscope on the infant's chest, listening for any irregularities of the lungs and heart.

With a gentleness that Cora remembered so well, David examined the baby, talking softly as he worked. He checked her eyes, ears, and throat, her fingers and toes, and ran his hands up and down her arms and legs. He checked her navel.

"You did good with the cord," he said to Cora, but didn't stop his exam.

She'd been a mother once, Cora wanted to say. But of course, he knew that. She kept quiet as he went about his business, ascertaining the child's health and progress.

Finally, David put his equipment away, placing everything gingerly back in his bag, and then he covered the baby with a light blanket. "She's a healthy baby." He stood and walked out of the room and quietly downstairs, the memories too overwhelming to allow him to stay any longer.

After a quick glance at his face, Cora picked up her granddaughter and brought her downstairs.

He was standing in the kitchen, with a worried look on his face, head bowed, his hands deep in his pockets.

"Thank you for comin' all the way out here," Cora said quietly.

"I'll write up her certificate," David said calmly. "You'll have to take it into Jackson to get the seal. I don't see where there would be too many questions asked. You know how these white folks are 'bout colored folks. One looks just like the next one to them." He kept his back to her.

"All right."

"Why didn't you tell me, Cora—about what happened?" His voice carried a brittle tone she had never heard before. "Didn't you trust me? Have I ever let you down?"

Her heart seemed to stop. He knew! Lucinda told him. Her emotions ebbed and flowed between fury, fear, and finally acceptance. Maybe this was her second chance, a second chance to somehow make up for what happened by not running away from it anymore. She would face up to her burdens this time.

"I—I was too 'shamed." She fought down the last of her reservations. "I didn't want you to know how horrible it was . . . what happened to me."

He turned toward her, startling her with the bitter tears that filled his eyes. "Didn't you know how much I loved you, Cora? Loved you enough to understand—to work it out—together. If only you woulda trusted me with the truth in the beginning . . . we coulda found a way. What we had together was strong enough to deal with anythin'. But I was made to feel a fool, tricked by the one person in the world I woulda given my life fo'."

Cora wept openly now. "Every day I've lived with what happened, the lie I told by not speakin' the truth. That one lie cost me everythin' I had. I was left with nothin' not even my pride. I paid for it wit you, this town, with Emma. I paid more than anyone should for somethin' that weren't my fault. I cain't pay no more. I won't."

David stared into her wide, luminous eyes that surprisingly weren't asking him to forgive, but to understand. In that instant, he understood the sheer strength of this woman he had loved for so long.

Without any further talk, he pulled a sheaf of paper from his jacket pocket and took a seat at the kitchen table. He looked up at Cora. "Do you have a name to call her?" he asked, with a slight tremor in his voice.

Cora stepped closer, the baby held tightly against her. She gazed down into the perfect face. "I want to call her Parris. It's where her mama said she was going."

David nodded. "Then her name will be Parris." He hesitated for a moment. "What about a last name?"

"I—I thought maybe my maiden name—Harvey," Cora offered.

David was thoughtful for a moment. "I'd be willing to give her our last name, Cora. If you are."

Cora felt her heart heave in her chest. She bobbed her head. "Yes. Yes. I'd like that, too. The edges of her mouth trembled. "Very much."

David reached out and took Cora's hand, maybe there was a way to put the past behind them, to find a way to heal the hurt. He wasn't sure if it was possible. But if there was a way that he could, perhaps it could begin today—with this one act that would bind them once again.

Thirty-one

~~~~~~~~~~~~~

At first David used his monitoring of the baby's health as an explanation for his daily visits to Cora's house. With the weather changing seasons, he wanted to be certain that little Parris didn't take sick, he'd told her. Cora only smiled to herself and welcomed him inside with a hot meat dish, buttermilk biscuits, and a cool drink. Most of his visits were short, at least in the beginning. However, as the days turned into weeks and the winter into spring, his evening visits lasted past sunset.

Cora didn't want to allow herself to think that his comings and goings were more than what he said. To do that would give her a hope she wasn't ready to believe in yet. But she'd grown accustomed to having him around again, feeling his male presence move about the small, framed house, hear him tell her stories about his patients, fix him dinner at the end of his day. So it came as more than a surprise when he told her he was thinking about moving.

"I've been thinkin' 'bout leaving Alligator," David casually mentioned one evening following a supper of smoked neck bones with lima beans and rice, along with Cora's special spicy collards.

Cora felt the jolt of his words as if she'd been shoved in the back. This was why she was afraid to hope, she thought, trying to keep her expression relaxed and unaffected by his surprise announcement.

"That so. I guess that be right nice for you to be livin' in a new place and all." She busied herself with clearing the table, washing the dishes, staring at the warm water running over her hands. Any distraction to keep from looking at him.

"I wouldn't say it was a new place." He paused for a moment. "I was thinkin' of comin' back to Rudell."

The plate she held in her hands slipped from her fingers and plopped with a loud splash back into the sudsy water. She didn't know what to think of his sudden confession.

"What do you think about that, Cora?" he asked matter-of-factly.

Her mouth had gone completely dry. "I—I think that would be fine, if it's what you want." She scrubbed the same spot on the glass over and over.

"It's important to me that it's fine by you."

"Why should what I think make a never mind?"

She heard the feet of the chair scrape across the wood floor. Her entire body went on full alert. She whirled around to find David right behind her, close enough for her to see the sparkle in his eyes. Her body trembled with anticipation. His gaze rolled over her face. " 'Cause I thought I'd move back here, Cora, with you—and Parris."

Cora's mouth opened, closed, and opened again, but nothing would come out. She blinked in rapid succession, completely dumbfounded by his statement.

"What do you think, Cora? Is that somethin' you want?"

"I . . ." A smile like a moonbeam shot across her face, and she suddenly looked as young as she did more than twenty years earlier. "Yes! Yes!" She wrapped her arms around his neck, raining kisses on his face. This was what she had waited so long for, the two of them together under one roof. A family. A second chance.

David laughed from deep in his belly. "I think our little Parris nbneeds both of us to help raise her," he said over his quick laughter, spinning her by the arms in a tight circle just like he once did so many years ago.

"Two of us." Cora sniffed. "Yes, that's just what our baby girl needs."

"That's what we need, too, Cora," he said in a solemn tone. "We were meant to be together." David finally stopped spinning her, held her by the shoulders, and stared deep into her eyes. "We're gonna do this right, me and you. We can make it this time, Cora."

Cora happily nodded her head in agreement. "Yes, we'll make it right this time." Then suddenly she frowned with concern. "What 'bout the neighbors? What they gon' say 'bout you livin' here?"

"We're still man and wife, Cora. That never changed. We're still married. That's the law so there's nothin' they can say. And you know what, I don't care. Worrying 'bout what other people think is what came between us before. I don't intend to let that happen again. All we need to worry 'bout is what *we* think."

Cora let the strength of his resolve sink in, then a slow, almost seductive smile eased across her lush lips. She gazed up at him. "Then if we still man and wife, that means . . ." Her observation hung in the air.

David's eyes crinkled with laughter. "I do believe you're right, Mrs. Mackey."

Hand-in-hand, giggling like schoolchildren, they ran to their bedroom and this time was like the first time, only better.

▲ ▲ ▲

Sometimes the rumors and whispers about Cora and David would tiptoe from one house to the next, sit right down at the dinner table passing from mouth to mouth on forkfuls of ham hocks and snap peas. Other times they would roll like all the ripples of the Left Hand River, float under the boats, and come right back home in the mouths of the hooked fish. Most times they would glide along with the breeze, real quiet-like, touching down every now and then to tickle an ear, turn a head, or raise a brow. But David and Cora would just walk right on through those whispers, unperturbed by the talk, flick away the rumors with a gentle toss of their heads. They were too caught up in the newness of being together again to pay anything else much mind. And the love that floated around them was like a cold, passing from one person to the next. After a while, the old rumors and whispers got bored with themselves, evaporated like dew under the glow of the sun, tired of not having a resting place to take root and grow. So they just stopped coming around, and folks couldn't seem to remember what all the fuss was about anyhow, especially when they'd see Cora and David strolling through town with nothing but smiles and good cheer for everyone they'd meet. The couple cherished their mornings of waking up together, the security of having the other lying next to them. They embraced the night, became one with the velvet blackness of it. They walked proudly through town, sat tall in the church, had a "good day to you" for everyone. They rejoiced in each day they were given, knowing how many they'd lost.

And everywhere they went, little Parris was right there with them. They held her up to the light for all to see, to accept, and to love. And Parris bloomed in Cora and David's love, in the love of the townsfolk, who had taken her into their hearts. Parris was more than just a beautiful, easy baby. She was a symbol to everyone. A symbol of second chances. In Parris, they saw possibility and hope that anything could change—even minds.

Growing up enveloped in love, nourished in hope, groomed in faith, Parris was destined to make a difference.

And she did.

Thirty-two

———⁓⁓⁓⁓⁓⁓⁓⁓⁓———

"Nana, what was my mama like?" Parris suddenly asked one afternoon while she swept the kitchen floor.

She wondered about her mother from time to time, the woman who gave her life. But for the most part she never truly missed her. Her life was complete with her Nana and Granddad. They provided her with everything a child, a teen, a young woman could ever need. A wonderful sense of belonging, emotional security, and support. And though her life was some-what emptier since the passing of Miss Lucinda, she would never forget the love and wisdom she'd shared with her over the years.

For as long as she could remember, she'd always felt special somehow, as if she'd been chosen. Her life was full and carefree. She had many friends and suitors. She spent her days studying because Nana and Granddad in-sisted that education held the secret to success, and that she would need more than the beautiful voice she'd inherited from her grandmother to survive in the world. They'd spent all their savings to send her to college to ensure that success. And she promised herself that she would never disappoint or fail them.

But at night she had dreams, restless dreams that took her away from all things familiar, into a world of sparkling lights, art, music, museums, theaters, plays—all the things she'd read so much about and watched on television.

She loved her life in Rudell. She wouldn't deny that. She cherished the quiet, easiness of it, the rock-steady feeling of community. However, there rested a hunger inside her that burned with a barely contained energy that needed release. And she understood that what she sought would never be found in Rudell. The thought that she must leave one day both saddened and excited her with the possibilities. It was those times, the times when the hunger burned so hot inside, that she thought of her mother and wondered if she'd ever had the same dreams.

Cora heard the question as she sat in her favorite rocking chair by the window, watching the sparrows hop from tree to tree. When Parris was little, it was easy to just say "yo' mama was a special woman" and leave it at that. That vague reply would temporarily satisfy her curiosity. But Parris wasn't a little girl anymore. She was a grown woman, who looked more like Emma with each day that God sent. But what worried Cora the most wasn't that Parris had inherited her mother's looks, but rather that Parris had inherited her grandmother's restlessness. She could see it some days in the faraway look in Parris's eyes. She knew she was looking far beyond Rudell. She could sense it in the way Parris moved her slender body, almost as if she heard a special rhythm in her head. She could tell it by the way Parris would scour through the magazines, settling her gaze on the articles with tales of glamour and the high life and listen to her bedside radio, the old Philco, late into the night. She could hear it in the raw power of her voice when she sang the Gospel in church and the blues at home. And it frightened her.

"Nana, are you listening to me or pretending that your hearing is going bad again?" Parris teased, taking a seat on the footstool in front of Cora.

Cora smiled. "Sure, sugah. I'm listenin' to ya." She took a long breath. "You want to know 'bout yo' mama."

"Yes." Parris put her hands up to her chin and rested her elbows on her thighs. "Did she . . . ever want to . . . what did she want to do with her life . . . before she died?"

Cora glanced away for a moment. She'd lived with that old lie of her daughter's passing for so long, she'd begun to believe it herself. If it hadn't been for the monthly deposits into her and David's savings account, she would have surely known it was true. The money had started coming about a year after Emma left for Europe. She wrote one letter with a Paris postmark, asking for Cora's banking information, saying that she wanted to be sure that she had enough money to take care of "the child." The money came regular, sure enough, but not another word from Emma. It was as if the earth had swallowed the girl up.

Cora still had the letter tucked away in her special box with all her important papers. She'd look at it every now and again, hoping to read something in between the lines, something she'd missed, one word that might help her believe that Emma had ever forgiven her. She never found it. And all the letters and pictures she'd sent to Emma over the years since were never answered. Eventually she stopped.

"And don't just tell me 'she was special,' " Parris warned, snapping Cora from her musings.

Cora stared out of the window. "Your mama was very beautiful. Just like you. Didn't have your voice though. You got that from me," she added, with a proud smile. "Truth is, your mama was a hard person to really know. Kept a lot of things locked up inside her, how she felt, what she thought. She was determined though. Once she set her mind to somethin', there was no changin' it."

"Was she happy, Nana?"

Cora inwardly flinched. "I don't think she was happy living here. This place weren't enough fo' yo' mama. She wanted somethin' Rudell couldn't give her and neither could I."

Parris was thoughtful for a moment. "That's how I feel too, Nana," she confessed. She released a slow breath. "Sometimes it just feels like I'm reaching and reaching and when I open my hand, there's nothing inside. When I went away to school at the university, I had a chance to meet all kinds of people, people I never see here in Rudell. Nana, I miss that. It opened up a whole new world to me. But don't get me wrong," she rushed on, clasping her grandmother's vein-lined hand. "I love my life here with you and Granddad . . . my job at the bank. I—I just want more. I want to get out into the world, see things, do things. I want to use my talents, Nana." Her green eyes tightened. "Do you know what I mean?"

Cora knew all too well what she meant, what that fire was that scorched her insides. She'd had it, too. The intensity of her dream had sent her up North in search of a way to put out the flame. And it had cost her so much. She didn't want that for her baby. She wanted to protect this child, to shield her from all hurt or harm. But she had no right to stop her. Like her own daddy once said: Children have to find their own way. That could only be done by living by their own choices, choosing their own road, and making their own mistakes.

Cora swallowed down the hard knot that was building in her throat. Slowly she nodded her head. "Yes, chile, I understand." *More than you'll ever know.*

▲ ▲ ▲

The day David and Cora drove Parris to the Jackson airport, Cora was sure her heart was breaking, that the pain of her baby's departure was more than she could bear. She wanted to warn her about the wickedness of the big city, just like her mother, Pearl, had warned her. But in her heart she knew it would do no good, wouldn't stop Parris from leaving, just as it hadn't stopped her. Parris would have to learn these things for herself. So she'd prayed tirelessly for weeks after Parris told them over dinner that she wanted to move to New York, the capital of sin and the devil's merriment, to find a job and hopefully get a chance to sing at one of the many night-clubs. She said she'd been saving her money and could easily support herself until she found a suitable job. She promised to write every week and call as often as she could. And Cora prayed, prayed until she was dizzy, but she knew this day was inevitable. And all the prayer in the world couldn't stop it from happening. Just as her mother's efforts had been futile in stopping her from ultimately going to Chicago. Dreams aren't killed that easily.

Cora stood in the airport fighting back tears, gripping David's hand for dear life, as she watched the plane take off with her baby. And all she wished was that Parris would find what she was seeking, the one thing that would quench the burning in her soul, that thing that had eluded both her mother and grandmother.

Maybe.

BOOK III

Parris

Thirty-three

～～～～～～～～

It was nighttime in the Big Apple, New York, or Noo Yawk, as her nana would call it. Everything started Uptown shortly after midnight, Parris quickly discovered, an hour that none of the folks down home would have even been outside. This cosmopolitan crowd stood outside of the club where the wails and throbs of the music could be heard out on the street. Yes, Harlem. Darktown after sunset. Parris could feel the beat of the metropolis, the vibration of the big city in everything around her, could feel it pulse magically through her veins, run up and down her spine like the nimble fingers of a piano master over the ivories.

The front door was opened just a crack, the golden light from within just a sliver, just enough to let out the buzz of the talking and cash register chatter from the club, the chuckle of a good joke, and the allure of a better drink. The people came looking for an evening of good sounds, of escape, of a place to revel in the joys of life. One after another they entered, making sure they made it inside before it got too crowded. Like in the good old days when Minton's would get jammed when Bird, Dizzy, and Monk performed, jammed in there on into morning. It was the memories of those golden, precious times that still haunted this well-heeled crowd. These grandsons and granddaughters of those sturdy field hands, who ran over each other getting inside, each making their own unique sound like horns speaking among themselves, then settling down like old friends to a hot meal of grits and salmon croquettes.

This is where she'd come. Alone to this mecca of melody and rhythm. To see for herself what all the fuss was about, to see what brought these

243

people out so late. Entering a New York nightclub held the same excitement and exhilaration for her that came with her first trip downtown on the subway express train. Everything was speed, acceleration, and movement. The music she heard possessed that same feeling of force and power. She sought to fit in, to be like the others. Most important, she didn't want anyone to know just how unsophisticated she really was when she inadvertently gawked at the bright lights of the towering skyscrapers or sat wide-eyed listening to the music. That same feeling came as she watched the women in their tight dresses wiggle past the men, who leaned like slick blades of grass along the walls and against shiny cars, waiting for just the right twitch of a curvy hip or alluring glance of an feminine eye.

She'd overheard talk about the club from several of the men and women at the Harlem-based law firm where she worked in the Accounting Department. The place had a reputation for fine music, good food, and a savvy crowd. Her years at the two-teller bank in Rudell, her business degree, and natural talent with numbers and ledgers made her job search a relatively easy one.

Parris stepped inside, stumbling at first when her eyes slowly adjusted to the sudden dimness and blue, smoke-filled air. She looked around in awe at the glitter, the long necks tossed back in laughter, the secrets whispered deep into gold-studded ears, the long, dark arms draped around slinky, bare shoulders, bodies huddled into tight corners.

"Bar or table?" a young woman who could be no more than nineteen shouted above the noise.

Momentarily startled, Parris looked around at the hostess in confusion.

"Bar or table," the girl repeated.

"Um, a table please." She quickly recovered, attempting to sound more self-assured in this new, mysterious environment.

"How many in your party?"

"Just one, thank you."

The young woman clad in a short, black skirt and tight, white blouse, snatched up a menu from its holder and said, "Follow me."

Parris was quickly seated at a small table in the back of the club, which suited her just fine. It gave her a perfect view of everyone and everything.

"Can I take your drink order?" the same woman asked, holding a pad in her hands and a pencil poised between her long fingers, her nine-inch-high Afro sitting like a black halo around her tiny face.

"A Coke would be fine, thank you."

The girl gave her a curious look before whirling away. *A square.*

Parris folded her hands on the white-topped, linen-covered table and instinctively bobbed her head and snapped her fingers to the music from the live jazz band, humming along to their rendition of "Smoke Gets in Your Eyes."

By degrees she felt her body begin to relax, move easily to the rhythms, forgetting that she was alone in a strange place, with people she didn't know, many of them in big platform shoes and multicolored shirts. She glanced briefly at her own attire, a simple red polyester sheath that hit her just above the knees, with a modest scooped neckline and short sleeves. She smiled to herself. Nana would have a fit if she saw her now, looking so whorish.

"You look like you're enjoying yourself." The voice was definitely male, smooth and full of baritone notes. Solid but not booming, like a horn's low, throaty sound.

Parris looked up into dark, shimmering eyes and a soft smile. The man before her was tall, a bit taller than her, and slender. She could tell by the way his obviously expensive black suit framed his body. The white shirt beneath was open at the collar, a signal of casualness that she instantly liked, and upon further inspection she realized that he was the sax player from the band.

"Yes, I am," she finally responded.

"That's good. I like to make sure all my customers enjoy themselves here at Downbeat."

Parris was certain the surprise of his proclamation registered on her face by the subtle smile that flickered across his mouth.

"Nick Hunter," he said by way of introduction, in that smooth, controlled voice of his. He was careful not to frighten her by standing almost on top of her as she'd seen many men do since her arrival here.

"Parris Mackey."

"First time here, Parris?"

"Yes."

"So what do you think of the place?"

"It's great. Nice music. I haven't tried the food yet, but I'm sure I won't be disappointed." She paused for a moment. "There is one thing missing though."

His right brow rose in question. "And what might that be?"

"You need a singer to go along with that great band."

He chuckled lightly. "We had one, but she quit and went on to bigger and better things, or so she said."

"Really." Her mind started to race.

"Know of anybody who sounds like Sarah, has the presence of Billie, can phrase like Ella, work the changes like Carmen, and will work for cheap?" he added, with a sheepish grin.

Parris lowered her head and bit back a smile. "Maybe."

"Then tell her to show up on Wednesday around six; we're having auditions. Tell her to ask for Nick."

Parris nodded. "I'll do that."

"Nice to meet you, Parris Mackey. Enjoy your evening. I hope to see you again." With that, Nick turned away with an easy grace and blended into the crowd.

I think you will, Mr. Hunter, Parris thought, as she watched him move from one patron to the other, shaking a hand, patting a back, planting a kiss, confidence and sophistication in each and every gesture. Yes, I do believe you will.

Thirty-four

~~~~~~~~~~~

Parris arrived at her desk promptly at eight. She liked being the first one in the office. It gave her the opportunity to relax with a cup of coffee, read the morning paper, review her workload for the day, and write her weekly letter to her grandparents.

She'd been in New York for nearly a year and hadn't missed one week of her letter writing. Some weeks she didn't have much to report, her life for the most part was simple and routine, except for an occasional Friday night at the club, and her ongoing relationship with Frank Carter, an up-and-coming attorney in the corporate law offices on the third floor. She'd written to Nana about Frank, describing in detail the nice restaurants he'd taken her to, their Saturday jaunts to the Museum of Modern Art, Broadway plays, and horseback riding in Central Park. Nana wanted to know how serious she was about "this fella," and the truth was, she really didn't know.

Frank was nice enough, handsome in a magazine kind of way, and a gentleman; but there was no real spark there, that all-over warm feeling she'd expect to have with someone who would be long term. Maybe in time, she'd told Nana. She only wished that Frank shared her dream. Unfortunately, that wasn't the case.

This morning she wrote about her solo evening at Downbeat. The rush of adrenaline she'd felt, the excitement—and the man she'd met, Nick Hunter, the owner of the club.

Although they'd only met and spoken briefly, there was something about him, a sensuousness that she couldn't deny, or forget. He made her feel hot and cold all at once, with no effort on his part. His smile made her skin tingle just to think about it, and his melodious voice had touched her deep in the center of her being.

He'd hovered in the back of her mind all weekend, sneaking into her thoughts without warning. She tried to describe the feeling in her letter, but knew she must sound like a babbling idiot. She smiled as she wrote. Her Nana would understand. The way she felt was the same way Nana described her feelings that day Granddad first came to First Baptist Church. Yes, it was like that.

If only she could find the kind of love her grandparents shared. You could feel it in the way they stole secret looks at each other, the way they touched when they thought no one was looking. Sometimes they would sit quietly for hours on the swing bench out on the porch, just holding hands and looking out onto the countryside. Yes, that was what she hoped to find one day. Someone to love her totally and unconditionally like Granddad loved Nana. Someone to share her dreams and her nights with.

Parris didn't tell Nana about the upcoming audition on Wednesday. She knew her grandmother's feelings about singing outside of the church, even though she reluctantly accepted Parris's desire to perform one day. She never quite understood her grandmother's adamant opinion, and Cora refused to discuss it. So she decided to wait with her news. If things didn't work out, there would be nothing to tell; and if it did well . . . She didn't want to think about it, at least not yet. Parris promised to call soon, signed her name with a flourish, and slipped the short note into an envelope to be mailed during her lunch hour.

By the time she'd finished her coffee, the sounds of office activity began to swirl around her. Good mornings met with the sounds of opening doors and jingling keys, in time with the hum of typewriters kicked back to life, and the giggles and whispers blending together to share weekend escapades.

"Hey, Parris," Gina Raymond, her coworker greeted.

Gina, a friendly woman with looks that eluded the mighty grip of time, sat at the desk right next to Parris and had quickly befriended her when she first arrived. She had showed her the ropes and filled her in on all the office gossip, which Parris made a point of avoiding.

"Hi, Gina. How was your weekend?"

"Great." Gina plopped down in her seat, her miniskirt inching high up on her trim thighs. She shoved her purse into the bottom desk drawer. "How about you? Do anything exciting?"

Parris debated about telling Gina of her trip to Downbeat, especially the part about her plan to audition on Wednesday. She told her office mate everything but the juicy details, which were sure to be repeated over coffee. Gina was sweet, but she was also notorious for having a big mouth. She loved to chat, especially about other people's business. And the last thing she needed was for Frank to get wind of it before she was ready to say anything. She knew his feelings about her goals, and a part of her understood, but it remained the central bone of contention between them. And in the months that they'd been seeing each other, it was becoming obvious by the day that he would never change his mind or his opinion. His view of women, and their traditional role in society, was unshakable.

Parris blew out the tiny lie on a breath of exhaled air. "Nothing special. Listened to some music and relaxed."

"You and Frank didn't get together this weekend?"

"No. He had to go out of town." She edited her words skillfully.

"You two make such a great couple," Gina stated, as she carefully applied her red lipstick without the aid of a mirror. "Frank's moving up in this firm." She lowered her voice to a conspiratorial whisper. "Rumor has it that he's up for a promotion as head counsel in the Litigation Department."

Parris's brows drew together. He'd never said anything to her about it, but she supposed they both had their secrets.

"That would make him your boss," Gina added, with a wink. "You'll have it made. Nothing like having your boyfriend as your boss."

Parris smiled weakly and turned her attention to the case files on her desk. Maybe having your boyfriend as your boss could work for some people, but she wasn't interested in whatever perks that coveted position might afford her. Everything came with a price. She wanted her accomplishments to be of her own making, not bestowed upon her because of her status in someone else's life.

If she'd learned nothing else from her grandparents, it was that hard work, determination, and faith brought its own rewards. Rewards earned could not be snatched away at a whim or a sudden shift in emotions. And she had worked hard over the years—at home, at school, in the church, and on her job—all with one goal in mind: to have a career one day as a singer. It was the same dream that had somehow eluded her nana, even if she never spoke of it. But Parris intended to capture if for both of them. And in two days, she would take her first real steps toward that goal.

▲ ▲ ▲

Sitting in the back recesses of the club, Parris was as nervous as an expectant parent, the one left in the waiting room. She crossed and uncrossed her legs, took nervous sips from her glass of water, and tried to concentrate on getting the blood circulating back into her hands and feet, which had mysteriously turned into blocks of ice.

They are good, she thought, listening to the would-be starlets who took the spotlight one after another. They all had a certain style and a presence that she'd never had the opportunity to acquire. It was easy to see that these sleekly dressed, bejeweled, and heavily makeup women had performed before more than a handful of pious churchgoers. Some were really seasoned professionals.

Oh, Lawd, maybe she'd made a mistake. She didn't have any business here. She was out of her league. What—

"Parris Mackey!" a woman with a clipboard shouted.

Parris felt every muscle leap against the skin.

"Parris Mackey!"

She jumped from her seat; the shock of hearing her name was like a sudden pin prick in the rear. Parris glanced briefly around, took a deep breath, tugged her suit jacket over her waist, and walked toward the stage.

"Good luck," a deep voice to her right whispered.

She turned toward the familiar sound. It was him. She hadn't seen Nick from her vantage point in the back, but he must have been there all along. Her pulse raced as she mumbled her thanks and stepped up on stage.

The piano player gazed at her expectantly. "Um, do you know, "Lover Man," the Sarah Vaughan version?"

"Not a problem. Same key as 'Sassy?' " he asked, referring to the song diva's pet name.

Parris nodded numbly.

"Would you rather sit or stand?" Nick asked, from the floor of the club.

Could he tell how terrified she was, Parris wondered, which only added to her angst. "Sit," she replied, over the sudden dryness in her throat, secretly thankful for the offer since her knees felt as if they would liquefy at any moment.

"Bring a stool for Ms. Mackey, will you, Tessa?" Nick asked of the clipboard girl.

Tessa disappeared behind the stage and returned shortly, carrying a three-legged stool.

Parris took the stool and positioned it in front of the standing microphone. She tried to make out the few deciding faces at the front tables, but the overhead spotlights and the darkened interior blinded her, which was just as well. She could pretend she was alone.

Parris cleared her throat and let her lids glide shut over her eyes. " 'The night is so cold, and I'm all alone . . .' " She let the music, the poignancy of the lyrics, and the familiar bounce of the song's sorrowful rhythms fill her. She became the woman crying for someone to love, someone to take the ache of loneliness away. How would it feel to be all alone? She wondered, as she gently rode the crest of the notes, sometimes diving deep, then rising up from her center, breaking free, the liquid clarity of her tone seeping into every crevice and crease in the room until it echoed with the haunting power of her voice.

Nick was trapped, transfixed. Her silky voice wrapped around him like a hunter's net, and he didn't want to break free. He wanted her to take him on the journey with her, give her what she was searching for.

Compelled, he picked up his sax, which was propped up against the chair next to him, and brought it to his lips, joining her as she bent and twisted those last plaintive notes, the cry of his horn heightening the soulful moan. " 'Lover man . . .' "

Nick wailed a few mournful runs as the song neared an emotional end, which left many of the musicians completely mesmerized. The final bottom notes of the tenor sax supported Parris effortlessly, while she reworked the dramatic closing words of the sad ballad, infusing them with as much raw feeling as she could conjure up. Someone gasped in astonishment at her range and power, and Parris slowly opened her eyes as if awakening from a dream and her gaze settled soft as a feather on Nick's face. He still held the sax to his lips as if he was unable or unwilling to break the spell. They simply stared at each other. Everything and everyone else in the room drifted meaninglessly into the distant background. It was just the two of them, caught in the special reverie of the moment.

"Nick! Can I see you please."

The moment was gone, broken by the tight voice of a woman who stepped out from the shadows of the partially lit room.

"That was great," Nick uttered. "Don't move. I'll be right back."

Nick rested his golden Selmer sax gingerly on the cushion of the chair and wound his way around the maze of circular tables to the back.

Parris's gaze trailed him, cataloging in her mind's eye the rhythm of his stride, the way his body seemed to glide in a smooth flow of graceful motion. Yet there was a muscularity in it, like the coiled force of a big cat, as if he worked hard at containing the volcanic energy that hovered just beneath the surface. It was nothing overt, but she'd caught it in his eyes, in the rawness of it that flared his nostrils and lit his dark skin from beneath. The look she expected would come into his expression while he was in the throes of passionate lovemaking.

A sudden heat rushed to her head. She blinked rapidly, her eyes quickly darting around in the dimness of the room, as she momentarily imagined that everyone could read her secret, erotic thoughts. She focused her attention on her hands folded in her lap.

"Who's that?" Tara Davis asked Nick, with a subtle lift of her chin in Parris's direction.

Nick could already hear the edge in her voice and wasn't in the mood for one of Tara's jealous tirades. He placed his hands on her shoulders and looked down into her upturned face. "Tara, she's auditioning for the spot, just like everyone else," he said, in a tone you would use with a petulant child.

Tara folded her arms beneath her small breasts. "Looked to me like she was auditioning for more than the singing spot," she stated snidely, cutting her eyes in Parris's direction.

Nick heaved a weary breath. The last thing he needed was a catfight in the club. More tension. He and Tara had been seeing each other exclusively for almost three years. They'd met when he was playing at an after-hours jam session with some of the cats in a nightclub in the West Village. The attraction, at first, was purely physical, nothing but sheer animal magnetism. Tara Davis had a totally devastating sensuality about her that was impossible to ignore. Over time he'd grown to care about her, and she made it a point to introduce him to her influential father, Percy Davis, and all of his high-powered Harlem associates. Percy had taken Nick under his wing. "Anyone who can catch my baby girl's eye is someone I want to know," he'd told Nick one night over drinks during a New Year's Eve dinner party at his posh digs on Shriver's Row. "I believe you have a lot of potential, Nick. I can make things happen for you in this town." He leaned back against the bar and studied Nick thoroughly. "What's your dream, son? If you had one wish, what would it be?"

Nick didn't have to think about it. It was something that had lived inside him for as long as he could remember. "I want my own business, my own jazz club." He sipped his dry martini and eyed Percy over the rim of his glass.

Percy smiled slyly, placed his glass on the top of the bar, patted Nick on the shoulder, and walked away.

About a month later, Nick got a call at home asking him to meet Percy on Lenox Avenue. When he arrived at the address, Percy, Tara, and two of Percy's business partners were outside, their limo parked at the curb.

"So what do you think?" Percy asked, with a brief wave of his well-manicured hand when Nick approached.

"About what?"

Percy stood back proudly, like a genie who had just made a wish come true, and faced the two-story, prewar building behind him. "About your new club, son."

Nick's thick brows drew tightly together in confusion. "New club. What are you talking about?"

Tara came up close to Nick, pressing her lithe body next to his, and placed her opened palms on his chest. "Daddy bought this for you, for us," she stated, in that sultry whisper of hers.

Percy grinned broadly. "It's all yours, son."

"What! I can't take this from you."

Percy pulled a pack of Rothman cigarettes from the breast pocket of his sharkskin jacket. He tapped out one of the English cigarettes, put it slowly to his lips, and lit it. He peered at Nick through the thin cloud of smoke. "Consider it a loan. When everything is paid off, the joint is yours free and clear."

"But, Mr. Davis . . ."

"It ain't right to refuse a gift," Percy uttered, his voice taking on a slightly ominous, gravelly tone.

His two stone-faced associates moved in around him. "And it makes Tara happy. I want to see my daughter happy . . . and I know you do as well."

Nick glanced from Tara to her father to the future that was mere feet away. To accept this "gift" would tie him up in dealings that he didn't want to think about. A gift like this always came with strings attached and big obligations. To walk away now, even if it was the right thing to do, could be worse. But beyond all of it was an underlying excitement he couldn't deny. This was what he'd longed for, dreamed about. Now it was his. His. He'd make it work, make it profitable, and pay off Tara's father, get him and everything he represented out of his life. He had to. He must.

That was more than a year ago, and his monthly payments to Percy Davis seemed to barely put a dent in the huge mortgage that was in his name, cosigned by Percy. Not only was he tied to him, but to his daughter, who was part of the tangled web of his life.

"You're not going to hire her, are you?" Tara demanded to know, a quality of aggressive control that had grown more insistent during the course of their relationship.

Her terse question pulled him back from the flight of his thoughts. "She's good. Better than good. I don't see why not."

"What do you know about her?"

"What do I need to know, Tara, beside the fact that she's one helluva singer," he tossed back, feeling his temper bubbling to the surface. "Listen, I need to finish up. I'll talk to you later." He turned to leave before he said something he'd regret.

"We're still on for tonight, right?" she asked, loud enough for Parris and everyone within earshot to hear.

Nick's step momentarily faltered for a beat. "I'll let you know." He returned to the front of the stage without looking back, knowing that all he'd see if he did was Tara's exquisite face marred by her irrational anger.

"Sorry I took so long," he apologized to Parris.

"It's fine. Really." Her heart beat faster as she prayed that the woman, whoever she was, had no real say so as to whether she would be hired or not. Because if she did, she knew what the answer would be.

"Why don't you come on down so we can talk for a minute," Nick said.

Gingerly, Parris stepped around the microphone, made her way across the stage to the stairs, and climbed down, joining him at the table.

"Please, have a seat." He pulled out a chair and waited for her to get settled. "So you were the one you were talking about the other night?" Nick asked, with a sparkle in his eyes and a half smile.

Parris ducked her head with embarrassment. "Yes. I was."

"I loved what you did up there."

Her gaze flew upward. "You did?"

"No doubt about it. You have talent. Where have you sung before?"

Her face heated. "Just in church, in the choir, back home," she quietly confessed.

"And home is . . ."

"Mississippi. A small town called Rudell. Very small," she added with a grin.

"Hmm. They let you sing like that in the church?" he teased.

She laughed openly now, her green eyes twinkling in the light. "No way. I did all my 'other' singing in the shower. Hymns are something you don't toy with."

Nick got a quick flash of her nude body, enveloped in steam, glistening with dewdrops of water. He shifted in his seat, then cleared his throat. "I'd, uh, like to make you an offer."

Parris nodded, too afraid to speak.

"Two nights a week for starters, Thursday and Friday. The pay isn't great, but you'll get plenty of exposure. How does that sound?"

"Sound! It sounds wonderful," she gushed and suppressed the overwhelming urge to reach across the table and hug him.

The soft lilt of her southern drawl floated like music in the air. Nick chuckled. "Then I guess we have a deal." He stuck out his hand.

Tentatively, Parris placed her hand in his and a sudden rush of heat shot through her as his hand covered hers.

He felt it, too. It was as if someone had lit a fire in his belly. He didn't want to let her go. He wanted to pull her closer, listen to that teasingly soft voice of hers, see her face light up. He wanted to know what she felt like, skin to skin, deliciously pressed against him.

Nick released her hand. His eyes looked everywhere but at her, lest they betray his thoughts. Finally, his pulse returned to normal. "Can you be here on Sunday at noon? We rehearse," he added, checking the questioning arch of her brow.

"Sure. I'll be here. Noon."

"See you then."

Parris stood. "Thank you for this opportunity. You don't know how much this means to me."

Nick rose from his seat. "I think I do."

For several moments, they silently faced each other, both trying to sift through the array of emotions that ran like unruly electric currents between them.

"I . . . I guess I'd better go," Parris said finally. "Thank you again." She turned away and walked toward the door, feeling instead like she wanted to skip with joy. Once, in disbelief, she stopped and glanced back at the stage, where the musicians were packing up their instruments, talking quietly among themselves.

Nick watched her departure and unconsciously counted the days until he would see her again.

From the back of the nightclub, Tara observed the two of them, her man and that woman. She'd felt the heat between them; everyone had felt it.

No, she didn't like what she'd seen. She didn't like it one damned bit.

Thirty-five

~~~~~~~~~~~~~~~

"Where were you last night?" Frank asked, as soon as Parris walked into the employee kitchen.

Silent, Parris poured herself a cup of coffee. She was buying time.

"I called you until almost eleven."

"I had an appointment," she replied curtly.

As if on cue, two other attorneys walked in, their voices humming in guarded conversation. Their entry momentarily derailed Frank's verbal assault, but he was not going to be denied for long.

Frank frowned. "What kind of appointment did you have until that hour of the night? Where could you be so late?"

"I'm not on the witness stand, Frank," she snapped from between her teeth, trying to keep from being overheard.

He blew out an exasperated breath. "I didn't say you were, Parris. I was simply asking a question. I was concerned. I still am."

"I'm sorry if I worried you." She started to move past him. "There's no reason to be concerned. I told you I had an appointment."

"So you're not going to tell me." He was adamant.

Parris stopped in her tracks, whirled around to face him. "I went on an audition at a nightclub. Okay. And I got the job." She turned and stalked out, almost enjoying the look of astonishment on his otherwise handsome face.

Why did he have to make her feel so damned guilty? Guilty for wanting what she wanted. What was so wrong with wanting a career as a singer? she fumed, tapping out a letter on the typewriter. He made her desire, her

256

one passion, seem so ugly and insignificant. And it wasn't. It wasn't and she'd prove it, to Frank and to herself.

"What is wrong with you, girl?" Gina asked, reading her face as she approached her desk and sat down. "You look like you had something bad to eat."

"Nothing," Parris mumbled. "Just thinking about all this work, that's all."

"Listen, take my advice. I learned a long time ago not to let it get to me. It's just a job, not my life." Gina popped her gum loudly and began typing.

Parris was thoughtful for a moment, then turned suddenly toward Gina. "Isn't there something you want to do more than anything in the world? Something you've dreamed of all your life?" she asked, with a breath of wistfulness in her voice.

Gina's long, manicured fingers halted above the keyboard. She pursed her red-painted mouth. "I know this sounds corny and old-fashioned, but . . . I want to get married, have a bunch of kids, and live happily ever after."

Parris stared at Gina's profile in surprise. Gina was the last person she expected to hear that statement coming from. It was common knowledge around the office that Gina Raymond was a gossip and a party girl, not someone who had a serious thought in her head or the girl you took home to meet Mama.

"Told you it sounded corny," Gina mumbled quietly, when Parris didn't respond.

"No, it's not," Parris said gently. "I was just surprised, that's all."

"Yeah. I guess anyone would be." She laughed, disheartened.

Parris swiveled her chair toward Gina. "Then if that's what you want, why do you run around from man to man and pass off stories along the way? It doesn't make sense."

"I don't know." Gina lowered her head. "I—just want people to like me. I want guys to like me. But after one or two dates . . ." She shrugged.

"Then you've got to give them a chance . . . not throw yourself at them. The most precious thing we have is our self-respect. My grandparents always said if you believe you're a lady, you'll act like a lady and you'll be treated like one."

"It's too late for me. You think I don't know what they say about me?" Her eyes began to fill and her bottom lip trembled. "I never slept with any of them. None. Never. I swear." She sniffed and quickly dabbed at her eyes. "But that doesn't stop them from lying on me."

Parris had the urge to scold her, tell her how stupid it was for her to keep repeating her mistakes, looking for something she'd never find in the people she surrounded herself with. But when she saw the look of pain, vulnerability, and loneliness etched on Gina's face, she knew a scolding wasn't what she needed. Gina needed a friend, a real friend.

"Hey," Parris said gently, "what are you doing later—after work?"

Gina sniffed loudly and patted her eyes dry. She shrugged a shoulder wearily. "Nothing really. I was going to go home and wash my hair."

"I was thinking of eating out tonight," Parris explained. "I don't feel like cooking. Why don't you come with me?"

"What about Frank?" Gina couldn't believe her good fortune. The women there talked to her, but none of them had ever invited her out for dinner.

"What about him? I'm asking you."

Gina stared at her a moment, trying to peer beyond the pleasantries, see what was really going on behind those strange eyes. And for the life of her, all she could detect was sincerity. Parris was genuine in her concern for her; she could see it on her face.

"All right," she agreed. "If you're sure."

"Absolutely."

Gina's expression brightened noticeably. "Have any place in mind?"

Parris smiled. "As a matter of fact, I do."

▲ ▲ ▲

The atmosphere at Downbeat was different than on Friday night. The after-work clientele chatted in sugar-coated tones, drank wine instead of shooters, wore business suits instead of clingy mini dresses, stylish sharkskin suits, and lizard shoes. It was a more sophisticated crowd.

Even the music seemed mellower, its riffs floating sweetly above the chitchat rather than shutting it down with finger-popping funk or high-stepping, blue notes.

Nick stepped up to the mike, fingering the keys on his horn silently before launching into a blistering solo. Critics had often compared his playing style to that of Coleman Hawkins, with its full-throated tone and mastery in all registers. He closed his eyes, improvising on the changes of the jazz anthem, "Star Eyes." One of his idols, Charlie Parker, was known for his various interpretations of the popular evergreen, a real crowd pleaser. The drummer used brushes on the high hat behind him, coloring the intervals in his blowing with soft, ever-shifting accents.

"I haven't been here in a while," Gina commented, as they were led to a table in the center of the room. "What made you pick this place?" She slid into her seat and put her purse on the table.

"I came here on Friday," Parris admitted in a faraway voice, her attention focused on the lean, dark figure at center stage.

"You're kidding. You? By yourself?" She smiled skeptically. "Still waters run deep."

"Something to drink, ladies?" the waitress asked.

"White wine spritzer," Gina said.

"A Coke for me," Parris added absently.

Gina followed Parris's gaze, then jerked back to her. "He is cute," she commented on the lanky saxophonist, who was doubled over with the sax, and waited for Parris's reaction. "I've seen him around."

"Have you?"

"Yeah. He used to play downtown before he opened this spot. I usually see him with the same chick. Her father is some big-time hustler, Percy Davis."

She had Parris's full attention now. "Who is she?" Parris asked, thinking immediately of the female fashion plate she'd seen at the audition.

"I think her name is Tara. Everybody knows she's connected. She's Daddy's little girl. What she wants she gets, including Mr. Cutie Pie up there. If she says she wants him under her tree for the holiday, Daddy'll have him gift wrapped in no time."

Parris frowned, disturbed by what she heard, in particular Nick's connection to less than savory individuals. What if he was mobbed up? He didn't seem the type. But what did she really know? She'd allowed herself to get caught up in an impossible fantasy; something that would never happen, especially since there was a woman in his life. Maybe this little talk with Gina was the best thing that could have happened. Thank God for Gina's big mouth. She blew out a breath. And she did have Frank. So why did she feel so disappointed?

Nick slowly lowered his horn, letting the last sheets of sound from his tenor reverberate in all their golden splendor throughout the club, and the attentive crowd showed their approval with hand clapping, foot stomping, and shouts for more. He acknowledged their appreciation by holding his sax in front of him and bowing slightly.

His gaze drifted around the packed room. There she was, and the sudden tightening in his stomach took him by surprise. He'd had to push her out of his thoughts just to get through the night. He'd never had a woman have that kind of effect on him, not even Tara in all her sexy glory. There was something erotically innocent about Parris that was more alluring than if she walked around nude. Yes, she was beautiful in a simple way, stunning really, but it went beyond that. And for the life of him, he couldn't figure it out.

Nick put down his sax and trotted down the steps off the stage as the band went into their theme before taking their first break of the evening. As every band knew, the first set was always the toughest because that was when you felt out your audience, much like a boxer in the early rounds of a bout. Tonight's crowd was smoking. As bop great Bud Powell used to say: these folks got ears. Nick nonchalantly crossed the room until he stood at Parris's table, slightly behind her. He didn't want her to get a direct look at him. She'd definitely see what he was feeling in his eyes, there was no hiding that.

"Didn't expect to see you so soon." His smooth voice slid down her throat, settled in her stomach, and spread through her limbs like the glow of a hot toddy.

"I thought I should get used to the place." She said it like a veteran singer getting the feel of a new room she would soon make her own.

"I'm glad you came." He shifted his attention to Gina, although he was talking to Parris.

Gina intently watched the intimate exchange, the body language, and all it implied. For all the people in the smoke-filled, wine- and perfumed-tinted room, it was plainly obvious that this man and Parris saw only each other. This was more than a work situation.

"So am I. Uh, this is my friend, Gina Raymond. Gina, Nick Hunter."

Gina extended her hand. "Heard a lot about you."

Nick didn't comment. He'd heard the rumors, too, that he was connected through Percy Davis, that his club was a front for Percy's numbers racket. None of which was true; but until he could free himself from Percy's financial stranglehold, the stories would stick to him like flypaper. At this moment, the man owned everything about him except his soul. It was only a matter of time before he made a claim on that, but Nick planned to cut all ties before that happened.

"You ladies enjoy your evening. See you on Sunday," he said to Parris, winking.

She nodded with a weak smile. Her eyes went to her restless hands, while Gina watched Nick walked away with something more than admiration in her stare.

"See you Sunday," Gina quizzed. "What's that about?"

"I, uh, have a job here." Parris was still mulling over the revelation that had come from Gina about Nick's possible underworld ties: a damn crook.

"What?"

"I'll be singing with the band." She turned to Gina with a bland expression on her face.

Gina suddenly slapped her hand down on the table, shaking the glasses, then burst into laughter. "Well, I'll be damned! You're going to sing—here? Get out of town."

"And don't you say a word. Swear to me." Parris didn't want her business getting around the office. More grist for the gossip mill.

Gina drew her fingers across her mouth, signifying that she wouldn't tell a soul.

"I'm trusting you, Gina."

"Okay. Okay. I swear." She leaned forward. "Did you tell Frank? Does he know?"

"No. And don't you say anything either."

"Someone is bound to say something. People from the office come in here all the time. Most of them are already curious about you and your private life. You don't come to the cafeteria and run your mouth like everyone else. You're a mystery."

Parris twisted her lips. "I'll deal with Frank when the time comes. As for the rest of the office crew, I don't really care what they think about me."

"Why don't you just tell him? I don't see what the big deal is. He should be happy for you."

"I wish it was that simple," she murmured. She silently remembered the various spats they'd had in recent weeks, some of them needless disputes.

"I don't get it. He—"

"Frank wouldn't understand, Gina. Believe me. He has very firm ideas about things, about women."

Gina was watchful for a minute. "Then—why are you with him?" she asked astutely.

Parris's gaze drifted toward Gina. How many times had she asked herself the same question, especially over the past few months. Yes, why was she with him? Where was the relationship going? In the beginning, it was exciting to have a successful, handsome, educated man show an interest in her, take her around town, introduce her to all of his friends, get her familiar with life in the big city. It wasn't until they were several months into their relationship that she told him of her desire to sing. They'd just come home from a dinner party at Wells Restaurant.

"Sing!" He'd begun to laugh cruelly, as if he'd just heard the greatest joke. "You're kidding," he'd finally stated over the choked laughter.

Parris stood before him, feeling diminished and stupid, her desire insignificant and trivial. By belittling her dream, Frank must have known that he was also belittling her, making her feel small.

"Singing is a frivolous lifestyle, not for someone of your caliber, Parris. Let's be for real." He strode over to the bar and poured himself a double bourbon over ice. "Those women are nothing but tramps who will sleep with anyone to get a record deal. Everybody knows what type of people are attracted to that wretched environment: the lowest of the low. The entire profession is drug-infested, full of crooks, and they'll work you to your grave for pennies." His tone grew more strident and bitter as he ranted on and on about the vices of the industry, seemingly oblivious to how he was affecting her.

"Believe me, I know what I'm talking about, Parris," he concluded, tossing down the drink in one long gulp, his light cream complexion flushed by agitation and the flood of alcohol.

"How do you know?" she challenged.

His jaw shifted from side to side as if the distasteful words were lodged there somehow. He averted his gaze and crossed the room—away from her. He slid his hands into his pants pockets and stared out the window, taking in the bright lights and silhouetted buildings that cut through the night. This was the town that had seduced her, destroyed her, and his family with its secret whispers of fame and fortune, its intricately threaded web that lured you to its poisonous center, draining you until you had nothing left, with promises of fast cash, quick highs, and instant celebrity.

His throat tightened with painful guilt and memories.

"Well—how do you know, Frank? You're so eager to tell me what a fool I am. I want to know why."

"It killed her. That's why!"

Parris jerked back. "Who?"

"My mother."

Parris shook her head in confusion. "Your mother?"

"Yes."

Slowly, Parris sat down on the couch and listened as Frank unfolded the story of his mother and her ultimate destruction. The years of empty dreams and living from one small town to the next, waiting for "the big break." And then they came to New York and everything came apart. Frank blamed it on everything and everyone. It never entered his mind that she'd made her own choices, walked knowingly toward her doom, and embraced the bitter consequences. The most important thing he missed was that *she*, Parris, wasn't his mother.

"I'm sure you have your reasons, Parris," Gina said, tugging her new-found friend back to the present. "But you can't dance around it for long."

Parris blinked, then focused on Gina. "I know. And I won't. I just want to get settled. Try it and see how things work out."

Gina stared at her for a moment. "Be careful, Parris. I saw how that Nick guy was looking at you—and how you were looking at him. You don't want to get mixed up with him. He's bad news. Everybody knows that."

"I can take care of myself. But thanks for the advice. Believe me, there's nothing going on with us. He's the owner, and I'm just an employee."

"Yeah, for now," Gina mumbled into her drink.

Thirty-six

~~~~~~~~~

After that first night together at Downbeat, Parris and Gina could be seen giggling at the water fountain, huddled over a salad in the cafeteria or one of the local lunch spots. Many evenings, they would walk to the parking lot together, swapping stories about their day and solidifying plans for the evening. Their new friendship was the talk of the office; Ms. Southern Belle and the Office Hoochie. What did they have in common was the unending puzzle, a puzzle that no one was able to put together.

Parris actually enjoyed Gina's company. She was funny, easy to be with, and had more under her cap than anyone realized. People had totally underestimated Gina Raymond. Parris was tickled to discover that Gina had a love for foreign films, collected movie magazines, and had begun writing a screenplay, which she hoped to eventually get produced. "Maybe if I turn it into a musical, you could be my lead singer," Gina had teased. Parris shared with Gina her wealth of knowledge about music. She told her tales of some of the early blues singers, like Ma Rainey, and Bessie Smith, and the more contemporary and controversial Billie Holiday, and incomparable Ella and Sarah. She was in heaven when she spoke of Duke, Coltrane, Miles, and Lester Young. She grew pensive when she recounted the tales of the early black musicians and entertainers and what life was like for many of them as they traveled through the segregated South, unable to get hotel rooms or decent meals. She explained how the hospitable southerners would open their homes, providing food and shelter. Gina sat in on Parris's rehearsals, giving her thumbs-up and applauding after each and every song; and she watched the sparks fly between Nick and Parris and she worried in silence. If there was one thing she'd slowly come to know about Parris Mackey, it was that she didn't revisit an issue. She listened, thought about it, made a decision, and moved on. Just like she'd done about the whispers and snickers that were now floating around the office about her. And it hurt Gina to know that the only thing Parris had done to deserve the verbal abuse was to be her friend.

"Do you really think I give a damn what those people think of me, Gina?" Parris asked during lunch in the employee cafeteria. Her green eyes darkened, highlighting the warm brown of her complexion. "In the beginning there was nothing to discuss; they didn't know me, so they talked about that. Now they assume . . ." She glanced at Gina for a hot, embarrassed moment. "Anyway, it doesn't matter. We're friends, good friends, and I wouldn't trade that in for anything they could offer me."

"Really?" Gina asked in disbelief. The concept of anyone standing up for her, taking her side, was something so foreign to her, she didn't know how to handle it.

"Yeah, really. Gina, you're a decent person who may have made some mistakes, but that doesn't take away from who you are inside. Believe me, it's their loss, not yours if they won't give you a chance."

"Thanks. Really." Gina was humbled by the compliment.

Parris waved off her gratitude. "Are you coming tonight?"

Gina grinned. "Of course, girl. I wouldn't miss your big debut." She leaned across the table and lowered her voice. "You excited?"

Parris grinned. "I haven't been able to sleep. I can't think. Sometimes I feel like running, not walking, all the back to Rudell and telling my nana just how crazy I am." She slowly shook her head, allowing the surge of doubt to subside.

"Have you told Frank yet?"

"No. After tonight. After I face the music; then I'll tell him."

"I can't believe you got away with it this long. It's a miracle." Gina's gaze drifted behind Parris's shoulder. "Speak of the devil," she whispered from between her teeth as she spotted her friend's estranged heartthrob walking toward them.

Parris briefly shut her eyes. She felt her entire body tighten. The tension that existed between her and Frank these past weeks had been unbearable. Between her secret visits to the club and giving Frank all sorts of reasons why she couldn't spend their usual Sunday afternoon together, along with her impending debut, she was a nervous wreck. She really wasn't up to another teeth-gritting conversation with Frank. Not today.

"Parris," Frank placed his hand on her shoulder. "Glad I found you. Can I talk with you a minute? Hello, Gina. How are you?"

Gina gave him a puzzled look and mumbled her hello. She knew she wasn't one of Frank Carter's favorite people, and he'd made his dislike of her apparent by his distant, almost condescending attitude toward her. This new, pleasant stance was a switch.

Parris glanced upward, surprised and relieved to see the open, pleasant expression on his face. He was actually smiling. For an instant, her heart softened momentarily. This was the Frank she remembered, the one who had captured her attention with his easy ways and old-school manner.

"Sure." She began to stand. "Excuse me, Gina."

"No problem," Gina uttered, still dumbfounded by Frank's behavior. She watched them walk away.

"Let's talk in my office," Frank said, as he gently guided Parris down the hall with his hand at the small of her back. "I've missed you," he whispered.

A shudder ran along the length of Parris's spine. She didn't comment.

"I know things have been strained between us, Parris. I want to change that. A lot of it is my fault. I've just been a bit overwhelmed and crazy lately, but that's all about to change."

She turned her head to look at him, but his face was unreadable. The elevator door slid open and they rode up to the third floor. Frank nodded amicably to the harried attorneys and paralegals who rushed along the hallways with bulging folders of case files tucked under their arms. Parris rarely, if ever, came to the third floor, the heart and soul of the firm. This was where the decisions and strategies for people's lives were discussed, dissected, and made a reality—or not. It was one of the few, powerful black law firms in the city, and the only one that possessed an entire department dedicated to civil rights issues.

Frank opened the door to his office and ushered Parris inside. She looked around. She'd only been there twice in the year that she'd been with the firm. It looked pretty much as she remembered it, with the single, towering window, hand-polished mahogany desk, the old grandfather clock that stood in the corner—a gift from his father Frank had once told her—the plaques and awards of merit, his degrees, and one long wall that was lined with law books. His accessories were minimal: a gooseneck desk lamp, a crystal paperweight, a gold Parker pen. There was no clutter to be found or any real evidence that someone worked in this office. Everything was in its place. It was almost sterile. Frank was not what you would

consider a showy, flamboyant person. He believed that good taste was mod-
eration, and that belief was repeated in his quietly stylish home, his sedate
office, and in his low-keyed, elegant mode of dress. Frank was the con-
summate example of the black bourgeoisie, which ran counter to the type
of law he practiced and the people he represented—the poor and illiterate.
At times Parris believed he did it just to show his clients how much better
he was than they were.

So it surprised Parris to notice a silver tray on his desktop that held a
chilled bottle of what looked like imported, expensive champagne along
with two thin-stemmed glasses.

Frank coolly locked the office door and walked directly to the tray,
expertly uncorked the bottle, and poured the first glass. Smoothly, he
turned to Parris and handed it to her with a mysterious smile.

"What in the world is going on?" Parris asked, completely befuddled by
Frank's uncharacteristic behavior.

He turned his back to her, humming softly to himself, and poured himself a glass of champagne before facing her to reply. He raised his glass in
toast fashion. "To us and to the incredible days ahead." He brought the
glass to his lips and took a short sip. Parris absently followed suit, watching
Frank's every move and reaction, hoping for some clue.

"I know you must be wondering what's going on." He placed his glass
down on the tray and stepped up to her, taking her glass gingerly from
her fingers. He set it down, perfectly, next to his. His hands slid around
her waist, and he eased her closer. The faint scent of champagne and cigarettes floated around him. "I got it, baby. I got the promotion. You are
looking at the senior litigating attorney for Russell and Wells, Esq."
He brushed his lips against hers. "I get my own staff, a new office, and decide which cases we take and which ones we don't. It's only a matter of
time before I make partner. And when I do—we can get married."

"Married? We never discussed marriage, Frank. And I—"

"I know it's down the road. And I know there are things we need to
work out between us, and we will," he said, misinterpreting the look of
escalating alarm that lit Parris's eyes for simple surprise. "I know I've been
a real bastard lately, but the pressure of waiting, trying to make sure I did
everything right, was seen at all the right places, with the right people,
making the right decisions, and winning my cases was really getting to
me." He stroked her cheek. "I'm sorry if I took my anxieties out on you.
But ninety percent of this job is appearances. If you look like a winner, act
like a winner, run with winners, then by consensus you *are* a winner." He

stared at her a moment, confused by her silence. "Aren't you going to say anything, congratulate me?"

Parris swallowed. "Congratulations, Frank. I'm happy for you. I really am." She lightly pecked his lips.

"Good. I want to celebrate. I got us two tickets to the ballet. Judith Jamison and the Alvin Ailey Dance Troupe are performing at the City Center. We have seats front row, center. You'll love them."

Her heart thumped against her chest. "When?"

"Tonight. And believe me I had to practically sell my soul to get them." He chuckled. "But nothing is too good for you." He kissed her again, pleased with himself.

Tonight. Tonight was her debut, her first night singing in front of a live audience. The night she'd waited her entire life for. What was she supposed to do? Her stomach lurched. There was no way that Frank could understand what this night meant to her. She should have taken Gina's advice weeks ago and told him what was going on. But it had always been one thing or the other that stopped her. Either they were barely speaking, which only stiffened her resolve not to say anything to him at all, or he was being uncommonly sweet and attentive, calling her in the middle of the day or sending flowers to her house. At those times, things almost seemed right and she hadn't wanted to upset the tenuous balance they'd regained. Now her feeble excuses had finally caught up with her.

"Frank, I—," she swallowed. "I—can't, not tonight." There, she'd said it.

His entire expression tightened into a hard mask of disbelief. The nerve under his left eye began to pulse. "What—why not?"

"I have plans for this evening." She said it as calmly as she could.

"Cancel them." He was firm with his reply, uncompromising.

"No. I won't." She stepped back and stood her ground. It was now or never.

His jaw clenched. She could see his nostrils flaring. "You won't?" His question rang with sarcasm. He began to laugh low in his throat. "You won't," he repeated, as if he couldn't believe what he was hearing from her, and began pouring himself another drink. He gulped it down. "And why is that, Parris?" he asked, in a dangerously flat tone.

"I'm singing tonight."

He glared at her with a malevolence that chilled her. "Singing? You?" He tossed another drink down his throat. "We talked about this. I told you my feelings."

"And I told you mine. This is what I want. This is my chance."

"Chance! What in the hell kind of chance do you think you'll have in that seedy type of life? None. Nothing." He stomped across the room. His lean body was a tight coil ready to spring. "I won't have it. You're not going. That's all there is to it." The veins in his forehead throbbed with fury.

Parris squared her shoulders defiantly and looked him straight in the eye. "The only people whoever told me what to do were the grandparents who raised me," she stated in a cool, even tone, her voice as sweet as honeysuckle. "And when I got old enough to figure things out on my own, even they stopped telling me what to do. I make my own decisions, Frank, just like you make yours. And hopefully we won't regret the ones that we make." She paused a beat. "Congratulations on your promotion, Frank. I'm sure you'll do well." Before he could respond, she turned to leave.

Frank saw his mirror cracking. Everything he'd put together piece by piece, step by step, was coming apart. This goddamned music thing had nearly destroyed his life once before. It was the one element in his life he actually feared, the one thing he couldn't control, and it had taken hold of Parris, the only person he'd allowed himself to care about. He couldn't let it take her away from him, too. Yet he knew if he forced her to stay, the fire that burned inside her would eventually engulf them both. But if he allowed her to leave, he would lose even more—his pride. And pride was the window dressing of every winner. A solid, confident front was all that mattered in this corporate world. He would never allow her to strip him of that, no matter what the cost.

"You walk out that door—and you'll regret it!" he shouted at her. "I swear you will!"

The intensity of his threat caused Parris to pause, her step halted a moment, but she quickly recovered her composure. She lifted her chin, the ramifications of his veiled words racing through her head. "It's a chance I'm willing to take." She opened the door, walked out, quietly closing it behind her.

Thirty-seven

"Are you okay? You look—calm," Gina commented sarcastically when Parris returned to her desk.

Parris inhaled deeply and turned her chair to face Gina. "Actually, I feel better than I have in a long time," she said, on a rush of renewed air and that hint of southern drawl. "And all I want to think about right now is tonight." She turned back around and calmly flipped through the letters she had to type.

Gina watched her for a moment, studied the steadiness in her hands, the completely benign expression on her face. That's how she knew Parris was lying. When most people ranted, raved, and shed tears if they were upset or angry, Parris was just the opposite. A kind of chilly calm settled over her, and she became the perfect picture of the well-bred southern lady, trained in the rules of camouflaging anything ugly or distasteful. She'd pay money to find out what had happened between her and Frank. And it must have been something heavy because Parris was almost smiling.

▲ ▲ ▲

It was three hours before her set. Paris arrived at Downbeat early, wanting to give herself plenty of time to get her head together and shake off the effects of the scene with Frank. A part of her felt a sense of relief, relief at being freed of a relationship that was destined to fail. She'd allowed her innate, accepting nature to take precedence over good common sense. Instead of walking away when the doubts and uneasiness began to take on

270

a life of their own, she'd stayed, convincing herself that tomorrow would be better. Convincing herself that Frank would come around. But Frank was trapped, caught in a fragile world of misconceptions and wounds that wouldn't heal. Because of that, there was an unyielding need to control, to mold and fashion his world the way he wanted to see it, to keep it from hurting him, to protect himself. If she stayed with him a dozen years more, the troubling elements of his personality that made him who he was would never change. She felt a deep sadness for him. Sorry for the empty space in his soul. Maybe, God willing, he'd find someone or find someway to fill it. Only he could heal himself, no woman or relationship could do that. She'd finally realized that she wasn't the one to do it.

Nick was rehearsing when she walked into the club. The rest of the band hadn't arrived and he was alone on stage. He stopped to change the reed in his mouthpiece, adjusting it, testing it with his tongue. Parris leaned against one of the pillars, out of sight, shadowed by the play of soft lights around the room. She didn't want him to see her. She wanted to watch him. There was something almost feline about him, the long, muscular stretch of his body, the predatory look that would often come into his eyes when they talked late into the night, the control of emotions that could so easily be unleashed with the right amount of provocation.

She listened to the cascade of notes as he traveled up and down the scale, working the fragments of sounds into a pleasing mix of tone, color, and emotion. He leaned back and let the horn have its say, measuring every interval, weighing each phrase. The big sound of his tenor sliced forcefully through the dimness, riding easily in the still air above the wood tables, swooping down between the legs of the chairs, vibrating through the emptiness. She hung breathlessly on each and every improvisation, feeling his muse lead through a revamped version of the ballad, "Stella by Starlight," in a way that owed little to the rendition made famous by Miles Davis in the 1950s.

Watching him, listening to the passion that came across in his playing, there was no doubt that Nick Hunter loved what he did, loved it from the center of his being. That was something she could understand, understand as well as she understood herself. It was what drove her, fueled her spirit, gave her days meaning and purpose. When she stepped up on stage, beneath the spotlight, and felt the music seep through her pores, when the words rose from the depths of her soul, it was magic, pure and simple. When she attacked the lyric just right, hit the phrasing on top or slightly underneath the beat, the spreading glow in her chest let her know that she was making the song her own. And that's what they shared, a love for something completely intangible to anyone who wasn't a part of it. The music, always the music. Because of that oneness, they were able to cross the bridge of class, education, and experience and find a common ground, a platform to share parts of their lives with each other. Theirs was a partnership, a unity that could not be denied.

Sometimes after rehearsal they would sit together in the semidarkened club and just talk, long after everyone had gone home, talk about everything from acoustic jazz, classical music, abstract art, to Beltway politics. He'd hipped her to the use of flatted fifths by Bird and Dizzy, the influence of music on painters such as Bob Thompson and Jackson Pollack, and the mathematics found in the classical works of Bartók, Ives, and Copland. She'd have him doubled over with laughter about the rural ways of the Delta, her secret forays to the juke joints and blues dens, her one night of sharing white lightning with a female blues singer from Yazoo City. She'd left him in stitches with her imitation of the riotous revival preachers, especially when she gave into the drawl that had never really left her, as she described the vast array of colorful characters from Rudell.

One night Nick was leaning back in a chair, totally relaxed in the afterglow of the session. His long legs were propped up on the table, ankles crossed, head braced by his linked fingers. His eyes were closed and there was a half smile gracing his mouth, as if he had some secret that no one would ever know except him. She imagined him reworking a tune in his head, going over the riffs, dissecting the long and short tones of the song.

"When I was a kid," he began slowly, his voice almost dreamlike, "growing up in the projects in East New York, I never thought this was where I'd wind up one day."

"Where did you see yourself?" Parris asked, her curiosity piqued by this man who seemed to have it all together and maybe did not.

"Locked up. Dead, maybe."

She was shocked into silence."

Slowly he opened his eyes. "Surprised?"

"Yes. I am. I would have never thought that about you."

He laughed lightly. "Sometimes when I look around here, I just think it's all a dream, ya know." He sat up, leaned forward, and lost himself in the softness of her eyes. "I grew up where the only thing you had to hope for was to last until your twentieth birthday without getting shot, or worse." He heaved a sigh. "My best friends were some of the busiest drug dealers in Brooklyn. My father, the little I knew of him, was a hired hit man, sold to the highest bidder. My mother loved the needle more than me, more than life itself. By all the statistics compiled by white folks about young, black boys in the ghetto, I was doomed to a life of crime and drugs."

Was that part of his life still engrained in him? Was that tainted past what made it possible for him to be tied up with a gangster like Percy Davis and all he represented? She tried to imagine Nick as a young boy, lurking in dark alleyways, running from the law along dank, garbage-strewn streets, and she couldn't seem to fit the person in front of her into that tawdry picture of criminality.

"What happened? How did you find your way out?"

"Sometimes, Parris, I wonder if I really did," he said somberly, as if he'd read her thoughts. "I guess it was the night I found a beat-up sax in an alley when I was waiting to meet up with a couple of my friends. I was about fifteen. I was leaning up against a wall, and it was colder than Christmas. I remember because all I could think about was making a score so I could get a warm jacket and some thick socks. I was smoking a cigarette and something shiny at the end of the alley caught my attention. I figured it was jewelry or something, ya know, and I got all excited thinking I could pawn it, get a few bucks, and I wouldn't have to go with the fellas on the next job."

Next job! She didn't want to ask what that meant.

"Anyway, I crept down the alley and dug through the clothes that were piled on top of it." He grinned. "When I pulled the thing out, I didn't even know what it was. Just some kind of horn . . ."

"Aw, man. What is this shit?" Nick turned it around in his stiff fingers, disappointment making his young temper flare.

He started to put it back, but something stopped him. He remembered having seen horns like this in the window of the pawnshop. He looked at it again. It was kind of scratched, and its shiny gold surface was a bit dulled, tarnished from neglect, but other than that, to his untrained eyes, it looked to be in good condition. It was worth at least thirty, forty bucks.

He looked around, then edged back toward the mouth of the alley, and peered up and down the dimly lit, snow-covered street. The fellas were nowhere in sight. He studied the instrument in his near-frozen hands, took one last look down the street, and sprinted off toward home, the cool metal tucked beneath his threadbare, wool jacket.

The following day he cut school, which was really no big deal. His foster parents barely paid him any attention, except at check time, and he usually caught the cutting cards from school before they came home. Just in case.

He'd put the horn in a black, plastic bag and headed for the pawnshop on Livonia Avenue.

"You back again, Nicky?" Walt, the owner, asked, as he placed a set of gold cuff links in the glass display case. He'd gotten used to seeing the young boy come into his store once a week. He never asked where he got the stuff he brought in. He didn't want to know. And he was pretty sure Nick didn't want to tell. Nick wasn't like some of the other thugs who frequented his flourishing business. He never boasted or tried to act tough. If anything, it was just the opposite. There was almost a shyness, an embarrassment on his expression when he placed his contraband on the counter and asked, "How much kin I get for this?"

Most of the time the stuff was pretty worthless, but there was always something hopeful in the dark eyes and lean, undernourished face. Walt could see how the used coat hung loosely from his thin body and how the cloth from his sneakers gapped open from the rubber soles when he walked. And yet there was a dignity in his shabbiness, a pride in the set of his narrow shoulders. So Walt took a liking to him and always gave him more than his junk was worth. It was the least he could do. Maybe one day Nick would use the money to buy a ticket out of this hellhole or, at the very least, get a hot meal to fill his belly.

Nick pulled the horn from the plastic bag and placed it on the counter. "How much?"

Walt's eyes widened. Gingerly, he picked up the instrument. He knew right away its value. It was an expertly crafted Selmer saxophone. One of the best. It was almost in mint condition, except for its abused reed and well-worn pads.

"Where did you get this, kid?"

Nick tried on a defiant stare. "Why? I ain't steal it, if that's what you sayin'."

"Where did you get it?" Walt repeated.

Nick shrugged. "In an alley around my way." He started to fidget, shifting from one foot to the other, his eyes darting nervously toward the door. Watching for the Man.

Walt placed the instrument gently down on the counter. He looked across at Nick, who at fifteen stood as tall as he did at an even six feet. He pondered his options.

"You ever hear of a dude named John Coltrane?"

Nick frowned. "From around here?"

Walt chuckled. "No, Nick, he's a musician. A sax player. A great sax player."

"Yeah, so what."

"Playing sax, one of these right here, made a life for him. Let him travel all over the world, made records, appeared at clubs. People come from all over to hear him play."

"What's that got to do with me?" Nick asked, becoming more agitated. He just wanted some money so he could get a sweater to go under his coat, not a lecture about some lame dude he'd never heard of.

Walt leaned on the counter. "You ever think of getting out of this place, Nick, making something of yourself?"

"Ain't nowhere for me to go, man. This is it." He jammed his hands into his pockets. "You gonna give me the money or what?"

Walt took a breath. "Tell you what, kid. I'll make a deal with you."

Nick cocked his head suspiciously to the side. "What kinda deal?"

"You keep the horn, the alto sax."

Nick's brows shot up. "What?"

"You bring it in here every Friday afternoon at six, closing time, and I'll teach you how to play. How to blow into the mouthpiece, how to master the fingerings, and all of that . . ."

"Aw, man. Come on, man. I don't wanna play no stupid horn."

"I'll give you twenty bucks after each session."

"Twenty bucks?"

Walt nodded. He knew the boy was hooked.

"How long is it gonna take for me to learn?"

"Depends on you. But until you do, our deal stands—twenty bucks a week after each lesson. If you work hard, you'll see results in no time."

Nick tried to calculate what twenty times anything was. He couldn't. But he figured whatever it was, it was better than nothing. And it would be steady. Maybe he could string this out for a while, take his time, and really make some cash.

"Awright," he agreed. "When do we start?"

"This Friday."

Nick looked at the sax, wondering if he would ever master it, and then returned it to the plastic bag. He glanced at Walt a moment, feeling uncomfortable, wondering why he cared, why he was willing to do anything for him. Nobody had ever done anything for him before. Something inside him shifted, that cold place that was building in his soul began to thaw. Maybe he could make something of himself like that Coltrane guy. Maybe people would pay to hear him play, too. Maybe he would make the people cheer for him, too. Maybe he would make big money, too. Maybe.

Nick blew out a long breath, drawing himself back from the frightening, early days of his youth, when day-to-day survival by any means necessary was the only thing that was important. When he felt so alone, so desperate not to make the mistakes he'd seen his friends make . . .

Nick slowly focused on Parris's face, which held the softest, most tender look he'd ever seen. Her eyes were all watery like she was going to cry, like she'd been right there with him.

Nick cleared his throat and flashed an embarrassed grin. It wasn't like him to show that side of himself, leave himself open and vulnerable to anyone. But for some reason, with Parris, it was all right. There was no reason to fear when he exposed his soul to her. "Sorry about that. I guess I get carried away sometimes."

"It's all right, really." She sniffed. "I feel honored that you told me."

Nick glanced away.

"So that's how you got started." She smiled softly.

"Yep. Good old Walt."

"What happened to him?"

"He died from a heart attack when I was about nineteen. And I promised him at the grave site that I would keep at it, make him proud." He chuckled. "I had the bug by then. I lived and breathed music. Practiced day and night, while all of my friends were out running the streets. Listened to the sides of the greats and transcribed their music and learned it by ear. Did that for years. Then started hanging out in jazz clubs and sitting in on jam sessions that would last until the sun came up. Got a few gigs, then a few more. Helped to pay my way through college. And I knew I wanted my own band, my own place." He shrugged and turned his palms upward. "So, here I am."

Watching him now, so cool and self-assured and knowing the source from which he'd sprung, made her marvel and admire him all the more. He made her believe that anything was possible. Although their backgrounds were as different as night and day, they were joined by a single, indisputable passion—the music, always the music. And the more she came to know him, the more hours they spent in each other's company, she came to realize that it was more than music that pulsed between them. It was in the looks they shared, the laughter at things no one else understood, the unspoken sync they had with each other, the unconscious touches that electrified and forced them to step back, shocked by their intensity. Yet neither dared to cross the invisible line that stretched between them.

That realization saddened her as nothing else in her life. Their caution weighed heavily on her, although she knew it was necessary to keep things from getting complicated and dangerous. The time just didn't seem right for any kind of move. So many things were unresolved, unsettled.

▲ ▲ ▲

Nick trotted down from the stage and was met by Tara, who ceremoniously draped her arms around his neck and kissed him passionately, full on the mouth. It was a gesture to announce to Parris that this was her territory, her man. Do not trespass. Look but don't touch.

Parris felt a sudden tightness in her chest, turned quickly away, and hurried down the corridor to the dressing room. Her eyes were filling with tears that she hoped no one would see. She shut the door firmly behind her.

Sitting in front of the mirror, Parris stared at her reflection, taking stock of who she was and how far she had come; and for the first time in more years than she could remember, she missed her mother terribly. Or rather she missed what it felt like to have a mother. Maybe if she would have been able to talk with her mother about her confusing feelings about Nick and how everything between them seemed so perfect and yet it wasn't, her mother could help her understand. What would you do, Mama? Would you have the strength or the courage to walk away? How do you know if the decision, the choice you make is the right one? This was a time in her life when she would have loved to look into her mother's face and see love and pride reflected there.

Nana often told her that she resembled Emma, had her determination, too. Emma, the mother she'd never known, the woman she felt deeply in her soul, the missing emotional piece.

Parris peered closer at her reflection, taking in the smoothness of her pecan-toned skin, the startling clarity of her green eyes, a feature that always puzzled her. Nana never discussed her father. She only said that her mother had kept him a secret, and he was long gone before Emma gave birth. They never discussed him, Cora had said. It was if any mention of the man was taboo, forbidden. She was not the only child without a father in her community. It wasn't unusual when she was growing up for fathers to be absent from the house, for children to be raised by grandparents and old aunts and uncles. So she never questioned her beginnings, the mystery of her missing parents. Not really. But there was always the nagging question of where Emma got the green eyes that she'd passed along to her daughter. It was a topic that Nana didn't discuss, merely said it was one of those things that happened to colored folk from time to time, a mixing of the races from back in slavery time.

Yet even as she'd listened to the pat explanation, there was an uneasiness, an element of caution in the expression on Cora's face. The way her gaze would wander away from Parris when she spoke of the mystery. The way her grandmother's slender fingers would quickly find something to do, to still their restlessness, and her voice would grow distant and cold.

Parris painfully began to realize that Cora might be lying—hiding the truth—a concept that she refused to accept. Because if she did, it would destroy the fabric of her life, diminish the one person she held most dear, and make her question all that she had been told. She wouldn't do that. Couldn't do that. So she stopped asking the questions, sealing off that confusing part of her life. It was safer that way. And everything could remain as it appeared, everything still in its place.

A light tapping on the door sent her lingering doubts scurrying into the recesses of her mind.

"Come in," she said, swiveling the chair to face the opening door.

Nick stuck his head inside the room, and she immediately felt her heart leap in her chest. He always had a surprising knack of appearing just when she needed to see him most.

"Mind if I come in?"

"No, not at all. I could use the company." She settled herself in the hardback chair and waited with barely veiled anticipation. She loved talking with him, learning about him, about the business. The almost stolen moments they shared together were precious to her. She couldn't count the hours in the past months that she'd sat enthralled by his stories as they shared a sandwich and a beer after a grueling rehearsal. And no matter how bone tired she may have been, she relished those times, looked forward to them, and was painfully disappointed when he'd leave with Tara's arm tucked securely in his. Without fail, Tara's face and body language let him and everyone around them know what she offered him, the security of a dream fulfilled, something that was banned to Parris.

"I figured I'd take your mind off the evening for a little while." He pulled up a chair and straddled it, bracing his arms across the top.

Parris grinned sheepishly. "Is it that obvious?"

"No. You're always so cool under fire. It's hard to tell with you." He studied her seemingly relaxed expression, searching for the cracks in the smooth veneer. She was a difficult woman to read, her gentle quietness impenetrable, totally inaccessible.

"Do you get nervous before you go up there?" she asked, steering the conversation away from her. She became nervous whenever he quizzed her too much about herself.

"Absolutely." He grinned. "For me, every performance is like the first one. I get the same rush. I think you need that," he added thoughtfully. "It keeps you fresh, sharp. I don't ever want to get so cocky that I forget there's somebody else out there just as good or better than me. Keeps me humble."

"Looking at you up there, I'd never imagine you had a nervous bone in your body. You seem in total control when you're on the bandstand."

His gaze grew suddenly intent, heating her. She drew in an unconscious breath. "I didn't know you watched me."

She wanted to tear her eyes away, but they were locked onto his, holding her in place. "I . . . I . . . I . . ."

"I watch you, too," he admitted. "It's impossible not to."

She swallowed. "What do you see?" she dared ask.

"I see a beautiful, talented woman with a lot of class and style. I see someone with a good soul. It comes out when you sing and floats around you like an expensive perfume when you don't." He paused a moment, uncertain about the rightness of what lingered on his tongue, vibrating there like the reed of his sax. But he needed to say it. "I've never met anyone like you, Parris." He chuckled lightly. "Sounds like a line, right?"

Parris tucked away her smile. It was an old line but still effective.

"It's not." He shifted uncomfortably in his seat, the first time Parris had ever seen him uneasy, off beat. The realization stirred the thin walls of her outwardly calm facade until it churned deep in her center.

"You're not like those women out there." He said tentatively, not looking directly at her for a second. "You're not out here to climb over anyone's back to get what you want. Success at all costs. What you want comes from inside. I know it 'cause I feel it, too—when I play."

"Do you?" she asked, the question suddenly like that of a young girl. "I've always tried to explain it to people, especially when I was in school. They may as well have just patted me on the head like a puppy for all they understood about my dream." She smiled wryly. "The only person who ever seemed to understand was my grandmother."

"You talk about her a lot. She's really important to you, huh?"

Parris nodded. "She's the most incredible woman I've ever known."

Nick glanced away to a corner of his past. "I never knew what that was like—have somebody that really meant anything to me. I guess the closest person was Walt. But there's nothing like family, real family, you know. There's nothing like blood."

The sense of melancholy in his voice, the heaviness of it, like a tuba playing its bottom note, touched her deeply. She wanted to ask him about Tara. She wanted to ask him if Tara filled his empty spaces, completed him, nourished him in the ways he needed most. But then that was a subject that she decided to avoid. She might not like the answer he gave. Instead she reached out and placed her hand lightly upon his, and a sudden surge of heat rushed up her arm. Her body shuddered as if she'd been tapped with an electric prod.

Nick's dark eyes flew to hers and set themselves on simmer. Neither spoke, both sensing that if they acted at that moment, the line of no return would be crossed.

Nick cleared his throat.

Parris drew her hand back, but Nick caught it gently in his. His strong grasp said what could not be spoken between them. What they felt went beyond the limits of physical desire or animal attraction. This was something else and very dangerous.

"Thanks," he said thickly.

"For what?" Her voice was a threadbare whisper.

He stared at the tiny pulse beat in her throat, memorizing its rhythm.

"For listening," was all he dared say, not that he was thanking her for filling all those empty spaces in his life, bringing some joy without strings, just for being who she was. He released a shaky breath. "I, uh, better let you get ready. I'll be in here running my mouth all night."

Parris nodded, still shaken.

"Break a leg tonight."

"You play; I'll sing."

He bent and lightly kissed her cheek, needing to feel the exquisite touch of her silky flesh again. Then abruptly he left the room before his body betrayed him.

Parris sat immobilized, still caught in the heart-pounding moment that had just passed between them. She didn't know how long she sat there staring at the empty chair Nick had just filled, still feeling his presence, inhaling the faint, lingering aroma of his scent, the final notes of his voice, the sensation of his mouth against her skin.

She shook her head. She couldn't let her runaway emotions and wild imagination take her someplace she had no business going. Exercise caution, girl. No matter how right it felt, how good and easy. He was another woman's man, and that was a web she refused to get tangled in.

Parris turned and faced herself in the mirror again. This time even her face seemed magically transformed, bathed in a strange glow, as if his visit had done something mystical to her inside. If only things could be different. If only she hadn't fallen in love with him.

▲ ▲ ▲

The stage was draped in semidarkness. Parris sensed the standing microphone in front of her, felt it more than saw it. The low, expectant hum of the crowd rippled along her spine, raising the hairs along her bare arms. Her heart raced. This was finally it, the real thing. She was certain she was going to faint.

"Ladies and gentlemen, welcome to Downbeat," Nick announced, the deep timbre of his voice enriched by the amplification of the club's costly sound system. "We have a special treat for you tonight—a very special lady, and I know you're going to love her. Parris Mackey! Give it up."

The audience applauded in a loud Harlem welcome—and then the spotlight hit her.

A wave of "aahs" rode along the crest of the room.

Parris stood, statuesque, in a fitted gown of white satin that slid seductively over her warm, brown body like the comforting embrace of a tender lover. She'd decided to wear her hair loose, letting the soft, natural curls fan around her face in a gentle halo. Her only jewelry was a pair of pearl studs that her proud grandparents had given her upon her college graduation.

Sammy Blackstone, the pianist and Nick's right-hand man, eased into the opening bars of the first number, a ballad, a Billie Holiday classic, "God Bless the Child."

Parris moved sinuously toward the microphone, cupping the cool metal in her hand. She closed her eyes, blocking out everything except the notes and the familiar lyrics that had become a part of her. "This is for you, Nana," she whispered softly, as she launched in the delicious low notes of the song.

One tune after another, Parris took the mesmerized audience on a soul-stirring odyssey of sound, nuance, and emotion. Every selection showcased another of her many vocal strengths, her mastery of the lower registers, her uncanny skill with hitting and maintaining the high notes. The band supported her throughout, providing her with the rhythm and spark for her musical flights. Once, during her rendition of "Laura," she turned slowly and winked at Sammy, the pianist, as he did something extraordinary on the ivories, comping in a way she had never heard before. She felt the energy, became the bent and spiraling notes, her body as well as her voice moving in a slow, erotic flow completely in harmony with the accompaniment that left her weak and spent as Nick matched her step for step during her final walk on the last, baleful notes of "Strange Fruit." The stage went dark.

For a moment, the awestruck audience was numbed into silence as the melodious combination of the satin voice and potent jazz drifted into their memories. It took them a few seconds to digest the miracle they had just witnessed. Then, suddenly, the entire room erupted into a unified, near-deafening, tidal wave of applause.

Parris covered her mouth to contain the scream of relief, propelled by the maddening pace of her heart. It was incredible! What a feeling!

The spotlight slowly silhouetted the single, triumphant figure on the stage. Parris, nearly blinded by her tears, bowed graciously to the appreciative audience that exploded in a new continuous surge of clapping and cheers. She bowed again and again, allowing their welcome salute to wash over her, reward her for every sacrifice she'd made to get here. Yes, it was worth it. All of it.

Regally, she waved one last time, turned toward the stage exit as the band went into their closing theme, and disappeared into the corridor that led to the dressing room. Once she was certain that she was out of sight, she collapsed against the cool wall. Her head whirled as the adrenaline rush slowly began to ebb. She'd done it! Actually done it. The final echoes of applause trailed her down the corridor as she made her way to her dressing room.

Standing in the middle of the room, Parris wrapped her arms around her waist and spun around in a circle in a kind of joyous victory dance. "I wish you were here, Nana, you, too, Granddad." She stopped spinning and looked at the gilded-framed photo of her grandparents. "As soon as I make some real money, I'm going to bring you both up here to live. So we can all be together again. I promise."

Someone knocked on the door.

She glanced quickly in the mirror and dabbed away the tears of joy. "Come in."

"A star is born!" Nick announced, his brilliant smile filling the room. "They love you, Parris. Did you hear them out there?" he went on, his excitement charging the room like bolts of lightning.

Parris's eyes lit up with delight. She tugged on her bottom lip with her teeth, clasping her hands to her chest. Her legs were still trembling as the rush of performing still clung to her. She would never forget this night, never.

Seeing Parris there, in that instant of unbridled joy and total vulnerability, the last vestiges of Nick's usually cool reserve melted and fell away. He desperately wanted to grab her up in his arms, hold her close, and let the happiness he felt flow from him to her. He wanted to, just for a moment, forget about the downside of his involvement with the club, Percy's cruel demands, and Tara's possessive jealousy, and give into all the wonderful emotions he possessed for Parris, the feelings of love that he'd been fighting to ignore.

At first he'd blamed it on their common appreciation of music, believing that was what drew him to her. Other times he believed it was only her unparalleled talent or her stunning beauty. But during the blissful months that he'd spent with her, talked with and laughed with her, shared stories about himself he'd never revealed to anyone else, he realized none of those things were what pulled him to her like a moth to a flame. It was Parris the woman, the person she was inside, that captured his heart. The sum and total of her. And he also knew that if he allowed himself to be drawn by that flame, he would inevitably get burned. The cost of it all was too great. Yet he believed more each day that it was worth the risk.

"Wonderful things are going to happen for you, Parris," he said sincerely. "You're on your way."

"You gave me the chance, Nick. I can't thank you enough."

Nick felt as if a storm was building inside him. He slowly crossed the room. He could feel the heat of her body radiate toward him. "Parris, I—we—"

"Oh, there you are. I should have known," a female voice said cattily from the doorway.

Nick turned to the sound of the voice at the door. He knew who it was, even before he pivoted in the direction of the familiar, sultry voice. Tara.

Tara stood framed in the archway, her short, black dress clinging to her every feminine curve, the tight fabric leaving nothing to the imagination. No emotion showed on her lovely face, but there was something ablaze and sinister in her eyes.

"I've been looking all over for you." She sashayed across the room, walking right up to Nick, insinuating herself between him and Parris. She turned to Parris. Her eyes rolled over her like the blur of knives in the graceful hands of a Japanese chef at a sushi shop. "Not bad tonight. Where did you say you sang before? Oh, right, I remember now, some little backwoods town, Rodell or something."

"Rudell," Parris said quietly.

Tara waved her hand. "Whatever. You could use a little more rehearsal though. I didn't think you were ready for a debut yet. You sounded a bit thin on a couple of the numbers, but the band covered well for you."

Parris looked down at her. "I thought the same thing. But there has to be a first time," she replied evenly, refusing to take the bait.

"She was more than ready," Nick cut in. "Now that you've found me . . . ?"

Tara moved closer to Nick, but she was not finished with Parris. This woman who was openly making a play for her man, her investment. "Well, the band can't make you look good every night. Remember, critics are a fickle lot. Tonight is a freebie, but you may not be so lucky tomorrow or next week. You're the flavor of the night. Enjoy your ten minutes of fame, honey."

Parris crossed the room to collect her belongings, avoiding the catfight Tara wanted to start to tarnish her glorious opening night. Sometimes passive resistance was best.

Seeing that her adversary couldn't be tempted into battle, Tara turned her laser stare on her beloved. "Baby, I'm ready to leave. Take me home."

But Nick surprised her. "I have some things to take care of, Tara. I won't be leaving for a few hours."

Tara pouted, cutting her eyes at Parris. "I'll wait." She kissed him full on the mouth, running her hand seductively down his chest, and walked out.

By the time Nick turned around, Parris was putting on her coat. "I'd better be going, too." She started to move past him. Nick lightly grabbed her arm, with that glow again in his eyes, the look that both weakened her resolve and frightened her to her heart.

"Wait. I'll walk with you to find a cab." He gave her his best smile.

"My friend, Gina, is probably out there waiting for me." Parris wanted to avoid another scene. This was her night and she didn't want it ruined.

"We'll let her know you're leaving. Maybe I'll get her a cab, too."

"Nick, I don't think—"

"Let me worry about that. Come on. Please."

She looked into his eyes, saw the determination and passion, knew there was nothing she could do to change his mind. And she didn't want to.

Thirty-eight

Parris felt as if she should slink out of the club like a sneak thief trying to avoid detection by the owners of the house she'd just robbed. She felt ashamed that her emotions seemed to be getting the best of her. Any notion that she was still in control of them was a lie, only superficial.

Nick, on the other hand, made no secret of their departure, stopping at several tables to chat with the clientele and introduce Parris. He was proud of her and really didn't care who knew it. He wanted to show her off, for others to share his deep feeling of respect and admiration for her.

Nervously, Parris tapped Nick on the shoulder. "There's Gina." She raised her chin in the direction of the petite woman seated several tables away.

"Great." He placed his hand on the small of Parris's back, excused them both from the seated couple, and approached Gina's table.

"Girl, you were . . ." Gina shook her head at a loss for words.

"Thanks, Gina. You, uh, remember Nick?" Parris swallowed.

"How could I forget. Good to see you again." She turned to her male companion. "This is Paul Winston." She continued with the introductions. "Paul and I went to high school together."

Paul, a nondescript, but pleasant-enough looking man, smiled benignly. "Gina wouldn't give me the time of day back then. I wasn't in her league."

"That's not so," she said in a teasing tone. "We didn't get together because you were too involved in being the class genius to notice me."

The couple both laughed, sharing something, a secret wrapped in a dim memory that locked out Parris and Nick. Still, Parris smiled a knowing smile, one filled with understanding. She knew exactly what that was like, a remembrance forged by time, and was happy for her friend.

"Parris was concerned that you were waiting for her and didn't have a way home," Nick interjected.

"I'll make sure Gina gets home if you two want to leave," Paul offered, looking hopefully at Gina.

"I'll be fine." She looked up at Parris and her eyes sparkled. "Really. You two go on. We're going to hang around for a while."

"Are you sure?" Parris quizzed, unsure of being alone with Nick. Inside of the club was one thing—it was a safe and controlled environment. Outside of its confines and security, there were no guarantees; anything could happen.

"Yes. Go on. Go on," Gina urged. "I'll see you on Monday, bright and early."

Nick stuck out his hand cordially to Paul. "Nice to meet you, man."

Paul stood halfway and shook Nick's hand. "You, too. Love your playing."

"Thanks. Well, good night. Be sure to come back."

"We will," the pair chorused, then turned to each other with a secret look and began to laugh and talk at the same time, quickly forgetting the presence of Parris and Nick. They were lost in their own world.

Nick ushered Parris toward the exit, weaving carefully between the tables.

"But what about . . . Tara?" Parris asked cautiously, as she pressed her hand against the glass door halting their exit. Tara was a matter that could not be ignored.

"Believe me, Tara will find plenty to do to occupy herself." He opened the door and they stepped out into a perfect, crisp fall night, with just enough chill in the air to remind you that winter wasn't far away. The leaves had long turned color and begun their earthbound trek.

Parris pulled up the collar of her coat and walked in unison with Nick.

Instinctively, Nick moved to put his arm around her shoulder, but quickly decided against it. "Cold?" he asked instead.

"Just a bit. I'll be fine."

"Let's walk down Lenox," Nick said. "I'm sure we'll find a cab on the way." He shoved his hands into his pockets.

They walked for a block in silence, adjusting themselves to each other's company outside of the familiar cocoon of the club.

"Why did you leave with me after all . . . she said back there?" Parris finally asked, needing to hear him say the words she'd only imagined.

"I wasn't ready to see you go. Is that a straight-enough answer for you?"

Parris didn't respond, surprised and secretly pleased by the candor of his reply.

"I could ask you the same question."

They stopped on the corner for a red light.

"You didn't leave me much choice," Parris said. "You were pretty determined."

Nick chuckled. "I can be a bit aggressive once I set my mind to something."

She wouldn't touch that one. She tossed out her next question instead, one that had been rolling around in her head from the moment she'd heard the rumors. "Is it true what they say about you and Percy Davis—that you're bought and paid for?"

Nick's jaw clenched in suppressed anger. "There's an all-night diner on the next block. You hungry?" he asked, stalling for time, not sure of how much to reveal, even though he knew it couldn't put off the inevitable forever.

Parris glanced at his taut profile, the hard set of his eyes, the new lines of tension around his mouth. "A little."

"Come on."

After they were seated in the diner and had placed their orders for burgers and fries, Nick folded his hands atop the table. How could he explain to her how he'd sold his soul to the devil and not have her lose whatever respect she had for him—that he had realized a bit too late that nothing given comes without a price, sometimes too costly for what is gained. But as difficult as it was to expose this dark side of himself, he'd rather that it come from him.

"Sometimes when you want something so badly, Parris," he began slowly, "you cast good judgment to the side and take what's offered to you, not thinking about the consequences," he said, choosing his words with great care. "By the time you realize what you've done, it's too late and the deal is set in stone. There's no backing out without paying dearly. Then all the strings attached to what you thought was a real bargain begin to strangle you." He glanced across at her intense expression. "I'm trying to untangle myself, Parris. Undoing what's been done won't be easy, but I'm trying. I hope you believe that."

"Nick, why does it matter what I believe?"

"It just does—all right."

Parris looked away, stared out the window at the few stragglers, a group of night owls who walked along the avenue. "Is Tara a part of those strings?"

"Yes," he stated simply.

"Was it always that way?"

Nick swallowed heavily, weighing the consequences of his response. "Not in the beginning, not before her father became a part of my life."

She turned suddenly to zero in on him. "Walk away, Nick. Leave it behind."

"If I could, I would. And I will. It's just going to take some time." He blew out a breath of exasperation. "This isn't what I wanted for myself. But I saw the gold ring and I snatched it. Am I paying for my choices?" He laughed sarcastically. "Every day. We all do. I knew it was all too easy, too good to be true. I knew that the bill would come due one day, but I put that out of my mind. But you know what, none of that mattered too much until I met you."

"Don't, Nick." She didn't want to hear a line; she wanted to hear the truth.

"No, listen. I need you to hear me, to understand. Until I met you, I just drifted through the whole process, went along with the program. It was easier that way. You compromise, sell off bits of yourself and never think of the damage to your soul. Since I met you, my thinking has changed about a lot of things. Now I understand that self-respect and character mean everything. That's what I've learned from you. There wasn't this urgency to break free before. Only realizing my dream mattered."

"And now?"

"Now there is a reason. You. I want you to see all the man I could be. This isn't what Walt wanted for me. Not what I wanted for myself." He paused a moment. "I know it's unfair of me to ask you anything, but . . ." He took her hand. "Wait for me. Give me some time. I'll work it all out."

"And then what, Nick? I can't build my happiness on someone else's hurt or loss. I won't be a part of it. Do what's right for yourself, Nick, not for any notion you have about me or anyone else; that's the only way it will really matter."

"Are you saying you'd be happy with me? Just what are you saying, Parris?"

"Here you go, folks," the waitress said, placing the food on the table. "Can I get you anything else?"

"No, thanks, we're fine," Nick answered for both of them. Parris cut him a searing look, which he luckily missed. Everything was not fine.

He turned his attention back to Parris. "Well, are you saying you'd be happy with me, Parris?"

"I—I'm not saying anything, Nick. There's no point—other than to . . ." Her sentence drifted off.

"Than what?"

"Than to make bad matters worst. You're involved with Tara—and apparently her father. To what extent I don't know and don't really want to know. I'm not going to put myself in the middle of it all."

"What if I was free, Parris, free from everything? What would you say then?"

She looked directly into his eyes. "When and if the time ever comes, that's when I'll know, that's when I'll be free to say what's on my mind and when you'll be free to hear it."

He couldn't argue with her. Everything she said was right. What was the point in torturing themselves with what ifs and maybes? But now he was determined to break free, get his life and his integrity back. Whatever that took. He respected her even more for not caving in to him, for demanding that he face up to the situation that threatened to rob him of everything he treasured most. He expected nothing less from Parris.

They finished their meal, making polite chat, steering clear of any topics that could spark heated debate or stir the unspoken emotions that brewed just beneath the surface in both of them.

"You were wonderful tonight," Nick said, as he opened the taxi door for her. "And I don't just mean your performance."

They stood barely a breath apart. He wanted to kiss her so badly, but again it was not the right time. Everything was on hold until he straightened out his life.

"So were you." She slid into the car, then looked up at him.

"See you at rehearsal on Sunday?"

"I'll be there."

"Good night, Parris." He leaned down, taking a chance, and touched his lips lightly to hers, lingering there for a moment beyond what was practical, then reluctantly pulled away. Heady with sensation, he shut the door, waved once to her, and headed off in the opposite direction.

Parris leaned back in the cab, watched him walk away, and finally shut her eyes. What was she going to do? How could she keep working at the club, seeing Nick day in and out, and know that he was out of reach? What if he could not cut his ties to Percy, Tara, and the club deal? How could she act like everything was normal? Like he was just another person in her life.

She couldn't. It was just that simple.

Thirty-nine

~~~~~~~~~~~~~

Between the tension at the club with Tara's catty remarks and the tension on the job—Frank doing everything in his power to make her look incompetent—Parris was an emotional wreck, and it was beginning to affect everything in her life. Something had to give.

"Are you singing tonight?" Gina asked, several weeks after Parris's debut. "Sorry I haven't been back down since your big night, but Paul and I—have been, well, getting to know each other," she confessed shyly.

"So things are working out between you two, huh?" Parris asked, thankful to talk about something to take her mind away from her own situation.

"I never thought I'd fall for somebody like Paul. He's so . . ."

"Regular?"

Gina laughed. "That's a good word to describe him—regular. He's the first man I've met in ages who's actually interested in me and not the 'gold' between my legs."

Parris inwardly blanched. At times Gina could be a bit crude, and she was working hard at getting used to it. "Glad to hear it, Gina. You deserve some happiness."

"So do you. But I don't think you've found it yet."

Parris briefly glanced in Gina's direction. "What makes you say that?"

" 'Cause I think you have a thing for Nick Hunter, and he's taken. Am I right?"

"I'd really rather not talk about it, Gina."

"Fine. But when you do, I'm here to listen. Okay?"

"Sure."

290

"Parris! I was expecting that report on my desk an hour ago," Frank boomed, suddenly appearing at her desk like a dark cloud.

"I'm almost finished."

"This can't continue. When you were hired, it was because it was believed that you could keep up with the volume of work. If you can't, maybe you should seek other employment."

Parris glared up at him. "I do my job, Frank, and you know it."

"Maybe if you didn't have people retyping the work a half-dozen times, things would get done on time," Gina cut in, with a distinct edge of disgust in her voice.

"This doesn't concern you, Ms. Raymond."

"If it—"

Parris held up her hand to halt the impending sparring match. "It's okay, Gina." She looked at Frank. "You'll have your report within the hour. Now if there isn't anything else, I need to get back to work."

"If I were you, Parris, I'd make sure it was on my desk on time." He turned on his heels and stalked away.

"Prick," Gina mumbled.

"Just let it go, Gina," Parris cautioned, pressing her thumbs to her temples to ward off the headache that was brewing.

"Fine, but all I can say is good riddance. You're better off without him," she huffed. "Do you need me to help you?"

"No, I'm fine. Thanks for the offer."

"So—what about tonight? Are you on?"

She didn't even want to think about the night ahead. "Yes. Ten o'clock."

"I'll be there."

Parris slipped out of her navy blue jacket and hung it on the back of her chair. She adjusted the headset over her ears for the Dictaphone and began typing. The sooner she got this thing finished, the sooner she could get Frank off her back. At least for a while.

Ever since their abrupt breakup, Frank's entire attitude toward her had deteriorated at a lightning fast pace. With his promotion, he was now head of the department she worked in. He went out of his way to pile more work on her than any of the other secretaries. He wanted it completed in a shorter period of time and complained in front of her coworkers when it wasn't done.

When everyone else in the office had knocked off for the day at five, she too often found herself working until seven or eight just to keep up.

Then there was rehearsal, where she had to deal with Tara. She'd tried to ignore her nasty remarks about her clothes, her country accent, her lack of real talent, and an assortment of other slights. Tara was careful though. She never made any of her off-color remarks in Nick's presence. And day by day Parris felt more alone and isolated as if it was her against the world. She couldn't even talk with Nick anymore, which was harder than anything else she had to deal with. After that night when he left the club with her, Tara made it her business to be right in Nick's face at the end of every rehearsal and every performance. It was getting to a point where she was seriously thinking of quitting the club and trying to find a gig someplace else. But then that old spark would kick in, and she'd remember the stories Nana told her about her great-grandparents, Pearl and Joshua, and all they'd endured because of their beliefs. They hadn't fought, struggled, and died for rights that were due them for her to walk away because her life was suddenly uncomfortable. She was better than that. Their memory deserved more than that. This was her chance, what she'd come to New York to accomplish. And she'd be damned if she'd let the likes of Tara Davis or Frank Carter take that away from her. Whatever she gained or lost in this world would be of her own making.

▲ ▲ ▲

As usual for a Friday night, Downbeat started filling up promptly at five, as the Harlemites left their places of business to find refuge with others like themselves. They came to forget about the jobs that didn't pay what they were worth, forget about the waitresses who took their sweet time in taking their lunch orders, or the boss who promoted the blond coed— recently graduated from some upstate university—over them, who they invariably had to train. Here, at least for a few hours, they could close out a world that demanded twice as much from them and gave even less in return. They could relax among their own, speak the language that was uniquely theirs, and shed the false faces of the happy-to-be-here Negro in a place that was accepting of who they were.

▲ ▲ ▲

The instant Parris walked into Downbeat, there was a sense of expectation in the air. She spotted Nick huddled at one of the tables with the band members, and all of the staff were scurrying around more than usual.

"Parris." Nick stood and motioned for her to join them.

"I have some really exciting news. Sit down. Sit."

Sammy stood up and gave her his seat.

Parris glanced from one expectant face to the next. "What is it? Tell me, tell me."

"Art Newhouse from Columbia Records called me today. He said he'd been hearing rumblings about a new performer that he'd been advised to listen to."

Parris's eyes widened. She dared to hope.

"You, Parris. He's coming to see you. Tonight."

Parris's hands flew to her mouth in astonishment. Her feet stomped up and down on the floor like a child delirious with joy.

Suddenly she reached over and squeezed Nick's hand. "Is this for real? Tell me it's for real. You're not kidding me? Tonight?"

Nick laughed, his face glowing with happiness. "This is it, Parris. Your night, babe, the one you've been waiting for."

She stiffened. All the joy drained from her expression. "What if he doesn't like me? What if he hates what I do up there?"

"No way. Not possible. If you put on half the show tonight that you've been putting on, you have nothing to worry about. They'll love you."

"You really think so?"

"I know so."

She looked around the table, at all the friendly, encouraging faces—the people who had become like a second family to her—and saw the love and support reflected in their eyes.

"Okay, fellas," she said on a gust of air, "we're gonna have this joint jumpin'."

There were high-fives and hand slapping all around.

Nick cut in on the precelebrations. "Can I talk to you for a minute, Parris?"

"S-ure," she answered, a hesitant hitch in her voice.

One by one the band members excused themselves until Parris and Nick faced each other.

"I, uh, I'm sorry to spring that on you. But I wanted to wait and be sure."

"That's understandable, Nick. Don't worry about it."

He glanced away, then looked back at her. "Listen, I know things between us have been pretty strained lately. We haven't had much time to talk."

"We're both very busy."

"I miss that. I've missed you."

Her pulse picked up. "Nick—please . . ."

"I just don't want whatever has been going on between us—with Tara—to affect you tonight. I know I haven't said anything, but I've seen how it has affected your performance. Sometimes it's as if you're not really there."

She looked away, knowing what he said was true.

"I want this for you, Parris, more than you know. I want you to go out there and knock 'em dead. Put all this other stuff aside. This is your night." He stared into her eyes. "Don't forget that."

"I'd better get ready," she said, then stood. "Thank you—for everything. I won't disappoint you, or myself." She turned and walked away.

▲　▲　▲

They opened with a jazz medley of tunes by Cole Porter, then segued to a collection of songs by Duke Ellington, tossed in some classics from the pen of Gershwin, then changed the tempo with a Chaka Khan ballad, "Your Love Is All I Know," and closed with an original composition by Nick, written especially for Parris's range and versatility, "Since I Met You, Nothing Seems the Same."

The applause was deafening, vibrating against the walls, the glass, slipping out the door to dance on the street, then run back inside to start all over again.

Parris did three more encores, and the crowd couldn't seem to get enough. Finally she made it to her dressing room as the band played their closing theme, elation running through her in waves that kept her pacing back and forth across the floor, reliving every instant of the set. Something had happened out there. She'd felt it. She'd become one with every note, every dip and curve. She was the music.

"Parris, Parris." Nick rushed through the open door. "Baby, you did it. I just finished talking with Newhouse. He wants to meet with you on Monday."

"Oh, Nick. I can't believe it." Her voice cracked with emotion.

"Believe it. Here's his card." He handed the card to her, and she stared at it in wonder.

"This is for real, Parris. I told you that you would do it. I knew it!"

Spontaneously, Parris threw her arms around him, and he hugged her to him in return. The moment was simple and pure as they let their happiness spill from one to the other. Then suddenly, the mood, the reason for the embrace shifted. They were no longer two people simply sharing a moment, they were a man and woman who had fought day in and out to keep a seal on their emotions for each other.

Nick felt the dips and curves of her body as they fit perfectly with his. He held her a bit tighter, burying his face in the pillow of her hair, inhaling the sweet scent of her. He felt her tremble; a soft moan escaped her lips. He leaned back and looked down into her upturned face.

"Parris, I—"

"What the hell is this?"

Nick pulled back, not completely releasing Parris's waist.

Tara stood in the doorway, her face a mask of injured fury. She stalked across the room.

"Tara, it's not what you think," Parris began.

"Shut the hell up, bitch. I've had about enough of your shit since you and your country ass come to town."

"Tara!" Nick shouted, his face contorting in barely contained rage.

"You—don't you dare. You have the nerve to do this to me—with her." Tara's voice rose to a screeching pitch. "If it wasn't for me and my daddy's money, you would still be a no-name musician running from club to club trying to put two dimes together."

"That's enough, Tara."

"You wasn't nothin' then, and you still ain't nothin'," she ranted on, pacing back and forth in front of them, pointing and tossing her head in dramatic fashion. "I made you, and I can unmake you. One call from me to my father and you're finished, do you hear me! You think I'm gonna sit still and watch this little no-talent, country hick mess up my life, take what's mine. Hell no. I'd rather see you dead first."

"There's nothing going on between me and Nick, Tara. There never was and never will be. You can't always believe what you see," Parris stated, with a calmness that belied the fury and humiliation she felt for herself and for Nick. "I came here for one reason and one reason alone, but you'd never understand that."

She snatched up her coat and purse and brushed pass Tara and out the door.

"Parris, wait!"

She turned, looked from one to the other. "I think you both have some things to work out." She closed the door quietly behind her and slipped out of the club unnoticed.

Forty

~~~~~~~~~~~~~~

It was well after midnight when Parris turned the key in the lock of her apartment on 120th Street. From her fifth-floor window, she could see the sprawling campus of the renowned Columbia University, where many of the great minds and talents from all over the world planned the future of society.

Most evenings when the sky was clear and full of stars she would sneak up on the roof and stare out across the incredible landscape of New York with its towering, twinkling buildings, mammoth bridges, and ceaseless traffic. It was true what they said about this city; it never sleeps. There was always music to be heard jumping from the opened windows of fast-moving cars or slipping out of the cracks in doorways, voices raised in loud conversation, spilling down the darkened streets, which played in time with the sounds wrapped around it. If you listened really close, you could hear the rhythm of the city—its secret pulse beat like a bass playing beneath the tar and concrete—keeping time. Every now and then the soulful wail of the sax would break through, and you'd want to close your eyes and let it take you where it would. Sometimes the piano would tingle up and down the scales to the tempo of slapping feet and finger pops and warm, brown bodies that moved with singular grace and style along the gray stone, imbuing it with flash and color.

Tonight Parris neither heard nor saw any of this—these intangible things that fascinated her about the city. Tonight the bass player, sax, and piano man were gone from their usual spots, replaced by blaring, toneless car horns, foul curses that knocked on her window from the street, the moan and screech of sirens, and the cacophony of voices, all off-key.

Absently Parris sat on the side of her bed and, with each blink of her eyes, the look of shame that slackened the fine contours of Nick's face flashed again and again. Shame. It took the starch out of his back and slapped the spark from his eyes. To bear witness to the stripping of his manhood brought to mind the stories her nana would tell about the countless colored men and women who were beaten, humiliated, treated without dignity at the hands of whites. But to see it being inflicted by your own was somehow worse. Tara's words lashed him as surely as a master's whip.

Parris felt a sickness in her stomach at having been in any way the catalyst for what had transpired; what disturbed her even more was that Nick was very much trapped in a situation that left few means of escape. He was like a sharecropper who worked for the landowners and never worked long enough, hard enough, or fast enough to pay off his debt. And Tara was the master's overseer. How different, then, was New York from the Delta? How much had changed from her great-grandparents day until now?

Nick had to find his way to freedom. Like those who dared to read under the candlelight, who eluded the hunting dogs as they ran toward a better life, who'd been hosed down on their way to vote—they'd had enough—enough of being under the control of someone else. Enough of being constrained and contained, beaten and humiliated, and they took a chance, risking everything, even their lives, for that taste of freedom. When Nick reached the point where the freedom of his soul was more important than the salvation of material possessions, he would break free. She knew he would—somehow.

▲ ▲ ▲

The balance of the weekend passed uneventfully. Parris was thankful that she had the rest of it off. It gave her time to just relax and do something for herself for a change. She decided to venture off to the West Village and browse some of the antique and novelty shops in preparation for Christmas, promising herself that she would get the jump on it for a change. She'd already put in her request to take a few days off during the holiday week so that she could return home and spend it with her grandparents.

It seemed like forever since she'd seen them, and now, after more than a year, the phone calls and letters were no longer enough. She needed to see her Nana in the flesh, hold her and inhale the gentle scent of her that always made her feel safe. She needed to feel the pressure of her Granddad's hand as he held hers, while they sat on the bench swing and shared his wise words as they made up Granddad and Granddaughter secrets. She needed to walk along the Left Hand River and watch the horny toads sit on uneven rocks and croak in an off-beat tempo, see the catfish leap out of the water, and smell the richness of the moist, dark earth. She needed to be replenished. She needed to hear the soft twang of the familiar, see a string of faces that didn't rush by her in a flash, but proceeded along like the meandering of a warm, summer night.

Yes, going home would be good.

By the time she'd returned to her one-bedroom apartment, loaded down with shopping bags, she was beginning to feel better; the heaviness in her chest had eased a bit. Picking out just the right item for Nana and Granddad had taken all of her wits and concentration. She'd selected a handmade shawl that reminded her of an Indian blanket for her grandmother and a stoneware set of teacups, because Cora loved her before-bedtime tea. For her Granddad she'd bought a pair of silk pajamas. She knew he would fuss up a storm at the idea of the expense and something so personal, but underneath his huffing and puffing he would love it and prance proudly around Cora as if he was a newlywed. She could almost see his handsome face, preening in the full-length mirror. To go with his new outfit, she bought him the collected works of Richard Wright, knowing that Granddad would appreciate the depth from which Wright brought his characters to life.

She tucked the shopping bags away, removing the few items she'd purchased for herself, and decided to relax in a hot bath, sprinkling the water with the scented bath salts she'd bought, just as the phone rang.

She crossed the room, sat in the comfy lounge chair next to her bed, and picked up the phone. She wanted to be in a relaxed position when she tried to explain to Gina why she'd vanished Friday night after her set.

"Hello."

"Hello, sugah. This is Granddad."

She sat up straighter in her seat at once, surprised by his unexpected call an instant before alarm set in. Granddad never called.

"Granddad, it's so good to hear your voice. I've been thinking about you and Nana so much lately. I'm planning on coming home for the holidays. Even did some shopping to get ready," she rambled, instinctively forestalling what she was afraid would come if she stopped talking. "I know you're going to be upset about how much things cost and all, but you two are worth it, every dime. So don't you worry none," she said, easily slipping into the comfort of dialect, needing to grip something familiar. "I know it's still warm back home; done turned cold up here already. Wearing a coat and a sweater," she said, laughing nervously. "But I think you'd like it, you and Nana. Gon' bring both of y'all up here to visit with me. Soon, real soon, Grandddad," her voice starting to break, and her heart felt as if it had swollen and was lodged in her throat.

"That's real nice, sugah, all those things." He paused for breath. "I'm calling about your Nana."

Her head pounded. She squeezed her eyes shut.

"You need to come home before Christmas, baby. Soon."

"Oh, God; oh, God . . ." The words wobbled out of her throat, nearly dying on her lips. "I need to talk to her, Granddad, ple-ase."

"Well, you know that the phone is in the hall, and yo' Nana is restin' in the bed," he said, speaking in slow and measured tones, as if he was running on a worn battery. "Restin' comfortable." And she could kick herself for not insisting long ago that they add a phone to the bedroom. "So you need to come soon as you can, Parris."

She heard the tremor in his voice and that was more frightening than any news he could ever share. She'd grown up seeing her grandfather as the tallest, strongest, smartest, bravest man she'd ever known and compared all other men to him. She couldn't see him as weak or capable of being hurt, even though there was a tenderness about him that belied his strengths.

"Granddad . . ." She wished she could touch him.

"Yes, sugah . . ."

"I'll be home tomorrow. Tomorrow."

"Good. That's real good."

"You . . . you tell Nana don't do nothing foolish . . . till I get there."

A poignant silence hung momentarily between them.

"I'll tell her," he whispered and hung up the phone.

▲ ▲ ▲

Parris spent the better part of the evening trying to get a last-minute flight into Jackson, Mississippi, where she'd transfer to a bus to Rudell. The only thing available was a midday flight the following day.

By the time she arrived at work, suitcase in hand, every nerve ending in her body was raw and screaming. She hadn't slept; she couldn't. All she kept thinking was that she'd arrive at the door, take one look at her grandfather's face, and know she was too late.

Gina took one look at her and knew something terrible had happened.

She immediately got up from her seat. "Parris, what is it? You look awful. Is it Nick? Did something happen at the—"

"It's my Nana," she said weakly. "I have to go home. Today. I came to tell Frank. I don't know how long I'll be gone."

"Oh, Parris, I'm so sorry. Is there anything you need me to do?"

Parris shook her head. "Is Frank in yet?"

"I just saw him go down the . . . here he comes."

Parris watched his approach, confident and assured. That was the image he worked hard to maintain. *Appear like a winner.* Words to live by.

Frank stopped directly in front of Parris's desk. For a moment his eyes were the warm ones she remembered, briefly reflecting concern when he saw the distress on her face, then just as quickly the darkness took over and his expression hardened, became devoid of humanity. He reached inside his pocket and pulled out an envelope. He dropped it unceremoniously on Parris's desk.

"I'm glad I didn't have to go searching for you in the cafeteria. After careful consideration, your services will no longer be needed. Consider Friday, your last day. You have a check there for two weeks' pay. I expect your personal possessions to be packed up within the half hour."

Appear like a winner. The best attack is the least form of resistance. A slow smile crept across Parris's full, rich mouth. "Why thank you, Frank. That was very generous of you. But you're right; this isn't the place for me. I'll always be grateful to you for bringing it to my attention." She turned to Gina, who sat opened mouthed with tears welling in her eyes.

"I'll call you when I can . . . and let you know," she told her.

Gina nodded numbly.

Parris picked up her briefcase and brushed passed Frank.

He'd done this; he'd sent her away, and now . . . "You'll never make it out there," he tossed at her back, needing to say something to justify the twisting in his heart, turn the hurt on her.

Parris glanced over her right shoulder, her green eyes cold and determined. "I come from a long line of survivors, Frank. I may have disappointed you, but I'd never disappoint them."

▲　▲　▲

The flight to Jackson was the longest one of her life. Every minute seemed to multiply by ten. Finally, the plane landed and she waited two hours for the last bus into Rudell.

She called the house when she arrived in Jackson. David assured her that Cora was hanging on. "She won't go anywhere until she sees you," he said, with the calmness of resignation.

Parris closed her eyes and prayed that it was true.

By the time she arrived in Rudell proper—the white section of town—twilight had begun its descent. She had to walk along the outskirts, follow the path of the river until she reached the black section—or colored as it was still called in those parts—or worse. Not much had changed.

Walking along the familiar rutted roads, she saw the lean-to shacks, pigs grunting in their pens, chickens pecking at the last of their feed, the glow of oil lamps flickering in the windows, the rich voices of the Delta filling the night air—this was the rhythm, the beat that flowed through her veins, and it always would. This was where everything began and ended—in the simple purity of nature's song. And for the first time she understood why her grandmother would never leave.

Realizing that, a sense of peace slowly began to fill her, quench her thirst for answers. This is how it should be, she reasoned, standing in front of her childhood home. With a soft smile of acceptance, she walked up the creaky front steps and opened the door.

Forty-one

~~~~~~~~~~~~~~

"It's sure good to see you, baby girl," David said, wrapping her in the embrace of warm words and the strength of his arms.

For a moment Parris allowed her mind and body to relax in the comfort and security of her grandfather. She could momentarily push aside the reason for her visit and swim through the stream of memories that kept her afloat.

David reluctantly released her and held her at arm's length. "Your grandmother is in her room, resting. She's waiting for you."

Parris looked into the sadness of David's eyes, saw the strain in the half-moons that hung beneath them, and knew how much of a toll this was taking on him.

"How . . . long has she been . . ."

"Months now. It started slow, but . . ." He released a shaky breath. "I don't want you to be shocked when you see her."

Parris swallowed, pressing her lips together to keep them from trembling. She nodded her head in understanding.

David patted her shoulder. "Go on," he softly urged.

Parris slowly mounted the stairs, her heart thudding in her chest. As she approached the partially opened bedroom door, a moment of paralysis seized her. She didn't want to go in, didn't want to face what awaited her on the other side. She knew she would have to be strong—for her Nana. But she wasn't sure if she had the strength she needed. What she really wanted was to be a little girl again, sit between her Nana's thighs and feel the strong, but gentle touch of her fingers as she braided her hair—"just

302

like Ms. Lucinda would do mine," Cora would always say. She wanted to
sneak down the stairs on Christmas Eve and watch her grandparents almost
reverently place her gifts beneath the tree. She wanted to look out from
the stage of her graduation and see their proud faces among the crowd.
She wanted to turn back the clock.

Tentatively she pushed open the door. At first she didn't see Cora at all,
until she noticed the barely moving sheet.

"Nana," she called out into the dimly lit room, cautiously stepping closer.
When she stood directly above the fragile body, she gasped in terrified
shock. Cora was no more than a shadow of her former self. Tears welled
in Parris's eyes and spilled unchecked down her cheeks.

Laboriously, Cora opened her eyes, inhaled heavily, and gazed unfocused
around the room. Parris was certain the frail woman who vaguely resembled
her Nana would break in two. The pain of seeing her grandmother was
like having her insides shredded.

"David?" Cora wheezed. "That . . . you?"

Parris knelt at the side of the bed and took Cora's paper-thin hand in
hers. "It's me, Nana, Parris."

Cora's glassy eyes began to focus. She turned her head toward the sound
of Parris's voice. A faint smile slowly bloomed across her mouth and she
almost looked like her old self—almost.

"You done come home, chile."

"Yes, Nana, I'm here. For as long as you need me."

Cora's mouth flickered. "Won't be needin' you too long, baby."

"Don't say that, Nana."

Cora patted Parris's hand. "It's true. You need to accept that."

Parris squeezed her eyes shut, the pain in her heart a searing burn.

"Let me get a good look at you." Cora reached out tentatively and stroked
Parris's cheek just the way she had done when Parris was a little girl. She
pushed the cascade of ebony hair away from her face. "No time for tears,
chile."

Parris sniffed and brushed the tears away only for them to become immediately replaced.

"You look so much like yo' mama. I wish I could see her again before
I go—make my peace with her. It's the only thing I regret in this life."

"Nana, Mama's dead."

"I did love her. Still do."

"Nana, listen to me, Mama's dead. You're getting yourself all worked up.
Just . . ."

Cora fiercely gripped Parris's hand. "No, you listen to me, you hear. I shoulda told ya long ago . . ."

Parris's heart began to race. She didn't want to hear this. She didn't.

"There was nevah nothin' I could do for my child to make up for her life, for the resentment and anger I felt at how she came to be. But it weren't her fault." Tears hung in the corner of her eyes. "The only thing I could ever do for her was the last thing she asked of me." Cora took a shuddering breath. Her forehead now covered with a thin film of sweat; she looked deep into Parris's eyes and cupped her chin. "She asked me to keep a secret . . ."

Reluctantly, Parris listened intently as Cora recounted her life, her one dream to sing and searching for that dream in Chicago. In halting words she unfolded the exciting, frightening, and life-altering circumstances that happened to her there, resulting in Emma. There was no regret in her words, only the proud remembrance of a dream gone awry.

Brick by brick the world that Parris had known came tumbling down at her feet. Everything she'd been led to believe all her life was a lie, built one atop the other. The identity she had embraced was shattered in a few sentences, but so many mysteries were suddenly solved. She no longer possessed a true sense of who she was; yet that empty space that had existed in her for so many years was filled. Most importantly, she felt real sadness for the dying woman lying before her. Her Nana. A part of her had known, had always known, that something was not right, that some piece was missing. And now she knew the entire, horrific story; her grandmother had been brutally raped by her white employer—her real grandfather. Her mother was half-white and rather than live under the burden of being colored, she'd crossed to the other side, leaving her daughter and her life behind.

A cascade of turbulent emotions ran rampant: fury, confusion, hatred, shame, and sadness. But as she looked upon Cora's ravaged face and saw in her eyes all that she'd endured, the sacrifices, the ridicule, the losses—all she could feel in her heart was love.

"You brought me so much joy, chile. More than you'll ever know. You comin' into my life even brought David back. You was my second chance to do right. I pray until my last breath that you'll find a way to forgive me for what I done. I nevah figured I had no other choice. Did the best I could."

"I know, Nana," Parris whispered. "I know. There's nothing to forgive."

Cora breathed deeply, closing her eyes, and a terrible panic tore through Parris. "Nana!"

Cora sighed. "I need you to do two things for me."

Parris leaned closer to the withered flesh of her dying grandmother, and then she pressed the beloved woman's hand to her lips. "Anything."

"I want you to look after yo' granddad fo' me. He gon' say he's fine and all, but you stay in touch wit him. Visit when you kin. That man been my happiness—" Her voice broke. She tugged in a breath. "And I want ya to do one mo' thang."

Parris couldn't even think what that might be. It was impossible for her to imagine a world without Cora in it, without her in Granddad's life.

"I saved the few letters yo' mama wrote me in the beginning. They in a tin box behind the stove."

Parris felt her heart constrict in her chest.

"I want you to find Emma. Find my chile. Tell her . . . tell her I'm sorry. Tell her I did what she asked. I did the best I could. Tell her I understand that she did what she had to do. Ask her to forgive me. Tell her I love her, Parris. Always did. Tell her that for me."

Cora squeezed Parris's hand and struggled to raise her head. "You forgive her, too. Yo mama had a life neither of us will ever know. We make choices in life, chile. My folks made theirs. I made mine, yo' mama made hers. It's yo' time now. We can only pray they the right ones, and if not, that we get a chance to fix it. No choice carries a guarantee. None of 'em comes without a price, even the right ones. My mama used ta always say that. Promise me you'll remember that."

"I—promise."

"Good." She released Parris's hand and sank back into the pillows, exhausted. "You go head now. Look fo' them letters. There's a picture there, too."

Parris pressed her head against her grandmother's chest, listening to the faint beat of her heart.

"Go on now, chile. You gon' be just fine."

Parris sobbed openly now. She'd held back the tears for as long as she could, but now she couldn't be strong.

"Dry up them tears now, and go tell yo' granddad to come set wit me a spell. Some things I need ta say."

Slowly Parris pushed herself up from the floor, terrified to leave, but good training made her obey.

"Yessum," she mumbled, and walked downstairs.

David knew the instant he saw Parris's face that Cora had finally told her the truth, and it felt as if a weight had been lifted from his soul. He crossed the room and stood in front of her.

Neither of them said anything. Now even the silence was comforting. Some things couldn't be expressed in words. Years of sharing a life, years of sharing secrets, gave them a special place in each other's hearts, bonding them in a way that most people only dreamed of. Gently David gathered her in his arms and just held her, letting her cry until she was spent.

"I fixed some supper for you. It's in the oven. I'm going to set with Cora."

Parris stood alone in the kitchen, looking around at all the familiar things; the butcher block table and chairs that Granddad built as a present for Nana on one of their anniversaries; the row of cast-iron cooking pots that hung from the ceiling; the floral curtains that hung in the window— the same ones Cora helped her sew. There were the rows of photographs of her growing up that held a place of honor above the mantle. There was the rope rug that she would sit on when Cora braided her hair. There were the sounds, too: the third plank on the sitting room floor that always screeched when you stepped on it, or the way the trees in the yard rustled just so when the wind blew. Or the smell of fresh biscuits or spicy collards. All those things and more were a part of this house, a part of her life, and neither would ever be the same again.

She heard the bedroom door above gently open then close and remembered her grandmother's instruction to look for the tin box behind the stove.

After a bit of digging around, she was finally able to wiggle the dented and dusty box free. For a few moments she simply stared at it, leery of its contents and the secrets that it might reveal. Yet at the same time, an eagerness to connect somehow with the mother she had never known prevailed. What kind of woman was Emma to give up her identity and her child? What powerful force could have driven her to do such a thing? *Choices*, Nana tried to explain, help her to understand, and hopefully there would be something in the letters that would reveal even more.

Parris sat down at the kitchen table and placed the box in front of her. Over the racing of her heart, she lifted the lid and took out the first letter. It was postmarked: Paris, France, nearly twenty-five years ago.

Gingerly she opened the faded white envelope, which had began to yellow at the edges, and lifted out the fragile sheet of paper. A sweeping sensation of unreality made her momentarily light-headed when she saw her mother's fine handwriting for the first time. Awestruck, she gently ran her fingers over the words as if they could somehow bring her closer, help her to touch the person who had only been a vague image in her mind.

Her eyes filled with tears of joy, loss, and acceptance as she began to read:

Dear Mama . . .

Forty-two

~~~~~~~~~~~~~~~

For the past three days Nick tried unsuccessfully to reach Parris at home. He'd left at least a dozen messages on her machine, but she hadn't returned any of his calls. He couldn't blame her. Not after what happened, not after what she'd heard.

What plagued him most was what her opinion of him must be, how diminished he was in her eyes. That hurt most of all. Even in his own eyes, he appeared compromised and weak, led by material gain and not his conscience.

No matter what the offer from Percy, no matter how succulent the fruit, he should have never agreed. He knew it then, but he did what was easy. He'd sold his soul, his integrity, and his free will for a dream that could never fully be his as long as it was controlled by someone else.

Listening to Tara telling him that night in no uncertain terms just what a pawn he had become made him ill, filled him with a sense of shame and humiliation. It was the same way he felt standing in front of Walt with his hand out, practically begging for whatever he could get no matter what the merchandise was worth. Like his own talent—bartered for less than its value. The difference between Tara and Walt was Walt's desire to see him do better and not continue to feed on his need for his own selfish reasons. Walt wanted Nick to stand on his own. Tara thrived on his dependence. It was obvious what she thought of him—a mannequin, someone to dress up and show off, someone to control, her prize—bought and paid for by Daddy. He had no one to blame but himself, and he would always remain the shell of the man Tara described as long as he allowed his emasculation to continue.

He had never fully understood just how jealous, vindictive, and spoiled Tara was until that night, or maybe he just didn't want to know. All her life she'd been given everything she ever wanted. She didn't know the meaning of struggle, of sacrifice—and sadly enough, he'd allowed that same mentality to poison him as well.

Yet even in the midst of the ugliness, Parris remained the lady, always the lady. She wouldn't let herself become reduced to Tara's level, and it increased his admiration for Parris even more. She inspired him to be more than what he had been, to live up to what Walt had instilled in him. How could he do any less than what was right?

He'd made a choice when he accepted Percy's jaded offer—the wrong choice. Now he would find a way to undo it no matter what the consequences. He would prove to Parris that he was worthy, the man he claimed to be. But first, he must prove it to himself.

In the car in route to Percy's office, he thought about how he would sever his ties to the gangster without getting into a long, verbal battle, which he knew he could not win. He imagined the many tricky arguments Percy would use to convince him to remain a partner in a shady deal that only undercut his character and left him at the mercy of a very ruthless man. It was no secret in Harlem that Percy Davis had made his enemies disappear. As Nick parked the car, he assured himself that he would stand his ground regardless of what Percy promised or threatened to do. The one thing he did know about Percy was that he only respected men who respected themselves. Once he knew he could browbeat and threaten, the unwitting victim became fair game. Nick stepped out of his car and faced the storefront office building. It was time he earned his own respect.

Percy's young, attractive secretary buzzed him inside, taking a quick glance at his face, which was set with lines of determination. The curtains were pulled shut when he entered the man's vast office, a complete contrast to the shabby exterior of the building—the perfect setup. The sole source of light was a small, desk lamp. Nick noticed that his soon-to-be former partner had his back turned to him, his imposing silhouette almost blending into the dark around him.

"Nick, what can I do for you?" Percy asked matter-of-factly, as if their meeting had been previously arranged and not impromptu. He took a cigar from an expensive-looking humidor on his desk, lit it, then blew out a thin plume of smoke.

"We need to discuss our business arrangement."

"What's wrong, son? Problem with your percentage of the take from the club? Maybe we can work out something where you get more of the gate or a larger share of the profits from the bar."

Nick stepped closer to the desk, locking stares with the older man. "I want out. The arrangement is over."

Suddenly Percy stood and walked around the desk until he was standing inches away from Nick. "Nobody tells me when something is over. Nothing is over until I say it's over. Let me tell you something, son. All I have to do is snap my fingers, and you're finished in this town. Finished. Now if you're all upset because you want a larger cut; then we can sit down and hash this out."

"You're not hearing me. I don't intend to spend a lot of your time and mine arguing about something I've already decided. There's nothing to talk about," Nick said firmly. "I've made up my mind. And I'm not your son and never will be. I've never been more than another hired hand to you. You bought me for your daughter like you bought everything else for her, but my part in that is over, too."

Percy inhaled more of the cigar smoke, but this time blew it toward Nick's face. "Son, do you know who the hell you're talking to? You walk out of this deal when I say you can walk out and not a minute before. As for my daughter, I won't have you making her unhappy. Do you understand what I'm saying?"

"Your threats don't mean anything to me," Nick retorted. "I'm finished with you, the club, and your selfish daughter. Do *you* understand?"

Percy stepped closer, his face twisted in a mask of fury. "Do you remember what I told you about Tara's happiness and what that means to me?" he hissed. "Do you remember what I said would happen to you if you ever did anything to hurt her? Do you?"

"You can't threaten me, not anymore. This isn't about Tara. It's about me." He pointed his finger at his chest. "I came to talk to you like a man, Percy, the man I'd forgotten I was. I'm out and I won't be back."

"Like hell you won't! You're fucking right I bought you, and there's not a thing you can do about it. Nobody twisted your arm to make you sign those contracts. You did it because you wanted to get something for nothing. Greed, just like everybody else. You thought you were suckering me, getting over on me?" he railed. "Who really got suckered?" He laughed bitterly. "You can't change the rules in the middle of the game. You're playing with the big boys now, Nick." He walked closer, looked Nick up and down. "I'd hate to have to force you to do the right thing."

Nick smiled, turned slowly, and began walking toward the door. "Percy, you do what you have to do. I'll do what I have to do. There's nothing you can possibly say that will change my decision. Nothing."

As the door was closing behind him, Nick could hear the old man ranting and raving in the office, hurling threats like daggers at his back. He didn't care. He'd done it! He was free, totally free of everything that sought to make him untrue to his values and convictions. The strings were cut. And no matter what Percy decided to do, it was all right. He'd deal with it.

Somehow the confrontation left him feeling energized, more alive and more serene than he could remember feeling since he'd first signed as Percy's partner. The thing that surprised him most was that he couldn't remember what he had so dreaded about this moment when it all felt so right and left him feeling human again. Now he could come to Parris as the man she deserved, the man he truly was—if she'd give him the chance to prove it.

Forty-three

~~~~~~~~~~~~

Emma returned home early to her villa; the bistro she'd opened with Michael's financial assistance was running well without her.

She smiled as she turned the key in the door and inhaled the aroma of freshly baked bread. Vivian, their middle-aged housekeeper, was working her magic again. Michael loved fresh bread. She knew he'd be pleased when he returned home from his business trip to London.

Strolling across the gleaming wood floors, the distinctive sounds of her heels clicked rhythmically. She gazed around, the wonder and beauty of her environment and her life never ceasing to amaze her. Original art by Renoir, Monet, and Picasso graced the stucco walls. Imported rugs dotted the floors. The two-story villa was adorned with the finest antique furniture that money could buy. All the things that Michael had provided for her.

After the deaths of his parents, Michael inherited everything and invested wisely, turning their already reasonably comfortable life into one that dreams are made of. "I want my beautiful wife to be surrounded by beautiful things," he'd said.

Her jewelry boxes were filled with precious stones. "Trinkets," Michael called them, when he'd bring home yet another velvet-lined box. "Because I love you," he'd whisper, as he'd clasp a diamond necklace around her throat or slip an emerald ring on her finger.

They'd shared nearly three decades together. Incredible years filled with joy, adventure, and all the love she'd ever craved.

Sometimes, less often now than years earlier, she'd think back to those early days, her life in Rudell: the poverty, the loneliness, the isolation. She'd envision her mother and wish that things could have been different, that somehow Cora could have found a way to love her. And she'd see her face, the look of pain and regret when she walked out of the door for the last time, leaving her infant daughter behind.

Her daughter. It was her one regret. Even now, at the oddest times, she could almost see her, feel her tiny fingers wrapped around hers. Her little brown baby with the thick, curly hair and startling green eyes. How had she fared in the world?

It was the one empty space in her soul that could never be filled—not with paintings, jewelry, cruises, and not even with Michael's unshakeable love. And because of her dark secret, because of the secret of her mother, it was the one thing she could never share with her beloved husband— their child.

Would she do it all again? It was a question that haunted her. A question she had yet to be able to answer.

Emma shook her head, scattering her melancholy thoughts, and brushed a wayward tear from her eyes. She sniffed and straightened her shoulders. "Must be getting sentimental in my old age," she muttered aloud.

"Ah, Madam, you're home early," Vivian greeted her as she entered the grand foyer.

Emma spun toward her housekeeper, putting her smile in place. "Yes, everything was fine at the bistro, so I decided to come home early—welcome my husband home from his trip." She smiled mischievously.

Vivian clapped her hands and grinned broadly. "It is good to see a couple still so in love after many years. You're a lucky woman."

"That I am, Vivian."

When she'd come to France so many years ago to await Michael's release from Germany, it was the longest, darkest two months of her life. Everything came into question. She doubted herself, her decisions. The fear of discovery, the guilt of what she'd done to her child woke her with cold sweats at night. For days she would wander the streets of Paris, watching mothers and fathers with their children, and an ache would well up inside her, forcing her to run to her room, where she would hear the sounds of a baby crying, crying for its mother. Surely she believed she would go mad with doubt and grief. Then finally, mercifully, Michael came home, and the terror, the emptiness slowly began to wane. And together they healed each other's hurts and built a life, this life. Yes, she was lucky. Wasn't she?

"Oh, Madam," Vivian pulled an envelope from her apron pocket. "This came for you today." Her small, dark eyes twinkled. "All the way from America."

Emma's stomach suddenly rolled. She reached for the small, white square of paper. "Thank . . . you."

Vivian returned to the kitchen and the preparation of dinner.

Emma stared at the envelope, at the familiar, precise writing, and her hand began to tremble. Suddenly, she couldn't breathe and a thin line of perspiration trickled along her hairline. She squeezed the stiff paper between her fingers, willing it to disintegrate.

Her mother had never written her in all these years. She'd kept the promise, held the secret. Why did she choose now to break them?

Blindly, she found her way upstairs and to her bedroom. On shaky legs she crossed the room to the bay window and slowly sat down heavily on the seat.

Every iota of her being told her to tear it up, get rid of whatever message was scrawled on the sealed pages. But if she did, the question of what rested inside would torture her.

Drawing on all of her resolve, she tore the envelope open, and her heart seemed to leap to her throat, pounding with a vengeance.

My dearest Emma,

By the time this letter reaches you, I will be gone from this earth. And it's time I made my peace with myself, you, and my God.

I know how much you must hate me for what I done to you. And I hope you will find a place in your heart to forgive me. I did love you, Emma. The only way I knew how. I know I should have done more, been more of a real mama to you, but I couldn't. That wasn't no fault of yours. It was mine. Ain't no pain greater than living with shame, living with secrets, and hurting the ones who love you, who need you. And that's what I done to you, passed on my hurts and heaped them on you. Wasn't right, chile. I know that.

Only way I could ever make that up to you was by taking care of your chile like I shoulda took care of you. And I did. Raised her up to be strong and proud of who she is, me and David. Yes, he come back to me, Emma. After all those years of living without him, being empty inside, he come back. I told him everything that happened and he done forgive me. And my life had meaning again. So I knows why you did what you did. Knows why you had to find your own piece of happiness, fill that dark place inside yo'self. Cain't fault you for that. I understand.

Parris, that's her name. Named her after that place you run off to. Well, Parris is a fine young woman. You'd be right proud to have her as your chile. Makes me proud every day.

I just want you to know that I took good care of her, gave her a good life, good education, and plenty of love. And I kept my promise all these years 'bout you. Until now.

Emma squeezed her eyes shut and the tears rolled unchecked down her cheeks. When she opened them again the letters waded in the waters of her heartache. Tenderly she brushed them away and continued to read.

I cain't leave from here with the weight of lies and secrets and shame on my soul. And this chile deserves to know that her mama and papa are alive. That she still got family after I'm gone.

So I done told her, Emma. Done told her everything. Ain't leave nothing out. Hardest thing I ever done besides watching you walk out that door and leaving that baby, knowing you was gonna carry the same secret shame right along with you.

I done told her where to find you. If you still there. Done told her she got to forgive, got to understand and make her peace with her mama like I's trying to make with you. It's time to make things right, chile. No matter what the cost.

If she finds you, Emma, open yo' heart to her. Love her. She gon' need you now. You got a choice, Emma. You can stay and wait fo' her, or you can run. But yo' past will always find you. Just like it found me.

I done said my piece. Done all I can. I can rest now.

The next time we meet will be in a better place, and my arms will be open and waiting to hold you.

Your loving Mama.

Emma's body shook as the sobs of absolute sorrow consumed her. "Mama!" she cried. "Mama." She pressed the letter to her breasts, reliving all the years she'd missed, the years she would never regain, the choices she'd made, the losses, the sacrifices—all to shield a secret, a past that would inevitably unfold no matter what course she chose to take.

She gazed down at the damp, crumbled letter and gently laid it on her lap, smoothing the wrinkled edges, conjuring up her mother's face.

"I forgive you, Mama," she whispered, the tears flowing in a silent stream. "I'm glad you found your happiness."

Her lids slowly rose and Michael stood before her, still as strong and handsome as the day they'd met, the gray in his hair and the extra few pounds only adding maturity to his good looks.

"Em, Honey, what's wrong?" He came to her, sat at her side and protectively wrapped his arm around her shoulders, pressing her trembling body firmly against his. He planted tiny kisses into the thickness of her still black hair. "Em, tell me what it is. Are you hurt?"

"Oh, Michael," she whimpered. Everything she'd done, everything she'd worked for, struggled for, hinged on what she would say next. *Your past will always find you.*

She gazed through tear-filled eyes into those of her husband.

Michael gently cupped her chin. "Whatever it is, you can tell me, Em. No matter what, I love you, more than anything in the world. Believe that."

Her mother had taken a chance, purged her soul, and finally found happiness. Emma could only hope that she would as well. She shut her eyes and slowly, painfully, the words began to flow, pouring out of her like a broken storm cloud. From her childhood days in Rudell—where the girls and boys teased her, shunned her, refused to befriend her; the hardening of her heart to keep from being hurt; the realization that she could pass for white; finding her father, the man who'd raped her mother; the birth of their daughter; to the death of her mother—she left nothing out. Nothing.

Michael didn't move a muscle, didn't say a word all the time that she'd spoken. The pain of her tale evident in her voice and the anguished look etched onto her face.

And with the telling came a sense of peace, a lightness in her soul that she'd never before experienced. Slowly she opened her eyes ready to face whatever confronted her.

Michael stared at her, trying to see her differently from the woman he'd known and loved for what seemed a lifetime. All he could see was his Emma.

His body shuddered as her pain seemed to transfer to him. Her losses, her struggles, her fears were now his. They were one, and the lines of color, the remorse of deceit, would not change that. And even if he left her for the lie she told, it wouldn't change a thing. He would still love her and be incomplete without her.

Slowly he pulled her to him, crushing her body against his, and their tears cleansed them.

"I only pray that our daughter will accept *us,* forgive us, when she comes," he whispered raggedly against her cheek.

Emma's heart soared with a true, inescapable joy, and she knew whatever the future held, she and Michael would face it together. "Thank you, Mama," she whispered.

Forty-four

~~~~~~~~~~

It was warm for January. Unusually warm, the folks of Rudell said—a sure sign of a long, hot summer. The sky was a beautiful cloudless blue, the kind of blue that can't be described or duplicated, and if you're lucky you see it once in a lifetime. The birds, tricked into believing it was spring, hopped from tree to tree, twittering their surprise and greetings to old friends. Every inch of the small plot of grassy land just behind First Baptist Church was covered with the feet of the parishioners, gathered together to wish Cora Mackey farewell. Even folks from Big Bethel came from upriver to pay their respects. Some came to speculate, see if they could dredge up the rumors about Cora and Emma that had torn through town like a brushfire more than forty years ago. But mostly no one really remembered or cared to remember. All anyone seemed to recall about Cora was how she'd lost her folks in that KKK fire, how hard she'd worked all her life, how much they loved seeing her and David together, laughing and fooling with each other like school kids, how she raised Parris, and most of all, the beautiful voice she had, which she'd passed along to her granddaughter.

Parris held on tightly to David's hand, both of them silent in their sorrow, each caught in their own recollections of Cora. In those final weeks of Cora's life, the three of them spent every moment together. Parris told them all about New York, her job at the law firm—and what had happened there with Frank. She told them in halting detail of Nick, her confusion about her feelings for him because of the situation he was involved in with Percy.

"If he's half the man you think he is, he'll see the error of his ways,"

317

David had counseled. "And if he doesn't, he isn't worthy of you. Don't ever forget that."

"Sometimes a man got to find his own path to being a man," Cora added, looking lovingly at her husband. "It ain't always easy. But it's worth the wait." David leaned over the bed and tenderly kissed her forehead.

That was what she wanted, Parris thought, as she laid a rose on her grandmother's casket, a love like that of her grandparents—one that would endure through time. Her grandmother was blessed to have a man like David in her life, someone whose love had never faltered even during those years that they were apart. And ideally, she had her place next to her own parents, Pearl and Joshua, whose love was the foundation upon which three generations followed: Cora, Emma, and Parris.

"Rest in peace, Nana," Parris whispered, as she stood and then turned away, walking slowly up the slope.

▲ ▲ ▲

Nick hadn't wanted to intrude, even as much as he'd wanted to hold Parris and absorb the pain he knew she was feeling. When he finally reached Gina at her office and found out everything that had happened, he knew he had to come, whether she wanted him there or not. He watched the congregation from the back steps of the church and immediately saw Parris, head bowed, as she made her way up the short incline.

When Parris looked up and saw Nick standing there, she immediately thought that yes, this was all a dream. Her grandmother wasn't being buried at all, she hadn't lost her job, and she hadn't witnessed the scene at the club. Everything was as it had always been.

But as she watched him come toward her, the long, slender figure, glimpsed the gentle sorrow in his eyes, and tender smile of comfort on his mouth, she knew it was all too real.

She stopped in front of him, her heart pounding. David stood alongside her and instantly knew that this was Nick.

"I came as soon as I found out," Nick said softly, reaching out to brush the hair from the side of her face. "Gina told me."

Parris's voice shuddered. "Granddad, this is . . ."

"Nick," David said, filling in the space. "Nice to meet you, son."

Nick shook the strong hand, and this time the name "son" sounded just fine. "You, too, sir. Parris has told me a lot about you."

David nodded slowly. "I'm glad you chose to be here," he said warmly.

"It says a great deal about you, son." He looked to Parris and smiled softly. "I'll see you at home," he said, and then to Nick, "I expect I'll see you, too." He patted Parris on the shoulder then continued on past the church with the rest of the flock.

"How are you?" Nick asked.

"I'm going to be all right," Parris said with conviction. "I really am." She looked into his eyes. "What about you?"

Nick drew in a deep breath. "I'm free, Parris. Finally."

"Tara?"

"That's over. Probably had been for a long time, and I didn't pay it any attention. It was easier to just go along."

"What about her father and the things Tara said?" she pressed, needing to know the answers to all the questions that plagued her.

"I did something I should have done a long time ago, Parris. I took out a bank loan and used my half of the club as collateral to buy myself out of the business and pay off any money I owed Percy. Funny, the irony of it all is that going into business with him actually made me credit worthy."

She smiled, as relief and hope rushed through her. "I take it we're both out of work?"

Nick chuckled. "I guess you're right. But it was worth it."

Her eyes rushed over his face. "Was it?"

Nick cupped her face. "It took falling in love with you to make me truly realize it, to realize that life is about choices and the consequences of those choices."

"And about second chances," she said, thinking about her grandmother's words to her and her request. "There's someone I want you to meet, Nick."

"Who?"

"My mother."

Nick frowned in confusion. "Your mother? But I thought . . ."

She took his hand in hers. "It's a long story. I want her to meet the only other man I've ever loved besides Granddad."

He gathered her in his arms and kissed her slow, deep and long, the way he'd wanted to since the first time he lay eyes on her. Reluctantly he eased back and looked into her eyes. "Where is she?" He glanced quickly around at the few stragglers.

Parris smiled. "I figured since we both had some time on our hands . . . we could find her . . . together. It's what my grandmother wanted," she added.

"I know I don't understand all this, but I have all the time you need.

And I want that time to be with you, whatever, however." He thought about the recording contract he had in his suitcase. All it needed was her signature, and her dream would be a reality, the circle would come full. He smiled to himself. He'd tell her all about it when they had some time alone.

Parris released a long breath and became infused with an incredible warmth. "Let me show you where my great-grandfather, Joshua, used to preach," she said, taking his hand and heading around to the front entrance of the church. "My grandmother told me that the townspeople of Rudell built this church plank by plank." She opened the church door and stepped inside. "This is where my Nana used to sing," she said wistfully. "It all began right here."

Parris and Nick stood in the narrow aisle, side by side, looking at the hand-crafted pulpit and the raised platform where the choir would sing. Nick gently put his arm around Parris's waist, as she rested her head on his shoulder.

And if you listened really close you could almost hear the rhythm of Cora's sweet refrain, "Swing low sweet chariot, coming for to carry me home . . ."